L.G. PACE III
VIGILANCE

Copyright © 2014 by L.G. Pace III
Cover design by Robin Harper of Wicked by Design
Formatting and interior design by JT Formatting

Printed in the United States of America
First Edition: February 2014
Second Edition: October 2014
Library of Congress Cataloging-in-Publication Data
  Pace III, L.G.
    Vigilance – 2nd ed
      ISBN - 13: 978-0-9889418-1-6

https://www.facebook.com/LGPaceIII

For Michelle, Holly, Bridgette and Kai.

Making every day of my life the very best of adventures.

PROLOGUE
CRUCIBLE

WHEN TWILIGHT FELL UPON HUMANITY it brought with it the sickly sweet stench of death. The long shadows of misinformation and censorship hid the threat until it was too late. When the truth came to light panic spread across the globe like a fear borne tidal wave. Even more dangerous than the outbreak, was how people reacted to it. Disbelief and isolationism drove humanity further into the growing darkness. As people hid in their homes or fled the cities, the fragile latticework of mankind was torn asunder. Power failed, supply chains ground to a halt, air traffic was grounded and people starved by the millions. First to fall were the sick or infirm. With no one to care for them they languished and expired as the world lost interest.

After the initial chaos those strong enough to survive tore each other apart. Previously abundant supplies like food, water and medicine became more valuable than gold. Psychotics roamed the land, terrorized the living that remained, working to destroy as much as they could before death could claim them. Dead bodies became commonplace in homes, apartments, cars, and even lying out in the open. The air became foul enough to sicken even the strongest stomach. And while the corpses festering where they fell were horrible enough, it was even more horrifying when a few would rise and began to shamble around.

Zombies, once thought the subject of late night movies and horror stories, came into our world with a whisper. In a world where new media screamed to sell you every last titillating detail the public had become jaded. The first unsubstantiated accounts were largely ignored. Online rumors of zombies stalking the living were regarded as just another hoax. Television reports got better traction but few of those remained on the airwaves long. They disappeared with no explanation or follow up. The worse things got in an area, the less information was available. News blackouts were thrown up in the most democratic of countries as governments fought to control the flow of information. The authorities had decided that the best way to keep the public calm was to suppress all evidence related to the threat. Their need to control the flow of information nearly doomed us all.

Brave, foolish or zealous people took to the airwaves to warn the public. Roving vehicles broadcast radio messages. Videos were blitzed over thousands of websites simultaneously, trying to give people a chance to see the truth. Several heroic souls risked everything to provide advanced knowledge of the threat. These warnings gave some a fighting chance to make the preparations needed to survive the coming storm. Rather than focusing on the danger, authorities wasted time trying to kill the harbingers of our doom. It is a pity that they were more successful at controlling the airwaves then protecting the public.

The lid blew off the cover up when flight 763 went radio silent en route from Beijing, China to Paris, France. In the days before terrorism gripped the world that plane would have splashed down in the northern Atlantic, following its autopilot until the fuel ran out. Not so with the security protocols in the modern world. They required any flight approaching a populated area to answer a radio call. When the plane did not respond fighter jets went up to see what the problem was. After numerous attempts at communication-and with no small amount of regret-the jets were ordered to shoot the plane down. It exploded into tiny bits and rained down over the city of Paris. Less than ten hours later the city was being torn apart by zombies.

There was no way for the secret to be kept after that, but for many it was far too late. Asia was already awash with the undead.

Europe soon followed. Africa fell as refugees from the two infected continents sought safety in the third world. Australia locked itself down, banning all travel and eradicating any sign of the infection mercilessly. North and South America fell to infection from flights being shot down in the ocean. What most military units did not realize until too late was that to combat the new enemy required a different kind of warfare.

Zombies do not breathe. They do not get tired. Walking along the bottom of the ocean floor is no different for them than walking on land. Shooting down planes or sinking boats was pointless. The ocean just spewed whole and partial zombies out of the surf a short time later. Within a month the infection was worldwide. In two months most governments had fallen. At the end of the third month over seven billion humans were dead. Only a fraction of them had been infected. The rest had died in the ensuing chaos.

Earth, our gleaming blue marble, went dark. With no one to keep the plants going, the electrical grid went down. The communications network failed as well, taking most of the Internet with it. There were still satellites in orbit but most of them required ground stations to run them. Roadways were clogged with abandoned or disabled vehicles. Survivors were scattered across the continents in makeshift sanctuaries. Refugees learned to shun the old cities, now teeming with zombies. To survive most had to learn to become self-sufficient, to live off the land and stay unseen. But some things from the old world are necessary. Medicine. Tools. Knowledge. The wealth of mankind was no longer the sparkling rocks and pretty metals but the accumulated information of the species. And most of it lay waiting in the places most dangerous to the remnants of humanity.

Of all the refuges in the world one sanctuary was ready for the fall. Vigilance. Renamed by the founder Jeremiah Kane, its name is a constant reminder to the residents of the price for their success. Kane's foresight placed Vigilance in the unique position of being well supplied for the approaching apocalypse with a population of skilled and learned people. Because of its remote location on a high mesa, the town was better suited for the new world, far better than many other refuges. With Kane's leadership the town was able to flourish while the world shattered around it. But the path into the new world wasn't smooth. No, there is always a price to be paid for survival.

Survival requires sacrifice, adaptation and the will to endure. The many tales from the old world reflect these tenets. As the world fell apart many survivors recorded their stories. Some for posterity. Others as a way to deal with what they were going through. These accounts, written as time allowed in a world gone mad, contain invaluable insight.

From the beginning Vigilance collected knowledge along with supplies and survivors. Any books that could be found were brought back to the city, including personal journals. They were carefully disinfected to prevent spreading the disease. Then they were read, sorted, scanned and recorded in the library's system. This made them available to anyone in the town that would wish to read them. Some books, those of a disturbing nature or that provided particular insights to those that travel the wastes, were not put into the public archive. These books were instead placed privately in what became known as The Hunter Archive.

Only those few who had passed the rigorous training of the elite Hunter cadre are allowed access to these books. To those Hunter Initiates, these books provided insight as well as perspective. It is hoped that these tales will aid you when you venture out on your graduation journey. Those of you that return successfully will be granted access to our most secure book, the Journals of the Stranger.

Unless you are an initiate of the Hunter Guild or a full Hunter you should not be reading this. Put this book down. Return to your home immediately and never speak of what you have read!

If you are a Hunter Initiate, these stories have been selected to help prepare you for the horrors you will face out in the waste. What is within should only be discussed with your fellow Hunters.

Beth Sanderson

YOU KNOW, I NEVER REALIZED how much time I wasted. There were so many things that I did simply to fill my day. Watching television was a big one. Then again, social media ran neck and neck for sucking my life away. Did people really need to know I was drinking a Caramel Macchiato? Or that my personal scone recipe was stupendous and the talk of my friends and family? In retrospect? No. These were all just time sinks to pass my day and to take my mind off my problems. But they were never as important as my one true passion in life. Reading. As we appear to have reached the end of the world, I would like to go on record as saying of all the things that I will miss, new books rank as number one.

Oh, my beloved books. Never again will I be able to pre-order my favorite author's new novel. Or argue the merits and shortcomings of instalove with my reader groups online. So many friends vanished without a sound when the electricity disappeared. The only comfort I have is that by the time the world flew off the tracks I had tons of paperbacks and unread eBooks. You know, I never realized how much I took power for granted until it went out. I have three e-readers, a cell phone and a laptop in my backpack right now. They don't weigh much but without a power source they are useless. I hope to find a way to charge them so that I can read all the books I have got on them. As they say, "hope springs eternal". I try and comfort myself with reading the best of my hard copy collection over and over again. I'm going to have to pick a few and leave the rest behind when I hit the road. It is like asking a mother to choose between her children.

Anyway, I guess I better start at the beginning. My name is Beth Sanderson. I'm twenty four. I lived in St Paul, Minnesota where I used to be a graphic designer. That's short hand for suffering through four years of college to sit with idiot clients who have no creative spark of their own. These clueless clods would come to me so that I could pour my heart and soul into their project. Once I was done, they seemed to revel in smashing my work like a two year old having a temper tantrum. It was exhausting to put myself out there day after day just to have the client never be satisfied. My therapist said this was why I had so much trouble staying in a long term relationship. That I'm so afraid of being hurt it makes me hyper critical of every man I meet. I told her it was more that I just keep meeting jerks. Heaven forbid I don't want a guy who lives in his mom's basement. Or some unemployed boy child that thought I was a cash machine or a booty call. I was holding out for a man. Then the end of the world came. It figures.

I had a great apartment on the top floor of an old converted brownstone. It was small but it had a lot of charm and was close to the subway entrance, so it was convenient to work. I loved that apartment. Men might come and go, mostly go, but that apartment and I saw a lot of good times together. I traveled to more worlds in my time there inside my books, on my old couch or under my comforter, than most people could hope to visit in a lifetime. My own story seemed like it was just about to start before this plot twist hit. The week before everything went to hell, a totally cute guy moved into the ground floor apartment and I think he liked me. He came up to my apartment seven times in three days to ask to borrow something. On his last visit he wasn't wearing a shirt. That six pack of his was worth way more than a cup of sugar. The last time I saw him he was moaning and reaching for me. Don't get the wrong idea. He wasn't lusting after me. He was hungry. Mr. Six Pack had become Mr. Zombie.

My clients had been canceling left and right, so my schedule was wide open when things got really bad. I hunkered down in my apartment watching the news and maxing out my credit cards. Plural. By my last calculation I ran up over seventy thousand dollars in charges in two weeks. I figured if the world was ending, the credit card companies could bite me. Pun intended. Every eBook that sounded mildly interesting or helpful ended up on my laptop. I then backed them up to my three eReaders and cell. By the time the power went out I was an expert on the outbreak, had the five closest refuges mapped out and had my electronics packed. The only problem I had was I had no idea how I was going to get out of the city. None.

So I went to the second floor to see if my neighbors, the Clark's, were home. Not only were they not home, they hadn't even bothered to close their door. From the look of the apartment they weren't planning on coming back. "Thanks for seeing if I wanted to come with you fuckers," I said to their empty apartment. When I headed down to the ground floor I saw *him* standing near the front door. At first I was overjoyed. Some part of my brain even started writing a romance novel about us overcoming impossible odds to escape to somewhere safe to start a family. Then he turned around. His face was no longer pretty. His nose was missing and his jaw was half ripped off. His chest and that perfect stomach were ripped open and his guts hung out like rancid spaghetti. Sue me. I screamed.

By the time I got my shit together, he was at the foot of the stairs grabbing at me. Luckily, I was halfway up the staircase, safely out of his reach. Behind him, I saw a package about the right size to be the solar charger I had ordered and desperately needed for my electronics. It was sprayed down with his zombie goo, totally infected and useless to me. That hurt almost as much as my hunk being a ruined fetid corpse. I ended up back in my bedroom rocking and crying under the bedspread. When I spun down, I realized I didn't have a lot of time. The power was out, it was going to be dark in about ten hours, and I didn't want to be out on the street with those things without at least being able to see them coming. Plus, I realized if I didn't get out of the city soon, I might never be able to escape.

First, I needed to get out of my building in one piece. Using the stairs was out with Prince Zombie down there literally chomping for a piece of me. Plus the news had been pretty clear about infection dangers. Any fluid contact and you were fucked. He'd turned the entryway into a bio-hazard by sloshing his goop all over the place. Not exactly the mental picture that had gone through my head when I pictured his fluids sprayed around.

There was a fire escape on the back side of the building, but I'd never used it. The window had been painted shut and in the end I had to break the glass. It was rusty and nasty out on the fire escape, but at least it was sturdy. Getting to the street was easier than I thought. I just didn't plan on the damn stairs of the fire escape shooting back up as soon as I stepped off. So much for going back. Out on Grant Street, it was bedlam. I saw a line of soldiers and police retreating from the dead towards where I was. One of them glanced back and saw me and did a double take. Yelling at the line to close up he came over to me.

"Ma'am! What in the name of God are you doing here? This block has already been evacuated." From my confused expression he seemed to realize I had no clue what he was talking about. Turning to his squad he yelled some orders and one of them came running over. It was a kid who barely looked like he was old enough to shave. "Masonholder, get your skinny white butt down to the evac point with this civi and get back here A.S.A.F.P.!"

The kid grabbed my arm and rushed me down the street. For the next two blocks I lived in some sort of first person shooter horror story. The soldier shot seventeen people, in the head, on the way. He didn't even hesitate, other than to reload. I looked at a few of them as we went past. I really shouldn't have. One of them was a little zombie girl, now missing half her face. I almost puked all over myself. He took me to a fenced in area with trucks that were loading people for evacuation. Pushing the gate aside, the soldier pushed me inside and yelled to one of the guys on duty who in turn grabbed me and shoved me into a line.

4

We were herded into a truck like cattle and then the trucks blew down the road like they were trying to set a new land speed record. People started throwing up which made the whole truck stink. I moved to the open edge of the vehicle and held on for dear life. About an hour later we found ourselves outside the city in a quarantine area. The next few hours were an absolute nightmare. I saw things that I'll never get out of my head. Stuff that put the worst horror movies to shame. Mothers turned and killed their own children. Kids ripped each other apart after turning. The head shots. The burnings.

Quarantine culled almost half the people. Families were shattered. Wives lost husbands. Children lost parents. Parents lost children. Sometimes they lost their minds as well. Soldiers had to shoot a few non infected people that tried fighting them to save their sick relatives. I went into survival mode, my emotions went numb and I tried to block out as much as I could. I failed miserably. The things I saw will haunt my dreams for the rest of my life.

The soldiers were running everything with typical military efficiency. One took down my name, address and occupation on a notepad. Then another moved me to a fenced area. It quickly became apparent that I'd been sorted into the loser group. It was just like high school. The cool kids, the jocks and the brains were all taken somewhere else. I was sitting in a big holding area with the adult version of art kids, medieval reenactors and band geeks.

It was hard not to notice the lucky ones being processed through to apparent safety. In a few rare instances they were even taken in the direction of the helicopters. Occasionally, I heard the distinct sound of a helicopter taking off. After an hour of this, I asked a soldier when I could leave. He ignored me. So I threw a world class, "ugly American style", fit. They pulled me out and straight marched me to their commander, a hard looking man named Davidson. He stared at me for a moment before looking at some paperwork.

"Sanderson, Beth. Graphic Designer . . . well that's a helpful skill." His derision for art was as obvious as it was confusing.

"What's going on here? I'm not infected. Why are we being held here while you evacuate others that arrived after us?" He gave me a withering look.

"Ms. Sanderson. This is a triage operation here. Do you understand the concept? We're trying to get the most valuable resources we've got left to safety. To put it bluntly? You're just not that important. We need the doctors, scientists, skilled craftsmen. No one is going to need any advertising any time soon. Once we have those people evacuated, we'll start taking the rest of you out." His attitude pissed me off. And it set my mouth in motion before I could stop myself.

"Well if you don't need me, then let me go. Keeping me here when I could be getting myself out is as bad as you killing me yourself." He looked at me for a moment and his hand dropped to a knife on his belt. A few seconds later he shook his head. Motioning to one of his men he pointed to me.

"Go put her in a private room...like a broom closet...before I do something to fix both our dilemmas." The soldier saluted and hauled me away bodily. Once we were around the corner he slowed down and I got a look at the man holding me. He was older, probably late thirties, and looked extremely tired. He led me away from quarantine down a long corridor. Leaving the main area he took me through a gate and into a small room that looked like it had been a storeroom at one time.

Closing the door behind us, he stood for a second and then gave a weary sigh. "What a mess," he said. Pulling his hat off he ran his other hand through his thinning hair. "Look lady . . . I have to obey orders. So I'm going to leave you in this room. I also happen to agree with you. Keeping you here is stupid. You aren't going to make a transport. So as long as we don't see you back inside the General should be happy. If I were in a situation like yours I might suggest that you get into these boxes and get dressed in something a bit more all weather and then see if you can find something out that other door to get you out of this city." He gestured to an exit on the far wall. Giving me one last meaningful look he left though the door we had come in. I heard the heavy click of the deadbolt being shot home.

Digging through the boxes, I found fatigues, insulated socks and underwear. It felt a bit surreal to dress in them, but the clothes were better than what I was wearing. I found heavy boots as well. Once I was dressed, I took the door he suggested. I found myself in a parking lot. At the far end of the lot were a big group of Hummers. Each one had the keys in it. There was no one around, so I got in one and started it up. When nobody came running I drove away.

Getting out of the city was horrible. People tried to wave me down, but after what I'd seen in quarantine I never took my foot off the gas. Even for the poor bastard that jumped in front of me. I ran him down like a deer and kept going. The sickening crunch of his head under the Humvee wheel sounded like a walnut cracking. He was infected. At least that's what I tell myself. Hell, he probably was.

Exiting the city I drove west barely above an idle. There were vehicles stopped on the road, some of them with bloody bodies inside. I tried not to look but sometimes I couldn't help it. I had to push some of the cars out of the way with the Humvee's bumper. You have to look to be able to steer. More than once I drove over dead bodies. I hoped they were dead. I really, really hope they were dead. I cried a lot during that drive. I thought about the people back in that cage. The ones that didn't realize that they were all expendable cattle. What would have happened if I had gone back and told them? Would the soldiers have evacuated us? Or maybe just shot all of us? Part of me will always wish that I had at least tried.

The gas ran out in the country and I was left crying in a Humvee in the dark. When the sun came up I got out and got ready to walk. Just as I was about to leave I thought about taking the gas can with me. When I tried to pull one of the two cans down I realized it was full. It took me a few moments to figure out where to put the fuel. Both cans went in and when I got back inside I had about half a tank.

7

That got me a little further down the road.

Then I was walking. It made me glad that I had always tried to walk as much as possible. But it still sucked. The boots I had taken were new and within a few miles I could feel blisters starting to form. There I was in the middle of nowhere with almost no food or water, no transportation, and no plan. I just knew I was going to end up getting eaten by a zombie.

My wandering took me pretty far from the main roads by the time the sun started going down. The big roads had a lot of cars and a lot of zombies. Infected people trying to escape the city got pretty far before keeling over. So I had driven the Humvee on mostly back roads.

It was luck that helped my find a place for the night. My refuge for the evening was a gas station, old and rarely trafficked by its look. It had likely been more successful back before the interstates went in.

The place was run down but still looked like it had been open recently. The doors were locked, but I could see food and water through the window. I stood there like an idiot for like an entire minute trying to think of what to do. Finally I decided to walk around the building. In the back I saw a ladder attached to the roof. It was one of those metal ones with screen locked over the bottom part to keep you from being able to climb up. I stacked up some crap and climbed up where I could reach the ladder. Then I tried to pull myself up.

Remember in gym class when we girls were humiliated in front of each other trying to climb the damn rope? No? Guess I'm showing my age. I was grunting and trying to climb, but it was no good. I stacked more crap up and finally was able to get up on the ladder. The roof was clear and I saw a trap door style hatch in the center. There was a lock on it but it wasn't hard to break, it was one of those flimsy flip locks that held from the inside. It seemed like it was more to keep the trapdoor from blowing open then keeping anyone serious out. Opening it, I saw another ladder going down. I took some gravel from the roof and tossed it inside. I'm not sure what I hit, but it made a hell of a racket. I lay there with my head down in the hatch and listened for any noise.

It stayed quiet which was a good sign. Zombies are attracted to noise and they're never patient. If one was down there it should have started towards the opening right away. Climbing down the ladder, I found some flashlights. Batteries were right next to them and pretty soon I had a light. I put two filled flashlights in my backpack with some extra batteries. Protein bars and water followed. Then I checked the store out. It was decent sized with a cooler in the back. I stayed clear of the cooler. With no electricity, things had gone bad in a big way. It reeked of spoiled milk and rotten eggs back there.

The sun was about a half hour from setting, so I searched the place looking for anything useful. Behind the counter was a pistol. One of the kind with a cylinder with shells in the middle. Now, I've never even held a gun before, but I've seen them used on television. It was surprisingly easy to open the gun. The cylinder slid out to the side and I saw it had bullets in it. My opinion on guns had been strictly neutral before, but now I am definitely pro-gun. I found a box with ammo next to the gun and a set of car keys on a little hook underneath the register. I grabbed them and headed back up to the roof. Sitting behind the station, just around the dumpster from where I had climbed the ladder, was an old pickup truck. I climbed down again and checked it out. The keys opened it up.

It was a simple single bench seat and the truck was from back in the sixties. It was a huge old gas guzzler but the gas tank was full. What is it they say? "Any truck in a zombie apocalypse." I loaded the truck inside and out with supplies before heading back inside. I decided to write some of this down before getting some rest. If I'm going to be traveling cross country, I'm going to get a good night's sleep.

I'M SO DAMN LUCKY TO be alive right now. It has been a few days since the gas station, but I've been too wired and busy to write anything down since then. I was sleeping. I don't know what time it was. I'd left a light on, a little flashlight lantern, because I didn't want to sleep in the dark. Glass breaking jarred me out of my nightmares into a living one. A zombie had smashed one of the front windows. There was a metal strip divider running up the glass and that had hung it up. Otherwise I would have woken up with its teeth in me somewhere. I scrambled around and down the aisle to the ladder. I managed to get up the rungs about one second in front of the next zombie. I slammed the lid down and lay down on the roof. That was when I realized that I had left my backpack behind.

My heart felt like it shattered. It didn't matter that the electronics inside were dead and likely would never be charged again. That they were just useless plastic and glass, that wasn't really the point. For me they stood for something else. They stood for hope. That one day I would be able to live a normal life again. With electricity and running water. It might sound stupid, but they were the one goddamn thing that was keeping me going in this fucked up world. And I'd be damned if some fucking shambling corpse got between me and them. By the time the sun came up the tears were gone and I was pissed.

I didn't see any zombies outside at all. I took a rock from the roof and threw it at the gas pumps. It made a loud crack when it connected and after waiting a minute I threw another one. From out of the station came three zombies. The one I saw before and two others. The one that almost got me was wearing a flannel shirt and work jeans. The other two were in t-shirt and jeans. Aside from their bad complexion and a little blood they could have been alive. They went to the gas pumps and stopped. I threw a whole handful of rocks and they headed further out towards the road. With a final heave I tossed more rocks and sped back to the hatch. Opening it I went down the ladder scanning for movement. I didn't see anything but I moved quickly back to where my bag had been. It was untouched. I had hung it up out of habit. I grabbed it up and moved back toward the ladder.

Apparently I'd made too much noise because when I got back to the roof I heard the trio of zombies moaning nearby. I looked over the building edge in time to see them disappear inside. Checking the back of the building, I saw it was clear. I went down the ladder and headed for the truck. Yet again I was stupid. I almost ran headfirst into a zombie coming around the building. Apparently all three of them hadn't gone inside. The gunshot rang in my ears and the zombie went flying back, its head half gone. I looked at the gun in my hand in shock for a moment and then sprinted to the truck. As I slammed the door shut I saw another zombie coming around the corner of the building.

I tried the key in the ignition, but it didn't work. After a panicked moment I realized I was trying the wrong key. Slotting the other one made the truck roar to life and I threw it in gear. The back end squirreled around on the gravel and swung into the approaching zombie sending it flying. I tore away into the dawn with my backpack on the seat beside me. I was shaking so bad I almost drove off the road twice. That near death experience was a wakeup call for me to focus on getting somewhere safe.

Watching all that television ended up working to my advantage. Especially since I have no desire to take refuge at any of the government run sanctuaries. Not after my experience with the army. Screw that and screw them. For all I knew, they had a standing order to shoot all us 'civis' on sight. I figure my best bet is a refuge in New Mexico. It's being run by artists and if there is anywhere that I can find a place to fit in this world it should be there. I'm going to head there and see if they'll take me in.

THE LAST MONTH HAS SUCKED. I held off writing anything because I've been too busy and I didn't want to dwell on what was going on until I had a chance to stop and rest. I've found a wellspring of strength that I never knew I had. Which is good, because life is a lot harder than it was in the old world. The smallest thing, like getting gas or collecting supplies is a huge ordeal. I've got to find somewhere with what I need, then lure away the zombies so I can circle back. This is a hell of a lot harder to learn how to do than you think. It is exhausting. Every night I have to find someplace to pass the night. And it has to be a place that I can park the truck out of sight that has a shelter with multiple exits. Those kinds of places are not so easy to find. There were days I stopped well before nightfall just because I found the right place. I raided gas stations for food but after a week of pork rinds and fruit pies I would have killed for a greasy cheeseburger.

On top of all of this I was having trouble finding a road south that didn't have a missing bridge, courtesy of the military I don't doubt. Each crossing had a ragged middle with charred and mangled edges showing where the missing span had been. Abandoned cars were parked on either side of the hole. It made me question if I was heading the right way since there were just as many empty cars on the far side of these bridges. As an aside, I have to say, even with all the stress and horror I have seen, New Mexico is beautiful. By the time I found my way to the artist run sanctuary, Peace Grotto, I was feeling a little more upbeat. This made what I found all the more horrifying, even after all I'd seen.

The place had been overrun. There were bodies everywhere. At first I thought it was zombies. But when I looked at the corpses, they had gunshots, not bites. I didn't get out of the truck but even from my vantage I could see corpses that had been left tied over barrels and railings. Based on the way the clothes were cut away they had been tied there by the living, for pretty obvious reasons. The place was a graveyard and I had no wish to meet the people who had made it that way. I backed the truck out and quietly drove away.

Three days of searching back roads led me to the perfect place. A secluded cabin high in the hills. I only found it by accident myself. I was backtracking to avoid a herd of zombies when I noticed a faint side rode and decided to follow it. It took almost a half hour of driving, and I had begun to consider turning around, when I saw the structure peeking out from behind some rocks. After the bullshit I had been through I wasn't taking any risks. It took almost three hours of quietly checking outside and then inside, but in the end I was sure there were no dead around. And no living either.

The cabin had high windows, something that I'd read about in a wilderness romance. These high windows, teamed with heavy wooden drop shutters, kept animals from gaining entry when cabins were empty for long periods of time. The house had an old fashioned hand pump and water came out when I moved the handle. There were large stores of dried and canned foods as well as a standing tank with gasoline in the carport. Having finally arrived at a safe place I let my guard down. I ended up spending the first night crying in an actual bed, once I had secured the doors and windows. The relief of not being on the road, in constant danger, was immense. For almost a month I rested in my new refuge taking care every day to go and scout to make sure nothing crept up on me.

I'd lost count of how many days I was at my new home when the depression hit me. The reality of all that I'd lost, co-workers, friends, my beloved books. I know it sounds heartless, but the books hit me hardest of all. It was sheer torture to know that my laptop, smartphone and eReaders were stuffed full of books that I could never read. Now, when I was safe and secure their loss was like an open wound in my soul. I went to sleep sobbing and when I woke the next morning the feeling of hopelessness made me start crying all over again. For two days I broke down to a gibbering mass of snot and tears. On the second day, dehydrated and needing to pee I went into the bathroom and caught my reflection in the mirror. I looked like Marilyn Manson's ugly stunt double. I laughed at my reflection, holding onto the sink as the absolute absurdity of my situation hit me. Right then and there I decided that I was going to read everything that I had if I had to power it off zombie goo.

I fueled up the truck and headed for the nearest big city, Las Cruces. By the time I reached the outskirts I had a plan. There was a sporting goods store, a giant one, out in the country by itself. This was the place where I would get what I needed. I knew they sold solar chargers. When the internet was still up I'd ordered one from that same company. Who knows? Maybe the package by my mailbox was from them. I never did get close enough to check. So, it wouldn't really be stealing if I took one from the store itself, right? Or twelve. It would be a good idea to have a backup so I never had to do this again.

With the store being outside of town I'd hoped it would be a bit more deserted than it was. Fat chance. One look at the parking lot told me that this wasn't going to be easy. There were zombies all over the place. The store looked to be infested. So not only was there a chance that the zombies themselves would get me, they might have gotten goo all over the store. I figured it was time to rethink my original snatch and grab plan. Early on, I'd made a protective outfit from odds and ends that let me go into gas stations and stores to get food and supplies without accidentally getting goo on me. It was rubber hip waders that went up to my chest, a rubber overcoat with a hood, a full faced gas mask and rubber gloves. The big yellow kind you used to do dishes. It looked ridiculous and made a hell of a racket. Rubber on rubber with rubber on top of it. I squeaked along in it like a new shoe. Going into a store full of zombies in it would be suicide. But without it I could almost guarantee infection.

Back outside of town I scouted, finding what I was looking for after ten minutes of searching. A gas station with a few cars. Luring away the dead there was old hat to me. Once they were gone I gassed up, filled extra cans and searched the cars. One of them lucki-ly had keys in it. I filled it up too. Then I drove my truck away and parked it about a mile from the gas station, up on a steep rise. I wanted to keep my ride safe and use the other one to go to the store. I figured if I had to I could use it as a ram on the dead and then abandon it. Jogging back to the gas station was terrifying. I kept ex-pecting to see zombies appear all around me.

Returning to the gas station I got in the throw away car and pulled to a safe distance before doing something I'd never done be-fore. I torched the place. And damn near killed myself doing it too. Who knew the explosion would be so big? I singed off some of my hair. I circled wide back around to the sporting goods store and true to form the little brainless undead were filing out and headed to-wards the big noise I had left behind. I waited ten minutes for them to clear out and then headed inside.

The store was dark as hell so I lit up some road flares and threw them around. The added light showed me something I hadn't planned on. There were still zombies in the store. Not a lot of them, but enough. They saw the flares and crowded around them. Moving away from the door I headed deeper into the store. I can tell you at this point I think I lost my mind. No sane person would go squeaking into a store full of zombies to get a charger to read romance novels. But the thought of leaving and going home to my dead eReaders was too much to bear. If the zombies got me or I got infected so be it. I was going to read those fucking books!

Creeping along I found a few zombies in my way. Their moan-ing, shuffling and generally banging around was giving me enough masking that they hadn't heard me. Though they hadn't spotted me yet I still needed to get to the other side of the store. Grabbing a few bottles from the shelf I threw them as hard as I could towards one of the road flares. The cans were compressed air and one of them broke open when it landed issuing a loud hissing. The zombies shambled towards it and I slipped past to the aisle with the solar chargers. I filled my bag with as many of them as would fit. When I looked back the way I had come there were zombies between me and the door. I figured I would try the same distraction to get back outside when the light was obscured for a second. Glancing over I saw zombies coming back in the store. Fuckity fuck fuck fuck!

I panicked and backed up against a rack, knocking over an entire display. The noise was horrendous. Every single zombie in earshot started to shamble towards me moaning. They were coming at me in a half circle. Blocking my path out, pushing me towards the wall. I was sure that I was going to die with a bunch of solar chargers in my hand. I lit my last road flare and it saved my ass. A zombie that was pulling itself along the floor was only five feet away. Backing up I spotted my salvation. An emergency exit! I hit the paddle and flew out the door narrowly missing a zombie.

My lungs almost bursting, I ran for the car. Having abandoned all pretenses of stealth I squeaked like a dogs chew toy, the noise making me a target for everything within earshot. Behind me the gates of hell had opened up and hundreds of zombies were shambling after me. Worse, there were some between me and the car. I was forced to dodge back and forth between vehicles to avoid them as they came towards me. Twice hands came out of windows and almost got me. I managed to get to the car ahead of the dead and high tailed it outta there. Looking down at myself I almost threw up. I had bits of goo on me. The car would be a total loss and I might already be infected. Fuck. I drove back towards where I had left my truck. Getting out of the car I pulled bottles of water from the back and rinsed myself off. I used all of it and then carefully pulled everything I was wearing off and discarded it on the road.

I pulled three giant bottles of antibacterial hand sanitizer out and wiped myself down like I was putting on suntan lotion. Fun side note? That shit burns like napalm. When I was done I carefully checked myself. I looked okay, but what did I know? The television experts had said even a drop could infect you. For all I knew I was a dead woman walking. I put on clean clothes and winced as it pushed hand sanitizer into some uncomfortable places. Shaking, I got into the truck and drove away. The drive back to the cabin was brutal. My stomach was roiling and I couldn't stop myself from obsessing. Was it a side effect of the change? Was I already dying? I felt like I was going to be sick. The cabin was only four hours away. When I got there I sat in the truck for a moment. I was no longer in danger of being ill, or of crying. Instead I found my hands beating on the steering wheel and screams of rage ravaging my throat. It was so damn unfair, to have come so far only to have the virus get me now.

Lucky for me the truck kept my noise muted. Otherwise I would have drawn every zombie for two states with that racket. I got out but stopped outside the cabin, afraid to go inside. What if I was infected? Sitting outside on a rock I waited for the next few hours. The sun was getting ready to set hours later when I finally snapped out of it. Enough time had passed. If I was infected I would have turned. I felt a huge rush of relief. I was going to live. Even better, I was going to get to read my books!

Going into that store was the most petrifying thing I've ever done in my life, but it had been worth it. Putting on new gloves I carefully removed the outer wrapping of each charger being very careful. It took me twenty minutes to strip the plastic and boxes off. When I was done there was a pile of garbage bags with suspect packaging and gloves in the ditch and twenty plus chargers safely in two clean bags. My legs felt like rubber by the time I finished and I carefully took my treasure inside the cabin, locking up behind me. When I woke up the next morning I felt an overwhelming sense of relief and joy. It was like the sun had come out from behind the clouds and was bathing my soul in light. For the first time since the outbreak I bounced out of bed looking forward to my day. After going outside and making sure there were no zombies around I got two of the solar chargers out.

Setting them up I found to my delight that they would charge items within ten minutes. I hooked up the three eBooks, smartphone and the laptop. An hour later I was reading the last book by Jillian Dodd. Well, at least I think it was the last one. For all I know she survived the zombies. But she might have more pressing things to do then write. Like trying to stay alive, for example. The next few days were glorious. I laughed, I cried, I raved in anger. I realized the absolute frustration of knowing that I would never know how a series would end because the author was likely worm food. Damn you zombie horde!

I've got to admit that the fucking zombies sneaking up on me was entirely my fault. I may have gotten a little lax in my scouting each day. I mean, come on, there are so many stories that need to be read and so little time. So imagine my surprise when I went out one morning and found that there were dozens of zombies scattered around the area. Two of them were wandering around the truck and a few of them were near the road leading in.

I had always been so careful, so meticulous, when I came back to the cabin. This time I'd been so shaken up about the possibility of being infected that I'd taken no precautions. So sue me. But now I was so royally screwed. There was no way of getting to the truck and no chance I was going to try getting away on foot. The cabin being so far off the main road it made a great hideaway. But there were plenty of level places between here and the highway that undead could be lurking. Not to mention the whole dying of exposure in the middle of the desert. In the end I flipped the zombies the bird and went back inside to read. Seriously? What the hell else was I going to do? Can't kill them, can't flee, might as well read.

I must have read through a chunk of stories on one of the eReaders when it occurred to me that I was going to run out of food before I ran out of books. Well, duh. I had enough books to last a few lifetimes. But in all seriousness my food was running out. I wished I had a second rubber outfit to at least try to make a break for it. I went back to reading, stopping only to check on my undead visitors from time to time. It was a few days later when the undead started freaking out. They all stumbled towards the west. They made enough of a racket that I decided to see what the big deal was. Putting down my book I made sure it was on the charger and the charger was square in the sun before heading outside. Ten minutes later I came upon the weirdest frigging thing I had seen in a long time. There was a dry river bed that the dead were shambling down towards this guy that was all swaddled up in protective gear.

I was too far away to be able to see him well but he seemed to have taken the same precautions I had against infection. The crazy thing was he didn't run from the zombies. He just slowly walked towards them. What a freaking nut job! Granted, I had seen footage of stuff like this before the television went off the air. Infected that decided to take out as many zombies as they could before they died. Or people who just snapped and started attacking the zombies. Crazies weren't really that rare in the city where I lived. We had a guy on my block who claimed to be the reincarnation of a cow and would rage against anyone he saw eating a hamburger. In retrospect I can sympathize with the cow.

Now, I sat on a rock high above and watched this insane guy wade into the group of undead. He held a machete in each hand and with each blow he smashed the head of a zombie, dropping it in its tracks. It was over so quickly I was actually shocked. I'd expected that the zombies would either drag him down or just rip him apart. He wandered around for a minute and then started yelling. I decided to get the hell out of there before he turned or worse, spotted me.

I hid out in the house, going out each morning to see if either the guy or his zombie corpse would show up. A few days later there was no sign of the guy but I saw a few zombies out on the horizon. Going back to the cabin I took stock. I was getting low on food, zombies were showing up, there was a crazy guy (who might already be a zombie) wandering around my neighborhood and I hadn't seen another human being besides him in way too long. So I packed up my meager possessions and hit the road. Making sure a solar charger was on the dash of course.

Three days later I'd just finished getting gas when I got hailed by three guys and a woman. I'm not ashamed to say that they scared the holy fuck out of me. After trying not to jump out of my skin, I pulled my gun on them and took cover behind the truck. The woman came forward after handing off her gun. Her name was Kate Wilson and she was a firefighter from Phoenix. She told me that they had no interest in hurting me but I was wise to take precautions. There were a lot of assholes preying on others these days. I kind of had a mini breakdown I think, hyperventilating. I might have laughed a little hysterically. She calmed me down and asked me about myself, what I did and where I was from. She seemed surprised to hear I was from St. Paul, even more so with how pissed I was at the military. She waved to her patrol and they came forward with their weapons holstered.

It took about three hours to get me to trust them. In the end I've got the zombies to thank. When one came out from behind the station, without missing a beat, one of the guys stepped in front of me, pulled an arrow from a quiver and shot it through the head. Glancing back at me he gave me this cheeky grin, like he wanted to show off for me. Within a few minutes of that we were heading off towards their camp. My hero rode with me while the others drove their jeep ahead of us. I found myself blathering like an idiot, but he didn't seem to mind. He jabbered right back at me. His name was Jack Reynolds. He was hot. Seriously friggin' cowboy hot. Like someone you would expect to see on the cover of a bodice ripper.

When we got to their camp they had me sit a bit apart from them and over the course of the evening we talked. All of them stayed well back from me. Kate explained that they had to honor an eight hour quarantine on strangers. Their camp was built on high ground with good line of sight all around. That night I experienced a different kind of quarantine than I had with the military. I was kept at a distance but treated with respect. Jack had me tell him my story from beginning to end, and he really seemed to be listening which made me a little self-conscious.

The solar chargers got a lot of attention as did the eReaders and laptop. My tale of how I got the chargers had him shaking his head. He gave me a look that seemed equal parts horror and admiration.

When he heard how many books I had on my electronics he was astonished. Here I've got to admit my fan girl came out and I gushed as the conversation turned to some of my favorite authors. He called the others over and we talked about books all through the night. When the sun came up, they asked me to wait for a moment and withdrew to talk. A few minutes later they returned and Kate asked me if I'd be interested in returning to their refuge with them. They were from a town called Vigilance, a remote sanctuary. I don't know why but I trusted them. I didn't even stop to think about it, I just said yes.

We stripped my truck of everything useful. Hoses, battery, belts, gas, they even took the seat out and strapped it to the roof of the jeep. A few days later we came to a line of cars. They parked the jeep and unloaded it. Everything got stashed up on a high ledge. We climbed up on the ledge and they knocked on a metal door hidden behind an outcropping of rock. When the door was open the gear was passed inside. Kate handed me a full body jumpsuit to put on over my clothes. Then she took me through a dizzying number of tunnel twists and turns before we entered into a series of chambers. Here I met Dr. Alice Carter. She explained that even though the field had quarantined me that we all had to go through a formal quarantine before we could enter the town.

The wait wasn't bad. I read three novellas and then took a nap. When the door opened it wasn't Kate or the doctor that stood there, but Jack. He led me to another room and introduced me to an older gentleman, Jeremiah Kane, the leader of these people. From the first time I met him I was struck by the presence he exuded. He seemed old before his time but his eyes were filled with fiery energy. He told me he was overjoyed to meet me. After a lengthy discussion he asked me if I'd like to stay and work as their Archivist. He needed someone with not just a knowledge of books but also a deep love of them. Of course it didn't hurt that I brought a veritable library with me and some solar chargers. I jumped at the offer. A lifetime of reading books? With a hot cowboy sporting dimples and tattoos?

Sign me up.

Mike Bealie. . ._

THEY SAY WHEN THE END finally comes the meek will inherit the Earth. I call that a load of horse shit. When the four horsemen start their ride, it's people like me that are going to be left standing. My name is Mike Bealie and this is my blog. Some of you may know me from my website - DangerZonePreppers.com where I and a few others sell our fine selection of prepping gear. Now I know that there are some of you out there that do not think we are ever going to have a problem. That is fine, live in your own little world with cotton candy clouds and rivers made out of beer. As for me, I am going to be prepared when everything goes to shit.

NOVEMBER 21, 2032 – Hope everyone is going to have a great Thanksgiving. My wife and kids are getting the house decorated and we are going to live it up. After all, eat drink and be merry for tomorrow we die. For those of you that want to work a bit on your holiday weekend we have our new mini freeze drying appliance available for next day shipping over at Danger Zone Preppers. Get it today and you can be saving your turkey day leftovers for when you really need it.

DECEMBER 5, 2032 – Well the fat cats in Washington seem to think they're pretty important. I got word through the grapevine that there is a sudden exodus from the capital to resort areas out west. All on the taxpayer dime I bet. Like they work so hard? Those bums are barely ever at work. If you or I acted like that we would get fired. I will just remind you all of their little holiday around the next election time, okay? Jan and I have finally finished our mountain stronghold. Everyone thought I was crazy when I bought an old copper mine but I got it for a song. They had pretty much tapped out all the ore they could make money on, but what is left is more than enough to provide protection in the event of nuclear attack or a solar flare. The final touches got put on this last weekend. A foot thick door that seals the compound off from the outside world. Between the hydroponics, water recyclers, freeze dried, canned and preserved food we could feed a community of a hundred for almost fifty years. I also am waiting on one more shipment of seeds and my seed vault will be complete. I would have been done weeks ago if it wasn't for all the goddamn red tape. Damn bureaucrats trying to keep me from protecting my family!

DECEMBER 22, 2032 – I hope all of you have a great holiday season. Or to be more politically incorrect, Merry Christmas and Happy New Year! But do NOT let your guard down. I got some weird chatter coming out of China and England. There is a lot of crazy crap going on over there but someone is working overtime to try and keep it quiet. I can see a lot of you are hearing the same things based on the sales from our website. One customer out of New Mexico just cleaned out our entire stock so the rest of you will have to wait until after the first of the year for the next shipment.

DECEMBER 29TH, 2032 – As we get ready to ring in the New Year I'm starting to get pretty worried. I had Jan take her family and our kids and go to the mountain. I'm going to be joining them there later today. First I'm backing up my website and blog posts, just in case we have a media blackout and they try to erase the truth. We have a pretty good system set up at the mountain. Solar, geothermal, and wind power with a backup diesel generator. I should be able to upload to the net even if the entire western United States loses power. Reading back over my old posts I now start to see the rats fleeing the sinking ship right after Thanksgiving. Did they know something they weren't telling us? You can probably bank on it. Bastards.

JANUARY 5TH, 2033 – Jan's family is pissing me off! They think I'm a kook. I noticed how quickly they ran their asses here when they thought there was a problem. Now that nothing is hitting the "lamestream" media they all want to go home. I told them if they go then do not come back. So far the lily livered cowards are staying put. I am so tired of people who cannot see the writing on the wall. I got a call from New Mexico and that customer that bought my entire inventory wanted to buy me out again. He offered me and my family a place in his refuge for it. I told him that cash will do and we discussed prepping. This guy is the real deal. He knows what he is doing. At least one person out there can see the coming storm. I do not know if you are reading this but Jeremiah you are one of the few that has taken the blinders off.

JANUARY 18, 2033 – So now the wife's family is glad they came. They wanted to know if they could invite their friends and I told them to screw off. The people that are here are the ones that are supposed to be here. They should be glad I let them in. I only did it for Jan. The web is on fire today. Media blackouts are failing worldwide and it is easy to see why. The "lamestream" media here in the US is still fumbling the ball, but I got the real skinny from my contacts around the globe. There is a virus going around that causes people to go insane. No cure, spreads fast and the governments have no idea how to stop it. We sealed the outside vents just in case it is airborne.

JANUARY 20, 2033 – The virus is not airborne but I am not taking any chances that it will not mutate. Besides, half the time scientists get it wrong. I have set up a revolving IP on my website because someone kept blocking the old one. I think the government is trying to shut me up. It is a good thing we left the house when we did. My web cams show that men came to the house several times looking for me. Screw you, you fascists! Good luck finding me and better luck getting in if you do!

MARCH 3, 2033 – I have been silent for a while, mostly due to someone jamming my signal up to the satellite. But they could not keep me quiet forever. I wrote this up and set it to burst transmit out to the website. Things are getting bad overseas. Our wonderful reporters over here still have no clue. But over in Asia whole areas have been bombed. There are even reports of areas getting nuked by China inside its own country. I have unconfirmed reports that some of the European Union countries have gone silent. I have got a few friends there that I have not heard from in some time. If you guys see this please get in touch with me. I am really worried about you. Jan's family has finally started giving me the respect I deserve. Instead of the wacko that likes building bunkers in the woods I am now the genius who saw a way to keep them all safe. Again, they would not be here if Jan did not love them. None of them have any useful skills at all. Well, except her dad. He is a hell of an electrician.

APRIL 1, 2033 – The damn jammers have been horrible. I have been trying to get a message out for almost a month. How fitting that on April Fool's Day the jamming disappears. I thought it was a joke until I turned on the television. Yep, the mountain has a full satellite television system with a protected dish. And what did I see on my screen? The head of the CDC, Dr. Johan Meiticoff, telling us all the horrible truth. Of course the jamming is gone. They cannot hide this from the people anymore. The facts about the virus are out and it is worse than I could have imagined. We are facing the end of the world. The Zombie Apocalypse people always joked about has finally come to pass. For those of you in areas that still do not have the details I will summarize what he said the best I can.

1) Infection can be spread quickest from a bite or scratch from one of the dead. A slower form of infection occurs when body fluid of any kind gets on you from them.

2) The incubation period ranges from a few hours (for bites) to four to ten hours for scratches or fluid infection.

3) Those infected get red around mouth and eyes. Complaints of weakness and fatigue are common. The victim loses all energy until they lie down and fall into a coma. After death the victim rises very quickly as one of the walking dead.

4) There is no known cure. All attempts to combat the virus have failed.

5) The dead are unable to climb. Even a steep sloping ramp can stop them. But given enough numbers they eventually will make their way through most barriers. They possess incredible strength and endless endurance. They have been known to follow an automobile for days and continue in a straight line after their victim unless they see a different victim.

All citizens are being evacuated by their governments to places of refuge. The fools! How are they going to filter out the infected from the healthy? Where are they going to put them? Have they given any thought to sustainability? What do they do when their food runs out, or water? They have no idea what they are doing. And it is the innocents that will suffer. Just like it always is when government throws their weight around without a clue about what they are doing.

APRIL 10, 2033 – Even I am amazed at how quickly things have gone to hell. It was only a few days ago that they declared Martial Law in New York and now the city is being abandoned. Zombies spread way too fast. The military is at best fighting a retreating action. How do you fight an enemy that has no fear and does not get tired? Whose blood flies out in every direction when struck and can infect an entire company when it is blown apart? Conventional warfare has been turned on its ear. At the rate they are spreading they could be here in Colorado by the end of the month.

APRIL 12, 2033 – I cannot believe the reports coming out of the east. The entire eastern seaboard has been abandoned. There are even military units that have been left behind because the chopper pilots are unwilling to take the risk that there is an infected among the soldiers. The system is breaking down. It did not even take that hard a shove to make it topple. The military is in complete chaos. There are people talking about the Army shooting uninfected rather than leaving them to join the growing horde of undead. Jan is still unable to comprehend that the end is here. She has a crazy hope that they will find a cure.

APRIL 20, 2033 – I am so glad that I installed that old HAM radio system. It is the only communication that is still reliable. Satellite television is out. Power is likely going out all over the country. I am sure that the internet is not far behind. The redundant power stations that keep it going are only meant to last a few weeks. I hope that anyone reading this is doing so from the safety of their own refuge. I am setting up a network of HAM radio operators, if you have a radio scan for us on the upper bandwidth. We hope to open lines of communication between the survivors. If nothing else we can trade knowledge and try and help each other with problems.

ABOVE ENTRIES WERE PRINTED FROM the worldwide web before it crashed. Founder of Vigilance has kept in contact with Mountain Refuge since the days of the fall. One of the few refuges still flourishing.

Nathan Brill

MY NAME IS NATHAN BRILL and I am alone. In a way, I was always alone. There was part of me that was never happy, so maybe on some level I knew this was coming. I don't mean to say that I am psychic. Or on the other end of the spectrum that I simply had the blues. No, I was unhappy on a fundamental level, almost on the molecular level. It started when I was about twelve. One day I was at school, in Mrs. Rantif's sixth grade classroom, when suddenly the realization hit me. I was not happy and I never would be. At the time, as you can imagine, the feeling disturbed me. I spent a lot of time looking up my condition in the library in my hometown. And I had to do it on the sly. There was no way I wanted my parents finding out their son was studying mental illness.

In the end, after an exhaustive search, I came to the conclusion that I was actually was nuts. The books listed my condition as severe clinical depression. The suggested treatment was mood altering drugs and perhaps a stay in a nice mental facility. Whenever the inclination crossed my mind to talk about my issues the thought of being confined kept me quiet. I did a fair job of pretending to be happy even though the best I achieved was to keep from looking miserable. My parents normally chalked it up to normal teenage angst.

I managed to maintain high enough grades to keep my parents off my back and the school counselor at bay. I could have been a straight A student, if I had put any effort into it. But I just did not care. There always seemed to be a black cloud hanging over everything. It kept me from taking any normal concerns seriously. My studies rarely interested me, although at times things would catch my attention. Like the semester they taught us to weld in shop class. Or the summer camp where I learned how to live off the land and make shelters from basic materials. My parents, bless their hearts, thought camp might help me work through some of my issues. If they had any idea how bad it was I am sure they would have sent me away to get electroshock therapy.

My years leading up to college were pathetic. I spent most of my time reading, working out and brooding. At least that is what my mother called it. What I was actually doing was desperately searching for a cure for my condition. No holistic methods helped for long. All my attempts left me feeling incomplete. I eventually was able to take pleasure in many things, but I could not quite shake my feeling of foreboding. Girls seemed to find my quiet serious air attractive. It was almost comical how many tried to capture me. After a few days or weeks, when they got tired of not being the center of my attention, they would leave in a huff. Still, women were one of the things that took my mind off my problems. But the minute my attention wandered I would find myself again sliding down a dark hole into hell.

The older I got, the more the future troubled me. With every passing day the specter of doom that had been haunting me seemed to grow more immense. I graduated high school, surprising more than one of my teachers who had expected me to drop out. One of the women I had loved and lost, Mandy, came to my graduation party. She had been a year ahead of me in school and was now pre-med. Her intro to psych class had given her some insight into my behavior, and she begged me to get help for my conditions.

I doubted that I could be helped, but at her insistence (and to keep her from revealing my issue to my parents) I went to see a psychiatrist. Her name was Emily Bickers. She told me that my condition was very treatable but I figured it would be a colossal waste of time. How wrong I was, the medication she prescribed did exactly what she said it would. Suddenly, the fear was gone. I felt better than I ever had. It was amazing. Like a switch being flipped, my dark concerns just disappeared. I headed off to college with a much more optimistic outlook on life.

The way the drugs changed me awakened a powerful curiosity to know more about how it all worked. After some study I decided to begin working on a degree in pharmacology. With my obsessive behavior now properly channeled, I managed to graduate early and began working at a local pharmacy. That is when Mandy came back and began interning at the local hospital. We started dating and before I knew it we were living together. When her internship was over we moved to Seattle. Mandy took a job at Seattle General and I went to work for a small pharmacy near the ocean. We had a daughter, Macy, and a son we named Greg. The future looked, for once, full of promise. It was wonderful, for a few years.

Then the first case appeared in the US. Mandy started hearing scary things at the hospital. One night she called me from the car on her way home with the kids. There had been reports of outbreaks in town and she wanted to leave right away for her parents place in Canada. I heard a crash and she stopped responding to me. Then I heard moaning. Then the screaming started. I heard my children calling for their mother just before the phone went dead. I went out and jumped on my motorcycle and raced towards the babysitter's house. Her house was only ten minutes away. I saw our car when I topped the rise about half way there. It was surrounded by people. At the time I couldn't understand what was going on. Now I look back and know with utter clarity at what was happening. They weren't people, they were zombies.

The windows on the car were smashed. The remnants of my wife and children were laying on the ground, zombies still gnawing on them. I blacked out. Lucky for me zombies can't climb. If they could I would have woken up dead. When I came around, it was dark and the hill was surrounded by the undead. There at the base of the hill were three zombies that I recognized, my wife and children. Mandy had been ripped open from neck to navel. Her guts were hanging out and trailed behind her on the ground. Little Greg . . . and

Macy . . . I cannot even bring myself to describe what happened to them. I barely recognized either of them. I started screaming and then I must have blacked out again.

When I woke up it was still dark. My dead family was gone as were most of the zombies at the bottom of the hill. I picked my bike up and rode home. We lived at the top of a hill and other than dodging a few monsters I had very little trouble getting there. Once I was inside I went to the medicine cabinet. I am not proud of what I did, but I was out of my mind. I took everything to the kitchen and poured all the drugs from the medicine cabinet into a mixing bowl. I took a bottle of whiskey out of the cabinet and swallowed the contents of the bottle and bowl together.

I woke up three days later in a pool of my own vomit, urine and feces. I stumbled to the bathroom and took a shower. I was halfway done washing my hair when the pressure started to go. I rinsed off as quick as I could and had just finished when the water disappeared. I tried the lights and found that the power was out. Going down to the garage I found an old weather radio, the kind with a hand crank for power. Grinding the handle I was rewarded with a squeal of noise but no signal. It took a bit of fine tuning but I finally got a channel.

The only thing on the radio was the emergency broadcasting system. And it sounded like someone had left it on a loop. All people were told to move to designated safe zones. The closest one to me was near the high school by the ocean. I went to the garage and fueled up the bike. Then, as an afterthought, I put my emergency fuel pump and tube in the saddlebag. Buckling the fuel can onto the back, I headed towards the school.

I had no idea what I was doing, I was running on autopilot. On the way to the school I passed wandering groups of undead that shambled in my direction. By the time I got to the hill overlooking the school I had a parade of zombies behind me. The school was on fire and there were zombies everywhere. Abandoned buses, army Humvees and military trucks were all over the place. I noticed a lot of the zombies down below were wearing fatigues. Putting out the radio I cranked it again and listed to the message.

The next refuge was either north or south. The thought of going north, like I had planned to do with my family, put me on the edge of driving my bike into a tree at high speed. I headed south. There was a refuge south of Eatonville. When I got near, there were a bunch of crazies firing off automatic weapons. The noise was pulling every shambler in the area to them. I decided to move on further south. When I got just north of Los Angeles I started getting another channel. A radio station from the area was telling people to avoid L.A. It was overrun with zombies and killer gangs.

After sitting at the top of a hill thinking for an hour I decided to drive off into the desert. But, there were fucking zombies even in the desert. Wandering solo dead as well as undead trios, groups and hordes. One of the larger hordes forced me due south as I got near Las Vegas. I should have known the City of Sin would be over run. If I were a zombie where would I want to go? Seventeen days after I lost my family, according to my watch, I was sitting in a bar on the top of a rise getting drunk. What medication I had in my system had long since washed out and the weight of my depression had me lower than I had ever been before.

The alcohol helped. It was harder to feel the pain when you could not feel anything at all. I woke up with a killer headache, feeling like I had been run over by a truck. If I am to be completely honest I had given up. The full realization of the loss of my wife, of my children, had finally settled on me. With my back pressed up against that rickety wooden bar I wept until I felt like I would break in half.

Mandy had helped me make the darkness go away. It had been wonderful, but what a price I had paid for momentary relief. I found myself wondering, if I had not been on medication would she have wanted to be with me? Would we have had the kids? Was it worth it? The scant years they had lived? The horrible way they had died? In the end they were gone and I was left behind with my pain. For all I knew I was the last human alive on a planet of zombies. The guilt was almost overwhelming. I found solace in drinking for a few days but eventually even the whiskey did not dull the pain.

My dreams haunted me even when I was awake. I woke every night from nightmares of my children, screaming in agony as monsters ripped them apart. Screaming "Daddy, why won't you save us?" over and over again. My wife looking at me with such angry accusation in her eyes. I would wake in a cold sweat, sometimes screaming myself hoarse. Even after waking my ears could almost hear the sound of flesh being ripped apart.

Despair greeted me each day with the morning dawn. I began sleeping less and less. The thought of facing my wife and children again, of seeing my guilt reflected in their eyes, was heartbreaking. I left the bar. I set it on fire to make sure I could never return. It was more of a symbolic gesture. There are empty bars the world over. None of their patrons would be returning after all. At least not to drink. I took the bike out on the open road, not really heading anywhere, just needing to move.

The fifth day out from the burned shell of the bar a sandstorm came up. I am a kid from the suburbs, so I had no clue what the wall of brown in the distance meant. When it spanned the horizon I realized I was in trouble. There were zombies around and being out in that storm would be just like being out in the dark. Fuck that. I might be crazy but I am not stupid. Nor was I going to sit up on a rock in a windstorm. At the top of a distant steep rise I spotted what looked like an old fort. I sped to the top just ahead of the storm. There was an old stone building with no roof. Inside the building there was a less dilapidated section with an intact room with a solid door. After checking to make sure it was empty I ducked inside.

The storm had started just before nightfall. The howl of the wind was hypnotic and before I knew it I was falling asleep. My nightmares were waiting to pounce on my as soon as my eyes were closed. My children appeared first with blood leaking from their eyes with bite marks all over their faces. Then Mandy, ravaged flesh hanging like a macabre parody of a wedding dress hanging from her body. Accusation burning in their eyes their hands reached towards me. I woke screaming and almost stabbed the woman leaning over me. It was instinct, I was still in the dream, but I still would have killed her.

Without hesitation she punched me in the face. I sprawled back on the ground in a daze. By the time I got my head together she was standing on the other side of the room. Pretty. That was the first thing that occurred to me. And she looked really pissed. Not that I could blame her. Someone trying to stab you should piss you off. I raised my hands. "Shit. Sorry. Sorry. I was having a nightmare. Sorry." She looked at me for a minute with this odd expression.

"Yeah, I guess we are all having a nightmare. One that never ends," she said. She turned towards the door while keeping an eye on me. It was still open and I saw shadows moving outside. Before I could speak four people stepped inside, two men and two women. The larger of the two men looked at her quizzically. She moved her hands rapidly and his expression changed to a knowing look. It looked like they were talking in sign language. Securing the door one of the women sat with her back against it and all of them stared at me. Then there was another flurry of silent hand conversation before the woman I had almost stabbed turned back to me.

"No offense intended but do you live here?" I looked at her in confusion before glancing around the room. "Here? Hell no. I just ducked in here during a dust storm and fell asleep while I was waiting for it to pass." She nodded as if I had just verified what she had already been thinking. Motioning to the others she introduced them one by one. Her name was Tina and the big guy was her brother Danny. Danny was a deaf mute. The woman near the door was her friend Bree. The other two were neighbors from their building, Tom and Betty Lou Davidson. They had all been friends before things went to hell. All of them had learned sign language to make it easier to talk with Danny.

Sign language had proven invaluable after the zombies showed up. It allowed them to communicate without making noise, an advantage when surrounded by the attentive undead. They set up their camp in the room and set a watch. To watch me as much as for trouble and I did not blame them. I was a stranger. Why should they trust me? In the morning they had another discussion and Tina asked me where I was headed. When it became clear I had no real direction they invited me to come with them. I almost said no. Part of me just wanted to wander until I died. Something that would have happened sooner rather than later if I was by myself.

In the end it was the encouraging smile that Bree gave me that made me agree. It was nice to have people around even if everyone was still wary of me. It took a while, weeks, but we got to know each other. This was how I rejoined humanity. It was a stilted comedy of errors and happenstance wrapped in a clusterfuck of coincidence. Had I not stopped there or if they had stopped sooner I would have wandered off into oblivion. Instead, I became part of a group that kept me alive.

Over the next year I learned to do more than not die. I learned to live again. Bree took a special interest in me. Our stories were similar. She had lost her husband, but they had never had children. Because, as she told me late one night when everyone was asleep, she wasn't able to have kids. This secret made us a perfect match. Because I couldn't imagine having kids again. Not in this world.

We traveled a lot during that year. Looking for food, water and avoiding danger. Searching for a place we could stop running. More survivors joined us and we had to set up a rough hierarchy to maintain order. I suddenly found myself not only in charge of people but required to keep them safe. My protests were overruled by the others. My surviving on my own was soon the stuff of legend among the new people. Telling them I fumblefucked my way through it all only made it worse. Some insisted I had an instinct for survival and for some reason people started to believe it.

Things were getting pretty bad towards the end of the year. I had been feeling down for about the last month we were out there. Food was getting harder to find. We lost one of our people to a fall. Margaret Templeton. She was about my age. We actually had talked a lot about music during our many hours together. Anyway, she fell and broke her leg. The bone got shoved right out of the skin. We did what we could but it was pointless. After she died I helped bury her. We stacked a stone cairn on top of her, just in case she considered getting back up.

My moods had been getting dark before this, but now they got downright black. Hope just seemed to be slipping away from me. What was the point? We scraped and fought and for what? To die when we take a fall? Fuck the world that fucks you. Bree had been trying to keep my spirits up, and when she was around things were good. But she couldn't be with me every second of every day. And when she wasn't…Well, things were getting steadily worse every day anyway, there was no arguing that. My nightmares had started up again and I had been sleeping with a rag tied in my mouth to keep from making too much noise.

I was off scouting one day. Well, to be honest I was off on my own brooding, when I ran into Hamilton Graves. He scared the living shit out of me. One second I was alone and the next minute he was standing there like a fucking bogeyman. Once I got my heart palpitations under control he bent my ear for a bit. At first I thought he was trying to pull something on me. He said we had been watched for a while and our plight had not gone unnoticed. Plight? Who in the fuck uses that word? It was like talking to a fucking dictionary. I like to think of myself as intelligent but half the time I had to figure out his vocabulary from what context he used a word in. The basic gist was a place in their refuge for all of us.

I went back to the group and told them about him. The offer was taken with a heavy dose of skepticism. We argued for quite a long time. Everyone was all for telling Graves thanks but no thanks. But they were ignoring the larger issue. We were in trouble, too many mouths to feed and no place of refuge. In the end the feeling of doom decided me more than anything else. I told them I would go with him. If it was a trick I would be the only prize. If it was a good offer I would come back and let them know.

Bree was not having any of it. We argued in front of everyone and she gave me an ultimatum. Stay or we were through. Even though my heart hurt to do it I stepped forward, took her face in my hands and kissed her. I told her if she changed her mind I would be back. She stood there with a look of such abject shock it was almost funny. Almost. I walked out and met up with Hamilton and disappeared into the waste.

He took me to his town, Vigilance. We passed through a dizzying array of landscapes, tunnels and one section I had to walk through blindfolded. Needless to say I would not be able to find my way back on my own. Then I had to go through half a day of quarantine before being allowed in to meet the guy who ran the place. Phillip Kane. Long story short he had something we needed, namely safety and security. We had something he needed, the sign language. Our ability to speak silently was something he thought would help his people greatly. At the time I figured he was using it as an excuse to bring us in. I learned later how wrong I was. The ability to speak silently over distances of a few feet or more can be invaluable.

So the silent came to Vigilance and began teaching everyone sign language. To her credit Bree did not hold my decision against me. Though she did make me pay for it. I had to promise her that I would never go out in the waste again. Not really a hard promise to make. Now if I could only get rid of that dark cloud that lives over my head. Things would be almost normal again. Almost.

Dr. Rachel Gralin

THIS IS LIKE LIVING IN a nightmare. The only reason that I'm still alive is because I'm a plastic surgeon. As far as I know everyone that I went to school with is dead, most of them in the first wave. This virus . . . it is like the worst things we talked about in virology class got together, had a gang bang and this was the result. No cure, quick incubation period and highly contagious. It hit the shores of the United States like an invisible army which quickly turned into a very visible undead horde.

My name is Dr. Rachel Graelin. I was just hitting my stride when Murphy's Law kicked in. I had just moved into my house in Malibu overlooking the ocean. There was a doctor, James Carson, who worked in the ER of Thousand Oaks. We were dating and it was starting to get pretty serious. Then the virus scare began, be we thought that's all it was, a scare. No one out on the west coast was really paying much attention. After all, we had mountains in between us and any problems. Then I got a call from one of the nurses that worked with James. Some crazy guy had come into the ER moaning. He started attacking a patient near the door and James tried to pull him off. The guy had bitten James and she said it was pretty serious. I jumped in the car and sped towards the hospital. Three blocks away I ran into a military blockade. They turned me around at gunpoint and told me to return home.

Even before I got back to the house one of my friends on the police force called my cell. He told me that James died from a gunshot wound to the head. But he was walking around without a pulse before he was shot. The entire hospital was quarantined and sealed up. He said he really wasn't supposed to talk about it. But he told me to get to out of town right away if I could. And avoid the freeway. Panicked people had put the freeways in gridlock making them parking lot smorgasbords for any zombies that happened by.

Looking out my window I could see the exodus ran in every direction. People migrated to the mountains hoping that the elevation would keep them safe. Or the sea hoping the vast waters would protect them. Those heading north and south likely had all sorts of reasons for where they were headed. Canada had fewer zombies, but later we found out that droves of people died from exposure when winter hit. Thirst killed just as many who headed south.

I sat in my house in the hills and watched the world tear itself apart. My neighbor Bob got shot in the face by a soccer mom who wanted the gas in his hummer for her minivan. I saw her do it. No hesitation, no remorse. Just pulled the gun out, shot him in the face and went on her way. After that I learned to keep to myself. I hid in my panic room with my food and water. Eventually the people all just went away. When I started to get low on supplies I ventured out. It was shocking how bad things had gotten in just a week.

Zombies were wandering the neighborhood. They were slow and had trouble walking over curbs or up hills so they were easy to avoid. And apparently a lot of people had retreated into their homes after being infected. I could see them shambling around inside. There were no living people around that I saw. I searched empty houses for supplies, but there was almost nothing worthwhile. I found a jar of peanut butter in Bob's house. He used to eat out a lot. Faced with the real concern of starvation I headed down the block.

Before she had taken off on her cruise, from which she never returned, Dale Myers had asked me to do her a favor. A real pushy bitch from the neighborhood, she wouldn't take no for an answer. At the time I was pissed. She was a member of the welcome wagon and insisted that we were going to be lifelong friends the moment she met me. Then she asked me for the favor a few lunches later. I should have known that there was a catch. She had an order coming in of expensive dried fruit and a cash register for her new health food store. The grand opening was supposed to be at the end of the month. I had met the delivery guy as she demanded, then locked up the store and hadn't given it a second thought.

It turns out that manipulative bitch saved my life. The store was full of all the overpriced new age stuff that yuppies spent way too much of their lives obsessing about. Freeze dried tofu, nuts, trail mix up the ying yang and all manner of healthy protein. Between that and the fact that no one knew it was there, I decided to move what little I had into the store.

Two months later I was turning into a crazy cat lady, minus the cats. That was one of odd things I noticed on day. All the animals that used to be around were gone. The shamblers got them or scared them off I guess. Even the birds were nonexistent. I found myself missing the annoying calls of the flying rats everyone called seagulls. And I hated those things before, the way they always shit all over your car when you went down to the ocean.

There was a private satellite dish on top of the store that got every channel that was being broadcast. The power went out at my place before I ran out of food, but Dale had put in a solar panel system so the store was powered up. She had metal hurricane covers set up for all the windows, part insurance thing part security system. I left them down. Metal would hold out both the living and the dead better. It also let me keep the lights on once I blacked out the little window on the door.

With power and television I got to see the eradication of the human race. I know enough about medicine to be able to read between the lines on the broadcasts. Authorities were panicking. That was enough to make me glad that I hadn't tried to go out in this madness. The outbreak was marching unchecked across the face of the Earth. Even on the channels I couldn't understand, the ones from other countries, you could see the truth on the news anchor's faces.

Things were going from bad to worse. One by one the channels started to disappear. Not sign off, just drop to static.

I found myself crying . . . a lot. Now, I realize that a lot of people probably wept oceans of tears after the fall started. But I was never a really emotional girl. Sappy movies didn't get to me. I never burst into tears at a wedding. Not to say that I'm a cold and unfeeling person, I just don't let things get to me. That's part of what made me one of the best, if not the best, plastic surgeon in the state. Seeing those channels drop away did something to me. Sobs, deep and painful, burst from me like they never had before. It was like watching hundreds of thousands of people blinking out as the stations became static.

When there were three channels left, I decided not to get out of bed. It seemed pointless to even eat anything. So I lay on the sleeping bag I had brought from my house, a gift from James the first time he took me camping, and waited for the channel I was watching to fade out. Suddenly there was a man on the screen. Old, gaunt, pale. He gave the camera with a grim look and began to speak.

The country had fallen to the undead. The president and most of the leadership was dead as well. Each general was taking personal command of his remaining troops. The man on the television was in charge of the West Coast. He was directing people to move to the Naval Air Weapons Station at China Lake just north of Ridgecrest. The terrain was conducive to holding the dead indefinitely. He urged all of us to make our way the best we could to that area. He warned that there would be quarantines to pass, but he was offering refuge to the uninfected.

The message started over again and repeated for an hour. Then the channel blinked off. This time there were no tears. It was like they came from a well that had run dry inside me. After a few minutes the sound of the static began to grate on my nerves and I got up and grabbed the remote. Flipping through the channels stations there was only static. No more stations. No more people. I might as well be alone on the planet.

I started talking to myself. Just a little here and there at first, but after a while with no television or news I had full conversations with myself. Two days after the last station went dark I started wondering if I should just take my chances with getting to the refuge. I went outside to see if I could find a car and the dead were everywhere. I went around back and saw what I had been hoping for. The pride and joy of that overbearing eco bitch's life. Dale's baby, an electric hybrid with solar charging. After tossing her entire office I found the keys on a nail right near the door. Loading the car with everything I could I got in and started to drive.

It was a pretty good little SUV with high clearance. This let me drive through yards, over bodies and even though a few wooden fences. I got pretty far using my local knowledge, staying to low populated areas and off large roads. By the time it was getting dark though I was coming into unfamiliar territory and the SUV needed a charge. So before the sun went down I parked on the top of a steep hill. I didn't get a lot of sleep that night. I kept expecting to look out my window and see the face of a zombie waiting to smash the window and eat me.

The next morning things looked better. There were no zombies as far as the eye could see and the road I was on, a side highway, looked to be clear of traffic. Two hours later I found out why. The entire road was blockaded by cement barriers. Semis had been turned sideways and had barbed wire strung through them. It was totally impassable. I sat there thinking for almost five minutes. Abandon the SUV and proceed on foot or backtrack? In the end I could not bring myself to get out of the car. Besides there is no way I could carry all the supplies. I went back and took the Pacific Coast Highway. I had avoided it because I had been afraid it might be blocked. Quite the contrary, it was smooth sailing almost all the way to Santa Monica. Then it was full of abandoned cars.

I had to take to the grass and drive around all manner of vehicles from smart cars to army trucks. Again, I found myself glad that the little electric had enough power. By the end of the day I had to pull over and figure out how to activate the motor power to recharge the batteries. The owner's manual was still in the glove compartment and I realized when I was done reading it that it was the first time I had ever read the owner's manual for a car. The vehicle came with a ten gallon gas tank, that I saw from the gauge was full. I would give you the option of running the engine when you got to half and quarter charge. That explained the light I had seen last night. All you had to do was push the ignition button on the dash to start the engine when that light came on.

This option was a godsend because I had to creep around the greater Los Angeles area. I kept to the suburbs and even then tried to keep to the outskirts. Luckily the SUV made almost no noise. There was a button to turn off the exterior engine noise when the motor wasn't running. Apparently the makers had an electronic engine noise built in to make the vehicle safer, for pedestrians, but I had no interest in their safety, so I turned off the sound. The few zombies that did follow after me lost interest when a noise caught their attention.

I took a side road to the northeast that said it led to Devils Punch Bowl National Park. I'd gone there once with a group of friends. James had taken me there recently to scout out locations for another camping trip. Thinking about him made my chest hurt so bad that for a moment I thought I might be having a heart attack. Then I realized it was just a panic attack. Taking deep breaths, I carefully drove through the trees. The downside of taking this path is that I was forced to use the engine most of the way. There just wasn't enough sunlight under the canopy. Thankfully, there were very few zombies around. Those that were there would have followed me regardless of any noise I made. I was the only thing around.

I ended up on top of a high hill on the side of the road that night. Again I slept fitfully, wondering if a zombie would come and smash out my windows. The next day a few zombies were waiting at the bottom of the hill but I simply drove past them. Their half-hearted moans did little to slow me down. I came out of the park later that day near Phelan. I took another road that led northeast towards Barstow. According to my map it was less populated and I could try and cut back through more rural areas up to the refuge north of Ridgecrest.

I stopped once along the way to steal two gas cans. They were on the back of a big SUV that was nose first in the ditch. I yanked the cans off and strapped them to my SUV's roof. By the time I was back inside a few zombies had started to shamble over. Other than that I didn't have any big adventures on my drive. At one point I did see another car in my rear view mirror but I sped off since I was able to see the road for quite some distance ahead of me. I don't know if they ever saw me or not. I got to Ridgecrest a few hours later. There was no one living there, but there were plenty of zombies. Best I could figure the place got overrun. Maybe they let infected inside. It didn't matter. I was out of luck. The one good thing I found was an army truck that was empty. There was a radio inside, the portable kind. I grabbed it, ammo and guns, and a box of water and rations before driving away. That night when I stopped at the top of a hill I worked on figuring out the radio.

The great thing about the Army is that they make things for the lowest common denominator. I was able to use the pictograms on the side of the thing to discern its operation. You cranked the handle on the side until you were so damn tired you wanted to die. Then it worked for a few minutes. I tried calling out a few times but no one responded. I broadcast that I would try in the morning and at night on several frequencies, than I went to sleep.

When I woke up I cranked the radio and tried again. This time I reached a Tom Meadows who was in a refuge in Hearst Castle in San Simeon California. Had I know they were there I would have gone the opposite direction and reached safety. Tom said that there were refuges all over, the closest one to me that he knew was still active was north of Las Vegas in what was known as Area 51. He told me coming to him now was not advisable. The dead had the place surrounded. They were in no danger but he doubted I could get to them safely.

I thanked him and felt a surge of joy. It had been so long since I had talked to anyone but myself. I hadn't realized how much I missed it. I headed southeast again before heading northwest towards Las Vegas. The abandoned cars made it clear I wouldn't be able to get through. The side of the road was so soft I almost got the SUV stuck twice. In the end I abandoned the thought of getting to the refuge at Area 51. There were too many vehicles and too many dead between here and there. I turned southeast and tried to get as far away from them as I could.

Each night I would use the radio, each morning I would use the radio. I collected gas cans, siphoned gas, scavenged food. I shot a man near Flagstaff Arizona. He was going to rape me, then kill me. Perhaps not in that order. He wasn't a zombie but he was a monster. I fled from his friends in my SUV across the desert, losing them in the waste. I got horribly lost. To be safe I stopped using the motor and only traveled during the day, stopping before it got dark to let the batteries recharge.

My food and water were running out when I got stuck. The left rear wheel slid into a soft spot of sand and went down to the hub. It pulled my front right wheel into the air and without warning the car stopped. Lights came on. Then it all shut down. I read and reread the owner's manual trying to make sense of it. Finally I discovered a safety feature to prevent you burning out the electric motors. When one wheel wouldn't move and another spun freely it shut the motors down. To reset them I had to free the wheel and turn the car off and on. The only problem was that after five hours of trying I couldn't get the wheel free.

I fell asleep crying and woke up to a living nightmare. The face of a zombie outside my window, at least I thought it was a zombie. The figure retreated and raised its hands. I reached down and pulled my .45 from beneath the blanket and pointed it. The figure remained still with its hands raised. It spoke and I realized it was a man. He told me his name was George Larson and he was not going to hurt me. After spotting my vehicle stuck he was trying to figure out if I was dead, or undead. He asked if he could give me a hand. Without taking the gun off of him I nodded. He moved to the back of the car and then asked me to put it in neutral. I did and he rocked the car right up out of the soft sand.

Once back on level ground I turned the car on, off and on again. The dash lit up green and I sped away. From behind me I heard the faint cry of "Your Welcome!" before he disappeared in a cloud of dust. I only drove a few more feet before I slammed on the breaks. If he had wanted to kill me he could have done it while I was asleep. Right? So I turned around and stopped ten feet away from him. He stood in exactly the spot I had left him in. We talked. Me from inside the car with the window down a few inches, him from right where he had been standing.

In an hour I let him come closer. In two hours he was sitting in the car with me, directing me towards a refuge. We are stopped for the night and he tells me we should arrive before noon tomorrow. He came from the town of Vigilance and they needed medical people, even a plastic surgeon is in high demand. The leader of their refuge has his people out looking for anyone that they could find. I suspect it is more anyone that can be useful. Not that I blame them. Safety is a commodity now, just like money used to be. Between me and what I have in the car he is sure that not only will I be made a full citizen but I will be able help them out quite a bit. I hope he is right. I would love to be somewhere that I don't have to worry about being eaten alive from one moment to the next. I'm tired of running. Hopefully, I'm coming home.

Weight Loss Journal – Helen Madison

Day 1 –

I'M GOING INTO THIS WITH an open mind. Dr. McEntyre said that if I want to take control of my weight issues I have to make myself accountable. This means no more cupcakes on my way home. No take-out, no chocolate, no calorie filled drinks. Water is my new best friend. Rice cakes will be my new snack of choice. I can do this. It's a new beginning. I'm going to get down to a size six before Janet's wedding. I will not be the fat bridesmaid, damn it.

Day 2 –

I CAN DO THIS. I passed up donuts at work today and have been sticking to my diet. Only two more days and my exercise program starts. I'm supposed to meet my personal trainer, Billie, tomorrow.

Day 3 –

BILLIE SEEMS NICE. SHE WAS really excited about my goals and wants to work out with me every day. I really hope I can at least lose some of the weight. I bought some comfortable workout clothes. God I'm a fucking cow. XXL? WTF? I'm so losing this weight.

Day 4 —

FIRST WORK OUT WITH BILLIE. God hates me. There are muscles I didn't even realize that I had that are hurting. I'm going to have to get a hot tub filled with Icy Hot. For now I plan on eating my rabbit food, curling up in bed, and crying myself to sleep.

Day 5 —

READING BACK THROUGH THIS I can't believe how quickly this has begun to suck. I now understand why the doctor wanted me to journal during this. To remind myself why I'm doing this. To keep myself honest. And to give me someone to whine to that actually wants to listen. I went back to Billie today and told her I was dying. She laughed. Then she took me through some stretches that helped. Who knew that stretching before and after our workouts was so important. I guess she figured I had taken enough P.E. to know that I am supposed to stretch pre and post workout. Now I'm sore and I feel like an idiot.

Day 6 —

TOMORROW IS MY CHEAT DAY. For the first time in a long time I've got no interest in eating anything. Instead I bought a bottle of vodka. I can drink half of it and still not use up my extra calories. And maybe it will put the painful fires out in my muscles.

Day 7 —

VODKA ROCKS. THAT IS ALL.

Day 8 –

VODKA SUCKS. I WOKE UP dehydrated, my head pounding and sand pouring out of my mouth. I guess I should have spent the twenty bucks extra and bought the good stuff. Apparently I bought turpentine someone mislabeled as vodka. Billie had absolutely no sympathy for me. The only time she let up at all was when I left the exercise floor to go puke my guts out. Then she smiled and commented on the dangers of over indulging. I fucking hate her guts and hope she gets eaten by rabid dogs.

Day 9 –

THE CLUB CALLED AND SAID that Billie was going to be unavailable and offered me a different trainer. They wouldn't tell me why. I probably pissed her off. Screw her. I've been thinking about getting away for a bit anyway. I've done the routine enough that I can exercise anywhere. Plus it would be a good time to practice my good habits away from home. Belle has been asking me to come visit her in Kansas City. Since she and her long time man Zack broke up my little sister has been kind of down. I think I'll go see her.

Day 10 –

OKAY, LET ME JUST SAY that air travel is turning into a goddamn nightmare. I don't remember ever being more stressed in my life. First, the security lines were crazy long. They were doing all sorts of weird tests, pulling anyone that looked sick out of line. Some nonsense about bird flu or something. Then I get on the plane and there is a huge delay while these guys in suits walk up and down the aisle looking at everyone. We finally get in the air and right before we land there is some sort of ruckus towards the back of the plane.

So glad I don't fly coach. Anyway we ended up having to disembark without a chance to get our things. Screw them. I already had my bag in my hands before we started our descent. Then they told me they had lost my fucking luggage. I filled out the form and grabbed a cab to Belle's. We are pretty much the same size. She is a bit smaller than me but close enough to borrow stuff to wear. Belle is really down. She barely listened to me telling her about the trip. I think she is still hung up on Zack. He just took off she said. No note, no call, nothing. Poor kid.

Day 11 –

IT IS EASY TO FOLLOW your diet when you're at home. But being in Kansas City with all this barbecue has made it a bit more difficult. I love barbecue. Belle took me to this great place and I barely kept from blowing my diet. Luckily Belle distracted me with her tales of work. She is a claims adjuster at a big insurance company. Apparently, they've been getting all sorts of weird reports from the east coast. Disappearances and odd accidents. Things just seem to be going to hell back home.

Day 12 –

I SAT DOWN TO WATCH the news for the first time in . . . well a long time. I can't believe what is going on. I actually pulled up the program guide to make sure that I wasn't on the SyFy channel. No such luck. New York City, my home was all over the news. The greatest city in the world was suffering from an outbreak. The specifics were still sketchy, the military presence was not. There were soldiers everywhere. And they were shooting people. At least that is what it looked like before the camera guy got shut down.

Day 17 –

BELLE IS DEAD. I STILL can't believe it. I was waiting at home to talk to her about what I'd seen on television. My cell phone rang. It was the police. They had me listed at her work as next of kin. They hadn't known I was in town. They sent a car by to take me to the morgue. She had been killed in a car accident. Some crazy guy lost control of his semi and hit her. She was killed instantly. I returned to her house and lost track of time. Between bawling my eyes out I talked to people on the phone and made funeral arrangements. After that I talked with the neighbors that stopped by. She had a lot of nice people in her life. At least I can take comfort in that.

Day 18 –

WOW. I TURNED THE NEWS on today and realized that a hell of a lot has happened. New York has been quarantined. Boston too. Most of the east coast seems to have been put under martial law and this infection has gotten bad. They're saying the virus causes the dead to rise from the grave. Like some bad horror movie on late night. If you get bitten or scratched you get a fever and die. Fluid transfer can also turn you, it just takes longer. Either way about eight hours after exposure you lie down as you and get back up as one of them. It is horrifying how fast the infections have spread. Europe is screwed, Africa is overrun, and Asia has tons of zombies. They've got a map up with red on it. Red on the map shows it a month ago, a week ago and then day by day. It goes from a few red dots to a wave of red spreading across the country. Air traffic has been shut down to the east coast. Reports keep coming in of plane crashes all over the world. For the first time I'm glad Belle is gone.

Day 20 –

THINGS HAVE GOTTEN BAD. THERE are reported cases of zombies here in Kansas City. The neighbors got together last night and talked. Dave Wakeson, a park ranger at Perry State Park, thought we should all get out of town. There are cabins at the park, he told us, up in the hills. They were normally used by the staff when they needed to stay over. There should be enough space for about a hundred people. We can hunt, fish and live off the land if we need to. The cabins have pump well service and fireplaces. It sounds like the best plan. Everyone is meeting early in the morning and we're taking the most roadworthy vehicles with only the things we absolutely need. Warm clothes, food and weapons. This whole thing is surreal.

Day 21 –

WE HAD A HELL OF a time getting out of town. Half the group is gone. I don't know if they're dead. Well, I do know that some of them are. We ran into the National Guard halfway to the western exit to town. They wanted us to return to our homes. The guys in front ended up getting into it with them and they fired on us. Innocent civilians. We took off in every direction and by the time we got back together there were a lot less of us. Then one of the cars broke down, I think it took a bullet to the radiator or something. It was blowing white smoke out. One of the other vehicles stopped to help and both got caught by a wave of dead that came out of one of the alleys. Most of them were torn apart. The rest of us drove away as fast as we could. A car full of people crashed going around the corner. I'm pretty sure the dead got them if the crash didn't kill them.

Day 22 –

DAVE WAKESON WAS INFECTED. IT must have happened back in the city during one of the attacks. He killed his wife and most of the people in his car. The last I saw everyone was taking off in different directions. So much for getting to the state park. The van I am in is an old cargo type. We have food, water, even a few guns. There are ten of us in the van. Mary Blaine, a twenty four year old newlywed. Her husband Dave, twenty five and a construction worker. Bob and Rhonda Davis, a forty something couple who had a home business. Mike Jefferson, a nineteen year old college student with some of the best pot I have ever smoked. Julie and Betty Aarons, thirty year old identical twins that were visiting from out of town like me. Danny Mansfield, a thirty five year old divorcee that worked as a welder. And our driver is an old guy named Randall Jenkins. He must be eighty or something but he drives like he was born behind the wheel. He got us out of more than one scrape where I figured we were zombie food. On the radio they're talking about an evacuation point nearby. We had a talk and everyone wanted to head that way. I can see their point but it seems to be a bit close to the dead for my liking. Especially with the speed that they are spreading. In the end it came down to a vote. I was the only dissenter. So off we go to have the government save us. This should work out well.

Day 25 –

I WOULD SAY I TOLD you so but it seems like a moot point. We've kept our van and supplies, mostly because the military didn't want to be bothered with taking them. The radio led us to an intake center. Traffic was backed up so far back we decided to park the van up on a hill off the beaten path and come in from a different angle. This worked to our advantage. We got ahead of a lot of people and got a view behind the curtain. What we saw horrified us. The military was putting people in dog cages, big dog cages but dog cages. People were being sorted with military efficiency. Roughly. We even saw what happened when people didn't pass quarantine. By the time we had seen enough and tried to head back to the van we were far enough in that our leaving was noticed. We lost the twins. Two army guys came out and grabbed them and threw them in a cage. I'm not so sure they were concerned with quarantining them for evacuation as for possible later use. Another one was giving me the eye so I told the rest of them they could either come with me or stay. Then I hauled ass. I've seen that rapey look before and as bad as I felt for the twins there was no way I was going to join them. By the time I got back to the van I not only had most of my people we had picked up a few friends. Folks from the neighborhood had made it this far and by the time we left we had about twenty people. Time to get the hell out of dodge.

Day 26 –

WE DROVE WEST ALL NIGHT. Once we got the sun back we made better time. You've got to go pretty slow when you don't know if a car or truck is going to be blocking the road. We found a gas station that still had power and filled up. We traded the guy there a box of ammo since we have seen how well they attracted zombies when you fired them. Hopefully he has better luck. We got as many gas cans and even some plastic jugs and filled it up with all the gas we could get. So far everyone is looking to me to figure out what to do. I figure we go west until we find a better place. Or we run out of gas.

Day 30 –

WELL, WE RAN OUT OF gas. There's a gas station we stopped at but there is no power, we tried siphoning gas but we suck at it. We need a pump or something. One of the guys is trying to make one with some stuff from the car wash attached to the back. Until he can get it to work at least we have food and water in the gas station.

Day 35 –

JUST ABOUT THE TIME MIKE Walker, a mechanical engineer from the neighborhood, got the pump ready the dead showed up. I cannot imagine where in this god forsaken place they came from. There isn't a house around as far as they eye could see. What, did someone bus them in? Twenty zombies showed up in the space of two hours. They came out of the darkness just as the sun was coming up. That at least was a blessing. No one got caught out in the open. But we're trapped. Some inside the van that is out of gas, some inside the station that has plate glass windows and no second floor. This isn't good.

Day 40 –

THINGS WERE TO THE POINT where I was almost ready to make a run for it. Then something odd happened. This guy showed up, just walked out of the desert like some ghost cowboy. He was all wrapped up in something. Like a bad ass from an action movie he wrecked our zombie problem like they were Jets and he was a Shark. When he was done with the last one he stumbled over and screamed at the people in the van. Something about a refuge. He kept pointing west. Then he took off just as a sandstorm kicked up. When it was gone there was no sign of him. Mike got the pump working and we gassed up. We filled every container we could with gas and took off. A map from the service station showed almost nothing out the way the man had pointed. Just this little town named Ten Talk.

Day 45 –

THIS DESERT IS A FREAKING parking lot. There are more broken down vehicles out here than you would expect to find in New York right now. Every bridge seems to be blown, we're out of gas and there are no gas stations nearby, and there is no sign of this town. I'm afraid. I think I have led us all out here to die.

Day 50 –

SUPPLIES ARE RUNNING LOW. WE lost the Davis's today. They were scouting near the edge of a canyon and the ground just gave way. They fell over a thousand feet to the bottom. At least they don't have to worry about coming back. Before it all went quiet the radio was clear that you had to be infected to come back.

Day 55 –

I WOKE UP THIS MORNING and despaired. Out of food, out of gas, low on water. We were walking back toward the last civilization we had seen, an old roadhouse. Then a man showed up on the road ahead. He stood calmly with his hands out to show us they were empty. The man introduced himself as Harold Nichols. Apparently he had been watching us for quite some time. Now that he was fairly sure we were all non-infected he wanted to take us with him to safety. The group looked at me and I acted like I thought about it. What choice did we have? We were out of options.

Day 56 –

ON THE WAY TO SAFETY we ran into zombies. Our guide took us to an elevated area, easily bypassing them. Eventually we came to some caves where his people were waiting. They had each member of our group strip down and put on new clothes. A member of the same sex watched us change, looking for bite or scratch marks. Then they locked us in separate rooms for over ten hours. I was starting to worry, thinking I might have made a huge mistake when the door opened. An older man was standing there. My first impression was that he looked so tired, so sad. He introduced himself as Jeremiah. The first thing he told me was that Randall Jenkins was dead. Somehow during our close encounter with the undead he must have gotten goo on him. No one had realized it at the time, probably not even Randall. He had turned in his cave and they had incinerated him. The news hit me hard. I fell to the floor sobbing. After coming so far, after getting us away so many times Randall had died on the doorstep of safety.

Day 60 –

JEREMIAH IS THE LEADER OF this community. He spoke with the others and tells me he's impressed with what he has heard of my leadership abilities. I've been offered a job in the new administration. My people have been given a place here and I hope to safeguard all our futures. I also found out that this journal really has worked. I weighed myself. I've lost just over sixty pounds in sixty days.

SGT MILES THOMPSON

STATUS REPORT – APRIL 2, 2033. SGT. MILES THOMPSON, 3RD PLATOON INFANTRY BRAVO COMPANY.

We were deployed to Atlanta Georgia by emergency Presidential Order. What an absolute nightmare. The better part of our first day was spent setting up a perimeter that got torn through in all of ten minutes. The zombies are worse than reported. They're slow and easy to kill but they are relentless. There is also something singularly dehumanizing about looking into the face of someone that could be your grandmother or little niece, then shooting them in the head. We've had casualties far beyond anything the brass ever guessed at. Beyond the men infected by bites, scratches or back spray there are the suicides. Today a private that was out of boot camp a year if he had been out a day pulled his sidearm and blew his own brains out. I can't blame him. War is hell. Our current situation makes hell look like heaven. This book is supposed to be for hard copy status reports. Really? Who the fuck am I supposed to send them to? Last I heard the chain of command had more pressing matters than reading my reports.

I had to start doing something. My lieutenant cracked up about an hour ago, started raving about the wrath of god and ran off down the street. He was a jerk, but he was decent commander. And he took the SAT phone with him and with it our chain of command. Our last order was to stay put and hold position. I figure it is worth the chance of being court martialed to get out of this meat grinder while we still have a few men left. There were forty men when we started this defensive action. Now we're down to thirty. I'm going to call a retreat and get the boys out of here.

THREE HOURS AGO I CALLED the retreat. Jacobs was too slow. A little zombie grabbed him and bit out his calf muscle. Looking back over my shoulder I drew, aimed and fired without slowing down. The first bullet took the zombie girl's head off. The second took off Jacobs. He did this great impression of Humphrey Bogart that was dead on. One more man lost to absolute fucking stupidity.

The dead love gunshots. It's like their own personal dinner bell ringing. The more often you fire, the more of them come shambling up. By the time I pulled the plug we had every zombie within a mile jonesing for our meat. So our attempt to make a break for it in one of the vehicles didn't work out so well. The truck bogged down on flesh, the dead jamming up into the wheel wells until they locked up. It was the damnedest thing. With the loss of forward momentum we scrambled onto the roof, most of us at least. Jackson and Perwalskie got grabbed getting out of the cab and torn apart. The rest of us managed to get up on top and jump over to a van roof, then to a fire escape.

When we got to the roof there were zombies up there. We wasted them quick and gave their remains a wide berth. I spotted a watch post four roofs over that had been decimated. The post itself looked clean but there were corpses and zombies nearby. We took the shamblers out and checked through the watch post. Luck was with us. We found a SAT phone and a cache of ammo. Paulson was able to use the phone to get through to command. They said we were to fall back to the top of the nearest high rise for helo evac. A few roofs over we walked across the top of a walkway that took us within a few feet of a high rise. We broke the window and did a sweep of the floor. It looked clear so we headed up. We were near the top when they started falling from above. Zombies. From the sky. Or in this case from the upper landings they had been standing on. The platoon started a full bore sprint up to the roof.

When we got to the top the guys stopped under the harsh glare of the stairwell's emergency lighting and one thing became quite clear. Not all of us were going to be getting on the helicopter. Half the platoon had zombie goo on them. Zombie goo. God I hate that fucking term. Coined by some glib asshole when the problem was still contained to Europe and Asia. Now I was staring at the faces of a lot of good men that were going to die. Or worse, turn. Most of them moved down the stairs on their own. Two decided to try and brazen it out. Milson and Kendrick. When they stepped forward I put a round in each of their skulls.

I stepped back out of the door and before it shut one of the men, Paulson, caught my eye and nodded. It was good to know that at least one of the men I was leaving behind knew their duty. We wouldn't be adding to the enemies numbers. I had my guys strip their outer layers and inspected them. They all looked clean. The helicopter dropped containment suits, just the plastic, we didn't need the breathers. In this case the suits were for the helo crew's protection, not ours. Once we were suited up they landed. The cockpit had a cage with Plexiglas over it. They blew through the checklist and took us to a base outside the city.

Here we entered military grade quarantine. The brutality of it was more than a few of the nearby civilians could handle. Screaming, crying, and carrying on. It was pointless. No one was going to let them out until the deadline passed. High powered hoses rinsed us off into a drain. Clothes were scrapped. Once we were naked and clean we entered an individual cell made from chain link and plastic. Seven hours later they shot and torched Sulentic. He must have gotten infected on the stairwell and never even known it. Or he didn't want to believe. Now he is a bit of ash and bone. And the world keeps turning.

When we got out the platoon hit supply for new uniforms and skivvies. New weapons and tons of ammo. Then we hit command for orders. General Blazton was now in command from the Pentagon. That place had been sealed up tighter than a ducks ass but the chain of command was still open. Orders were to go out to recover targets of value and get them to refuges. In our area there were over twenty thousand people that were considered vital to human survival. I requisitioned a few new men and grabbed a helo. Rubber suits were the new outer uniform. They were uncomfortable, hot and started to stink almost right away. It was worse than being in the desert. Death by zombie or drowning in my own man gravy. Great choice.

THIS WAS A SNAFU FROM the jump. Take a helicopter in wearing a full body condom and evacuate one or two people from groups of hundreds. The noise drew the zombies, the people all thought they should be taken, no one was happy when they were told no. I've killed more humans in the last six months than zombies. It doesn't matter how much I tried to convince command that we should at least be evacuating the children. They said no. I was told to grow a pair. Fucking Blazton. He hasn't ever had to look in a parents face and tell them you can't help their kids escape.

The men are coming apart. Drinking has become the favorite pass time. There are drugs as well, I found out from one of the other sergeants that his guys deviated to a police impound and brought back everything they could carry. He wanted me to help him take it away from them. I talked him out of it. If they want to overdose then we save a bullet. Who are we to tell them how to spend their final days? I am about a day away from drinking myself into a stupor. Or just eating my gun.

THE WHEELS HAVE OFFICIALLY COME off the bus. We were having a teleconference briefing with Blazeton when the dead breached his facility. No one really knows how it happened. Who cares? It's done and so is he. The man told the regional commanders to take control and continue as they saw fit. Then he blew the Pentagon. Got to admire the bastard. He went under his own terms. And he made sure to follow his main directive, don't add to the zombie army.

Our new commander is Colonel Benjamin Raton. He is a gnarled old son of a bitch. But he knows how to command. The drugs and alcohol are gone and discipline is back. The list of evacuees is getting shorter and shorter. It doesn't help that a few of the sites we were sending them to have fallen. All that hard work, all those men lost in the field, for nothing. At least they got a better handle on the screening process. If you have a fever you're not coming with us. We also know that the eyes and edges of the mouth start to redden on infected. There are still the occasional oddities but most infected fall within the rule set.

Casualties are way down and quarantine rarely shows a resident turning while waiting. Things have gotten better in a lot of ways. It's too bad the world has gotten worse. Other than the military bands there are only HAM radio operators on the airwaves. They're who we are getting most of our intel from. They talk about the dead tearing down refuges, starving people out, swelling their numbers. Worse are the reports of the living. Bands of armed men and women who destroy refuges for what little they have. Or just for the fuck of it. Madmen preaching on the airwaves about the end of times. Man's inhumanity to man. Some say that the Lord will strike down the dead once the wicked are destroyed. This is why I have never been a religious man. God is, man does. Fucking deal with it or get out of the way so I can.

WE'VE BEEN UNABLE TO FIND the last ten targets we went in search of. All we found were shambling dead waiting to greet us. That is the least of our concerns right now. Colonel Raton got killed by zombies that crashed a perimeter fence. The place was never meant to hold back a flood of bodies like that. Eventually the relentless force of the horde pushing on the fence bent it down. The demo guys managed to drop some structures in the hordes way to slow them down but it's just a matter of time until they get through. We're fighting a delaying action to give people time to get as many supplies and personnel out as possible. Evac is going to Fort Riley Kansas. That site has hardened fences set atop raised barriers. The dead shouldn't be able to take them down. I've set our heavy weapons on rapid fire, pounding the outer perimeter. My hope is that we do enough damage to at least slow them down.

IF HE WASN'T ALREADY DEAD, I would kill Corporal Jack Mayer. The son of a bitch disobeyed a direct order to retreat with the men to the helo while I held the line. Instead he knocked me out with his rifle and had the men carry me out. Our door gunner reports that Mayer got ripped apart by the horde that charged right through his M2 gun fire. That damn fool. He was only twenty five.

The medic has me on light duty for the next few days in case I have a concussion. Light duty? There is no such thing anymore.

Once my boots hit the ground here I had a confab with the commanding officer, Colonel James Betterson. He has placed me in charge of turning our civilian population into an effective fighting force. Maybe he wants me to herd cats after that? Or walk on water? There are almost a half a million people on this base that are civilian. Of those, maybe a hundred thousand are physically fit enough to be a soldier. What a mess.

I MET SOMEONE TODAY. GAIL Strand. She is a feisty old lady. Just turned seventy when the shit hit the fan. While I was giving the orientation for the men of the first training group, she burst in the door. She lit into me like a Rottweiler on a soup bone. I haven't gotten my ass chewed so badly since I was in boot. And the worst thing? Lady had a point. Her issue was that we had dismissed most of the civilians as useless for combat. In the old days, carrying a pack, doing hand to hand, forced marches we would have been right. But combat has changed. If we get to close quarters we've already lost. What we do need are people that can hold a watch use rifles to kill zombies. That old lady stood in front of God and everyone and told me she could out shoot any of my new recruits. I was so pissed I took her up on it and marched everyone out to the range. Well, she proved me wrong, so I've got to rethink the entire strategy I had for our new civilian military. It's a good thing too. I'm not sure we could hold this place with so few on the perimeter.

THE FIRST CLASS HAS GRADUATED and the Colonel is impressed. This is the first class to train with the new weapons our researchers made us. Air guns. How very high school, right? But they take a zombie's head off at a hundred yards with pretty good accuracy. The down side is they are only good for about twenty shots before we have to switch over to regular ordinance. Each private can hit a melon shaped target at one hundred yards with the air guns. This gives us the ability to man far more of the perimeter than we could before and keep the dead at bay. In addition to the new class I've recruited older members with experience from the population for an officer class. Gail was my first recruit. I'm hoping they'll be able to take some of the day to day pressure off the military soon so that we can get back to recon and resupply runs. Winter is going to be here soon and I'm worried. We don't have nearly enough housing, clothing or food for the long haul. We've planted crops but it is pretty late in the season and we don't have all the things we need for farming. That's going on to our list of things to get on our next supply run.

Zombies are beginning to show up in big numbers outside the far perimeter. The air guns are a godsend. They allow us to take them out quietly. With the distance limitation there has begun to be an actual zombie barricade growing just from the corpses. If we can keep it up we might be able to build a secondary line of defense just by killing the enemy.

THE TWENTIETH CLASS OF PRIVATES and the fifth class of officers graduated today. The Colonel promoted me to Major and Gail to Command Sergeant of the civilian force. The military can now focus our full attention on resupplying and none too soon. The weather has turned and we got a taste of what is coming. There are a few builders here that clued command into a warehouse near St. Louis in the country. It was the staging area for Patchwork Homes, a nonprofit that sent houses to third world countries. They shipped them in kits that went together easily. Each had solar panels for power, a waste system, and water purification and was well insulated up to +150 or -50 Fahrenheit. One of the builders, Jon Feadid, said he sat on the board. They had at least ten thousand kits in that warehouse, maybe more.

We took a risk and sent a scout party there. They landed on the roof and brought back three of the kits. They worked as advertised. The next group took cargo helicopters and they cleaned the place out. Unfortunately we reaped a harvest of undead because of it. They followed the helicopters back to base. After we realized that we sent the helos on a fake trail, and then had them go high enough to escape zombie notice. But the damage was done. We ended up with every available hand killing zombies on the eastern perimeter. When we were done we were dangerously low on air gun ammo and had a pile of undead big enough to see for miles.

All helo traffic will now fly away from base, rise to high altitude and then fly back to base. I wish we had thought about it sooner.

HOUSING IS BETTER, BUT OVERCROWDING is still a problem. Civilians are getting upset that big buildings like the hangers are kept for machines while they shiver in the cold. The simple fact is the machines are more valuable and need to be protected. Without them we'll starve. Just last night the guys brought back a huge amount of food from one of the big box stores. It was outside of Des Moines, Iowa and had been closed before the trouble started. Three helo's of dried food, two more of canned and glass. Enough to get us through the winter and then some. The entire refuge has given a collective sigh. Tensions are down, but with one problem being solved there are always three or four more popping up.

The kit buildings are outstanding, big enough to fit a family of six. We have moved most of the families into them which cut down on some of the more unsavory problems with having large groups of people sleeping together. There were not enough of them by any stretch of the imagination. We have army tents set up and they provide adequate protection against the elements. But it sucks to get out from under your blankets. I've been in one of the kit houses to tour it before they turned it over to a family. The sooner we can get housing like that for everyone the better it will be.

Colonel Betterson kept one kit back for the eggheads to use as a template. Most of the materials it's made of are easy to acquire, well they were back before zombies ate the world. Back then you could have pulled up all the information within seconds on a computer. Now it takes a bit more legwork. I spent better than three days talking with Jon Feadid and a few of the others with the right information. One of the old timers that worked in our supply group used to work for the distribution company that supplied one of the Patchwork Home factories.

Of all the warehouses the company had, only three are not located in heavily populated sites. The rest are deep inside port cities and the risk is too high to go into an infested zone. The closest viable target to us is southwest of Kansas City. It's far enough from the city to take a chance on. Ten helos should be able to bring back more than a warehouse full. Hopefully it'll be enough to jump start our housing problem.

Gail has had her first test as commander of the civilian force. A few good old boys decided they didn't like being led by some "old biddy" as they put it. One of them had the bad idea to lay hands on Gail. She shot him in the crotch. I can barely write that without laughing. The look on his face as he died with no balls! It goes without saying that no one is going to put their hands on the old lady again. Just to make sure I took the liberty of assigning two bodyguards for her. One male, one female. They should have been there in the first place. Damn sloppy of me to forget the world, even with the much lower population, is still populated by assholes.

The zombies out on the perimeter keep steadily increasing. Two of the wiz kids came up with a way of making hardened glass balls from the massive amounts of sand we have on base. The grunts have dubbed them Death Marbles. The damn things work like a charm, and it isn't like we need to use them more than once. The armory has been churning them out like crazy and we use them almost as fast as they get made. The piles of corpses are making a pretty good second barricade about a hundred yards out. If we keep this up, we can keep the dead at bay with the bodies.

I LOVE SCIENTISTS. THE RECOVERY group that went to the warehouse came back with more than we ever expected. Not only are there enough components to make plenty of housing for the residents of Fort Riley, there are also the tools to make more. Our egg heads have started figuring out what raw materials they will need to set up production. They are also working on improving the design. Not a bad idea since the original houses only had a twenty year lifespan. We're going to need something a bit more permanent. Colonel Betterson has put all further air travel on hold until after the winter. He's from Kansas and told me I've got no idea how bad it can get. Snow blowing down a flat landscape? Yeah I think I can guess.

The helos are locked up and being serviced in the hangars. With the temperature dropping we have put all hands into making the Patchwork Homes. Many hands make light work and all that. I requested a few modifications for the military. We're still going to need dorms. Units need to sleep together, but with the changes in our world they'll need a new designs. Single sleeper units with head and sink. People sleep deeper when they can lock themselves inside a room. One that has two exits. Also, a common area for all of them to share. Hopefully it will maintain unit cohesion without changing the way we do things too much.

Adjustments have to be made. The designers liked my ideas so much they've said they're going to use the same idea for the normal homes. Even married couples have stopped sleeping in the same room these days. It is sad in a way, but survival is a strong driving force. There might not be the ability to spoon but at least you don't have to worry about your spouse biting your face off.

I've also decided it's a good idea to give people something to do. Having a bunch of folks sitting indoors idle is a recipe for disaster. So this winter we are going to do some cross training. Non-military are going to get some military training and the military are going to take some civilian classes. I figure it is a good idea for everyone to know how to do as much as they can. It eliminates the severity of casualties a bit if you aren't losing the only guy that knows how to repair the A/C. At least to the rest of us. I'm sure the guy dying still thinks it sucks.

There is so much we still have left to do. The civilians have organized some planning for crops when spring comes. Our recovery groups need people to help sort out everything that has been brought back. It's hard to say what they may have brought back along with everything else. I'm hopeful that all the activity will keep people sane during the winter. It's like planning for taking your kids on a car trip. Only this time if the kids get out of hand they might kill each other.

WINTER IN KANSAS SUCKS. FIRST it was so damn cold that I couldn't feel my feet. Then it warms up, the snow melts and packs just enough for the zombies to stumble over the wall of their dead friends. We now have a giant damn horde such as I haven't seen outside a major city. We don't have enough ammo to shut them down. Right now the air guns are running low and we are moving the heavy guns into place. The noise of them will bring even more undead but what choice do we have? We're so beyond screwed. I'm going to put this book in a Ziploc bag inside a foot locker. Hopefully, if we all die, someone will find this and know our story.

WELL THIS HAS BEEN A fun filled month. We ran out of ammo. Totally out of ammo. I never thought a military base could do that. I really didn't. Everyone that could was making Death Marbles around the clock. They made them, we shot them and still the dead came. After three weeks we had a huge pile of bodies and even more moving behind them. When it became evident that we were going to have a fence failure, brought upon by the massive number of dead bodies making a natural ramp, we set up a secondary fence. It wasn't hardened or designed to hold back so many dead. So we reinforced it with the trucks we rarely used anymore. Colonel Betterson and I held a conference with the other commanders and came to one horrible conclusion. Sacrifices were going to need to be made.

What's the only option when you cannot fire on undead? You kill them in hand to hand. That meant definite exposure and death for anyone that joined the fray. My brigade was going to spearhead the initiative with some civilian volunteers filling in the ranks. Operation Deathmarch was set to start when we got reports of a strange man out near the eastern perimeter. The dead were thinner out there, but the activity was drawing them away from the east. The danger of breach was dropping. I ran all the way to the observation tower to see who it was, which one of my men had sacrificed himself. Looking through the binoculars I could tell it was a man, but he was all wrapped up.

He had machetes in each hand and was an efficient exterminator. One hit, one kill. Between his work and our air guns the dead were decimated over the next twelve hours. By that time he was a giant red gore caked mess. There was no doubt in my mind that he was dead. One way or another he was infected. He was a god awful mess.

He finished off the dead in his area and walked straight around the camp to the last stragglers. When the last one fell he started back to the west. He stopped midpoint and appeared to be yelling at one of the guard towers. Gesturing wildly to the west he stood there for a few minutes and then turned and continued walking. There was no response to the guards that yelled their thanks to him. I suspect the poor fellow knew his time was slipping away and was trying to get somewhere to die in solitude, with dignity. I told the guards if he came back as a zombie to shoot him and then let me know.

I double timed it over to the guard tower where he had paused. Spc. Sara Marshall, a cute blonde that I made a note to look up later, gave the report. The man stopped and yelled at her. A lot of what he said she had trouble hearing over the air gun fire. She caught something about a refuge over and over again. From the parts she caught it seemed to be a sanctuary off to the west, in the direction he was pointing. Maybe that is where he was from. If so his people deserve to know about his sacrifice. I'm going to get with the Colonel about doing some recon in that direction in the spring.

I had the men wait until morning and then we sprayed some phosphorus onto the zombie bodies and burned them to ash. I asked to have the research guys come up with some sprayers that will reach out to at least fifty yards. We need to make sure we keep the perimeter clear. There are enough chemicals on base to burn a few million corpses.

IT'S THE FIRST DAY OF May and I'm astounded at what has happened so far this year. When winter broke we got to plowing and planting with all hands pitching in. Surprisingly, it didn't take as long as forecast to finish. Colonel Betterson was all for the recon to the west. If we could find another refuge we might be able to set up trade. I went out with fifteen men and two helos.

Instead of me finding the town their radio operator contacted us. He warned me to keep a three mile distance or they would fire on us. Nice folks but a bit skittish. We were directed to a plateau a few miles to the east. It was pretty easy to find since we flew over it on the way in. A man named Phillip met us when we landed. He asked us to keep our distance while we talked to minimize the risk of infection and all that. The city of Vigilance was a closed city. No uninvited guests allowed. Hence the surface to air missile warning.

Contact is to be made by radio in advance and they would meet us at this site. There are a lot of things the two communities can offer one another. They are interested in our knowledge and housing. They have a large supply of high quality pipes as well as a vast library. I gave them our frequency and told them the colonel would be happy to talk to them. It's nice to know we aren't alone out here. Maybe there's a little hope out there after all.

JOURNAL DONATED TO HUNTERS LIBRARY at the death of Colonel Thompson. First in six volume set. Colonel Thompson is credited with the idea for Safesuit. Worked with Vigilance research group to develop close combat gear that would keep soldiers safe. That led to the current suit system that all Hunters currently wear.

SIMON BILLOWS

THE LIGHT THAT NORMALLY COMES in from under the door is gone along with the mechanical noises that normally spun through the building. There is a hum that you almost never noticed until it is gone. Electricity has its own living voice when it is present, and that voice has just been silenced. It's like losing an old friend that you've taken for granted your entire life. Only realizing what they mean to you when they're gone. I waited for almost a full minute listening. The lights stayed off, my old friend electricity didn't return. All I heard was the rush of my own breathing and the hammering of my heart in my chest. This was the instant, the exact moment that I realized I was truly boned.

The building I live in is the oldest dorm on the campus, Merlot Hall. Built just after the millennium it's a bit run down. No elevators or escalators in this building, oh no. Old school steel and cement staircase complete with wide landings. And security lights that apparently hadn't had their batteries changed since they were installed. As far as I could tell the hallway was pitch black and this was going to be a problem. You see when I barricaded myself into this room it was because the hallway was full of flesh eating zombies. Writing that makes me sound like I'm a mental case that should be locked up and God knows I wish I was. Unfortunately, the three freshmen in the hallway, the very ones that had been sick earlier in the day, had been zombies. They tore Myers from next door out of his room and ripped his guts out right in front of me. I barely got the damn door closed and locked. For good measure I put both dressers, bedside tables and bed frames in front of the door as well.

Now I sit by candlelight and write what I figure are my last words on this planet. If anyone finds this, and my parents are still alive, see that they get this. I want them to know that I was thinking about them towards the end. Just in case whoever finds this hasn't got any idea who I am I suppose I better fill in some blanks. My name is Simon Billows. I'm working on my masters in nanotechnology here at the University of Arkansas. Until everything fell apart I was developing a chemical process that would help power a new generation of nanites. The medical and military applications were so exciting that I had my own secret service detail. Fat lot of good they did me. One got eaten on our way back into the building and the other one got infected. The last I saw of him he was telling me to run and facing off with three crazy zombies near the door to the stairwell.

My situation is dire. There's no food or water in my room. There is only one door, the aforementioned exit to the zombie filled hallway. I'm on the third floor and my secret service detail is either dead or walking corpses. Boned, boned and boned. Still, if I was the genius my test scores told everyone I was I should be able to come up with a way out. When it was still light out and I could see people still out on the quad. People, not zombies. They were walking way too fast and staying in groups. Cars were driving out onto the grass and picking people up. If I could get downstairs I might be able to get away.

At this point I'm stumped. I have spent the last two hours trying to figure out what to do. Statistically the best chance I've got is to open the door and make a break for it. Not going to happen. Not. Going. To. Happen. I have no desire to get my face eaten off. Breaking the window and throwing myself out has only slightly better odds of survival. If I had bedding in here I could make a rope of sheets but of course I had to send them and my laundry out to be cleaned before heading back home. Way to go genius. Lol. God this is stupid! I'm going to die in a crappy dorm room of starvation. Unless I toss myself out the window. That is if I could break the window. It's made out of impact glass so I would have a better chance of smashing out a car windshield

I WOKE UP A FEW hours later to the window exploding into the room. Two men in black tactical gear came through in a fast roll with assault rifles. After a lot of yelling and me nearly pissing my pants, they identified themselves as secret service. Apparently the infected agent lasted long enough to make sure help was on the way. And here I was thinking he was a horrible bodyguard. The two guys hook me up to a harness and I get yanked out the window. A few seconds later I'm in the chopper and glad I haven't had anything to eat in a while. I'm sitting in a cage with weapons trained on me. Nice. Very homey.

They took me to a military base and I ended up in quarantine. This consisted of sitting in a steel wire cage for seven hours. Then they send someone to examine me that is wearing a full on rubber containment suit. Then two hours later I'm let out for a full on examination and I finally get some food and water. Then a shower and a nice warm bed. The next day I sit in a room with a colonel who asks me questions over and over again. When he was satisfied that I knew nothing he sent me over to the spooks. I figured there was a reason they came up to find me.

The problem was that what they wanted was just not in my head. Trust a bunch of government types grasping at straws to not have the whole picture. They want me to give them a process or a formula that will let them create some sort of science fiction cure for the virus. To rush off to a lab and make a vial of nanites that will fix all the zombies and make them people again. They're out of their goddamn minds. We were working on something to manufacture things and what they want is at the edge of theoretical science. When

I told them this things got really bad. One of them beat the crap out of me and told me I had better figure it out. This is almost as bad as being trapped in the dorm.

I've been laying here in bed crying for the last hour because I can't give them what they want. I'm smart enough to know what is going to happen next. I'm going to die. If I can get some sleep I will try to figure out a plan in the morning for staying alive. Right now my ribs just hurt too much.

IT HAS BEEN A FEW days and I'm no longer at that base. One of the spooks came in and walked me out to a helicopter that took me to Fort Riley Kansas. There's a lab here that he wanted me to start working in. He introduced himself as Carl Weathers. Like I have never seen any of the Rocky movies? I could tell he was lying about his name. Not that I would have expected anything less from an intelligence agent. At least he didn't hit me. He apologized for the rough treatment and explained that they needed the best that I could give them.

When I got to the lab I was overjoyed to see they had state of the art facilities. There were also a few colleagues there, people I had worked with before. Among them was Dr. Karen Bowers and Dr. James Kenner. Dr. Kenner was an older, balding, potbellied man with a perpetually ruddy face. He was one of the pioneers of nano-technology and someone I always considered a mentor. Karen was a few years older than me and had been a secret crush of mine since the first day we me. She treated me like a younger brother and I dreamed of ripping her clothes off.

As a matter of fact she was the inspiration behind me designing nanites that would literally take someone's clothes off in less than a second. I figured if I 'accidentally' deployed them on her when we were alone at the least I would get to see her naked. This adolescent endeavor ended up proving far more important to the human race than it ever should have. Karen surprised me when she saw me by giving me a long hug and sobbing into my shoulder. I held onto her far longer than I think was appropriate but I couldn't help myself.

When we finally sat down at the table I discovered it was Dr. Kenner that I had to thank for my being brought to Fort Riley. He had convinced those in power that the magic bullet they were looking for was simply beyond our capabilities. Further, he told them that someone of my abilities should be on his team trying to help in ways that were actually possible. From that first day we were working long hours. There were so many things that needed attention. New challenges required new tools. And a new enemy required a different way of fighting. Gunfire, while highly effective, also drew new zombies. The noise was the problem. What the military needed from us first, before we did anything else, was a way to fire projectiles quietly. Another group was working on cheap and effective sound suppression. I suggested we try something simpler.

One of the most common pastimes on campus was disc golf. I loved this game and played it every chance I got. A bad throw led me off the path to a ridge overlooking a nearby business, a paintball range. Here boys from the school fought mock battles with air guns. I thought it looked like fun so went down to try it. After getting shot in the ass twice by some jerk I decided to call it a day. Rick Garrett, a thick necked jock, though my sore ass was hilarious. I returned to my dorm to plot my revenge.

Three days later the air gun kit and supplies I had ordered online arrived. I carefully constructed an air gun that looked just like all the others. This one however had a modified pressure system that allowed me to fire an almost endless amount of ammo. At least that was the way I had designed it. The problem was I never fully tested it and when I went up against Rick he ended up in the hospital. The paint balls I shot at him actually broke the skin. I had made a minor error in calibration which caused extreme pressure over long term shot capability. This mistake was the basis for a military grade air gun design.

By using a mixture of chemicals we could provide a portable weapon good for about twenty shots. These guns would be able to fire most anything round, from a ball bearing to a rounded pebble. Any object with weight and strength could be used. A secondary system was designed off an air compressor system however the noise of the compressor would draw nearly as many zombies as gunfire. If the compressor was soundproofed, as it could be in a base location, you could run hoses from it to wall installations. The military loved the design and set people to manufacturing the weapon as soon as possible. Dr. Kenner made sure that everyone knew that it was my idea. He went out of his way to make sure that I got the recognition I deserved.

With work on the air guns completed we joined a group working on another problem. Housing. The base was never intended to support as many people as it currently held. There were some prefab kits brought in from a warehouse out in the waste that were originally intended for the third world. Funny now that most of us would give a lot to be in the third world, instead of the zombie world. They gave us a kit for study.

THE HOUSING THING HAS BEEN a bear. It makes me feel a little guilty that I've got such a nice room. It's small but it's also dry, warm and secure. There are a lot of people living in army tents outside, in the cold of Kansas. So I've put some long hours in. I figured out a way to alter nanites to manufacture some of the less common components for the houses. Mostly the inner workings, what you never see. I also redesigned the capacitors and computer system so they use a lot less energy to run. Karen found a way to triple the purification capacity of the original design and Dr. Kenner worked out how to alter the floor plan in any way you want.

There are a lot of great people working on this with us. I'm told they're going to scout out a warehouse that should have a lot more materials and tools for us to move from design to production. In the meantime Karen and I have been working on another problem that popped up and I think we have the answer. The military has been complaining about a shortage of ammo for the air guns. The solution ended up being right beneath their feet. Sand. There is a ton of it all around us. Karen and I designed a simple device that you pour sand in the top of, it melts, drops down onto a revolving plate with sphere molds in it, they cool and fall out the other side. You can make ten marbles a minute with the machine. We sent it off to the manufacturing group so they could make some more.

THE RECOVERY CREW CAME BACK with more than we could've hoped for. Tools to make components for houses, most of the raw material we needed and tons of schematics. We'll have more than enough to get the ball rolling. We've been getting a lot of input from the military on what they want for their people. Most of the suggestions are pretty common sense and I have proposed we implement them for the civilian housing as well.

This is going to be a busy winter. It will take all of us working together to get everyone in decent shelter before the temperatures drop too low. I hope that I get to work more with Karen. Even being near her without talking makes me happy.

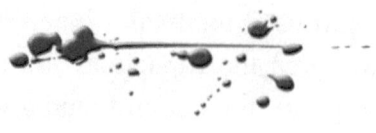

JUST WHEN I THINK WE might be safe we have things go to hell. We had just put the housing issue to bed when we had an unexpected warm up. The snow melted and then refroze making a natural ramp out of the zombies lining the perimeter. This allowed the dead previously milling out of range to not only approach the Fort but come right up towards the fence. We spent the last few weeks making as many Death Marbles as we could. That is the name they gave our glass ammunition based on their ability to kill a zombie with just one. Just when we thought things were going to fail some guy walked out of the snow and saved our collective bacon.

I don't know the details but the gist is he came in, killed enough zombies for us to catch up on making ammo and then walked off by himself to die. Sort of makes an atheist like me believe in miracles. Then I look out at the piles of zombies and realize if God does exist he has a twisted sense of humor.

THE WINTER IS HARDENED OUTSIDE. The upside is that zombies are frozen out there. The commander sent a few patrols out to skull crush any that they find. Two of the patrols came back and had members that didn't pass quarantine. The commander suspended all patrols after that. He came to Dr. Kenner and said that this situation is unacceptable and we need to find a way to protect his people.

Soldiers keep running into situations time and again where they risk infection. It's far too easy to become infected while fighting, especially in close quarters. When zombies are killed they sprayed fluid in every direction. We theorized it's because their cell structure hardened to allow for retention of moisture while leaving liquid at the core mass to provide flexibility for movement. The result was high pressure zombies. Any rupture causes them to spray infected fluid, or zombie goo as it was commonly called, in every direction.

The bio suits that we have are too bulky and fragile for field work. Further, it's often difficult to see infected fluid on these suits. Even if you spotted the fluid it was difficult to remove the gear quickly and without the possibility of flicking fluid off onto surfaces or people around you.

Using nanites to constructs weaves of cloth we tried to overcome many of these issues. We have had some initial success. It was easy enough to create cloth that would be bio reactive. Cloth that turns red whenever biological material gets on it. Then we altered it to turn red only if infected biological material gets on it. A few minor alterations caused the fabric around the infected area to turn white, showing a rough bull's-eye of the problem. Next we tried making it strong enough that bites and scratches wouldn't penetrate. It took mixing Kevlar and other strands in however by the time we were done it was fairly bite, claw, blade and bullet proof. Bullets were only stopped from a distance greater than fifty feet. And it does nothing to negate the kinetic energy.

Our next challenge was trying to make a removable suit that would come off quickly, easily and without dispersing infected fluid about. The latter we did by embedding absorbent chemicals into the fabric that locked fluid in place inside a gel like substance. This protected both the wearer and those nearby. We locked a never wet substance on the interior that kept fluid from passing through. This worked too well and our test subjects began passing out after a while because heat was unable to pass out of the suits. This hurdle required us to engineer a molecular wave tube that would allow heat and air to pass through but filtered out any contaminants.

So we now had a durable, protective, wearable suit but to make it practical we had to find a way to put multiple layers of suits on a wearer and find a way to make them tear away while maintain integrity until you were ready to remove them. While this sound simple enough these past few paragraphs are condensed years of work done by our team with a few others that joined us later. In the end it was Karen and I becoming a couple that finally solved the problem.

After one late night romp we were telling each other about our past, something she assured me is quite common among couples. I admitted to her she had once inspired me to create my 'naked nanites' just for the chance to see her naked. She had laughed and then gotten really quiet. I was afraid I had upset her when she kissed me and we spent the next half hour doing very little talking. Afterwards she told me I was most definitely the smartest perv she knew.

She had the idea to integrate my 'naked nanites' with a trigger mechanism. In effect half the nanites would be embedded into each side of the neck of a suit. The other half would be embedded in the gloves. To remove the outer suit you would reach up with both hands, grasp the neck of the suit with your thumb and forefinger and hold it for a few seconds. The nanites would activate, disassemble preset bonds on the suit and you would be able to pull it away. Each layer would take less than a few seconds to remove and each new layer would be completely clean.

Quite a breakthrough and command is quite excited by the possibilities. Within a few years we should have the bugs worked out and be outfitting our military. It will be nice to know that the men and women protecting us will be less at risk for what we have accomplished here.

WHEN WE STARTED THIS JOURNEY, I never realized how far it would take us. Karen and I have been married now for almost four years. Karen has given birth to two children, a boy named Isaac and a girl named Stephanie. Our refuge here at Fort Riley has flourished thanks to our breakthrough. The protection offered to our troops has not only allowed them to keep the dead at bay but also survive a few incursions by the living. I found out in a meeting today that we are going to provide our anti zombie suit, which the military has originally dubbed SafeSuit, to all the military units still active. Further it is going to be the cornerstone of our trade with other refuges. Makes me wonder what would have happened if that thug back at the first military base had ended up killing me. I've got to say, I'm glad he didn't.

Zack Montgomery

SO I FOUND THIS NOTEPAD in my bag, I think it must have been there since grad school. I guess if I'm going to die out here I might as well put down my thoughts. Not that anyone will probably ever read them but I have to do something. It's odd to have actual down time for once. Back before the fall there was never a single second when I wasn't busy. My alarm clock went off before the sun even thought about coming up. I was at work before anyone else, I left after everyone else and I sacrificed everything to get ahead. After twelve years of school, four years of college, a year internship and two years as a junior associate I finally made my bones. I got the big corner office, the juicy accounts and the parking spot. The company even leased me a sweet Tesla, the original all electric model. It was so cherry. Within another year I was living in a luxury loft apartment with a view of Lake Michigan. Yeah, I was living the life. Eating at the best restaurants, dating the hottest women, and taking the best vacations.

I'm not making excuses. I fully realize that I was so wrapped up in myself that I wasn't paying attention to the world around me. The whole zombie thing kind of caught me off guard. I was sitting at Beris, an exclusive micro eatery downtown, with a few friends when the subject came up. At the meal were Joey Fante, John Baker, Samuel Walters, Terry Graeson and Paul Davidson. We all worked in the business world together and had fought our way through the financial trenches together.

Joey Fante, was the best guy for electronics company trades that I had ever known. John Baker was the go to guy for corporate merger stock deals. Samuel Walters, a shark in the world of organic foods and renewable energy, sat at the far side of the table. Terry Graeson, the cosmetics trade king, was working on his second martini. Paul Davidson, the communications trade czar, was sitting at the far end obsessing with his smart phone. It was Joey that brought up zombies.

"Sorry, what?"

"Yeah, my doorman said that the military is talking about martial law and mass evacuations in New York and the same thing could happen here."

"Seriously? Zombies?" Joey looked at me like I had grown a second head.

"Man, I told you that if you didn't take your nose out of your computer for five seconds… you haven't noticed all the weird shit going on? Haven't you been watching the news?"

The rest of the table joined in the discussion and before we left that night I had every intention of checking the news out that night. Then I ran into this girl in my building and got distracted. Ahem. In the end I suppose it wouldn't have made that much of a difference in how things turned out. As I'm about to do something monumentally stupid I figure I should make a record of it. After all, what good is it if no one ever knows what a moron I am? My name is Zack Montgomery. I'm thirty years old and up until a few days ago I was a Mack daddy. Okay, that looks a lot stupider on the page than I thought it would but here I am at the end of the world with no whiteout. I suppose I better explain that so it doesn't seem nearly as douchey.

I have worked my ass off my entire life to be where I am right now. Hell, where I was before things went to shit. I achieved more in my short life so far than most business people do in their entire career. All my clothes are custom made Armani down to my underwear. I worked out every day and have six percent body fat. In short I'm the hot guy that every girl wants and every guy wants to be. I am, or I guess I was, the leading expert in the field of manufacturing.

My ability to read the market made money flow into my clients accounts like floodwater. Two days before the world started its slide into the sewer, a few days after our group met for dinner, I noticed things going screwy. A few huge accounts sold everything off just before the market got closed.

In the end, my years of hard work and sacrifice evaporated in front of my face. The stock market worldwide shut down, which should have been my wake up call. Instead I went home and got hammered. I lamented the fact that I had spent so much of my time working to be exactly what I was, one of the most powerful young men on Wall Street. And all that amounted to jack squat when the defecated material hit the rotary cooling device.

When things went bad they didn't go slow. It was like a cart full of dynamite being pushed down the side of a mountain. Business crashed and burned. Public transportation and car services became unavailable. Restaurants closed and supermarkets ran out of food. I had never kept a lot in my apartment so before long I had to go out to get supplies. That decision almost cost me my life.

Walking was not something I normally did unless I was on a treadmill. But the streets were packed with cars that barely moved. So I set off for the store on the corner. Mr. Chen was standing behind the counter like he always was when I came in. This time though instead of holding his usual spray bottle and rag he gripped a pump action shotgun in his hands. I did a double take just as he fired it at a guy stumbling down the aisle at him. The guy sprayed everywhere but luckily not towards me. He did get all over Mr. Chen who didn't seem to notice. I followed his gaze and saw three more people shambling up the aisle towards him. The back door was open and I saw another one coming in from the alley. I ran back outside, grabbing some beef jerky from the stand near the door.

When I got back into my apartment I called the guys and told them to get over to my place ASAP. I felt like an idiot for not being cognizant enough to have seen the trouble building around me, especially after our dinner conversation. Since we all lived in the same neighborhood, in the best penthouse in our respective buildings, I knew it wouldn't take the boys long to get to my place. While I waited I turned on the television and flipped to the news. It was like the Romero Channel. All zombies, all the time. I like to think of myself as a fairly smart man but I have to admit I felt pretty stupid right then. The people in the corner market? Zombies. The guys I avoided on the street that started following me on the way back? Zombie.

I had gone from Wall Street to the end of the world, without even noticing. The footage showing from all over the world was the same. More and more shambling people, strike that zombies, moving through the streets. Here in Chicago they said we were still at stage 1 of the infection. But the virus moved fast and from what I saw at Mr. Chen's, things were going to hell quickly. It might only be a day or so until Chicago was overrun.

The boys showed up a few minutes later, only there were twenty people at my door instead of five. My friends had brought some of their friends. Introductions all around were the first order of the day. Joey had three people with him. He vouched for all of them. John had three people with him. Again he assured me they were five by five. Samuel had four people with him. Good guys he said. Terry had two women with him. Go figure. Terry always did have more girlfriends than anyone I knew. Paul had a guy and two women with him. All clear and solid. Whatever that means in a situation like this.

My penthouse takes up the top floor. So there are a lot of rooms. Lucky for us. The afternoon was spent trying to figure out what to do. Leave town or stay? How to defend ourselves against the zombies. Watching more of the news helped fill in more of the blanks. You had to stay away from the dead. Even getting a little blood or fluid on you meant you would turn. The infection was slower that way than a bite or a scratch but it still killed you. I realized that Mr. Chen was probably already dead. But he was also probably still walking around. A few of the guys headed off to sleep and we decided to call it a night. And what a night it was. I was shown the true value of the hardwood doors I had installed more for vanity than function.

Around midnight I was woken up by a crashing sound. I checked the hall and saw a lot of people peering out their doors at me. Joey and I went down the hall and identified the two rooms that the crashing was coming from. When we stopped to listen at the doors we heard moaning. Joey opened the door to one of the rooms and the zombie inside that used to be Terry Graeson started shuffling towards him. Before he closed the door I caught sight of blood all over. What looked like the remains of the two women lay on the bed. The room across the hall was where two of Sam's guys had bedded down. We didn't even bother to open the door.

Nobody felt much like sleeping after that. There was a little panic, a little shock, and a whole lot of terror to go around. I will admit that I snapped a little. I showered, shaved and dressed in my best Armani suit. I figure if I was going to die it should be in my favorite suit. Besides, it isn't like I have a lot of other clothes. I went to my closet, to the back, and opened the storage chest. Besides the bag I found this notebook in the chest contained the only things that still tied me to my childhood. The items that make me more than the Wall Street giant that I was. Nestled there among the scrapbooks and mementos I sat down on the floor and lost myself in the past for a while.

When I was six years old I remember sitting on the back steps of my house crying. My father was supposed to take me camping that weekend. He had called my mom and told her that he had to work. I heard her ask him about the camping trip. From her side of the conversation it was obvious he had forgotten all about it, and me. I didn't know it until she told me about it much later in life but mom had stood there in the kitchen and watched me crying out the window. Three weeks later she told my father and I at dinner that we were joining the Proud Braves.

The Proud Braves were a father/son organization based off the Native American tradition of fathers teaching their sons the ways of their people. Braves were taught to live off the land, fish and shoot a bow. The group was amazing. There were a lot of high profile business people who were members. This was probably the way mom got dad to join. So we would go on weekends together and after spending the day with together dad would spend the evening around the campfire, networking.

We spent a lot of time together at first. Then, when dad had exhausted the networking options in the Proud Braves, he stopped coming as much. By that time I had made a lot of new friends and didn't miss having him around. The skills they taught me were simple, yet important. How to gather food from the land. How to catch fish, then clean and cook them. The making and use of bow and arrows. This last bit was something that I excelled at. Crafting bows seemed to call to something inside me. Putting them together was effortless I just had a natural talent for seeing how they should be formed. This insight gave me an edge when it came to firing bows as well. Among my friends I quickly stood out as the best shot. When the Proud Braves had a tournament I won it hands down. I went to the National Shootout and won that. My father got some great contacts out of that trip. I remember it was one of the few times he told me how proud of me he was.

Mom told her friends about me and one of them got her in touch with a local archery group. They were so impressed with my skill that they sponsored me on the path to professional competition. My ability grew with practice which garnered more praise from my father. It was like a drug. The better I did the more places it took him. The more access he got the better he did in business. At the time I only saw my father being proud of me. I put everything into competition. I gave up the Proud Braves and my friends there. My GPA went up to over 4.0 as I dedicated myself to doing my absolute best at school. Mastering my classwork allowed me to breeze through my homework before I even left the building. This freed me up to practice as much as possible.

All through high school I pushed myself, desperate for a moments praise from my father. My junior year I tried out for the

Olympics for archery. The day I was supposed to leave for the trials mom collapsed. Cancer. She had been hiding it from my father and I for some time. She said she didn't want to distract us. Dad fell apart. I would never have suspected that he was capable of such strong feelings. I had never seen him so upset. Archery was forgotten as I watched my mother start her slow slide to the grave. My father faded. That is the best way I can describe it. As mom slipped away the air seemed to seep out of my dad.

A little over a year and a half after mom was buried I got a call from my father's lawyer. I had been at Harvard for about six months. With my first semester under my belt I was just starting the second when I got the call. Dad was dead, heart attack. The school gave me all A's for the rest of the year. They told me to take time to grieve. I was gone for a week and then I came back. I made up everything I missed. My adviser had to have a few meetings to get the academic waiver removed because my existing grades were higher than 4.0.

My week away from school was hell. Dad had taken his last year putting mom's affairs in order. Looking back I realized he had put his own in order as well. He liquidated stocks, sold off vacation homes and cars. Retired from the boards he sat on. I left the lawyers office with a vast fortune and a letter from my father. Bland advice from him on business and a closing line about how he was always proud of me. It felt hollow, empty.

The only thing I had left from my childhood was archery. Harvard had given me a scholarship for academics but I joined the Archery Club the first day on campus. They had the best range I had ever seen, on par with an Olympic practice range. Every spare moment I had was spent on that range my freshman year. Even later, when my schedule was much more hectic, I found time for the range. When I was shooting I found a tiny island of peace in the chaos of life. Even though I never tried out for the Olympics again I never lost my edge.

Moving aside photo albums and setting them on the floor I took out my bow. Four quivers of arrows followed. Two I strapped to my back. One each went on my legs. They had slotted tops to allow smooth arrow pulls without allowing any of them to fall out on their own. Each arrow had a hunting tip, perfectly balanced, which required a small twist as you pulled them out. I got in the habit of using them when I was in college. I had found it was better to practice with the same arrow you hunt with. I took a small backpack and loaded it with my tool kit from the chest. I could fix my bow, making repairs up to and including replacing pulleys. In a pinch I could use the kit to make bows from scratch, although making strings would be a pain. Looking out the window I can see the sun is coming up. I think it is time to get out of town.

TIME FLIES WHEN YOU ARE running for your life. It has been a few weeks and I figured I might as well record my thoughts while they are still somewhat fresh. When I went back out to the living room, I got a few wolf whistles. I told Joey that I was going to head out of town. He asked me where and I told him that I figured, based off the news, that the best bet was to head west. The infected were coming from the east so the further away from them you got the better. Suddenly everyone was scrambling for their stuff. After last night no one was too keen on hanging around. Not having any better ideas I think they felt safer with someone that could drop a zombie for a good distance. And our moaning friends from down that hall were getting on everyone's nerves.

The hallway held our first obstacle. Two zombies shuffled around down at the window. I dropped them where they stood and we went in the opposite direction to the stairs. Down the stairs we were clear all the way to the street. Once we exited the building we were greeted by chaotic bedlam mixed with pockets of hell. People were running everywhere followed by shambling monsters. I took us west, but went one street over first. I wanted to avoid Mr. Chen's.

It was a long walk. From where we were, the edge of the city was a trek. The first day didn't go well. Even with the bow, there were just too many dead. Two of our people got taken out by zombies falling off of roofs. As in, dead guys take a swan dive off a building trying to get to the living below. Death from above. One of the guys got crushed by the zombie. The one next to him got splattered when it smashed into the ground. I held an arrow on the guy, he looked scared as hell, and told him he couldn't come with us. We left him behind with the dead and after that we kept to the middle of the street. All things considered we did get a lot of ground covered that day. We ended up spending the night on a rooftop after scrambling up a fire escape.

The next morning it was ten times worse. There was no way we were going to make it out of town this way. I remembered that my company kept a boat at the marina nearby. If we could make it there we could sail out of the city instead of trying to walk out. Keeping to rooftops whenever we could we made better time towards the waterfront. The dead were everywhere but I only shot when I had to. Even so I had emptied two of my quivers by the time we stopped for the night. Towards dusk I made my way down from everyone by rooftops to a sporting goods store at the edge of the block. I had to kill twenty zombies but I got through to the archery section. I took all the bows, arrows and archery gear to the roof. Before we set out the next day I outfitted the group with crossbows. Modern crossbows are really easy to load, aim and shoot. As easy as firing a gun. Having people armed could only help, plus my quivers were refilled and I had extra arrows packed in bundles.

We hit a few other stores on the way out of town. The group was able to get outfitted in all the outdoor gear they needed. This was good because it was cold out. I traded my Italian leather shoes for heavy boots. My suit stayed but I covered it with some outer gear. We reached the marina and the company boat was still there. I had to take down a few zombies but we were able to get aboard and cast off. Our boat was huge, big enough for all of the people with us, and it was still well stocked with food. Steaks, beer, canned goods. We went from being third world back to first world just by boarding.

The cruise was amazingly surreal. You could almost imagine that the world wasn't ending, until you looked at the shore and noticed no traffic on the roads. Or looked up in the sky and saw that there were no planes. Sam Walters told me that his company had a cabin on the far shore of the lake. The cabin was set on a flat area but was ringed by a high rock ridge. The only approach was from the water, so we thought we were safe. We were stupid.

For a few weeks we lived comfortably. Then they came up out of the water. They caught a few people away from the cabin. I got on the roof and shot enough of them for people to get clear. We grabbed all we could and raced back to the boat. On board I made it clear that anyone that felt ill or got tired was going down into a cabin and the door was going to be closed. If they turned they weren't going to surprise anyone. We sailed back to the west and landed north of Green Bay. One of the women and one of the guys went into a cabin on that boat and never came back out. The moaning and thumping made the rest of the voyage extremely unpleasant. When we landed we pushed the boat back into the water. I'd knocked a hole in it below the waterline. It would sink leaving our two dead friends trapped inside. I didn't want to take the chance of someone using the boat and getting eaten. We skirted the city and kept traveling west. Hopefully we can find a safe place out here somewhere to hole up.

IT WAS GOING PRETTY SMOOTHLY until we got near Wichita. Outside the city we ran into some pretty bad people. There was a compound, for lack of a better word, that was chock full of crazies. The First People of God. I guess it should have put us on our guard that we had not encountered any dead for a while. The lack of zombies was unnatural and we should have known that hadn't happened on its own. The good people of God had taken it upon themselves to cleanse the world around them. They ambushed us just as the sun was coming up. Three pickups full of men roared up and surrounded the garage we had taken refuge on top of.

An old grizzled man stepped out of the first truck, a big black four by four, with a bible grasped in his hand. He began what sounded like a well-practiced speech. We were wanderers in the waste and the Lord had sent him to judge us. If we were good folk, willing to submit to the will of the Lord then we would find a place among them. If we were wicked we would be cleansed. I really didn't like the sound of that. He got pretty worked up when we didn't rush right out to greet him. After several attempts to get us to surrender to his will he told us we had chosen to die. His men began advancing with their rifles and shotguns. Their intent was pretty clear.

I dropped the old man first, followed by the biggest guy with a rifle. My priority was the rifles. Shotguns would have to get pretty close to do any real damage. It was over in less than a minute. Two of the trucks roared away leaving ten of their dead behind. We packed ourselves in the truck they abandoned and drove as far west as we could get before the gas ran out. One of the girls showed us how to siphon gas from other vehicles. Being able to get gas kept us on the road, even if it did lower our arrow supply taking down shamblers.

Big sporting goods stores provided supplies, both arrows and food. We got another pickup at one of the stores, keys left above the visor. The further west we got the worse the roads got and the fewer stores we encountered. By the time we got to Colorado we were low on food, ammo and gas. The trucks had to be abandoned, it was just too hard to find gas and no one wanted to risk going to a gas station. I found some decent wood and started making arrows.

The carbon fiber bow had way too much torque to use with homemade arrows. With no other choice, I packed away my state of the art, one of a kind, custom made bow. I couldn't hit the broadside of a barn with the new arrows using it. I found a few suitable pieces of wood and started building a new bow, an old fashioned wooden recurve. I was amazed at how quickly the bow came together. The arrows were much more suited to it. I was able to tweak the design for accuracy. Pretty soon I was dropping the dead nearly as well as I had with my old bow.

Finding wood that was suitable was hard, especially the further west we got. Most of the trees became decidedly crooked. I was forced to reshape bigger twigs into suitable arrows. It took forever to make the damn things. It made us put false value on the arrows themselves. On the second week one of the guys was practicing and shot an arrow into the ground. He pulled it back up and got something all over himself. Then the ground started moving. A zombie sat up and one of the others shot it. Later that night the guy, Greg Wilson, turned. I put him down. After that the rule stood. If you shoot an arrow, even in practice, it's gone. Forget about it.

Every day I took time to show everyone how to select rocks while we walked. They needed to be flat and suitable for shaping. Each night I showed them how to turn the rocks into arrowheads. It was excruciatingly slow but it gave us something to pass the time. It also gave us the ammo we needed for everyone to practice. It turned out to be a good thing that I was a decent teacher.

There was a gas station out by itself. It looked empty but when we got inside and were stocking up on supplies the dead started showing up. Jamie Bennett was up top on watch and saw them coming. She called down to us and we threw all the supplies we could up top. Hell we practically emptied the store. The dead had apparently been following us for quite some time. There were a few, then ten, then nearly a hundred. I did a quick tally and realized the dead outnumbered the arrows we had two to one.

More than two days we sat up there eating chips and drinking beer. We set up a few tarps for shade. I figured we were done for and was racking my brain to come up with a plan to get everyone out. I had nothing. A few days later I quit drinking and decided to sober up. The water and rest did wonders for me, but at first I thought I was still drunk. There were a lot of bodies down below. Bodies that weren't moving. It took me about two hours before I realized that someone was walking out among the dead.

Wrapped head to toe in leather the figure stalked from body to body whacking them in the skull. One hit dropped a zombie to the ground. Over and over he crushed the skulls of the shamblers. He ignored their claws and killed them. It was mesmerizing. Watching the figure move through the dead was inspiring. By the next day it was clear he was going to clear the field.

When it was over, the figure walked slowly towards the convenience store. He looked up at Jamie, the blond that had been on watch when the dead approached. This close you could tell he was a man but it was impossible to see anything of his features. He screamed and ranted about a town to the west called Vigilance. Then he turned and walked away. Nothing we yelled made him stop and turn. When we got below, we had to skirt the bodies of the dead. We followed in the direction he went, but we never caught up to him.

In the middle of the desert, away from any roads or signs, we became hopelessly lost. The food and water wasn't going to last forever, but I had no idea which direction to go. I had a compass so I took us west. It seemed as good a direction as any. It turned out to be a pretty good choice. Our second night out we camped on top of a big flat hill. That is when we got a visit from another mysterious stranger, this one not covered in gore.

He appeared at the edge of the firelight and said hello. After everyone settled down he introduced himself as Ken Benson. I stepped forward and made our introductions. He tossed a bag that landed with a hefty clunk at my feet. Opening it, I found canned goods and dried meat. I handed it behind me and the group started making dinner. The first real meal we had in weeks. While we ate he asked us about ourselves and our journey. He seemed to perk up a bit when someone told him about our bows. He asked me about how I made them and how long it took. By the time we got done with our conversation he was smiling.

When we bedded down for the night, he stayed. The next morning he led us to a different campsite and asked us to wait. Two hours later he came back with a younger man who introduced himself as Phillip. We spoke for about an hour and he inspected our bows. After talking to the rest of the group he seemed to come to a decision. He bluntly told us that only I had any skills his people would value. They needed bows and arrows which made my knowledge important. If the others would agree to work as my assistants, making bows, then he could extend us an invitation to his refuge.

He left us alone to discuss this. There was a lot of shouting and anger. People don't like being told that they have no value. Hell, it hit me hard in my pride that they only wanted me for my bow building skills. I could only imagine what it was like for the others. But we had been through a lot together, and come to depend on each other. By the time Phillip returned everyone had agreed to his terms.

I was asked to go back and finish this journal by a woman known as the Archivist. She is kind of the historian of the refuge of Vigilance. Each person who comes to live here writes the story of how they came to be a part of the group. Archivist Sanderson says that with the world in the state it is now every story is precious. Because you never know what you will learn from someone else's journey.

Betty Simmers

MY NAME IS BETTY SIMMERS. My husband Robert was a cop, a lieutenant in the Greensboro SCPD. We lived in a quiet neighborhood in a restored foursquare. The house was everything we had always wanted. Beautiful, historic, filled with character and completely updated. We'd been talking about starting a family soon. I had just started working as a real estate agent a few years before we met so I told him I wanted to pass the five year mark before I went part time to raise our kids. Now that seems like a pretty intuitive choice. I can't imagine the horror of having a baby on board when the world ended.

That day started just like any other. Robert went off to work. He'd been tossing and turning because of all the craziness going on in New York. Before I even rolled out of bed he had showered and was on his second pot of coffee. He gave me a peck on the cheek as I was heading into the bathroom. Knowing what I do now I should have wrapped my arms around him and kissed him properly. Or improperly. Or just dragged him back to bed. I wish I had never let him leave that morning. But I did. Every day since then I have lived with a heart full of would have, should have, could haves.

I had a showing nearby, a beautiful restored Victorian that just went on the market. I drove over and was going through emails when someone slammed into my window. I started to unbuckle my seat belt to get out but then they threw themselves against the window again. The woman standing there was slashed up with one of her boobs hanging out of her housecoat. Teeth marks were all over her exposed flesh and her face was torn up. Milky white eyes stared at me blankly as she slammed her body over and over onto my car. I clicked my seatbelt, started the car and peeled out of there. Calling my client I got her voicemail. I left her a message telling her not to go to the house. I hope she got it.

As I raced home, I tried getting hold of Robert all the way there. He never kept his cell on when he was on shift. I left him twenty or more voice mails before I got to the house. I couldn't get out when I got there. There were a few zombies wandering around on my lawn. People from the neighborhood, or at least they used to be. As I drove out of there at a crawl I occasionally saw someone running away from the dead. A few even tried to wave me down, begging me to stop, but I didn't dare.

My heart pounding, I drove to Robert's precinct. Even if he wasn't answering his phone, they should be able to get him on the radio. The building he worked in was very modern, all steel and glass. It let the public look right inside and see everything that was going on. Robert always jokingly called it the Fishbowl. When I got there all the glass was broken and bodies lay everywhere. I flipped off my IPod and the first station I tuned in was talking about zombies. Getting bitten or clawed could kill you in hours. But just getting some of their "goo" on you would infect you. Within ten hours you would die and come back as one of them. They stated that noise attracts the zombies. Based on how they were attracted to my car, I bet gunfire must really get their attention.

Looking at the number of corpses around the precinct, I figured I was right. A lot of the zombies walking around were in uniform, with guns in their holsters. I couldn't' help myself. I started scanning the zombie's faces, looking for Robert. And I found him. Near the outside perimeter was Robert's car with his body inside. The top of his head was gone, just gone. I could see gore coating the inside of the car. I felt my heart wrench in my chest. Tears threatened to overwhelm me, but a zombie slammed the side of my card. Others were crowding in towards the car. My survival instincts kicked in and I slammed the gas.

From that moment to the next things kind of blurred. I remember driving aimlessly. I ended up outside of town, pulled over on a roadside overlook. It was all just too much. Losing Robert, zombies, the world ending. I cried until I fell asleep. I woke up the next day to a knock on the window of my car door. An Army soldier stood outside my window watching me uncertainly. After he figured out I wasn't a zombie he asked me how long I had been there. When I told him all night he told me there was an evacuation point was a few clicks down the road. I have no idea what a "click" is but before I drove a mile down the road it was blocked by stopped cars. I got out and hurried forward with the other evacuees. Behind us gunshots rang out, some of them were pretty close.

I joined a line of people snaking into a chain link compound hastily set up in the parking lot of a large chain store. The soldiers took anyone that was injured or sick out of the line. The rest of us were examined and then placed in individual holding cells. It didn't even occur to me to object until I was already locked in. The soldier who put me inside just ignored my cries and walked away. I sat there for over eight hours. In the end I was glad to be locked in. Some of the others lay down and I thought they were sleeping. That is until they got back up and began weakly pushing against the chain link, moaning. The woman next to me huddled on my side of her cell as her neighbor, a fat man of about forty, gnashed his yellow teeth at her.

Sometime after that all hell broke loose back in the main holding area. Gunfire erupted and then a soldier came running up to the cell area. She quickly let out anyone that hadn't turned and told us to head to the far side of the compound. I never saw her again. We went where she told us to only to find a few trucks with no one in them. All the soldiers appeared to be fighting or had fled. One tough looking woman grabbed an M16 and some ammo and jumped into the driver seat of one of the trucks. She told everyone to grab a gun and get in one of the trucks. I grabbed a few handguns. They were so much heavier than I thought they would be. Jumping up in the back of the woman's truck, I watched as everyone picked a vehicle and did the same. Our group was mostly women. I guess most guys didn't want to ride with a woman driver. The one exception was Francis. From his flamboyant speech he must have figured he would be more welcome with the females. There was less chance of being shot by a homophobe.

Our lady driver knew what she was doing. She tore a hole in the fence without taking her foot off the gas. While the other trucks sped away, overtaking us and disappearing into the distance she kept an even pace. We passed one of the trucks overturned and burning an hour later, so her caution turned out to be justified. After an hour she turned off the main road and headed up a back highway. There were fewer cars in the road here and before it got dark she took the truck up a steep hill, parking at the top. The woman introduced herself as Daisy Mae Fields. She was ex-military and knew a thing or two. After we all took turns introducing ourselves Daisy explained how it was. We might all be infected. There was no way to tell. We all needed to spread out and keep some distance between each other until the night was over. Then we would know. She picked a few of us to keep watch with her. Surprisingly she picked me and another woman that had grabbed a gun. I told her I didn't even know how to fire it and she gave me a crash course. Loaded, unloaded, safety on, safety off, point at the head and fire. But she told me to make sure I was back far enough to not get hit by any goop. And to be sure no one was behind my target.

"Bullets like to keep going," she said.

I sat on top of the truck roof and we waited for the dawn. It was a full moon that night which was helpful. Two of the women got up in the night and shambled toward their neighbors. Daisy got one of them, I got the other. After that no one slept much. Two others got back up sometime later but we were more than ready when they did. By the time the sun came back up we had zombies at the base of the hill. The gunfire really drew them out. I mean we were in a really remote countryside but we have six zombies show up?

Daisy drove the truck back out onto the road and put some distance between us and them. Francis started crying about an hour later. His cell service was out, but the last text he got was from his boyfriend who was still stuck in New Orleans. He had been away for business and couldn't even drive back with the military shutting down the highways. His last text was to tell Francis he loved him and would never forget him. Francis's crying set the rest of us off and by the time Daisy called a break later that day we all looked horrible. Daisy laughed and told us she had good news and bad news.

The good news was no one was around to see how shitty we looked. The bad news was the truck was about out of gas and we were going to be walking soon. About an hour later, when it did sputter to a stop, we stripped anything useful from the vehicle. Then we walked for hours until Francis spotted a turn off with a sign that had fallen down. When we picked up the sign, it was for an old hotel off the main road. Daisy took the sign and threw it in the woods. Then she had a few of us help her grab old tree limbs to cover up the side road entrance. It wasn't that hard, the road didn't look like it had been used in years.

Once we were done she took armfuls of leaves from the woods and spread them all around, covering all signs of our passing. None of us questioned her at the time. We were too shell-shocked and exhausted. After that she led us up the road which wound back and forth up a steep incline. A few times we had to go single file in areas where rocks had slid down onto the road. We never would have gotten the truck up here. Eventually we came out into an open area with an old fieldstone wall running about waist height around an old two story building. There was a dilapidated barn off to the right inside the fence line and what looked like an old well off to the left. Two giant chimneys sat at each end of the building which appeared to have been built at the turn of the last century. The windows were high and small and the entire structure had a wraparound covered porch. There were missing panes in the windows and the general sense of neglect made it a unique fixer up at best.

Daisy went into the building alone and came out an hour later advising us that it was clear. She told us to be careful until we knew how solid the place was then she went off to check the barn. After that I saw her disappear into the tree line and she came back a few hours later to gather a few of the girls to help gather fire wood. Francis had gone into the kitchen and begun cleaning it. There were plenty of pots, pans, cups and dishes and the stove was the old wood-burning kind Once he had it cleaned up the kitchen looked like an antique collectors dream. A few of the more handy women found things to shut up the broken windows with and two even fixed the front and back doors so they would securely close. Before nightfall we had wood in the house for cooking and fires, the doors and windows secured and our supplies stowed.

Water drawn out of the well was tested (I'm not sure how, but we had a few very smart women with us) and was good. So we had water, food, shelter and warmth. We were high enough up in the hills that the nights got pretty cold. I remembered that from camping here as a child. There was a distinct lack of bedding or blankets in the house. So the fires got built up that first night, we set a watch and went to bed.

The next day Daisy told me that she was going to take a few of the ladies on a supply run. She took four of the rougher girls and a few guns. Their first stop was going to be a general store we passed a few miles back. We hadn't stopped at the time because we weren't sure how much further we would be going. Hauling supplies would have slowed us down. Now, it was imperative that we got at least some blankets and food soon. They were not back until an hour before dusk. Daisy had us open a pack of rubber gloves she brought back to handle everything. I was given the dubious honor of inspecting everything to make sure it was clean and rub down the hard items with soap and water. The clothing, bedding and such we washed in big metal tubs filled with boiling water and soap. We found the tubs in the basement along with some wire that we used to make a clothesline. The soap we had was old. It had been powdered at one time, then solidified. It still worked well enough to get things clean. But the new soap they brought with them worked so much better.

The five who had gone out sat in the woods with ropes tied around their waists. Daisy said if they accidentally got infected the ropes would keep them at bay. We waited for ten long hours. After dark Jan Redon fell asleep and a zombie got back up. I shot her in the head. I hate this world. I hate what it has forced me to become. Instead of a bringing life into this world I am now tasked with eliminating unlife. How long before I can kill the living as easily?

We spent a somber night and the next morning Daisy called a meeting. We talked most of the day away discussing our situation. The discussion turned to how to prevent infection and one of the women, Penny Grace who was a nurse, suggested rubber gloves and sacks. New sacks and gloves would be used each time. This made getting a supply of them a priority. Daisy said the general store had a bunch of them. Anything that got brought back was to be washed in soap and water before being rinsed and dried. And everyone who went out would wear something over their clothes that they could throw away. Daisy had brought back some painters coveralls, the silly disposable kind. They would serve for now until something better was found.

Two women who knew Jan Redon told us all they knew about her. We told stories, cried and laughed as we remembered the woman that we had lost. Now it is time to get to work to make sure we don't have to lose anyone else.

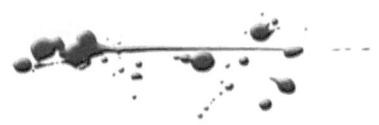

THE LAST FEW MONTHS HAVE been hard, but things just gotten harder. We had built ourselves a home gathering what we could from nearby stores, empty houses and in one case, a barn. As time progressed, our people had to go further and further afield to find supplies. Winter was approaching fast and we were worried that we might not be able to go out once the snows came. Daisy and I went out two days from the hotel and found a small town with an intact grocery store. Inside we found dried, canned and preserved food. There was enough for years. Daisy insisted we only take the canned and preserved food back to the hotel. The dried food she and I secreted in a cave high up on a cliff face and sealed it shut with rocks.

At the time we thought we were pretty clever to have put aside a reserve just in case. After what happened next I realize that it was like the hand of fate giving us a break. We spent a cozy winter in our new home. As it was turning from winter into spring the snows melted but then we had a cold snap. We had to keep the fires going day and night and ran low on wood. Daisy took a group out to gather firewood. She had been gone two days when the men showed up. The outer scouts reported them coming up from the road. They stumbled on the road entrance, probably took the wood off the road for their fire. It was stupid of us, we had stripped the surrounding area and of course the dead fall on the road would have been attractive wood for a fire. We should have put rocks down there before it snowed.

They came up to the house and laid siege from the woods. The entire contingent was made up of men. I didn't see one woman among them and it gave me a feeling of foreboding. Their leader was a handsome enough man who introduced himself as Major Terrance Montague. He told us that his men meant us no harm. They were the remnants of the 23rd infantry. For over fifteen minutes he extolled his men's virtues and praised our ingenuity. He offered his protection and proposed joining our two groups together for a common purpose against the zombies.

One of our scouts, Daria Reynolds, came in and told me the men were flanking our position, trying to surround us. I called a quick meeting and told the women we needed to go. Francis was the first to agree. He didn't like the slick way that man was talking.

"That boy is trying way too hard to convince us that he is a good guy," he said suspiciously.

A lot of the women were hesitant. They didn't want to abandon what we had built. Some thought it would be easier if we had some men around for protection. I cut the meeting short with an ultimatum. I was leaving. Those that were coming should come and those that were staying were fools.

A minute later I was out the back door and through the woods with half the women. The rest had either decided to stay or hesitated too long. Before we were even out of hearing the men took the hotel. The screams of the women who had remained behind left no doubt in my mind that I had made the right decision. I took the women to the cave up on the cliff face and unsealed it. Leaving them inside, I went after Daisy. I found her and the others on their way back with wood. She cursed the women who had stayed behind and the men that had taken them.

The two of us returned to the hotel. What we found sickened us. The men had moved right in and used the women who stayed behind horribly. Two bodies, barely identifiable as women lay like cord wood outside the back door. Daisy threw up. I was so numb it was like I was looking at the entire scene in a movie. It seemed unreal. We retreated back to the cave. For the next few days we stayed hidden. Daisy went out scouting and when she came back her face was white as a sheet. The men had brought the dead with them. An enormous horde was walking up the road from the direction the men had come from.

The woods were no longer safe. Soon they would be swarming with zombies. The dried food was now a godsend. It was light and easy to carry. We packed it all up and set off away from the horde. The going was tough, the woods were soon over run and we had to blaze a trail. Scouts that checked behind told us that the dead had laid siege to the hotel. Anyone still inside that place was never getting out. That night we camped atop a high ledge and we mourned those we had lost. For three weeks we walked those woods headed west. When we emerged from the trees there were less than ten of us. Daisy was among those we lost. Two days before we found our way out a large group of zombies surprised us, coming out of the underbrush.

Daisy could have escaped but instead she stood her ground and mowed them down. She killed them all but got sprayed by goo during the battle. The last I saw of her she stood under the trees with a handgun with two bullets in her hand waving goodbye. Leadership fell to me. Out of the forest we came to a road. Against my better judgment we followed it. After an hour we came upon another blessing of fate. A station wagon parked on the side of the road, filled with gas and locked. The keys were sitting under the back bumper. From the dust on the glass whoever had planned on using it never got a chance. After giving the vehicle a careful inspection to make sure there was no zombie goo inside we stuffed ourselves in.

Two days and over a thousand miles later we knew we were in trouble. The car that started as a blessing had become a curse. Every zombie we passed started after us. By the time we got out in the western part of the country we knew there was a river of undead following us. Tabetha Balchav, a CPA with a love of strategy games, told me that we needed to decoy the dead so they wouldn't follow us. When the next group of shamblers showed up I let them follow us until we got to a southern turn. Then we turned south. After an hour we turned back to the west. When the car ran out of gas we took off on foot.

The desert is no place for a stroll. Even with the stores we found along the way water had to be rationed. Then there were the zombies. We had no way of killing them without attracting more to our location. So we had to run and keep ahead of them. But we were only as fast as our slowest member, Mary Lou Tennalis. She had been a secretary and was pushing fifty. The problem was that fifty was pushing back. The longer we walked the slower she got. Melody Staein fell back and tried to help her, but it did no good. She just kept slowing down.

I was finally left with a choice. Keep going and leave her behind or find a place to hold up. Everyone took a vote and decided to hold up. Daisy would have told them to leave Mary Lou and keep moving, but I wasn't strong enough. Instead, I agreed with the group vote, even though I knew it was a mistake. We found a house out near the edge of the road. We got inside and tried to rest up for a day. The next morning when we woke up Mary Lou wasn't even able to stand. She told us to leave her and god damn me we should have. Within another day the dead were upon us. Then the question of leaving was no longer important.

The house was on a flat slab, so the dead were able to push right up to the walls. Within a week the house started to creak and groan under the strain. I tried to tell the women that the house would fail, but they either didn't believe me or maybe they just figured it didn't matter. When the house buckled Mary Lou was sitting too close to the wall. Hands reached in and grabbed her hair. Before anyone could act she was pulled out a hole in the wall that she was far too large to fit out of. Her screams went on for an impossibly long time. The rest of us climbed into the attic and bashed out one of the vents to crawl out onto the roof.

As I write this I am stranded atop the roof. The dead have us trapped. I don't know how we will get out of this. There may be no escape. If it comes to it we will use the last of our ammunition to end it. They will not have us. I will see my beloved Robert soon. We will never be afraid ever again.

JOURNAL FOUND ON ROOFTOP OF house to southwest of Vigilance. Area around was trampled badly, signs of horde in area. On
the roof there were ten women, all with self-inflicted gunshot
wounds to the head. Journal was in a bag sitting next to bodies. No
body fluid on bag. Also in bag was survival handbook and almanac.
Taken to Archivist.

Bobbie Grader

IT WAS DARK WHEN I woke up. Not just night, but so black that you couldn't see the slightest detail around you. No streetlights, no 'urban glow' of large commercial districts which was the norm near where I lived, just absolute blackness. All I could hear was a scraping and the sound of my own breathing. It took me a second to get my bearings. I was in the closet of my bedroom with the door shut. That explained the darkness and also why it felt so close in there. From outside came the scraping again and every hair on my body stood on end. It all came back in a sickening rush. How I ended up in the closet…and what was outside the door.

My name is Bobbie Grader and I'm 19 years old. I lived in Ames, Iowa and I started this journal to write down what happens in case I don't make it. Even if I do I doubt anyone will ever read this. But I had to do something. I've got no one to talk to and I kind of feel like I am losing my mind. Things have gone to hell and I've got a front row seat. I went from being a slacker that was struggling to find his purpose in life and fighting with his parents about going to college to a lonely orphan in a nightmare.

It started on a Tuesday of all days. The most boring day of the week most of the time, right? Everyone and their brother was swamping the stores trying to get everything they could get their hands on. I worked at a craft store. Yarn, crochet gear, sewing patterns and scrap booking crap. Yeah, I know. Not exactly the place a guy would pick for a career right? The owner was a friend of my mom's. When I opted out of college and needed a direction mom made a call. A week later I was working behind the counter of Batlin's Crafts. It kept my folks off my back and gave me some independent money. And hawking craft gear is normally a pretty sedate activity.

Why would you need any of it in an emergency? I've got no idea. The crisis should have meant that our store was the last place someone would come. Instead we had people pulling everything they could off the shelves and just throwing money at us as they ran out the door. It was a step below outright theft because they paid, but running out with merchandise wasn't a normal shopping habit. Maybe they thought they could crochet a zombie trap or scrapbook their way out of the apocalypse. Who knows? Mrs. Batlin finally just closed the metal drop gate out front and we left out the back. She offered me a ride home, anxious about all the chaos going on. I wanted to say yes. I really did. But I knew I was going the opposite direction from her and she had her own family to get back to.

When I left her, she was crying and turning on the ignition of her car. That image has stuck with me ever since. I wonder if I'll ever see her again. The walk home ended up as a run that took me well outside my normal route. Some crazy bastard started after me right after I turned up the street from the store and after that it seemed like I ran into psychos at every turn. Everything from a homeless guy to a preppy in a full on business suit, they all came at me in a shamble that gave me the creeps. By the time I got to the house I was spooked. All I wanted to do was get inside and lock out all the weird.

The house was quiet which should have been my first clue that things were fucked. My house is normally one decibel short of outright bedlam. Between dad blasting the game, mom fighting back by blasting her music and my sister yelling at both of them it was enough to wake the dead. Maybe they did. I headed into the kitchen and saw my parents working on something on the counter. When I got closer I realized what they were working on. It was our next door neighbor, Gale Baker. And by working on her I mean they were tearing into her with their hands. As I came in I must have gasped or made a noise because they turned. Both of them were covered in

Gale's blood. Mom had a bit of Gale hanging from her mouth, still chewing. We stared at each other for a moment and then dad shuffled towards me stretching out his hand and giving a low moan.

I pissed myself. Right there in my family's kitchen I pissed my pants. To tell you the truth I was surprised I didn't shit myself as well. I mean, there are some things that no amount of life lessons and horror movies can prepare you for. Having your parents turned into the living dead that start eating the neighbors? That was bad enough. Dad shuffling towards me with an eye towards chewing my face off? There is not enough therapy left in the entire world to fix the mental scarring bouncing around in my head.

I'm not ashamed to say I bolted for the one refuge still available to me. My bedroom upstairs. Soiled pants and all I ran in slammed my door and started changing. Here is an interesting bit of trivia for you. The door to my bedroom is slightly warped. My little sister and I had a water fight and the door didn't fare well. So when I slammed it the door shuddered but didn't latch shut. I had shucked my clothes and just pulled on new underwear when I heard the door creak open. I turned with my new jeans in hand, to see my baby sister standing in the doorway. Not really a baby, she was only two years and a few months younger than me.

She had just celebrated her 17th birthday a few days before and it turned out that was going to be the last one she got to enjoy. It was apparent from the bite marks on her that she hadn't been as lucky as I had in avoiding the parents. With a low moan she shuffled towards me and I backpedaled right into my closet and slammed the door. She thumped against the outside of the door and I heard her fingernails scraping against the wood. That was the sound that greeted me upon waking, that and her fucking zombie moaning. I'm glad my closet door latched tight because losing consciousness (I refuse to accept that I might have fainted) in the face of zombie attack would have ended my day right there.

Now this is not a big closet we are talking about. It isn't a walk in luxury model. There was not even enough room to stretch out your arms unless you reached up. Up. I pulled the clothes bar out of its bracket, dumping everything to my feet and stretched up. The ceiling of my closet gave a bit as I pushed on it. Dad had opted out of remodeling the closets when he redid the house and that little nugget of cheapness saved my ass. Pushing up with the rod I broke through the old plasterboard. I had to chip a few holes to climb up the wall but in the end getting into the attic was surprisingly easy.

It was a treasure trove. A veritable fucking horde of bounty. Well, that isn't really true. A lot of it was garbage. I mean, how useful are a bunch of Christmas lights and a fake tree? Or plastic Easter baskets we haven't used in a decade. In reality our attic was like a time capsule of all the useless things we had abandoned over the years. But dad had gone through a macho phase and that was what saved me. In the far corner of the room near a window that overlooked the street was everything I needed. In containers marked DO NOT OPEN.

Ripping open the smallest container I found a small lock box. It broke open easily enough. A glock 9MM, three clips and two full boxes of ammo spilled out. Another box had an ultralight backpack full of survival gear. A crossbow and a few bales of bolts and a flashlight with a solar charger. I almost left the crossbow and if I had I would be dead. The attic had one other feature that aided my escape, a chain link metal fire ladder. Once my bounty was packed into the backpack I put the gun into my coat pocket. The crossbow I strapped to the outside of the pack.

Then I just sat there. I made the mistake of taking a moment to think, to reflect I guess. Most kids do this when they're leaving for college, not when they're preparing to climb down the outside of their house in a zombie apocalypse. I realized right there, one leg over the window ledge that my life as I knew it was over. My dad, the guy that read me stories when I was little, talked to me about everything, hell he was one of my best friends. Now he was a murderous zombie with Gail all over him. Mom. I couldn't even think about her without tears spilling down my face. And Abigail, Abby for short, my little sister. Where was I when she needed protecting? Selling yarn to a bunch of idiots.

There would be no more family dinners, no more holidays. I was on my own and would have to watch out for myself from now on. And I never got to say goodbye. The last thing I said to my mom was telling her what sounded good for dinner. Dad and I had talked about a sports trade. I don't even remember the player's name. Decomba. Marvin Decomba that was the guy's name, a pitcher. And Abby and I had talked about hitting the movies next week to see something. Tears blurred my vision as I sat on the windowsill and lost my shit. I'm not sure how long I was there but by the time I was done I had to go back into the attic to find something to wipe the snot off my face. Going back to the window I took a final look around then slipped through the window and climbed to the ground.

Down at ground level there were more zombies. At this point the existence of walking dead in my neighborhood was an indisputable reality. Lucky for me they were slow. Really slow. Like I would have to sit down and wait ten minutes for them to get here and eat me slow. But there were a lot of them. By the time I got to the edge of the neighborhood I knew I was in trouble. There was gunfire everywhere, screams, and lots of smoke. Abandoned cars blocked almost every street that I crossed and there were a lot of unpleasant noises coming out of shadowy areas. Chewing noises.

I turned onto Fifth Street and found the way forward blocked on one side by a burning bus and the other side by a mass of shambling undead. The other way wasn't much better. Most of the lights were off and the darkness looked pretty damn unappealing. As I stood there wondering what I was going to do a guy yelled at me from a nearby fire escape.

"Hey! Stupid! Get your ass up off the street before you get bit!"

I looked up at him and he motioned to the fire escape above my head. Jumping up I grabbed the bracket of a drainpipe and climbed up to the bottom level and none too soon. From out of the dark came a mob of zombies. Packed wall to wall they shambled towards me.

The group looked almost comical if you didn't remember they had been people a short time ago. A fat woman wearing a jogging suit. A skinny guy with a Bite Me t-shirt (well I guess he asked for it.) But all the humor escaped me the second I spotted the first kid. There were lots of little zombies.

From geriatrics to toddlers the undead shambled around under my perch moaning and reaching up. They stared up at me, straining to reach me and I suddenly knew how a cow felt going to slaughter. If I had been a little slower getting off the street I would have been dinner for the group below. I turned to shout my thanks to the man on the fire escape across the way but he was gone, disappeared back into his building I would guess. The building I was on looked to be an office of some kind. Old brick with wood framed windows it was only a few stories tall. Barely big enough to need the fire escape on which I stood. Still I was happy to have it.

Going up I checked and didn't see anyone on the roof. There weren't a lot of places for anyone to hide but just to be sure I turned on my flashlight and shone it around making sure the coast was clear. Once I was out of sight on the roof I heard the group below quiet down. Then there was an explosion from down the street when I peeked over the edge they were all shambling in that direction. The roof of the building was a flat tar and gravel type. There was an old metal table and chair set sitting on top of a faded green all weather carpet near a door in the center. Walking over I tried the knob and it swung open easily. Stepping inside I played the flashlight around and saw that the stairwell was clear. At the bottom was another closed door.

Carefully holding the railing, because we all know stair safety is paramount during the zombie apocalypse, I made my way down. I opened the door, half expecting to see a rotting zombie's face on the other side. Instead, I saw an empty hallway. Shining my light before me like some lame lightsaber I quickly checked the floor. It was office space, thankfully empty. The stairs to the first floor had a wide landing and on it were two zombies wandering back and forth. When they saw me they tried to climb the stairs but kept falling down. They got back up and tried again and again to get to me but couldn't make any headway. I didn't stay around to find out if they would get the hang of climbing stairs and once I was out of sight they seemed to settle down.

The one good thing I found was a break room area with vending machines. One of the machines was a drink machine, another had refrigerated stuff in it (which stunk, likely bad due to lack of power), and there were two candy machines. The spiral wire feeders with the glass fronts. I broke the glass and emptied the candy, gum, chips and trail mix into a garbage bag. I tried to get into the drink machine but after busting the plastic off the front I realized it wasn't going to happen. Not without the key to open it or electricity to run it. I was feeling pretty upbeat about my find, after all I had food, the water was still on in the building so I had water, and I was safe for the moment. I took up residence in one of the offices and slept until it was light out.

When I got up the reality of what was going on hit me. There were no people out on the street, only zombies. No vehicles moved up and down the roads, instead abandoned and sometimes burning vehicles filled all the lanes. From where I was in the city it was a good fifteen minute walk to the nearest highway and there was no way I was going to make it with all these dead around. I decided to try exploring the rest of the building. I went back to the landing and shot the two zombies in the head. Blamo! Man the gun was loud. At least watching all those old movies seemed to pay off. I poked the bodies with a flagpole from one of the offices and made sure they were really dead before I went down the stairs. I was really careful to avoid touching anything, the television news had said any contact with zombie fluid would cause infection.

The main floor had twelve zombies. Like an idiot I killed them all, wasting ammo and making a huge fucking racket. There was nothing useful downstairs and I ended up back on the roof. It should have come as no surprise to me when I looked down at the streets they were all now packed with zombies pushing against the building I was in. The noise of the gunshots had attracted every shambling asshole for blocks. I congratulated myself on being an absolute idiot. Of course they were piling up. They were attracted to noise. I sat on the roof with my head in my hands for a while trying not to totally lose it.

When I had my head screwed on straight again, I started to look around. The building I was on shared a portion of its roof with another building. That building was only two stories so it would be a drop to get to it, but if I did I could make my way to the end of the block without going to the street level. Going back downstairs I yanked the cloth towel dispensers apart. Using all my finely garnered knowledge from my time in the craft store I twisted the towel length and knotted it. The twist made it strong enough to hold my weight. Something I tested by hanging from it a foot off the floor and bouncing. Tying my new rope off to a heavy pipe I lowered myself down to the next roof. The entry hatch to this roof was more like a trapdoor. It was locked tight, as were the next two. Near the end of the block the roof one building in from the next street was open. But when I opened it I saw shamblers moving about and quickly closed it.

The last building on the block faced onto a side street that had a few zombies moving about. There was also a fire escape across the street for the next row of buildings. The ladder looked newer and more difficult to climb. It was the kind that you needed to use a metal hook to pull it down from the street, kind of a higher security fire escape. If I got down there and couldn't get it down I would be in real trouble. In the end it was the futility of my situation that forced me down to the street level. That is when the fucking bag lady almost got me. In my defense I did look before I leapt. She was just lying there buried in garbage. The only thing I can think of is that she was sick and hid there to die and reanimated right around the time I showed up.

When I hit the ground her hand flailed out and just missed grabbing my ankle. I sped across the street and realized quickly that the fire escape was out of reach. So here I was with a zombie bag lady between me and my retreat and no way to reach the fire escape above me. Then I saw under the far side of the fire escape, the part that didn't swing down, my salvation. There was a utility truck with a ladder strapped to it. Racing over I climbed on top and unstrapped the ladder as the bag lady zombie approached. By the time she reached the truck I had the ladder loose and propped up on the fire escape. When I got up I pulled the ladder up behind me, why abandon something that might still be useful right?

The row of buildings I was on was newer. Each building had a roof door leading presumably to a flight of stairs. But they were all steel doors that were locked up tight. The rooftops were thankfully empty of the dead and I made my way three streets over before I reached the end. I couldn't make out any nearby street signs but there was a fire escape leading down and I could see the street was mostly clear of cars. On the far end of the street I saw people heading in the general direction I was travelling and that gave me some reassurance that I was going in the right direction. Well, that or we were all going to die in the same general area. Odd that that should be comforting.

I took the ladder down and left it next to the building's base in case I needed to come back this way. By the time I reached the street the other people had vanished, a few shamblers moving along in their wake. There was an open avenue closer to my right and I went that way hoping to avoid more of the dead. The next few hours were like a living horror movie. I moved from roof to roof taking refuge up high whenever the dead got too close. Unpleasant chewing sounds came from almost everywhere now.

From a distance, not far enough for my tastes, I saw three toddlers eating what looked to be a woman's body. One kid had on a cookie monster shirt that was caked in gore. That image is going to wake me up screaming for the rest of my life. I wonder who the woman was. Was she their mother? Their babysitter? Just a random person they attacked and killed? Where were they from? What happened to them? How were they infected? These and a million other questions raced through my mind as I moved on.

I scampered like a flighty squirrel from roost to roost seeking safety. A trip that should have taken me less than a half hour ended up taking me four hours. I had to backtrack more times than I can count. I was constantly hiding from small and large groups of shambling undead. When I was spotted I had to lead the zombies in a random direction before doubling back safely out of sight. It was exhausting. When I reached the edge of town I was wondering if I would be able to get far enough away before dark. I didn't want to be caught out in the open after the sun went down. I had never really traveled out of the city much. Just a few family vacations. And most of those we flew. I had been so focused on getting away I hadn't thought about the next step. Now, at the city limits, I suddenly realized I had no idea where I was going. Then inspiration struck.

Outside of town there was a big car dealership, I'd gone there recently with a friend who was lucky enough to get a job there washing cars. From where I was the dealership was a straight shot so I decided to head that way. Maybe I could take a car and put some distance between me and the chewing horde. When I finally reached the dealership I could see I wasn't the only one with the same idea. A few dead zombies showed bullet damage to their heads near some open bay doors leading into the main building.

I headed for the smaller building further back on the lot where my friend had worked. He'd shown me how they detailed the newly purchased cars and gassed them up from a tank under the building. The door was locked but going around the side I found the door that the smokers used to sneak out unlocked as usual. Turning on my flashlight I checked before I entered and listened. No noise, no shuffling. So far so good.

The room I entered was the break room. The vending machines had already been emptied although the drink machine was open and some bottled water and orange pop still remained. I took a second and added them to my garbage bag of vending treats. They weighed me down a lot more but if I was leaving town I knew I would need the water. Stepping out into the bay I saw three vehicles sitting there, a mid-sized sedan, a full sized pick up and a compact. I was torn. I needed good gas mileage but I also needed to be able to get around blocked roads. In the end I decided on the truck. Thinking back about the jammed up streets I figured it would be a good idea to have something that could go off road. The keys were in the ignition and the tank showed full. I tossed my bags on the passenger floor and went looking for anything else useful. I found a tool area that had a manual crank hand pump.

Taking it and two five gallon gas tanks back I put them in the back of the truck. The fuel tank had an electric pump, but it also had a manual crank. Filling the tanks in the back of the truck I threw everything in the back that I thought might be useful. Mostly it was tools and a few extra truck tires already on rims. As I dropped the last tire into the back I heard it, the noise of my activity had covered it up to this point. Moaning. A lot of moaning. An almost deafening amount of moaning.

I didn't think, I just acted. Jumping in the truck I slammed the door just as the first of them shambled through the doorway. The damn smoker's door. It was the only one that swung in and like an idiot I hadn't made sure that it was latched. Even if it had been the amount of dead streaming in might have blown it right off the hinges. I started the truck which really got them going and then slammed it into gear. Pushing through the garage door screwed up the paint job but I didn't give a damn. I mowed down the dead in my way and took off across the grass.

One look over at the interstate and I turned the other way. That route was a freaking joke. Even if I was a better driver the entire thing was clogged with broken down vehicles and crowds of undead. There was an old highway that looked fairly clear. The dead were coming from the east so I headed west. Turning on the truck's radio I got the emergency broadcast system. It was advising residents to head for refuges. I decided to put some distance behind me and headed for a refuge they mentioned in Kansas. Fort Riley, an army base.

By this point I'd gone numb inside. I wasn't thinking about the past, my zombie family or anyone that I had lost. Or even what I had just gone through. The horror that surrounded me had already started to harden me. I doubt the old me could have calmly mowed down children zombies without a second thought. Being alone was hard. It was quite possible that I started going crazy. I began talking to my-self. Somewhere in my ramblings I came up with the following.

Bobbie Grader's Rules of Surviving the Zombie Apocalypse.

1) There is no longer any normal. Trying to act like you did in the old world just doesn't make sense. It's like trying to act like if gravity reversed itself you wouldn't have to completely rethink things. In short, the rules have been suspended.

2) Don't get infected. This may seem like a no brainer but since besides getting bit or scratched you can get dead from body fluid it limits your options for fighting the undead. Guns are great except the noise draws more of the freaking things in droves.

3) Trust truly has to be earned. Like the guy that saved me by yelling at me to get up on the fire escape. Helping is great but you can't blindly trust people.

4) Never let yourself be cornered. The dead don't

get tired. They don't get bored. They'll stand there looking at you until you starve. So don't be stupid enough to get trapped.

5) The dead are stupid. They don't reason, they don't think. They simply follow noise and movement. So they are easy to distract, easy to leave false trails for and lure away. Use this to your advantage.

6) It is better to live together, than to die alone. The last rule is the most important. With what the world has become it would be easy to retreat, to put up walls and never trust anyone again. But if we're going to find our way past this we'll need to work together. If we can't do that then our species will vanish into dust.

Reading back through these I feel a little stupid. Maybe these rules are bullshit. But working on them got me though a lot of lonely nights. And took my mind off a nagging problem that just seemed to get worse. I was running low on gas, there were a lot more zombies around, and I couldn't find an intact bridge to take me in the direction I needed to go.

At first, I thought that the bridges had been destroyed by accident. But after the third one I realized that someone had blown them on purpose. From the dead lingering on this side of the gap I had a pretty good idea of why they had. Once my tank dropped below half I found a place clear of dead and put both gas cans into the tank. The next few gas stations I passed that were too full of dead to check but I finally found one that was empty and that thankfully had diesel. I filled the tank, the two gas cans and three more I found there.

I found an atlas on the counter and with a few road signs I was able to figure out where I was. I was in the middle of bum fuck with no good alternatives. The best I could do was head west. Three days later I was out of gas and out of luck. I had checked twenty different gas stations, even chanced a few with zombies, but couldn't find any gas. In the end I abandoned the truck and most of my gear and headed off into the desert. The nice thing about it was that there weren't a lot of shamblers around. I walked for days. Moving parallel to the road, taking shelter in barn lofts or on top of big rocks at night.

I kept the main road in sight so I wouldn't get totally lost, but kept back enough to avoid any zombies. From time to time I raided gas stations for water and food, shooting zombies when I had to. Most of the time I was able to lead them in the opposite direction that I was traveling and then circle around. Hence my rule about the dead being stupid. I had no way of keeping track of time. It seemed like I was out there forever.

Nights were cold. I took all the tourist t-shirts I could find and piled them on. I even raided a truck stop full of zombies to find some warmer clothes. I barely got out of there alive. Then I thought I found salvation. I came across a walled town called Maxten. I approached cautiously and kept out of sight but called out to them. I ended up talking to a woman named Karen. She sounded so nice and kind. After ten minutes of her promises of safety, a warm bed and food I almost went out of cover to her. Then I heard something. Something that made me glad my paranoia had made me chose a place of safety both from humans and zombies. I was up on a high ledge with a shallow cave.

Below me two men with handguns were creeping around behind where I had first called out. The bitch was keeping me busy while her friends snuck up to kill me. I stayed quiet and very still for the next ten hours. They retreated well before dark when a few zombies showed up and that gave me a great idea. I had a few wind-up toys from one of the gas stations that were loud as hell. I waited until just before dawn to hatch my plan. Winding up two of the toys I threw them as hard as I could towards the front gate of the town. The zombies turned and shambled enmass towards the gate and I took off in the opposite direction. As I fled I noticed a great many backpacks and bags thrown in a nearby ravine. Some of them were still attached to the bodies that had been carrying them. It should go without saying this is where my well-formed trust issues come from. So as I said, trust must be earned...or not.

I hope the zombies kept coming until they ate every last one of those fuckers. They were going to kill me for five bottles of water, two guns, sixty rounds of ammo and some ratty clothes. What a wonderful world. If I could have I would have figured out a way to let the dead in to kill them all before I left. But I had to content myself with thinking nasty thoughts and running like hell.

Nearby I found a few dirt bikes with gas cans attached. It looked like someone had hidden them to use later. I popped the tires on all but one, loaded up the gas cans and hauled ass. Granted the noise attracted every zombie for miles but I loved the distance I was putting between me and Camp Asshole as I had come to call the walled town of murderers I was leaving behind.

I was able to travel this way for the better part of two days before the gas ran out. I kicked myself for leaving the hand pump behind with the truck. I probably could have kept going indefinitely if I still had it. I left the bike propped against a telephone pole somewhere inside the New Mexico border. I had been traveling in a generally west direction but had followed one of the roads I was on more south than west. Now I found myself low on water, without transportation and suffering from a painful amount of sunburn.

With limited options, I decided to chance hitting a gas station. It was a risky proposition because out here most of the zombies were centered in towns or gas stations. Still, death by zombie or thirst wasn't much of a choice. I got inside the building and it seemed pretty quiet. There were flats of water just inside the front door as well as a display of sunscreen. I quickly transferred as much of both as I could comfortably carry and then took a water and opened it. The snap of the plastic cap was like a rifle report going off in the quiet stillness of the shop.

Queue the moaning band of freaks scattered all over the place. They rose like the nightmarish parodies of humanity that they were, stealing just a bit more of my sanity in the process. It had been awhile since I had seen one up close and I can tell you I hadn't missed them. The guy behind the counter had been about my age. He didn't have any visible marks on him. Not true for the three women who came out of the next aisle up. They looked like rover's used chew toys.

Running out of the store I saw more of the dead had wandered up from almost every direction. The sound of the bike must have been drawing them to my general area and they just kept walking after the sound stopped. It was clear from a glance around that I was in deep shit. They were everywhere. Granted, there was only about thirty of them in sight but they were close enough to get a hold of me if I tried to run between them. Frantically, I searched for an escape route. The only thing I saw was a semi parked nearby. Scrambling up the side, I found the door locked. Pulling myself up on handholds I climbed up on the cab roof. There was a sunroof that I easily smashed. There was no one in there and after triple checking to make sure no zombie was lying on the floor or sitting in one of the seats I lowered myself in. I had hoped that the dead would lose sight of me and wander away.

No such luck. They all gathered around the truck like sinners at a tent revival. Their low moans and the scrape of their hands was only out creeped by the occasional snap of their teeth. I checked and the truck had gas, but there were no keys. It made a fellow wish he had hung around with a lower class of people. Offhand I could think of at least ten guys that could have taught me how to hotwire a car. Oh well, misspent or in this case non misspent youth.

The only thing I had going for me was that I had kept hold of my bag. So I had water. And the inside of the truck was actually pretty comfortable. It did have the close smell of a camper but the broken sunroof helped air the place out pretty quickly. My search also turned up a pretty good stash of beef jerky, chips, canned fruit and candy bars. There was also a stack of porno movies and skin magazines. The former were useless but the latter were a real morale booster. Until I realized I would probably never see a living woman again much less anybody that hot.

By the time I woke up the next morning there were over thirty more dead around the truck. They had almost doubled their number in the darkness. Great. So at this rate they should resemble an outdoor concert crowd by the time I died of thirst. I again ransacked the truck in a vain hope that the owner might have kept a spare key inside somewhere. I checked the glove compartments and other than a really obscene birthday card from someone named Misty there was nothing of interest. I spent the day looking at magazines. Part of me already knew I was dead. The other part, the one that never wanted to give up, was trying to think of a plan.

The next day there were more zombies but not as many as I had feared. There were about seventy total. Just standing there like a bunch of groupies waiting for me to appear again to take a leak or look around. After another day of looking at magazines I realized that this was probably it. I was going to die in this truck, surrounded by undead. The only comfort I had was that I still had my gun and I still had bullets. Not enough to shoot my way out of course, but enough to end it so I didn't suffer.

The question then became when I would kill myself. I've got to admit my teenage streak of procrastination kicked in at this point. Deep down I just wouldn't give up. I was naive and hopeful enough to think something could still happen to save me. First, I set the benchmark of finishing the magazines twice before I thought about it anymore. Than it was when my water ran out. That looked like it was going to be the true trigger, pardon the pun. I had read once about dying of dehydration. That wasn't the way I was going out.

There were three bottles of water left when I woke up to find something had changed. There were zombies streaming away from the truck. They headed off behind the building attracted to something I couldn't see. Once the last of them were gone I checking out the passenger window. When I saw the coast was clear I unlocked the door and slipped out, being careful to avoid touching anything. I ran back and grabbed some water from a stack near the gas pumps. I had plenty of time when I was sitting in the truck to study the layout. Hindsight being twenty-twenty I'd laughed when I had seen the stacks. I could have avoided going inside at all. I never thought a store would have any of their stuff outside. But I guess water in the desert is a different matter. I still had plenty of food so I just took off.

It was about three days later that I got ambushed. The girl that surprised me was pretty good. She must have seen me coming and just waited for me to come to her. I walked around an outcropping of rock swinging wide to make sure I didn't walk into any corpses. Instead I found myself instead staring at the point of a notched arrow. Looking past the arrow, with some difficulty, I barely realized that she was a girl. She was wearing a strange collection of clothes with a camouflage rain jacket over the whole thing.

"Are you infected?" she demanded in a low menacing tone. So much for small talk. I'm ashamed to say the first thing that came to mind was the magazines I had been looking at and I immediately wondered what she looked like under all of that stuff.

"No. I'm tired, sunburned and utterly sick of the scenery but I'm not infected." Gesturing to the bow I nodded behind me. "Look, I don't want any trouble. You may be a dead shot with that thing, you might not. But if you shoot me I'm going to at least be able to get one shot off at you with the gun I'm holding behind my back. I might not hit you but it will bring every shambling prick for miles here. So how about you just go your way and I will keep my stuff and go mine?"

She hesitated for a moment before letting the arrow center on my forehead. "First off, if I shoot you it will be in the head. In which case that gun you are holding will just drop. Second, if I wanted to rob you I could have killed you without you even knowing I was here. Last, but most important, we are on an elevated ridge here. The only walkable approach is the one you just came up and it is too steep for zombies."

Looking back the way I came I realized she was right. Slipping the gun back into my waistband I raised both my hands palms up to show her they were empty and she relaxed a bit. The arrow still remained firmly centered on my forehead.

"Okay, let's start over then," I said. "What do you want?"

"Obviously I wanted to talk to you. Since you say you're not infected have you got any special skills?"

"Well, I can play a mean air guitar." I was getting irritated. It was hot and I had been traveling too long to stand there and play twenty questions with someone threatening me with being shot in the head. She pulled the poncho hood down and I was struck by how pretty she was. Deep green eyes stared out of a very pale face framed by dark red hair. Pursing her lips she gave me an appraising look.

"You seem pretty young, but you managed to survive so far. Where are you from?"

"Ames Iowa. The home of the Cyclones." The blank look she gave me confirmed that here, like everywhere else, women didn't follow college football. "Look lady, I got by the best I could. I've been on my own the entire time. Now is there a reason you wanted to talk or do you just hold everyone that passes this way at arrow point?"

The derisive way I said it got a smile out of her. She lowered the bow but kept the arrow knocked. Motioning to a rock she settled on one of her own. "Take a seat. My name is Stephanie Caste what is yours?"

"Bobbie Grader." She snorted a laugh.

"Aren't you a little old to be called Bobbie?" I bristled at her tone and then shrugged it off.

"At this point in the apocalypse who gives a shit? My mom liked Bobbie. That is actually what she named me. Not Robert or Rob. Not Bob. Bobbie. And she threw a fit when anyone called me anything else." With a smile she returned the arrow from her bow to the quiver before resting the bow on her leg.

"Okay Bobbie, just asking. Look, this may seem odd but I come from a town nearby. We have been coming out looking for any survivors that are wandering through. There haven't been any new people showing up for quite some time. So when I saw you I figured I would come say hi and introduce myself."

"And the bow? I suppose that's how they say hi around here?" She glanced away and then looked directly into my eyes.

"A lot of survivors don't react well to being approached. We've found it is better to introduce ourselves in a way that avoids us getting shot." Thinking back about the last town I had interacted with I figured it would be best to avoid this one too. It must have shown on my face because she raised one of her hands palm up to placate me. "Hold on now. I know you must have gone through a lot in your travels. We have all sorts of folks that have come to us. Based on what they have told us things have pretty much gone to hell in the world. But our town is different. If you can pass quarantine, if you truly are not infected, then you can come be a part of our town. The only other thing you have to do is your share. Everyone fights, everyone works. It is a whole lot better than living out here on your own. Don't you think?"

It was an interesting few days after that. Once I agreed to the concept of what she was talking about we got down to details. I would be required to make a leap of faith, something I wasn't sure I was able to do. To be allowed into their city I had to give up my weapons and submit willingly to being locked up. She said everyone coming into town, Hunters included had to spend ten hours in quarantine to make sure they were not infected. If they were they got a head shot and incineration. I had a few hours to think about it. The thought of just taking off back down the hill went through my head more than once.

I broke it down logically. If she had just wanted my stuff, she could have shot me before I knew she was there. If they just wanted slave labor, there would have been more of them and they could have taken me pretty easily. In the end, logic didn't win the argument. Instead it was that silly little hope that lived inside me. The part that refused to accept that everything good had gone out in the world. If I was wrong I probably wouldn't have a lot of time to complain about it anyway. Even in a world when everything has gone to hell, you either have faith in people or you die alone. It is a pretty easy decision when you think of it that way. And I was so tired of being by myself. Talking to her was the best thing that had happened to me since this all started.

A few hours later, with her in possession of my guns and ammo, we arrived at a rock structure that didn't look any different than those around it. Climbing up, we were met by three men who seemed to know her. They led us to stairs that led down to separate stone rooms. The rooms seemed like old Indian houses. The rock around was red but the rooms themselves were blackened by fire. In the center of the room sat a rough wooden stool. The men admonished both of us to touch nothing and to sit on the stool. Each room was sanitized between uses but unnecessary touching might still lead to infection. Likewise, our shoes would be disinfected when we left the room.

Soon the experience ended up being boring. I sat there for ten hours, occasionally singing show tunes. Yeah, I was that bored. Then they had me walk up the stairs, sprayed my shoe soles with disinfectant and I rejoined Stephanie. She led me through a winding path through rock formations until we reached a metal door set up on a ledge. She knocked and a man answered. Leading me through an electrically lit tunnel we emerged in the basement of a building.

She took me into a long room with a card table set up in the center. A man sat at the table playing solitaire. It was such a normal thing to see, such an everyday thing in the old world that I almost laughed. Then he looked up and the laugh died in my throat. His eyes were almost magnetic. I stopped in my tracks and just stood there. For a moment our gazes remained locked and then he smiled.

"Hello there. My name is Phillip Kane." He motioned me to sit and we talked. Well, I talked and he listened. I told him my story starting with the shop and he listened patiently. When I was done he asked some very detailed questions. About my knowledge of sewing, knitting, all manner of craft work. I answered honestly. I had skills because I had to learn to do my old job. He seemed happy to have found something that he considered useful that I knew how to do. It took a while to go over everything but he nodded eventually and smiled at me again.

"Stephanie? Why don't you show our newest resident to the orientation hall? Bobbie? The people in the orientation hall will take you through what you need to know to make your final decision, but I think you will be a fine addition to our little group."

Stephanie took me through some more twists and turns and we went up a long staircase that led me out into the sunlight again. Turning to me with a warm smile she gestured at the bustling town behind her. "You're home now Bobbie. Welcome to Vigilance."

ORIENTATION JOURNAL OF BOBBIE GRADER. Donated to Archivist upon death of citizen.

Father Charles Batten

THERE ARE NO WORDS TO describe the hell I'm now living in. It's hard to imagine that three short weeks ago the world was so different, so full of promise. I've lost count of the bottles of whiskey I've drunk. And how many hours I've wasted contemplating why all this happened. Was it a government conspiracy? Some terrorist group that made a monster they couldn't control? Sometimes . . . normally towards the bottom of the bottle, I wonder if the man upstairs just had enough of our ugliness and decided to visit us with some of his own. I was a priest in the old world. My congregation was small but devout. When the trouble started we gathered and prayed. That is until the week that Mason Graesser quietly died in the last pew, reanimated, and attacked one of the ushers. After that attendance suffered. Go figure.

I must confess it here, even if I never said it out loud. I was a shitty priest. On paper at least the job is simple. You preach the word of God, have faith and guide your flock. As easy as that should have been half the time I was a rotten shepherd. It's hard to give a shit when most of your congregation not only sins regularly . . . they revel in it.

Judge not, that ye be not judged. Perhaps I have been judged and this is my punishment for failing them. Maybe I was supposed to save them. It's too late now I guess. Last I heard they were all dead. I was evacuated by the National Guard when the town was mostly overrun. Penterad MO, population before the outbreak was around 1100. By the time I rode out in that military truck there were easily triple that number of zombies.

We evacuated to a refuge with about a hundred other people. The National Guard units were local boys and they were doing their best. It was just too damn hard to weed out all the infected. Night was falling when the first "sleeping" person rose up and ripped a chunk out of someone. The camp went to hell pretty damn quick.

It was chaos, pure, End of Day's chaos. I half expected to see the four horsemen riding across the sky. Instead a panicky guardsman drove his jeep over a bunch of people while trying to mow a zombie down. The camp splintered into small groups fighting to survive. I ended up with Randy and Jason Trase, age ten and twelve following me out into the night. The older one told me that their parents got infected fighting to keep them safe. A group of zombies had surrounded them and the parents got the kids free, killed most of the zombies too. But they got goo all over themselves doing it. Their last loving act was to send their lambs away to safety with the guard. Now they were in the dubious care of a failed priest.

I would love to say I acted heroically by saving the boys that night. But that would be a goddamn lie. I was terrified and fled instinctively for survival. The boys, for better or worse, decided to follow me. Likely from the misguided perception that I had a clue of what to do. Later that night the three of us were huddled on the second floor of an old barn. I went to the other side of the structure to smoke a cigarette. So I don't know exactly what happened. There was a loud scream and by the time I got back the two boys were locked in mortal combat on the ground. The younger one was moaning and snarling while trying to bite the older one. He must have been infected back at the camp during the confusion and never even realized it.

I'm ashamed to say I never hesitated, I just ran. It's the logical thing to do. Save yourself when the other person is already lost, so it's silly really to feel ashamed. There was no doubt the other boy was a goner. He would at the very least be infected. My trying to save him would have just gotten me infected as well.

Words. Just words. They bring me no relief, no solace. Nor do they quiet the voice in my head that calls me a coward. What good does it do for a man to gain the whole word if he loses his immortal soul? God has surely abandoned me now if he hadn't before. How else can I explain my survival other than his punishment being visited on me? He has seen fit to punish me for my transgressions. I will live a long and miserable life with my cowardice. It is enough to drain me of what little faith I have left.

Yet I still can't stand to take my own life, or surrender myself to the mercy of the dead. So I have retreated to Calvin's Fine Liquors. Located atop a hill it was unsullied by the dead. Its isolation was enough to keep it unoccupied by the living. What day is it? Oh, who the hell cares? I should just mark the passage of time by empty bottles. So it is two and a half cases that I have been here. I have blacked out so many times I have lost count. There is food here as well, though I have eaten little of it. Pork rinds, chips, nuts, cured meats and even some canned fruit. All taste like ash when I put them in my mouth. I am going to put this journal down for a while.

IT HAS BEEN A FEW weeks since I bothered to write anything in here. What is the point? I get up, I go outside and check to see how many undead are gathered at the bottom of the hill. I relieve myself in their general direction and then go back inside. The only relief to the monotony is the old boom box under the counter. There are more than enough batteries here to keep it running indefinitely. Each day I flip through the stations. But there are fewer stations every day, today I was only able to find one that was active. The automated message of the Emergency Broadcast System. It was telling everyone to try and make their way to high ground and giving details on the dead. Most of it I already knew. The incubation period would have been helpful to have known about earlier, to say nothing of the tell-tale signs of red rimmed lips and eyes. I remember thinking the young boy had been crying about his parents back in the barn. Now I know he was succumbing to the infection.

There is a stack of bottles in the corner of the store that is an impressive monument to my self-pity. There has to be five cases there, at least. Not top shelf stuff either, there are actually two bottles called Turkey Whiskey. I checked the price on the shelf. It is ten dollars a gallon. That explains why I feel like crap, well that and borderline malnutrition. Since I have failed to drink myself to death I should probably decide how I want to spend the rest of my days. First order of business is to take stock of what I have and what I know.

The world has arrived at its final stop in hell. The train has left the tracks and we're all on our own. The government has fallen on its face and isn't even communicating with the population anymore. Electricity appears to be out, at least as far as the eye can see at night. There are no cars, trains, buses, planes or helicopters that I've heard since I left the camp. The automated voice on the radio is pretty faint. I think it is being broadcast from one of the larger cities nearby. Maybe even the state capitol. I haven't seen another living person since I left the camp, no one has come by and I don't expect to see anyone. The dead are sitting at the bottom of the hill waiting for me to come down. I've got nearly an unlimited supply of booze, food and a decent shelter. If God has sentenced me to Purgatory he seems to have at least provided for some creature comforts. I added to my sins by beginning to smoke again. It is a filthy habit that I had not practiced in over a decade. But lung cancer is now the least of my concerns.

There is a van parked out back, it is gassed up and the keys were in the cash register. I could load it up and head out if I was inclined. But who knows how far I would get before I would find my way blocked. How many miles can a tank of gas take me? Where would I be going to? It isn't like I have anywhere to be for the rest of my life.

Writing in this notebook has served to help clarify things. I see it now. Back when Mason attacked Jerry Bates, the usher, how I snapped. It was hubris on my part. To actually rail at God and wonder aloud how a loving God could allow all this suffering to happen. I'm as bad as any of my congregation.

God doesn't do anything to us. He created the Heavens and the Earth, gave us life, and set us in motion. Never did he claim it would be easy, nor did he claim to be at the controls. The universe is spinning and we are spinning along with it. Our father gave us existence, and choice. Those are the only things that we have that can never be taken away. I could have chosen to die with those boys. I could have saved the older one from his dead brother and become infected. I could've spent my last hours comforting him before then myself succumbing to the disease. Instead I chose to live. It wasn't a great set of options I had but I did have a choice. So I made it and have to live with the consequences of my actions. My actions, not Gods. I of all people should have known better that to blame the creator for my shortcomings.

How many times did I admonish my flock? Don't blame the lord for your failures or thank him for your successes. He doesn't hold you in greater favor than he does your rival but instead loves you all. In simpler parlance? You roll your dice and you take your chances. The best you can hope for at the end of the day is to be able to look at yourself in the mirror and say "I did the best I could with the choices that I had." But there are things that you have no control over, such as chaos. Nothing you do is going to fix it and nothing you say is going to change it. Blaming the creator of everything for your having a bad day is like breaking your television because you don't like the movie that is on. You only end up hurting yourself.

The realization that I've been acting like a spoiled child has been swimming around my head for a bit now. So, now that I've accepted that I made these choices and have to live with the consequences I have to figure out what to do. Maybe I'll find a new flock. Or I could fall and break my neck looking for a four leaf clover.

Who know? The only thing that is certain right now is that I live in a new world. I better get used to the changes and figure out where I go from here.

I LAUGH AS I READ back over what I have written. I put this book down and spent the last few days cleaning myself up. No booze was the first order of the day. There is plenty of bottled water here so that is my new drink of choice. Second, I needed to take stock of what was available to me in the store. A more thorough search turned up a combination for the safe in the office and a box of questionable substances. I believe they are illegal drugs but with no point of reference I left them where I found them.

The safe was disappointing, although I did get to pretend I was James Caan from the movie The Thief for a brief moment. It had stacks of cash, a big box of condoms (why these are in the safe I have no idea) and an address book. The cash was of no use to me, nor I might add are the condoms. The address book I decided to flip through just out of boredom. Inside I found many female names listed along with a star system based from what I could tell on how sinful the girl was. I tossed it back in the safe with the overwhelming desire to wash my hands.

My stock of food is far from infinite. I estimate that even if I conserve it I have perhaps three months' worth of food. So, today, I came to a decision. It is time to go forth into the wilderness and put my faith to the test. No, I'm not going to trust that the Lord will deliver me. I'm going to deliver myself. I'll pack the van with all the food and water it can carry, as well as a few cases of the better alcohol. Not for social drinking. I'm done drinking for fun. However, if I find myself trapped in the van I would rather drink myself to death than starve. Plan for the worst, hope for the best.

IT'S BEEN THREE DAYS. IT didn't take me very long to load the van or empty the shop of what I was going to take with me. I lit the shop on fire and drove away. The explosion of the remaining alcohol going up was impressive. The dead were drawn back to the explosion and I had clear traveling for a bit. It was smooth sailing for the next few hours until I came over a rise in Kansas. I was somewhere east of Wichita on a nice level plain. There before me, stretching as far as they eye could see, were zombies. Big ones, little ones, fat ones, skinny ones. It was like a hideous parody of the cornucopia of life. A cornucopia of shambling death.

They had been milling around but when I topped the rise I suddenly became the center of attention. A shambling wave of undead began undulating towards me like Satan's wiggling tongue. Turning the van around carefully I retreated the way I can come. The first chance I got I turned south and drove for hours. Then another group of dead forced me west again.

Eventually, I ran out of gas somewhere in the middle of an open red dirt road in northern Texas. I haven't seen any zombies for a while but I know there are some behind me following me. I'm loading myself down with food and water. Hopefully I can make it to the next town on the map. It is only ten miles away.

IT HAS BEEN MADE CLEAR to me that I have a purpose. The Lord does work in mysterious ways and if we are patient he eventually gives us our nudge. I entered the town of Barnhart at the end of my rope. A will beyond my own led me here, buoyed me in my despair and kept my feet on the path. Here I found a flock in need of a shepherd. Three hours after I entered the town and climbed to top of the hill where the church lay the child came to me. Beautiful blue eyes stared fearfully out of a grimy face framed by greasy blond hair.

"Are you a priest?" Her voice wavered in fear but I had to hand it to her, she was brave. I judged her to be about ten years old. Careful to keep my hands out to my sides I nodded. "My name is Father Charles Batten." My voice sounded heavy and ponderous, like that of an elderly man. Clearing my throat I turned and sat heavily on the step leading up to the pulpit.

A haunted, hunted look in her eyes made me fearful of spooking her so I sat and waited for her to speak. For a moment she seemed to consider bolting then leaned sideways against one of the pews. "I need help. My parents, they told me I can't trust anyone. But I need help. They need help." I waited patiently. Her wariness lasted another moment and then the dam of words burst. The story was horrible. The town had been raided. Her father had been killed. Her mother, sister and friends had been taken.

"What can I do to help you?" She seemed surprised by my willingness to assist her and wariness showed on her face.

"I need you to get them free." My shock must have been apparent. "You're a priest. You could talk to the men. You could tell them they need to let everyone go." The innocence still inside her showed in her eyes and touched a part of my soul I had feared dead. To her it was the simplest task for a man of God to shame evil into doing the right thing. We talked for hours. I tried to convince her to look for a new refuge, she doggedly asked me to help her rescue her family. At one point I fell asleep.

When I awoke she was gone, as was any trace that she had been there. The floor of the church held only one set of footsteps in the dust. Mine. Turning this over in my head I realized that she had never drawn close, had never touched me. Nor had I heard her come in or seen the pew move when she leaned against it. I worried that I was hallucinating. Just as doubt began to cloud my mind a brilliant beam of sunlight came through the stained glass causing the window to glow. The scene depicted by the multiple bits of glass was Christ on the cross during his crucifixion. Never had I received a clearer sign.

In the office off the main hall I found food, water and a shotgun. The latter was an odd discovery in the house of the Lord. Perhaps the local father liked to shoot skeet, who knows. I loaded the gun and went to search the town. Most of the dead were the non-moving kind. The few shamblers present were easy to avoid. I have watched enough late night action movies to see how the assault on the town played out. The people had built barriers against the dead, nothing against the living. Heavy vehicles, likely pickup trucks based on the size of the holes in the fencing, had broken the perimeter. Gunshot bodies told the tale from there. Brutal, relentless and efficient. The attackers had killed mostly men, a few older women and taken the rest. For slave labor or worse.

I found a station wagon back near the church, fully fueled with keys in the ignition. I drove following a trail of corpses. It looked like the captors had made a few object lessons to quell their prisoners. Driving around the victims of the town I traveled for a few hours through recently cleared roadways. I had no trouble finding their camp. The smoke from their bonfire was visible for miles. When I got close I nearly drove straight in but something moved me to turn off onto a side road.

Down this barely visible dirt road was a maintenance shed with several heavy vehicles. Two dump trucks and a snow plow. The plow had keys in the ignition and a full gas tank. It was this vehicle I selected to drive down through the remnants of the road into the back of the bandit camp. Tearing through barricades and fences I smashed a line of pickup trucks and scattered the bonfire. Gunshots tore into the cab, shattering the glass. One of the slugs hit me in the shoulder. The pain was blinding for a moment then my arm went blessedly numb.

Twisting the wheel I smashed through the front gate, noting that I would never have been able to get through it from the other side. Behind me angry shouts rose up and engines roared to life. Checking the remaining side mirror I saw at least a dozen trucks following me. Roaring down the highway I headed east, away from both the camp and the town. Gunshots rang out and the remaining side mirror shattered in a hail of bullets. I felt cold and cranked up the heater. Blood was running down and pooling on the floor near my feet.

From a rip in the seat I tore some foam out to stuff in my shirt, hoping to slow the bleeding. I came up a rise and saw a sea of salvation in the form of undead. The plow blade let me shunt the zombies aside and I cut a fast swath through them. The trucks behind me made good headway at first, until the bodies bogged them down. When I left the horde a half mile down the road I swung into a large parking lot and turned around. The sight I beheld was awe inspiring. Every single pickup had been caught in the horde. Some had flipped. Others were stuck atop a mass of still writhing corpses. Zombies battered the windows until they broke and were already pulling some of the bandits out to their fate. I passed back through the horde, the blade of the plow clearing my path like the hand of God.

Returning to the camp I found a mere handful of bandits remaining. Most of those were patching the gate. When I blew back through the barrier many of them were crushed. I stepped down from the truck and dispatched the rest myself. I admit my sin in killing them with the shotgun. I pray the Lord forgives me for sending the wicked to his judgment. With failing steps I walked to the cages and freed the captives. Once they were out they scrambled to collect enough vehicles to get everyone safely away. I felt a heavy weariness stealing over me after my ordeal. One moment I was standing, the next I was being loaded into the back of a pickup wrapped in a blanket.

That was two days ago. My shoulder is infected. Red lines are running up and down my body. One of the women is a nurse. She thinks I have blood poisoning. They have found a refuge nearby that they are trying to get to, a place they trade with from time to time. I fear the Lord is calling me home. I asked them to find me this notebook so that I might write my story down. When I'm done I told them to leave me behind, I'm unnecessarily slowing their progress. Leslie Grady, a warm hearted woman who has taken these people in her charge, told me to shut up and concentrate on getting well. But we both can see the writing on the wall.

When I meet the Lord I hope he will forgive me. He gave me one task upon this Earth. A calling to guide my flock and make them ready for his embrace. I failed him. I failed him because of my weakness. I have broken his commandments, I have sinned . . . I have killed. I pray for his forgiveness but even more I pray that he watches over these people that he guided me to. I ask that he would deliver them to safety after I am gone.

JOURNAL OF FATHER CHARLES BATTEN. Given to Archivist by group of refugees brought into Vigilance. Group included medical personnel, farmers, pharmacist, botanist and multiple skilled crafts people.

the journal of catherine bellon

THE FIRE STARTED BECAUSE SOME idiot decided to try and kill a shambler with a Molotov cocktail. I happen to know this because I watched it happen live on Channel 4 News. The zombies got the dumb ass anyway. Then they walked around on fire for a while setting most of the block ablaze. One of them walked into a gas station. Boom! There went the entire neighborhood. Thousands died within hours. Just because someone didn't have the sense that God gave a jackass. Is it a good idea to burn infected bodies? Sure. But maybe you should have made sure they were incapacitated first. The city of Indianapolis went up like a tinderbox. It had been a dry winter and there wasn't a lot of snow on the ground. It was like throwing a match into a powder keg.

I was at work. I'm a 911 dispatcher and I was coordinating emergency squads. Between the walking dead, the fire, the panic and general chaos it was like shoveling sand up into the air just to watch if fall back down on you. To make matters worse no one showed up for the next shift. Most on my co-workers just got up and walked out. Not a word to anyone. My boss Frank Jerriton came out and told me to pack up and get to safety. Then he was out the door as well. In the end it was me and my old friend Marty Franks that remained behind. Marty is a good guy. Only twenty five he washed out of the firefighters because of a bad shoulder. He's sat next to me for the last year. He asked me out three months ago. I wish now that I had said yes. At the time the only thing I could think of was that I was ten years older than him. Now that really doesn't seem like a big deal.

For an hour we tried in vain to keep services working. There were multiple fires going now all over the city. It was moot if they had been set or caused by burning zombies, they were all getting out of control. Fire Captain John Matterson came on the radio and did an all call. All remaining firemen were to abandon their fires. Any that were not returning home to their families were welcome to join him at a rally point outside of town. He said there was no point containing the fires anymore. The word had come down that the evacuations were now mandatory. Indianapolis was being abandoned. I sat there in shock for a minute and then asked him to repeat that. He was alarmed to hear that Marty and I were still in the command center. The area was overrun with dead and he told us to get the hell out of there. The fire nearby was heading our way, courtesy of the shambling dead.

We jumped up and checked the window outside and sure enough the lot was full of zombies, some of them on fire. I looked at Marty and he gave me a reassuring smile. Then it changed to an evil grin. Running back over to the dispatch table he rummaged through a drawer before crowing triumphantly. He turned towards me with a pair of spare keys in his hands. Taking me by the hand he rushed me out to the garage area. The doors were all closed. The dead hadn't gotten inside yet. There were a few staff cars there and one FD Humvee. Pointing the key fob at the hummer he pushed a button and I heard the doors unlock.

Before leaving I convinced him to load up the truck with whatever we could carry. Medical supplies, spare gas cans and emergency food and water from the lockers. The back end was pretty stuffed by the time we were ready to go. We belted in and Marty clicked the garage door opener stuck to the visor. The metal doors slid up out of the way quickly and quietly. Marty slapped the Humvee into gear and roared out the opening. We mowed down some zombies and bashed a smart car out of the way before Marty got it under control. He is one hell of a driver fitting us through gaps I never would have attempted. He also knew which vehicles we could shove aside with the truck. I think he was showing off for me a little and I have to say I didn't mind one bit.

The Humvee had a CB in it and we used it to find a good route to the rendezvous. When we got there we have fifteen fire trucks and fifty men. A lot of guys had gone back to get their families. The chief said we weren't waiting around for them. He had the guys mount up and we headed for the nearest evacuation center. By the time we got there it had been abandoned. The chief got on the CB and found out the next one was a day's travel west. We decided to caravan that way until we came up with something better. Behind us we could see a strung out line of undead following along in our wake. Our passing attracted them like flies to shit and the flow stretched all the way back out of sight.

At first we tried following the interstate. The fire trucks could push almost everything out of the way. But then we started running into more zombies as well as big rigs blocking the road. The chief decided to take us to the back highways which had less traffic and less undead. The side highways led southwest but pretty soon we ran into other problems. These fire trucks were never intended for road trips. They guzzled gas like a middle age man drinks beer. By the time we left the state we had abandoned four of the trucks. The chief came on and told us that there was a state police yard in Missouri we could stop at. When we got there one of the guys broke the padlock with an ax and we drove inside. The place was abandoned. The chief took the liberty of breaking into the armory there and outfitted everyone with weapons. We took enough ammo to start World War III. They also had power, water and gas. After gassing up the trucks we found every container we could and loaded up the fire trucks with portable gas cans. Then everyone showered, ate and grabbed some sleep.

The next morning we awoke to shamblers arriving outside the fence. Luckily they weren't near the gate. Score one for us. The zombies are too stupid to walk around to the gate. They just massed up near the fence closest to us. After a quick check to make sure we had everything we needed we drove out the gate and shut it behind us. The chief said it made sense to leave it as secure as possible in case we needed to double back to it. After that we made good time. The roads were mostly clear and we got to Kansas in no time. We started picking up a broadcast on the CB about a refuge nearby. Fort Riley was a military base that had been designated as a refuge. Anyone that could make it there would pass through quarantine. But it was supposed to be a safe place. The chief had a course plotted through back roads and we hauled ass in that direction.

Every road we went down had undead. They were drawn to the sound of the engines like a dinner bell. Every time I looked in the rear view there were more of them. We were driving through small towns because the old roads passed through them. When we did the trucks had to smash other vehicles out of the way. The noise brought zombies out in droves. It was inevitable that we would run into trouble. Our luck ran out in a small town in Kansas near the border of New Mexico and Texas. The Arkansas River runs from west to east on the southern part of the state. We got to the town of Garden City only to find the way west blocked by semis, the way south over the river missing. The bridges had all been blown away. The dead from the city swarmed out to greet us.

We lost some of the trucks trying to turn around. Then we had a few that lost tires on broken glass and steel on the road from accidents. It went from bad to worse when the shamblers caught up to us. People panicked. By the time we go out of town we had lost three trucks and ten men. The chief was among those we lost. His truck hit something on the road, lost its tires and flipped. The zombies swarmed the vehicle before anyone could get out. Without the chief to lead us we decided to try and find our way west. Marty and I went out by ourselves, using the radio to let the guys know what path to take. We proceeded at a crawl because we had to make our way without the big engines to push vehicles aside. Then it happened, we were trying to go around a truck sitting in the middle of the road when we hit a soft spot. The Humvee slid sideways and rolled down a steep embankment. We came to rest half way down. The truck was dead, the CB no longer worked and Marty had been hurt pretty badly. I tried to patch him up but he died right there in my arms. I shoved him out of the cab. I couldn't risk him coming back and killing me. I have been crying for so long it felt like I was breaking. I decided to try and make my way out in the morning. I feel so tired.

IT'S NIGHT AGAIN. I MADE my way back up the embankment this morning to find zombies all over the place. I ran until I felt like my lungs would burst. My head hurts and there is a weird pain in my back to the right of my spine. I have found a roadhouse, some old skanky bar. I climbed up on the roof and will sleep here. I'm really starting to feel like crap.

I'M NOT SURE WHAT TIME it is or how long I've been up here. The pain in my back has gotten so bad I can barely walk. I think I've got internal bleeding. Makes me wish I'd paid more attention in emergency medicine class. Then again that's why I became a dispatcher, because I sucked at the EMT classes. I know I shouldn't but I have to sleep. I'm so tired.

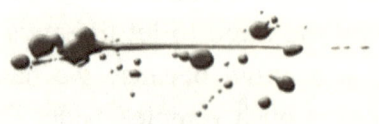

HUNTER JACKSON ENTRY – JOURNAL FOUND on roof of Tommy's Tap. Body of woman found dead on roof. Journal listed cache of medical supplies in Humvee. Located supplies. As for body of deceased male mentioned that had been pushed out of vehicle I did not go to bottom of embankment to verify. Supplies are extensive and include many needed drugs. Location of police yard documented. Information can be traded to Fort Riley in area in exchange for part of the take or equal value.

Dan Thomas — Superhero

IF YOU ARE READING THIS, you have survived. Congratulations! My name is Dan Thomas, a survivor of the zombie virus outbreak from Hollywood CA. I am also a post-apocalyptic super hero. In the spirit of historical responsibility I have chosen to chronicle my adventures for those that come after me. I hope that my humble actions can inspire those of you that read about them in the future. As is the case in fictional superhero origin stories I come from humble beginnings.

I was orphaned when my mother died in childbirth. I never knew my father but suspected that he was a great man who never knew about my existence. Why else would he have never come back to see me? My childhood was unremarkable, but happy. I was lucky enough to be adopted by a wonderful family, the Jacksons. I was their only child however Martin and Grace had spent their thirties trying to have children and had worked hard on being the best parents they could, reading all the books available. When they found that Grace was unable to have a child they moved swiftly into the adoption process.

My life with them was wonderful. Each of them taught me many things and supported me in everything I tried. It was Martin who shared his love of comic books with me and Grace who taught me to always try to be the best I could be. She was instrumental in helping me build the strength of character that has bolstered me during these dark times.

They were with me through my first year of college. I lost Grace to heart disease and I think when Martin passed less than a year later it was from a broken heart. I dropped out of college and used my inheritance to buy a small business, Jumping Jehoshaphat Comics. Set not far from the famous Hollywood Walk of Fame it kept up a brisk tourist business. In addition I had many local loyal customers. For four years before the zombies came I worked in a field that I loved, bringing the stories of heroism to the world. The month before things went awry I was even working up the courage to ask out Amy, the girl that worked at the coffee house next door. She was a vision of blond, perky magic. No matter how busy she was she always made sure to greet me warmly. Her demise started me on my journey to superheroism, thought the experience itself was the worst day of my life.

It was eight in the morning and I was going to get my coffee when I saw the man. Shambling along, covered in blood, he looked like a homeless person that had been mugged. I started towards him to offer my help just as he stopped in front of the window of the coffee house. At the time I thought he was reviewing his appearance, alas that was not the case. Instead he was eying the occupants inside. With a lurching lunge he bashed through the plate glass window of the establishment. At first I thought he might be having a bad trip, it was not unheard of to have an addict on a rampage in our neighborhood.

It was when the man grabbed Amy, who had been standing near the window, that I realized something was terribly wrong. I tried to get to her but before I could he bit her, his teeth ripping the skin and flesh from her throat. In that instant my entire world seemed to screech to a halt. Everyone started screaming and I stared in horror into Amy's eyes as she stared at me in shocked confusion. Then her eyes closed and she fell limply to the ground. The blood had stopped gushing from her throat and I realized she was dead.

The man, nay the monster, turned as I screamed my denial at what I was seeing. Raising his hands towards me he began shambling in my direction. Without further thought I fled back to my store in terror. There is a metal garage style door on the front of my building which was still down. I ducked in through the back door and sat inside sobbing. I am not afraid to record here that I cried. I mourned for Amy and what could have been. I cursed my slow action that allowed her to be so cruelly stripped from my life. Sitting there among the racks of super heroes I mourned what I had lost.

I am not quite sure how long it was before I got myself under control. I turned on the television and saw to my horror that the menace was widespread. I had not watched the news in days as I had been working my way through a new Blu-ray series. What I saw boggled the mind. The entire world had been falling down around me and I had been blissfully ignorant. My obliviousness had already cost me dearly and I was transfixed by the information I was given by the newsman.

The threat had started overseas somewhere. All attempts at a cure had proven ineffective. The virus was spread by bites, claw wounds and bodily fluid. Bites and claw wounds would turn someone quickly, within an hour or two. The fluid contamination was more insidious. It could take up to eight hours for someone infected in that way to turn. This had caused many seemingly safe havens to be overrun by dead when they unknowingly let infected people inside.

Governments across the globe had all but collapsed. Military forces were scattered and proving unable to contain the outbreak. Residents were being advised to evacuate to refuges but they were not able to say with certainty if the refuges they had listed were still safe or if they had any room. Footage showed people, women and children, being torn apart. The news recapped at the ten minute mark and began laying out the details on how to kill the dead.

Head shots. But of course, it was a well-established part of zombie cannon that you have to destroy the head to kill them. They were slow, unable to climb even steep hills. They were attracted to noise. One video showed a military unit shooting zombie after zombie but then cut to an aerial shot that showed every zombie within earshot of the noise turning and moving in their direction. Guns were incredibly effective killing tools, but they made a lot of noise.

After watching for an hour the information started to be completely repetitive. I turned the set down and sat thinking. I had no one to call, no one to warn. The only person that I had cared deeply about was already gone. There was nothing to live for, no reason to fight for my survival. For a few hours I wallowed in self-pity and contemplated my mortality. I went up on the roof. To be completely honest, I was thinking about jumping but I quickly realized that the height was probably not enough to kill me.

On the roof I had a great vantage point to see the carnage below unfolding. The single zombie now had quite a bit of company, including a pretty walking corpse with blond hair and a torn out throat. I waited for her to walk near the building and dropped a cement block, normally used to prop open the door, on her head. She dropped like the stone I used to fell her and remained motionless. I would love to say that this act of compassion gave me the inspiration I needed to proceed with my heroic work. Alas, all it did was generate another round of grief.

A short time later I was shaken from my tears by someone calling for help. Looking down I saw a man standing atop his SUV surrounded by zombies. When he saw me he implored me to assist him. Granted, his vernacular was far saltier and peppered with many colorful adjectives. Still, I could not in good conscience deny his request.

I began making noise which did attract a few nearby zombies to me but those around the SUV remained in place. Apparently the prospect of a meal so close was far too enticing. Going downstairs I retrieved my MP3 player and portable speaker and returned to the roof. Turning on the loudest heavy metal album I had I cranked up the music. This worked better than I had ever dreamed. Not only did it draw away the dead from the man's SUV, it also drew all others that could hear it. The man waved as he jumped in his vehicle and drove away and I saw a few others break from inside buildings and take off in their cars.

When I turned off the music, the dead remained below, waiting for me. It occurred to me that while I had saved the others I had put my own neck in the noose. Returning to the store I took stock of my situation. I had limited water and food as the store only sells a bit of candy and has a cooler of bottled water. There was thankfully a restroom in the store as well as a couch to sleep on. So short term my comfort was assured. However, it was obvious that I would need to go elsewhere soon or die of thirst.

In searching the office, I came across a slingshot that had been a gift from a regular customer. With it were a small collection of bullets he had given me to practice. At the time I had laughed and thanked him for his gift before putting in the desk drawer and forgetting about it. It would turn out to be the single most important gift I had ever received. I spent a few hours practicing and found that I had a knack for the slingshot. By the time I went to bed I could hit the target from twenty feet more often than not.

The next morning I took the slingshot to the roof to dispatch the dead. Most of them had wandered off during the night. It was easier than shooting fish in a barrel. Fish might move. The biggest concern I had was splashback from the head shots. Luckily I was high enough that gravity worked with me to keep anything from reaching me. Returning to the store I packed the remainder of the water and food in a backpack with twenty bags of marbles. The marbles had been a promotional giveaway item for a new card game. Luckily the game had tanked on release and I had enough marbles as ammo to carry me through hundreds of dead. Now what I needed was a way to carry them away from the shop. I emptied a large sling bag I normally used to carry my lunch and filled it with marbles. Adjusting it across my back I headed to the roof.

From my lofty perch I made sure that the area was clear of dead before retrieving my MP3 player and speaker and placing them in my bag. Then I headed out towards my apartment. I kept to the middle of the street but still had to shoot twenty zombies before I got to the stairs of my apartment. Once I was safely inside my place I flipped on the television and dropped down onto my futon. The news was even bleaker than it had been the day before. Most of the country had fallen to the virus, the military was pulling back, and everyone that could was asked to get to a refuge. The nearest one to me was a military base. I decided to sleep before I made any life altering, or ending decisions.

That night I had a dream. Amy came to me, more beautiful than ever, and asked me what I thought I was doing? When I asked Amy what she meant the look she gave me was beyond furious. She chastised me for thinking about killing myself. I felt shame and guilt to the point where I could not look in her eyes. Her hand came under my chin and she raised my face up so she could look at me. I thought she might kiss me and she seemed to know what I was thinking. She told me we could never kiss, because she was dead. We could not be together but that didn't mean that I should lie down and die.

I saw we were suddenly standing in my comic shop. She gestured behind her and as her hand swept from up to down the books flew off the racks. Each title transmogrified into the superhero it was named for. They all started giving me encouragement, telling me that I was a real life hero and that the world needed me. Amy looked on with such pride on her face that I could barely stand it. When the light of dawn woke me I nearly wept from losing her all over again.

Instead, I rose that day determined to make Amy proud. Taking warning from the information I had gleaned from the news I created my costume. Rubber boots, pants, gloves, a poncho and a full mask. It was horribly hot but the protection it provided would allow me to close with my enemy if necessary to save an innocent. When not in use I kept the suit open to keep from overheating.

Leaving the apartment I went to the roof to see if I could locate anyone that needed aid. Two buildings over someone had hung a bed sheet out that simply said HELP. Taking aim I dispatched five zombies that were wandering below before quitting the rooftop to investigate the marked building. Once inside it became clear that not all the residents were alive. Moans and shuffles came from behind most of the doors and I had to vanquish more than one walking corpse. At the apex of the structure I found three survivors. Two young boys, Jason and Joaquin Peterson and their babysitter, an elderly woman named Margaret Tames.

Margaret wept when she saw me. She told me that she had been keeping the boys safe for two days. Their mother had gone to work and never come home. The look she gave me when she said that told me she already knew their mother was gone. Why else would she not have come back for them? She asked me what we should do and I realized what Amy had been talking about. This was my purpose. I was to save as many people as I could from the Shambling Menace.

Taking charge I had her and the boys collect food, water and whatever clothing they could carry. I advised her there was a haven two buildings over where they could rest up while I located a sanctuary for them. The trip back was quick and uneventful and I soon had them cozily ensconced in an empty apartment adjacent to my lair. I then set out to discover if any of the local refuges were still intact. To do this I was forced to acquire transportation. Although the vehicles available did not belong to me I am sure their former owners would not begrudge my using them for the greater good.

In the street outside my apartment building there were three vehicles that were unlocked. One of them was a gas hybrid SUV that belonged to a neighbor. The key was hidden under the floor mat where he normally kept it. I had not seen him for several days. I assume he is already lost. It is a pity. He was a good man, always kind to me. The tank was full of gas when I started the vehicle. After driving through yards and on sidewalks for an hour I was able to make my way past three of the local refuges. All of them were either empty or over run. I flipped on the radio and scanned through to see if the emergency broadcast system was still on. It was and there was a looped message. It listed refuges that were still available. Sadly, two of them I had already verified were overrun. The third though held promise.

Outside of the city, up in the mountains, there was an old camping community. A collection of cabins and houses that normally only saw traffic during the summer months. A refuge had been established at the most remote of these locations. I drove towards that area. As I neared the outskirts I was stopped by a roadblock. Someone had parked a bus across the road, blocking all access. There were no zombies apparent so I exited my vehicle to see if I could find a way around the impediment.

A voice stopped me in my tracks, telling me to freeze. I could feel the heady air of violence hanging all around me. Looking up I saw a man standing atop the bus with an automatic weapon pointed at me. He introduced himself as Sam Wilson and asked what my purpose was. I told him that I was searching for a refuge for some survivors. He seemed dubious and asked where they were, as he could see my vehicle was empty. I told him they were in a temporary safe house and I wanted to verify that this place was secure before I brought them here.

We talked for almost ten minutes. He felt it necessary to question my outfit and my purpose. I understood his reticence and was completely honest with him. I was a superhero and I was attempting to rescue some survivors. It was pretty straight forward. I simply needed a place to rescue them too. Although I could tell he doubted my credentials as a hero, I honestly think he thought I was insane, he inevitably realized that I was serious about bringing survivors. They had apparently had more trouble with the living than they had with the dead and he wanted to make sure I was not an advanced scout for a raiding party.

In the end, we were able to come to a compromise. I would allow him to take me prisoner so that he could show me that the refuge was safe. He, in turn, would return me to the SUV unharmed and allow the survivors in, once they passed through quarantine. It was an act of faith on my part. He seemed surprised that I would allow myself to be taken prisoner. He told me putting myself in others power was a great way to get killed. I pointed out that he could have shot me at any time during our discussion so it was more of a calculated risk. The people depending on me were worth it.

His refuge did, indeed, pass inspection and I was soon back on the road. I waited until the next day to return with Margaret and the boys. It was far too dangerous traveling uncertain roads in the dark. Sam seemed surprised to see me return. He said he thought I was a kook and had written me off. I took his derision without taking offense. In the world we now live in it is quite natural to doubt those around us. I asked if I might bring others to him and he tossed me a long range military radio. He said if I found any others to call him up on a specific frequency and he would arrange a meeting. All new comers should be advised of the long quarantine and of being required to pass it before entering the refuge. I agreed and bid the boys and Margaret a fond farewell. The boys each hugged me and thanked me for saving them. Margaret kissed my cheek and told me to stay safe.

I returned to my duties with a renewed sense of purpose. This is what I was born for, to save the innocent. To ensure the survival of the species. For once in my life everything that had ever happened to me had meaning. All the pain and suffering I had endured had served one purpose and one purpose alone. To forge me into the man I am today. To make me into a real life superhero. To make me into, The Rescuer.

My first task was to gather what I needed for my work. First I collected a few hybrid vehicles and what I needed to refuel them. Then I entered toy stores and took every marble I could get my hands on. Ball bearings from auto supply stores worked as well. Rocks were less suitable. Most did not have the penetrating power necessary to drop a zombie. In a pinch though I have been known to make them work.

I set up a new secret lair and a string of safe houses. Sam's warnings about crazies bent on destruction had been clear. If they found me, or more importantly the people I was trying to rescue, things would get nasty. These places required food, water, medical supplies, blankets, and clothing, anything a victim might need. I made a point of stockpiling supplies in central locations for later re-trieval. This allowed me to continue my mission of taking someone to safety and then getting the supplies on my way back to the lair.

Within a few weeks I had established a wide ranging network of safe houses. The people I saved climbed into the thousands quickly. Some required rescuing directly, others simply needed to be pointed to a refuge. I met many people and was in contact with several of the remaining refuges in our area. A few I avoided. Most that had ex-treme views, like the religious camp, were not welcoming to outsid-ers. Others, like the hedonistic camp, had worldviews that most sur-vivors had no interest in sharing.

Everything was going well, until I fell afoul of the dreaded Banefool gang. The remnants of an antisocial motorcycle gang, they swelled their ranks after the fall of the world. Every two bit creeper, psycho, or deviant found their way into their group. They loved to capture and torture innocents for fun. One day I returned to a safe house to retrieve a group of refugees. The place had been destroyed. All that was left were the bodies. The sadistic and brutal ways that they had been abused before their deaths made me apoplectic. I fol-lowed the gang's trail, quite easily the largest path of destruction I have ever seen, back to their hideout.

Sneaking up on them I saw two of the refugees, two young women, were still alive and unharmed. I got close enough to over-hear a few of the men talking about the party they were going to throw in the girls honor. The things they planned on doing to them caused me to lose all control. Leaping out from my hiding place I stabbed both of them in the throat. Before I even realized what I was doing their blood was all over the ground. Pulling myself together I freed the girls and we escaped their camp. Before we had gotten far the bodies were discovered and the group gave chase.

They men were led by a monstrous fellow named Vanity Jones. He was by far the ugliest man I had ever seen so I could only assume that it was an ironic name. We were three miles away from camp and I was loading my charges onto a minibus when he and his men topped the rise on their noisy dirt bikes. I instructed the girls to drive the bus towards a refuge fifty miles away. They had more than enough fuel to get there. Then I turned to face the ruffians.

Have you ever had a moment of perfect clarity? Something crystallizes in your mind at the precise moment that it needs to and you are blessed with a bit of cosmic insight? I had one of those as the girls were pulling away. The men coming towards me had automatic weapons. I had a slingshot. I was going to get murdered in the middle of nowhere by a bunch of half-wit rapists and murders.

Ah, if only I had thought of that before the girls drove off. Still I drew a bead on the first man, a skinny, sickly looking fellow, and let fly. The marble took him in the eye and drove straight through into his brain, killing him instantly. For a moment my mind rebelled, I had just killed another human being. Someone that was living a moment ago now lay on the ground unmoving. When it was a zombie I could kill without hesitation. But another human? The two guards had been in the heat of the moment. This was a premeditated kill.

As quickly as the thought occurred I quelled it. These men were no better than the Shambling Menace that I normally killed. If anything they were worse. The dead were driven to kill, these men chose to. Bullet after bullet I shot from my slingshot killing a few of the men, wounding others. I fled before them seeking better cover and that is when Vanity managed to shoot me in the back. The bullet tore into the flesh near my spine feeling more like a burn than a bullet wound. I flew through the air and rolled into the ditch, coming to rest inside a large cement drainage culvert.

I heard the group getting closer. They called out warnings to each other. I might be playing possum. It was funny because at that moment I was dragging myself through the culvert wondering if there was any zombie goo in the pipe. If so would my zombie self be able to get out of the pipe and hurt anyone? I saw the light from the other side of the culvert suddenly interrupted and I froze. Someone was there and they would only need to fire down the pipe to end my life. Then the light returned, disappeared, returned. I looked up and saw figures moving past the culvert. Slow, shambling figures.

The fools had brought zombies down upon them with their noisy motorcycles and gunfire. I heard the first cries of alarm and then shots rang out. The noise started to diminish and I realized that Vanity Jones and his men were retreating. I had been saved by my nemesis, the Shambling Menace. Or perhaps I had been looking at them all wrong. Once understood they were no more dangerous than any animal. And animals could be used to your advantage.

It took me days to get out of that culvert and find a place to heal up. Luck was with me when I stumbled across an old ranger station. It had decent medical supplies and I took a map that showed all the other stations on it. They would be excellent additions to my list of lairs. A few weeks of healing and I was ready for action again. While I was recovering, I heard on the radio that Vanity had taken down two refuges and was threatening a third. I headed in the direction of the imperiled sanctuary with a plan forming in the back of my mind.

I had cleared many places in my time looking for survivors. One was an old tourist trap off the main road. I stopped there now and collected all manner of noise making toys. It is a testament to man's greatness that crappy plastic toys continue to make a racket long after the fall of civilization. I then went and found the largest group of undead in the area. Activating a toy I tossed it down and moved on. Once zombies gathered near the toy, I dropped another. Repeating this activity I made an undead interstate using toys as beacons to drawn them after me.

Once in the area near the refuge it took me very little time to find Vanity Jones. On a rise high enough to avoid zombies and sheltered by an overhang that kept the living from firing on them they sat waiting. I set a path of noise making toys from the edge of the overhang back to the waiting horde of zombies. Then I withdrew to watch.

The undead slowly shambled along the path I had laid for them, finally ending up near the edge of the drop off. It quickly became apparent that the plan would stall there. The men below were not making enough noise to attract the zombie's attention. Instead the shamblers were milling about happy to be around the noise the toy was making. I decided it would be necessary to push them along.

Making my way around I took up a position between the refuge and the bandits, praying no one from the stronghold would shoot me in the back. I had on my full costume, sans cape. The dead have a tendency to grab loose clothing. With my mask in place I stepped from behind the rock and yelled a challenge to Vanity Jones. The Neanderthal did not even respond verbally.

Instead, he grabbed a rifle and shot at me, taking some rock chips off near my head. I ducked behind cover, popping up in a different spot from time to time to encourage him to continue his target practice. A few of his men decided to join in and the cacophony of gunfire was truly deafening. And that is all the encouragement that my undead pets needed to try and fly.

As one, they turned and walked right off the edge. Before Vanity and his men knew what was happening it was raining zombies. Many of them died by destroying their heads on impact but as more dropped the landings became cushioned. Soon they were rising and shambling after their prey. The problem for Vanity and his men was that to flee the zombies they had to run into the line of fire of the refuge. Most of them didn't hesitate to run straight into the gunfire.

I guess they figured they had a better chance of surviving a gunshot. Or maybe they thought it would be a cleaner kill. Either way, within moments most of Vanity's gang was dead on the desert floor. Vanity himself, and a few others, made it to the bikes and roared away, drawing most of the undead in their wake. Those that were left I used pebbles from the ground to dispatch. Heading up above I removed the noise making toys being careful of the goo on them. When things were quiet again I approached the refuge under a flag of truce.

The leader of the stronghold asked me to stay. I told him I cannot. There are too many others out there that I need to save. I have asked him to hold this book for me until I return. It will stand as the first volume in my chronicles. Tomorrow I leave to track Vanity Jones down. I cannot let him continue his reign of terror. The Rescuer will make sure that evil finds itself thwarted by my mighty slingshot of justice.

BOOK DONATED TO VIGILANCE ARCHIVES by refugee from Refuge Sondoan. The refuge suffered a second bandit attack led by a Vanity Jones. Entire refuge was destroyed.

Pastor John Makon

THE LORD HAS LEFT ME here upon this world to shepherd his remaining flock and I'll do my best to keep his word alive in the wilderness. My lambs were far from home when things began to go bad. I'm so very proud of them and how they have handled themselves. My congregation was from the Johnston Baptist Church, from Johnston Idaho. Our little town only had about three thousand people in it. The congregation was two hundred strong, the choir twenty five plus a piano player. Our little group practiced night and day for two months for the state competition in Boise. When we were named to go to the national competition I felt humbled by the work the children had done. I made sure when we arrived in St. Paul Minnesota that the choir focused on the event and shut out distractions. The end result was that we won the competition, not that anyone in our hometown probably ever knew that.

We were onstage after they had announced our victory when the power failed. The people in the audience panicked and rushed out of the building. Hundreds were hurt, some were even killed. My choir was traumatized so I took them out the back of the theater to the hotel. Thankfully, the competition was held at a location near the airport and also housed our hotel. We had to walk up ten flights to our rooms with the elevators out. There were so many of us we took up almost the entire floor. The other occupants of our floor never came back to their rooms. For a day we stayed up there waiting for the emergency to get resolved. I went down to the lobby a few times. Each time there were fewer and fewer people. The last time I went down there were no people, only a few zombies that shambled towards me.

I went back upstairs and gathered my flock. It was time for us to go. We got down to the airport but found the gates closed and chained. One of my choir, Nabian Franks, found a bus that he managed to get started. I didn't press him on how he knew the way to do this without a key. Everyone fit on board, just barely and we started to drive away from town. The radio in the bus worked and the stories coming over it were not encouraging.

Outbreaks of a horrible virus were reported all over the country. It changed people into what was being described as zombies. The creatures were highly infectious and could only be killed by shooting in the head. Chaos was rampant all across the country. Government control was breaking down. People were panicking and doing unspeakable things to each other. It made my heart heavy to hear the pain in the voices of the poor men and women reporting the events. Tears were flowing down my cheeks as we moved further out into the countryside. I think Nabian had every intention of driving us all the way home. Sadly, the road was filled with abandoned cars. We were forced out into the open again, one group among many refugees.

The chaos of this new existence was hard to adjust to. Behind us, the low moans of zombies signaled that our passing had not gone unnoticed. An hour later, just as the suburbs were starting to fade around us a group of the monsters came out from an alleyway. Uniform privacy fencing hid their presence until the last moment. Our lead vocalists, Mark Mills and Tara Sontae, were out in front leading the group. They never had a chance. Everyone ran in different directions while I yelled at them to stay together, to head out of town. Mark and Tara were pulled into the horde and ripped apart screaming. For as long as I live I will see Tara's eyes, staring at me, begging me to help her. But there was nothing I could do.

The rest of us grouped back up and ran as fast as they could away from the creatures. I was slowing them down and told them to hurry on without me, I would catch up. The children refused to leave me, bless their misguided hearts. When we stopped to rest I looked back and could see the horde of shambling corpses moving in our direction. They were probably ten minutes behind us but that was no comfort. We would get tired. We would get hungry or thirsty. They would not. Like a plague they would spread across the face of the Earth until no living thing remained. Perhaps I had missed the signs. This very well could be the Day of Judgment that was foretold. But until the Lord tells me otherwise I'm going to fight to keep my lambs alive.

The suburbs, with their high fences and looping streets, were if anything more dangerous than the city had been. We kept to the middle of the road, avoided vehicles and anything that the dead could be concealed behind. At the edge of the suburbs we found salvation in the form of a bicycle shop. Nabian and his friend Tyrell Johnson smashed one of the windows and started handing bikes and helmets out to people. I smiled as I watched the choir dutifully put on the headgear. Even during the apocalypse we should not forgo basic safety gear. The children grabbed other items from stores located in the strip mall with the bike shop. There was a sporting goods store that had camping gear and cold weather clothing. They found clothing and outerwear that made our traveling much more bearable. The camping gear including portable stoves whose packaging professed high heat from small amounts of fuel.

They found a three wheel bike with dual rear baskets for me. It was surprisingly easy to ride and soon we were speeding away from the suburbs into the countryside. There were zombies out here as well, most of them near the road, but they were slow moving. We were able to ride around most of them with ease. Occasionally, one of the boys would pull to the side and make noise to draw the dead away from the road so we could ride through. Then they would ride in a wide circle and catch up to us. The system worked well, though I had to keep warning the boys not to get cocky. The infection spread so easily I didn't want them getting too close.

When night began to fall, I realized we would need someplace to safely rest until first light. A road sign showed there was a church up ahead however when we got to it the level ground it stood on made it unsuitable for our needs. Nearly an hour later, when I had begun to fear we would have to continue riding all night, Tyrell came rushing back with a wide grin. He said he found a place up on a hill that would be perfect. It was deserted and had a few ways down so we should be able to get away in the morning. The place was dark and the light was dim so I did not realize what the building was until we got inside. It was an adult book store.

The boys used a crowbar to break the padlock on the front door and we took the bikes inside. Row after row of dirty movies, magazines and 'marital aids' ran the length of the building. I had the boys move all the racks to the walls and admonished them on taking anything. We spent a night of relative comfort in this den of ill repute and rose early to be on our way. By the light of the sun we saw the base of our hill awash with zombies. They moaned and swayed as those behind pushed those in front down. Instead of crawling up the hill the fallen simply stood back up and were pushed over repeating an endless loop of movement. I gave a silent prayer of thanks to the Lord that the zombies were capable of climbing.

Looking down I saw the other side of the hill was similarly infested. The boys told me they were going to set up a distraction and we should get ready to ride soon. After admonishing them to take the greatest of care I took the rest of the choir to the top of the hill and we prepared the bikes to leave. Behind me I heard the boys break into an R&B version of Walk the Dinosaur. It was very well done. Probably something they had rehearsed on their own for something outside of church, but the performance was lost on their audience. Other than to attract more and more zombies to the base of the hill where they sang.

Twenty minutes later the far side of the hill was clear and I called the boys, now starting to get a little hoarse, up to the bikes. We set a rapid pace that day and managed to get just north of Northfield, MN. Tyrell came back from scouting ahead and said the town was too big and there were too many zombies, we would need to turn west. We had found an atlas in an abandoned gas station during our ride and with it I was able to find a small paved road that would take us that direction. There were no towns listed on the map but I was sure we would find somewhere to pass the night. Before nightfall one of the boys came back with a suitable barn set atop a small rise. We took the bikes inside after checking to make sure it was empty and secured the doors.

The next morning we found a few zombies lingering nearby and were forced to decoy them before we could be on our way. The bikes proved themselves a true blessing, as did the children who knew about them. Whenever we had a tire go out they patched it or replaced it with spares they had taken from the bike shop. Hand pumps kept the wheels inflated without the need for electricity. Spokes were tightened, seats adjusted, minor damage repaired, all enough to keep our little caravan moving. We were able to bypass barriers that had been set on roads, apparently by local and national authorities to prevent vehicle travel. With the bikes we were able to go almost anywhere and travel swiftly and silently. Before long we had fallen into a routine. Get up, decoy any zombies, ride, stop and forage along the way for supplies, find a refuge for the night to sleep. Then get up the next day and do it all over again.

We avoided any towns that we came near. Even if it meant walking the bikes through fields. Each of us now had rubber boots we carried on our bikes so when we had to walk we could do it without the fear of soaking our feet. The blessings of the Lord had given us the bounty we needed to survive and escape from the dead behind us. As we pushed further west we seemed to encounter more and more issues with roads though. The maps of the atlas showed me that rather than making progress towards Idaho we were steadily being forced south.

There were snarls of traffic on interstates that had left infected spread all along the roadways. This made it impossible to move west at times, sending us south. Then we found entire bridges that had been destroyed, with center spans missing. We even found one roadway that was entirely blocked by multiple barriers of razor wire. I have to give the choir credit here, they organized scouts to ride ahead and behind to make sure we did not get boxed in by any zombies when we hit these dead ends.

In the end it was sickness, not infection mind you but influenza that stopped our journey. With constant exposure to extreme conditions a few of the choir got sick. The colds got bad enough that they could not breathe well enough to ride. We were forced to take shelter in a farmhouse in western Kansas. It was the only high ground for miles and the area had multiple fences. For two weeks we rested, ate soup and canned goods from the house and wondered about the people who had lived here. Turns out they were never that far away.

At the end of the second week, just when the choir was starting to question whether or not we should try and make a home here we heard something we hadn't heard in a while. An engine. A big black truck with dents all over it and a big metal bumper on the front came roaring up the lane. It pulled to a stop and a man got out. He seemed shocked to see so many people and pulled a shotgun out of his truck. This was his mother's house and she had been staying with him because of the trouble. He wanted us gone and gone quick. I noticed he never came out from behind his truck, almost as if he were afraid we might have a gun trained on him.

I tried to talk to the man, tried to reason with him. But he was adamant. We collected our things and after I thanked the man and told him we would by leaving he got in his truck and backed out of the driveway. He sat out on the road and watched as we got on our bikes and pedaled away. The choir was dispirited then, but Tyrell and Nabian soon had them convinced that it was a sign. That we should continue on to our home in Idaho. We turned to the atlas and looked for a way north through Colorado. But then the weather turned on us and we had to go south within a day.

It got colder than I have ever experienced. We were forced to keep moving during the day just to stay warm. That night we camped in an old barn. We spent a miserable night shivering togeth-er in the loft before setting off the next morning. The one bright spot was that we hadn't seen any zombies in quite some time. The mood lifted a bit each day that went by without us seeing one. The choir started wondering if the dead had finally gone back to their graves.

We were somewhere south of Lamar CO, not far from the bor-der with New Mexico, when we spotted zombies. It wasn't a horde, just a few off in the fields and ditches. The cheerful mood that had buoyed us during our last week was destroyed like a balloon being popped. The dead forced us south towards a national park. We were almost to the entrance when Tyrell came riding back telling us the way was blocked by a big group of zombies. He had seen a lot full of RV's and the dead were swarming around them. Even in this remote place the people who had fled had brought the virus with them.

With the zombies at our back we were trapped between the two. The only refuge we had was an old steel building. I sent the boys to check it out. One of them came back and told me it would do, we could close it up. But it sat on a level lot. The dead would be able to surround us. As I looked around I realized that the dead already had. In each direction I looked they were closing in on us, they were still in the distance, moving closer with every moment. I didn't see an alternative so I followed the boys back to the metal shed. Once eve-ryone was inside we wrapped chains around the door handles to help keep them shut. Then we waited.

I led them in prayer, quiet and fervent prayer. We prayed for the Lord to deliver us. We prayed for our enemies to pass us by and leave us in peace. For hours we prayed. Then the din being caused by the zombies beating their hands against the steel building became too distracting to continue. There was a ten foot wide area around the second floor of the building. It circled the top and provided some storage. I went up there and looked out the windows at the dead be-low. Soon all the members of the choir moved up there as well. Some came to see for themselves, some because they could not bear being down below any longer.

We moved our things, except the bikes, to the second floor and set up camp. It was cold. The metal building almost seemed to magnify the cold outside. The dead massed outside, beating their hands against the metal siding. I continued to pray even when most of the choir gave up hope. If I was to meet my maker, as I suspected I soon would, I would do so with a clear conscience. Knowing that I had done all I could for my flock both physically and spiritually.

I felt my will begin to ebb on the tenth morning of our captivity. Food was running short as were tempers. I had been forced to break up three fights the night before and I was wondering how long it would be until someone snapped. I rose and prayed to the Lord for salvation. I prayed for him to send me a sign, tell me how to save my children. But the Lord was not feeling in a chatty mood so I was left with my own thoughts.

The ground floor of the building had nothing of value. I fervently wished they had parked a big dump truck in here so I could load up the kids and mow down the zombies in our way. I could hear a girl crying somewhere above me and felt my stomach drop. The time had come to accept that we were going to die. No great heroics would save us, no divine intervention. There wasn't even a way for us to save ourselves. The only viable exits were too close to the zombies to slip out and beyond them there were more undead. No, I decided it was time to get the flock ready for the next world.

Returning to the second floor I called the choir together. Solemnly I told them what they already knew. We were trapped, low on supplies and the nights had been getting colder the last few days. Without a way to stay warm or food we would die of exposure or starvation soon. They all reacted differently. Some cried, some raged, a few just sat there in stunned silence. I knew my statement was no great revelation. They all could see the dire straits we were in. None of them had wanted to say it out loud. When they were relatively calm again I started talking to them. Not preaching, they were in no condition to hear a sermon, just talking.

I asked each of them to tell us about themselves. Not just what they had wanted people to see. But their hopes and dreams. What they had planned on doing before the world ended. What they would do now if they were given the chance. The results were surprising. Many of them had faced a hard road in the old world. Small town life didn't offer a lot of opportunities. The choir experience had been the most exciting thing they had ever done. Most were afraid that music would die out in the new world. Along with most of humanity.

We spent days talking and sharing in the cold metal building. We ate what food we had, drank all but one large gallon of water and shared our lives. I have to admit being so distracted with what we were doing that I didn't even notice the din of the dead had nearly disappeared. When I looked out the window I nearly had a heart attack. There below me was a man singlehandedly slaying the zombies that had held us captive. Like an avenging angel this willing sacrifice put his dual machete to good use. One swipe of each weapon and a zombie fell, its head split open. His work surrounded him with a cloud of blood and fluid leaving no doubt in my mind this heroic fellow was already infected. He looked to have clad himself in a heavy coat made of oilcloth, almost like an old fashioned cowboy duster. His head was wrapped in leather and he had heavy goggles over his eyes.

The amount of gore he was spilling would find its way through a wet suit, much less the patchwork gear he had on. The choir noticed my absence and joined me at the window. We all watched over the next few hours as he tirelessly cleansed the zombies from the grounds outside. When he was done he walked around the building twice. Maria Lenox looked at me and started to cry. I could see in her eyes how moved she was by the man's sacrifice, how heartbroken she was for him. The man stopped beneath the window we stood at and looked up.

It sounded like he called Maria by name, I nearly fainted away right there. He berated her for allowing herself and the children to be surrounded. The others sounds of surprise drown out part of what he said but I was able to make out one word. Safety. The other members of the choir made so much noise that I missed most of what the man said after that. By the time I quieted them he had turned and was walking off into the trees. I called after him but he never slowed, never turned around.

The ground outside was covered with gore. Luckily the man had killed the zombies on one side of the building so we were able to carefully carry our bikes out the other side back out to the road. We back tracked and took another road, one that led almost due south. The temperature rose considerably as we traveled and that night we slept atop a hill in a snug barn. We had no trouble finding food and as we sat around one of the camping stoves the children turned to me with questions.

Was the man an angel? Had he been sent in answer to our prayers to deliver us? How had he known Maria? Why had he simply walked away? The discussion went well into the wee hours of the morning. In the end I told them the truth. I do not know. The Bible tells of many miracles that the Lord has performed over the centuries. In the end it was Tyrell who seemed to capture the moment best with a surprising quote from Shakespeare. "There are more thing on Heaven and Earth, Horatio, than are dreamt of in your philosophy."

Over the next two weeks we traveled south. We were much more careful in our travels trying to make sure we were not cornered again. This served us well in avoiding three separate zombie hordes wandering the area. It also protected us from a few groups of rough men that I think would have done us harm. The former we avoided, the latter we hid from. In the end we find ourselves with full supply bags heading into the desert. Like the Israelites going to wander the waste. The only thing that concerns me is the living we have seen recently. Hard, desperate people seem to be thriving in this new world. I pray the Lord keep us safe on our journey.

JOURNAL FOUND AT SITE OF battle in basket of three wheeled bicycle that had been run over. Multiple bikes found on site and salvaged for Hunter use. Various books, sheet music and letters found and sent to Vigilance Master Archivist. From the remains at the site it appears that the group was ambushed by bandits in trucks. Only nine bodies on site and over twenty bikes. Age of the site makes it unlikely that any of the captured would still be of use to Vigilance if they remain alive.

**Addendum—Master Archivist—Cross reference to Pental journal for additional information.

Tim Thompson

MY NAME IS TIM THOMPSON, and I am infected. When the fever begins to rise I am going to blow my brains onto the wall behind me, after I put this book in a safe place. I have chosen the only intact structure left in my home, the Wild Blanket Refuge. I will leave this book in a clear plastic tote on the landing on the first floor. Then I will end myself far enough away to keep the mess contained. The best thing I can do for this world is make sure that there is one less fucking shambler around to muck everything up.

Since this place has been destroyed I want to be sure that there is a record left behind to tell our story. There were a lot of good people here. People that just wanted to make a life for themselves in the belly button of hell. Fat lot of good what they wanted served them in the end. What is the old saying? Shit in one hand, want in the other and see which one fills up first. I came here with my sister and father when I was ten years old. I figure I'm about fifty now, I never was one for celebrating birthdays. What's the damn point? "Hey I have lived in zombieland for ten years! Let's throw a party!" What a crock of shit. Just like the world we live in now.

I don't remember a lot about the fall. I do know that my mom died of natural causes. Breast cancer. I remember her. She had the most beautiful eyes and smelled of lilacs. Her face grew more skeletal until one day she went to the hospital and never came back. My father did his best, so did my sister. Both of them tried to keep my spirits up, but they shouldn't have bothered. At the time I didn't understand. I thought mom was just away on vacation. I was sad that she was gone and wondered why I couldn't go with her. It was later that I understood what her absence meant.

When things went bad my father kept my sister and me out of school. He kept talking to a few friends of his and before I knew it we were driving across the country. My sister was crying a lot, trying to hide it from both me and dad. My father was overly cheerful. It was so fake. Even a ten year old could tell something was up. We came to the first refuge of our new world. The military base outside a big city. We weren't there very long. Dad didn't like the way that they were treating people so we moved on. The second refuge was much nicer. We were there for a week. Then dad decided their defenses were weak. He drove us up to a heavily wooded area and met up with some friends that he said were old college buddies.

These guys had been doomsday preppers back before things fell apart. Once the facts about the threat were made public they adapted their plans. This became our new home. There were thirty people there in the beginning. They had taken over a valley and converted it to a stronghold. It was elevated with multiple exits and an area suitable for farming. The area around it was too steep for any undead to get past. They could grow crops and had planted an orchard of fruit trees. It was a great place. There were a few other kids to play with and life became almost normal again. For a while.

I was about thirteen when the first raiders came. They stripped the trees, killed two people and kidnapped three women and two girls. After that the place got bad. No more playing, everyone tense. Dad started arguing with people. He wanted to build up the defenses. The others didn't want to listen. When the second attack came they almost got Lily, my sister. We left shortly after that. I'm not sure, but I think that dad took a lot of stuff from the refuge he wasn't supposed to. A guy followed us on a motorcycle. Dad got out, they talked and then they scuffled. The guy fell down and didn't get back up. When dad got back in the car there was blood on his arm. He wiped it off with a rag then drove us away.

Three weeks later we found our way to this place. Wild Blanket

Refuge was hidden way up in the mountains. It had been started by the remnants of refugee groups that ran afoul of either the military or bad guys. To this day I don't know how dad found them, or got them to accept us. No doubt my sister and I figured into it. When I was twenty my sister married a guy named Frank Harrison. Dad was overjoyed. He kept hinting that there were a few girls with their eye on me. I didn't have the heart to tell him. I had no interest in ever getting married, ever bringing children into this world.

Dad died when I was thirty. I think he had a heart attack. One second he was talking, next he was slumped over. Everyone thought he might have been infected and freaked for a bit. When he didn't get back up and try to bite anyone they realized the truth. We buried him under a cairn of stones, more to make sure he didn't get back up then for any honor it did.

My sister got pregnant and died in childbirth. Frank took it hard. He felt like it was his fault. And it was. What kind of idiot plans to bring an innocent child into hell? And make no mistake if you are reading this. You are in hell. I was pretty good at picking up skills so I found myself quite welcome even after my family was gone. When raiders came I killed more of them than anyone else. My prowess got me respect from my friends. How little they suspected the truth.

I wanted to die. At least if the raiders killed me it would be a clean death. No lingering guilt about being a corpse walking around trying to eat people. So I threw myself at my foes like a madman. Stabbing and bashing I killed with abandon. None of the raiders seemed to expect the kind of crazed defender that I had become. I never let any of them escape. No survivors, no return attacks. We did pretty well. As the years went on the attacks slowed and then stopped completely.

We were foolish enough to think that when the living stopped bothering us that we would be safe. Our settlement was high enough that we did not fear the dead getting to us. None of us knew the mountains as well as we should have. The outpost was built at the site of an old mine. When the railroad took over the area they used some of the old mine tunnels for trains through the mountain. None of us knew that there was a door that led to an old maintenance tunnel for the railroad in the wall near the gate. The dead found their way into it. Maybe they destroyed a refuge in the tunnels themselves. It doesn't matter at any rate.

It was late one night when I heard the screams. I ran from my room and saw zombies flooding out of the door. Broken chain and plaster littered the area and a broken chain hung from the wall. It looked like the dead had pressed the door out from the inside with enough force to snap the weakest link of the chain. The people were soft. They didn't stand a chance. Nor did I, the great survivor as my people called me as the oldest citizen warrior. I jumped in and killed the dead without any consideration for the consequences. For all the good it did.

The dead got them all. By the time I killed the last of the zombies I had to start bashing the skulls of my fellow citizens. I could not let them rise. They deserved better than that. Hell, maybe even I deserved better. But shit in one hand…

HUNTER CRANDALL RECOVERED JOURNAL, SEALED in plastic tote in largest building. Normal contact by Hunter patrol to trading partner. Body of Thompson found with single bullet wound to head. Hunter Crandall buried bodies under large rocks and debris from refuge. Thirty five layers of Safesuit used during burial detail.

Dana Crendall

I DON'T REMEMBER MUCH. THE time gets mixed up in my head when I try to play things back in the order they happened in. Doctors here say that writing this down will help me get rid of the nightmares. They're wrong. The nightmares will never end because we're still living inside of them. I lived in the town of Bakerstown Maryland. My daddy was a happy man that gave me piggy back rides. My mommy baked cookies and tucked me in with a story at night. I had a big brother named Pete and a big sister named Mira. We lived in a pretty house on a quiet street. I used to go outside and play with my friends. That was before everything got scary.

Daddy stopped going to work. Mommy helped him board up the windows. We weren't allowed to go outside. A lot of the people in the neighborhood started packing up their cars and driving away. They never came back. Daddy went outside one day and never came back inside. I heard some screaming that sounded like him but Mommy said that it wasn't. Pete was crying, he never cried. Mira just sat on the floor and rocked. Two days later something broke the board on the window and got Mommy. Hands came in and pulled her outside. There was a lot of blood and I started screaming. Mira slapped me so hard I fell asleep.

When I woke up her and Pete were arguing. He said we should run, she said we should stay. I stopped them and told them I was hungry. We ate the rest of the stuff in the refrigerator. Later that night I woke up and it was really dark. Mira woke up when I started crying and tried to turn on the light. I heard it click over and over. We were sleeping up in Mommy and Daddy's room, me, Mira and

Pete. She woke him up and they started whispering. I couldn't hear what they were saying but I was so scared I didn't say anything. If they were being quiet maybe they thought the boogie man was here. I didn't think he was real before. But that was before he got Daddy and Mommy.

When the sun came up Pete said we had to run, otherwise they'd get us. I figured he must mean there was more than one boogie man nearby. I had only thought there was one up to that point. Mira didn't even argue, she just helped me pack my backpack. Pete took some food and water in his backpack. Then we ate a big breakfast. They both told me they weren't sure when we would be able to eat again so I ate a lot. Pete put his laughing toy in the front hall, the one Daddy hated because it laughed really loud every time you walked by it. Pete pointed it towards the broken window that Mommy got pulled out. Something was moving out there and the toy started laughing. I saw a hand with blue nail polish just like Mommy had come through the window just as Pete pulled us back into the kitchen.

We went out in the backyard and went out the back gate. They'd told me to be quiet and I was careful not to make any noise. I didn't want the boogie man knowing I was outside. Just being out of the house I was so scared I was about to pee myself. We walked for what seemed like hours. Then we stopped to rest for a minute. We kept doing this all day. Pete went into a store and brought out some chips, soda and cookies. We spent the night on top of a garage. Pete lay on one side of me, Mira on the other. It was like camping, but I had trouble sleeping. I wasn't sure if the boogie man could get to us up there or not.

The days blurred after that as we moved out of town and into the country. Mira made Pete avoid other people saying something about them being infected. All I remember is that I wanted to be able to sit down and not have to walk for even a day. We avoided towns when we could but we had to eat so Pete would leave us and go by himself. I remember the day that he came back and told Mira we had to go on alone.

He stopped ten feet away from us and threw a bag to her. She laughed and told him he could have just handed it to her. I noticed he was wearing a big yellow glove on his hand. Like Mommy used to do dishes with. He didn't smile or laugh. Mira started to walk towards him and he told her to stop. The way he said it she just froze. They whispered back and forth but I heard him say he had gotten infected. Mira started crying. Pete looked over at me and told me he loved me. I started crying. Pete never told me he loved me unless Mommy made him. He told me to be brave and do what Mira said. Then he turned and ran away as fast as he could. Mira grabbed my hand and rushed us in the opposite direction. I never saw Pete again.

For weeks Mira kept us moving. I never seemed to get any sleep, never had enough to eat or drink. But pretty soon I could run and run and not get tired. We passed into West Virginia and then Kentucky. At least that is what Mira told me. She had an atlas and said she was taking us towards a safe place. She was awake when I fell asleep at night. When I woke up she was still awake. She was really getting thin. Every time we found food she had me eat most of it. She told me one night we were close to the safe place. She called it Gabriel. When she had listened to the news at home it was one of the places that people were going too. I asked her why we didn't go to a safe place closer to home. She said we had passed a lot of those but Pete had gone to check them and they were no longer safe.

That night we slept on top of a metal shed a little bigger than the one at our old house. When I fell asleep Mira was there next to me, snuggled close. I woke up the next morning and she was gone. I saw her shoe down on the ground near the shed. It had blood on it. Some of her hair was caught in the metal of the roof, near the edge. The boogie man had gotten her while I was asleep. I hadn't heard her scream or anything. I figured if he got her he was coming to get me next. So I ran. I ran as fast as I could in the direction she told me the safe place was. If I was close I might be able to get there before he got me.

I found it. Or I should say one of the people saw me passing by and called out to me. His name was Daniel Perek. He was a nice old man with lots of wrinkles and kind brown eyes. There was a big camper with a ladder that he had me climb on top of. I was told to stay there for the night and they would let me inside in the morning. I started crying. I told him that the boogie man got my Daddy, my Mommy, my big brother and last night he got my big sister. If I had to stay on the camper then the boogie man was going to get me too. Mr. Perek told me that he and his friends would watch over me and if the boogie man came near they would kill him.

I stayed awake as long as I could. When I woke up I was surprised I was still alive. I looked down on the ground and saw a lot of bodies that weren't there when the sun went down. Mr. Perek was back at his post and they lowered a ramp of wood down to me and had me climb over to where they were. I saw it was a wall that they had built up out of almost everything. He told me I was safe and that I was going to stay with him and his wife Grace. That was the first day I spent in Gabriel Missouri.

I was nine years old when I came to town. The Perek's adopted me, cared for me, treated me like their own. They couldn't stop the nightmares, but Mrs. Perek held me when I woke up screaming and told me things were alright. I went to school, not like my old school. The new teachers made sure we knew how to stay safe, how to find good food and water, and how to recognize if someone was infected. I learned how to make candles, to dry and preserve food and how to tan animal hides. I already knew how to read so I helped teach other kids who didn't. We also did practice drills. They were like fire drills back in school. But these were about zombies.

I had learned in my years in Gabriel that the boogie men were called zombies. They were slow, but really strong. If they got a hold of you then you were dead. If they got their goop on you then you would die and turn into one of them. But they were dumb and you could fool them pretty easy. There was a drill for if someone was infected. Another one for zombies passing by (we all were supposed to be real quiet). The big one was for a wall fail. We would all get to high ground and then take the escape routes. Anyone who fell behind would get left. There was no way to save people in this new world. Just run and don't look back they said.

It was a nice sunny day when the wall failed. I had just celebrated my fourteenth birthday with the Perek's. There had been a lot of tension for the week leading up to that day. Hushed whispers among the adults. I'd started sleeping on the second floor of one of the buildings with access to the escape route each night. But I was helping to stack firewood when the shout went up. I knew it wasn't a practice because they would not have yelled like that with zombies that close unless it was real. I tried to get to my escape path but found zombies coming towards me.

Sheriff Taylor, a nice man who had always been kind to me, started shooting the zombies. He stood between us and the horde while we rushed to safety. I scrambled up to the top of one of the sheds just as the boogie men of my childhood rushed toward me. Some people were not lucky enough or quick enough to get away. Many of the elderly got ripped apart. I saw Mr. Perek defending his wife as she tried to get to the staircase of one of the buildings. They were overrun by the zombies. I saw my new parents get torn apart and taken screaming out of my life. I ended up sitting in the middle of the roof rocking back and forth.

By the time I came out of it most of the people were gone. Those that remained were stuck like me. We were too far from the escape routes to get away and in my case there weren't even any buildings to get to nearby. Just a bunch of hands reaching for me from the edge of the roof. As night fell, I remembered how Mira had died and sat with my legs crossed, arms pulled in. I tried not to sleep at all but I ended up dozing off and on. When morning came the truth of my situation began to set in.

The people who were trapped with me were at least far enough from the dead to rest safely. I was on a fairly small roof. If I lay down in my sleep I would be pulled off and eaten. The screams of some of those caught by the horde, my new parents and Sheriff Taylor included, had gone on for what seemed like forever. I knew I was going to die on that roof. Tears started spilling silently down my face as I stared at the zombies gathered around.

I heard noise from the far side of town. Someone was banging pots and pans and making a racket. The dead moved away from the shed and towards the noise. When they were far enough away I made a break for it. I got to one of the buildings and raced up the stairs. Once I was on the second floor I entered an empty room and closed the door. I checked my shoes and they were surprisingly clean. Just in case I stayed in the room all that night and the next day. After that I figured I had not been infected and went up to the roof. There were ten others besides me. Twenty people had been left behind. Three had been pulled from their roofs, five died trying to get to safety and two got infected during their escape.

There was plenty of food and water and if the zombies could be distracted we might be able to get to the escape path. The problem was we could not reach anywhere from our location that would let us pull them away from where we needed to go. And no one wanted to go down among them. We stayed up on the second floors of the building for almost a week. Then one day I noticed there seemed to be fewer zombies. The day after that I was sure that there were less of them. Within another week they had gone from a horde to a small crowd. Within a few more days we found out why. Outside of town a man walked among the zombies. He killed them one at a time, never seeming to stop to rest. Gore coated him and I found myself taking steps back from him even though he was really far away.

He stopped near one of the girls and yelled at her. A lot of what he said was hard to hear but he was really mad. When he was gone we carefully made our way to the escape path, avoiding the zombie corpses. The girl he yelled at was named Tamara. She was freaking out when she got up to the path. She could barely talk he had scared her so badly. All we could get out of her was that the man had told her we should all be at the refuge and he kept pointing to the west. Tamara was always brave but she looked so white I was afraid she was going to pass out. Jeff, one of the older boys, slapped her to try and calm her down and she beat the crap out of him. Like I said, Tamara is normally not a fraidy cat.

We broke them up and followed the path to the evacuation point. The others were gone. They had left backpacks with food and gear behind. Not because they thought we were coming. You can only carry so much. We each took two packs and the food from three others. After a short argument between me, Tamara, Jeff and Bob (the oldest present) we decided to stick together and follow the others on the path to the next refuge.

For two weeks we headed parallel to the direction the stranger had pointed. The second week we ran into the remains of the first band of refugees. They were running back towards us. They told us there was a large horde ahead. No one knew what to do. People were arguing. Fights were breaking out. A few were even talking about heading out on their own. It was too much. I couldn't stand the thought of what was left of my family scattering out into the wastes to die alone.

I told them all to shut up. As quickly as I could I told them about the stranger who had saved us and the refuge to the west. A few argued and I told them if they didn't want to come they could face the horde or try to get back to our village. No one argued after that. The next few weeks were very hard. Zombies were everywhere. It was impossible to stop for longer than a half hour before one showed up. A day or so before I figured we were all going to collapse from exhaustion there was a giant racket behind us. It sounded like someone banging a whole lot of metal together. The dead went after the noise and left us alone.

We camped up on top of a tall rock before it was even late afternoon. People were too tired to keep going. The rock itself was enormous and it took a bit to get everyone up there. We didn't even set a watch. It was stupid. Anything could have happened, including one of our own turning and killing us all. The next day I woke up and did a head count and saw everyone was there. No one had turned during the night. A few hours after the sun came up a man appeared on the rock next to ours. He was careful to let us know he was there. I suppose he was afraid of getting shot. But none of us had a gun.

The man asked us to tell him our story. The others pushed me forward and I told him what happened to our refuge. I told him about the stranger, how he saved us. That got his attention. He asked a lot of questions after that. When he left he said he would come back towards noon, when the sun was highest. A lot of the others thought we should leave. They thought maybe he was going to get friends and come back to kill us. I figured we didn't have enough for anyone to go to the trouble of killing us. Besides, if he had just waited we would probably have died in a week or so on our own.

The man came back with friends but not to hurt us. They brought food, water and new clothes. We were asked to get rid of our old stuff in case it had any zombie goo on it. The new clothes were nice and they brought soap and water for us to wash off with. It felt good to be clean. Even back at Gabriel it was rare to be able to get cleaned up. We were asked if we wanted to come back to their refuge, Vigilance, with them.

It was weird. I still don't understand why they are so nice to us. I keep waiting for them to do something bad, but they haven't. I can take a shower here every day if I want to. I have clean clothes that are nice. We eat pretty good and all they expect is for us to do our chores and help out in some way. A lot of the people took the younger ones in as part of their family. I live with three other girls in a small house. We take care of ourselves.

This place is run by a really nice man named Phillip. When my group came here he came and talked to me while I was in quarantine. He asked me about my life before the other refuge and since. We talked for a long time. When they let us out of quarantine he was the one that brought me to the doctors so they could help me get better. So here I am writing my story. I am glad to be in Vigilance. I am glad to feel safe from the boogie man once again. I am glad to have a new family. A strong family. I will not let anything happen to this one. I promise.

PRIVATE JOURNAL OF DANA CRENDALL. Donated to Archivist stores upon Dana's death.

Danny Filoraate

MY NAME IS DANNY FILORAATE. Before all this happened I lived at in the 2300 block of 5th Ave in Brooklyn. There is nothing there now but some burned bricks. When the infection came to the Big Apple it took a giant bite out of the population. I was in fourth grade and we had just started the chapter in science about viruses. We were learning all about how they spread, how hard they are to treat, that kind of stuff. The news was starting to get pretty odd and one of the kids in my class, Mary Harford, didn't come in one day. No one knew where she was, not even her best friend, Tanya Benson. They had talked on Sunday and Mary hadn't mentioned being out of school to her. The next day three more kids were missing. When I got ready for school the following morning my dad came into my room and told me that I was staying home. Things were just hinting at how bad they were going to get.

Dad and mom went to work. Dad was a bus driver on the local route and mom worked at the bakery on the corner. They never came home. Around five in the afternoon I started to get worried and called their cells. Dad picked up and I could tell right away that something was wrong. He told me that he had been bitten by one of his regulars and that he wasn't feeling so good. He said I should stay inside and lock the door and wait for mom. Then the line went dead. I switched over from the cartoons I had been watching to the news. It was like a live action horror show.

The streets of New York were filled with people. Soldiers, civilians, and the undead. I watched army guys shooting zombies in the head, just like in the old horror movies. People were screaming and running. The newscaster was on top of his news van surrounded by zombies. Before long the camera cut out and a new one, showing a wider shot from a rooftop, replaced it. I stood up and looked out the window and came to a sickening realization. Neither of my parents were ever coming home again. Alive that is.

For the next week I hunkered down inside the apartment just like dad had told me to. When the army guys came knocking I didn't answer. When the neighbors came knocking I didn't answer. I was doing okay until the television stations disappeared one by one. It was like some sort of electronic countdown. I watched movies on the DVD player with the sound down until the power went out at the end of the week. It was so quiet. I could actually hear the collective moans of the zombies in the streets below. After that it was hard to pretend my world was not a shattered mess.

My food supplies were running low when the water shut off. I had filled the bathtub, sinks and every container I could find in the house. Dad had always told me stories about past disasters in the city and how water was sometimes the first thing to go. I decided to take a chance and ventured out into the hallway the next day. I made sure the door wasn't locked so I could get back in quickly before I stepped out into the hall. Uncovered windows at either end of the hall gave me a little light to see by. I had just reached the next door neighbors door and was about to knock when I heard the moaning from inside. Zombie moaning. More was coming from down the hall from down around the corner. And it was getting closer. I back-tracked to my door and glanced back in time to see Mrs. Kristoff from 3B shambling around the corner with half her face chewed off.

Back inside my apartment, I locked and chained the door and then stuck a chair under the knob. A short time later I heard shuffling right outside and the low moan of a zombie. I think it was Mrs. Kristoff but I wasn't going to look. Thumps against the door rattled it but it held firm. Going over to the window I was glad we had a fire escape, otherwise I might have been stuck in the apartment until I died. Unlocking the deadbolt on the window I slid it open and after looking up to make sure it was empty I headed for the roof.

The city stunk. Not like the New York stink that I'd grown to love. It smelled like shit, rot and rancid meat. The streets below were filled with dead both moving and unmoving. Legitimate corpses, most with head trauma, lay all over bloating in the sun. The stench was unimaginable, making the air feel almost greasy as I breathed it in. Moving up the fire escape I attracted the attention of zombies nearby who moved below me, patiently waiting for me to fall. I peeked up over the roof and saw a boy sitting near the chimney stack. Robbie Patson. One of the kids from the neighborhood I had known all my life. I tossed a rock from the edge of the roof towards him. He spun in fear and locked eyes with me. We were wary of each other, mainly because it was hard for us to know if the other was infected.

Hours later, but before the sun went down we had come to the conclusion we were both safe. During the wait we filled each other in on what we had gone through. Turns out Rob had the same sort of story that I did, except his mom was a florist and his dad a fireman. Neither one had answered their cells, but he figured they were dead. Otherwise they would have come back by now. He lived on the top floor and it was clear of zombies, unlike my floor. But unlike me he hadn't filled containers with water. So we decided to hatch a partnership. His food, my water and safety in numbers.

It was good to not be alone. You never realize how quiet it is until the television and radio is dead and you have no one to talk to. Once we got situated on the top floor Robbie and me started getting serious about survival. We searched the apartments, well the empty ones, and found all the food and water we could as well as more containers for what was in my bathtub and sinks. Then we built bridges over to the buildings within reach. It was hairy at times, more than once we almost fell off the edge into the zombies below. But after a while we got a system down.

First we scouted an area getting a lay of the land. Then we searched out anything worth taking and piled them in collection spots. Finally we separated the take into equal parts and hid them in top floor apartments near our building. After that we would expand our bridge system and move into a new area. Sometimes we found zombies and marked those buildings with red paint so we knew to avoid them. For a month we survived pretty well. That is until it started to get cold.

There was a nice apartment on the top floor of our building. At one time it must have belongs to the owners or something. It had a fireplace so we stayed there and burned a lot of useless furniture to keep warm. A week after our first fire we got invaded. Twenty adults descended on our kingdom. They had a few kids with them and plenty of guns. Before we knew it, Robbie and I were evicted from the refuge we had built and subjected to the adults rule. The adults kept telling us how ingenious we were, while they were eating our food and drinking our water. I made the mistake of telling them to get the hell out and one of the guys belted me. Knocked me out cold. He apologized when I woke up, but the apology was bullshit and we both knew it. The message was clear. I'm small and he's big and he'll do what he wants to me if I mouth off.

Robbie wanted to take off. He said we could rebuild somewhere else. I should have listened to him. Instead we stayed there. The leader of the new group was the guy who had hit me. His name was Nathan Walton, a heavily muscled tattooed freak with anger issues. Within a few months they had eaten the food we had put aside to get us through winter and most of the water. Then things started getting ugly. Nathan wanted us to go out and collect more supplies. And he didn't want excuses as to why we couldn't find them.

The guns were put to use way too often. Sometimes when it wasn't even necessary, like when Nathan would sit on the roof and shoot zombies in the street for fun. Each time he did it he attracted more zombies. He didn't stop even after the mass of them smashed through the ground level he just laughed and asked me if I ever saw a zombie climb stairs. In the end he learned his lesson the hard way.

A bunch of us were out collecting, adults too, when it happened.

I figure the dead broke a stove loose or damaged a gas line. I watched a show once about how gas leaks into a basement and then a house blows up. What we saw was a little bit bigger than that. The explosion tore off the roof, blew out the walls and killed everyone that was there. So much for zombies not being able to climb stairs. They took the building down anyway. At least Nathan died. Prick.

We got back to see the main base gone, the buildings nearby on fire, and most of our supplies burned to a crisp. The next few months were hard. We survived but it wasn't pretty. One adult after another tried to take charge and lead the group. None of them would listen to me or Robbie and after the third time someone almost got us all killed I had it. Robbie and I stole the weapons and ammo from all of them and hid all but two handguns. We leveled these at the adults one morning and explained that we were leaving. Any of the kids that wanted to come with us were welcome. But the adults were not. And if we saw them again we would shoot them just as quickly as if they were zombies. Hell, they were more dangerous than the dead. There were some tears and a few threats but in the end most of the orphans came with us. All the kids with parents in the group stayed behind.

Robbie and me led our band to a new base we had been setting up ten blocks away. The trip there was dangerous. We had to pass through two areas where there were no close buildings which meant taking to the streets. Luckily the explosion had drawn most of the dead to the old base so other than a few shamblers we were free and clear. The new base was in a ten story building that had a few buildings on either side and had a walkway over the street for pedestrians. We blocked off the bottom of each staircase and built bridges to fire escapes nearby. Then we started the arduous task of rebuilding. By this time we had gone through a winter and were back into summer. Scented candles and air freshener became a necessity. The top floors of the building were the best living quarters as they kept us above most of the smells.

For years we rebuilt our base. Then Robbie and I decided to

start another base further out. We left a small contingent at the old base and spent a year building the new one. We kept doing this, bringing more people into our group as we expanded. By the time we had six bases we had grown to over a thousand members. All young people that survived with no adults allowed. There were problems of course. Someone messing around with someone else's girl or boy. Fist fights. Stealing. We set up a group of peers at each base to deal with that crap.

Eventually we ran into a problem eventually that we couldn't solve. Supplies. We'd been living in the city for almost ten years when it became clear to me that we were slowly running out of places to scavenge. It was so bad we started going ground side to search. The first time we lost someone on a raid I pulled Robbie aside for a talk. I told him that we needed to think about getting out of the city. Try to find a place where we could grow our own food that had a supply of fresh water. He looked at me like I was infected. Robbie had gotten used to being able to do what he wanted when he wanted. A few guys had managed to hook up some batteries and solar cells and we had DVDs and video games we could play. So the thought of heading out into the wilds to rough it just didn't appeal to him. His idea was to set up some greenhouses and grow our own food on top of the city.

I could see his point of view but his plan had a couple of big holes in it. Like who was going to set up the greenhouses? Where would we get the materials, dirt or fertilizer we needed? I asked him how we would clear the building tops and get water to take care of the crops. We argued. Then we fought. Then we argued some more. In the end neither one of us would give an inch. I figured we would talk it out, we always had before. Then Tanya Williams, a girl that I liked, came and told me that Robbie was planning to take me out. She heard him discussing it with his crew, how I was a pain in his ass that needed to go. But he wanted it to look like an accident.

Over the years I had led most of our scouting parties so I was pretty good at moving quietly. I snuck up on one of his planning sessions and what I heard made me sick. My friend, my buddy from the old neighborhood, was a rat bastard fink. Using a tried and true plan I stole everything I could get my hands on. Guns, ammo, survival gear, food, water and medicine that I put it in two different hiding places in the city. One was close to the edge of town and one was near our original base. By the time anyone caught on to what was going on I was ready to leave.

Robbie tried to accuse me of betraying the group. He actually tried to play the part of the victim. Too bad for him I had a few people on my side that had heard him scheming to take me out. It helps to have friends that move as quietly as you do. When his little speech didn't work he pulled a gun on me, and found six trained on him. I took his piece and told him that I divided all the gear. Half I was taking and half I had hidden for them. I was leaving and my scouts were coming with me, along with about half the group. When we got to the edge of town I would leave a note telling him where they could find the map that would lead them to their part of the stash. He got all belligerent so I told him since I had collected most of the gear with my people we actually could take more of it, if he wanted to keep bitchin. That shut him up pretty quick.

Getting out of town was easier said than done. I had scouted out a school near where we were leaving and found four busses that were gas/electric hybrids. They were big enough to load all our stuff and people and to clear the road of most things that would be in the way. The big problem we had was none of us knew how to drive. I was forced to recruit a few drivers from a small adult group near our old haunt. They were more than happy to submit to my leadership. Out of the hundreds they had started with less than thirty remained. Most of them were the kids we had left behind but six adults that could drive were with them.

Our first stop was the mountains to the west. Foolishly, I thought that the worst thing we would need to protect ourselves from was the dead. The living ended up being a much bigger threat. The world had deteriorated to the dead trying to eat you and the living trying to do worse. By the time we reached the mountains we had used up most of our ammo on the living. We hit a sporting goods store off the beaten path. Most of the ammo was gone, but they had crossbows, bows and arrows. We cleaned them out and got all the survival gear that was left. Then we headed to the mountains. After a failed month of trying to build shelters I scouted out an old resort high up near one of the lakes. The cabins were solid, with fireplaces. We moved in and stayed there for almost two years. The fishing and hunting was good. All of us got really good at firing the crossbows and bows. But a few still used guns and that ended up screwing us.

The dead arrived one afternoon a few at a time. Pretty soon they were coming up the road in an unending river. I figure they were drawn by the gunfire. Thankfully, I had never stopped the practice of setting guards. We had more than enough time to pack up our crap, gas up the busses and go. Every time we stopped though we knew they were back there, stalking us. Every place we considered stopping at long term had a fatal flaw. We traveled for a long time, backtracking to avoid zombie hordes, route around destroyed bridges and blocked roads. More than once we cleared service stations to refill our gas tanks and cans using electric pumps connected to the bus's electrical system.

Outside of St. Louis, one of the vehicles failed and another one started to max out at thirty miles an hour. The writing was on the wall. We had no way of fixing the buses, our food was getting low and we were in the middle of the plains. While there were places to hide we couldn't survive in the open. I didn't have any interest in having us trapped in an unfamiliar city. When the third bus died we packed everyone onto the remaining one and drove. Something blew out in the engine on the last bus outside Dalhart, TX, in the panhandle. We raided the town, killed the zombies we found there and picked the place dry. Then we moved on, traveling by foot. It was brutal.

Most of us had grown up in the city and had no idea how to survive in the desert. For example, drinking soda and beer isn't a good way to stay hydrated. We started losing people left and right until I ordered everyone to stick to water. Each small town we hit was cleared of undead and picked clean. People started getting infected. I was forced to put my girl Tanya down. After that I make it clear that people needed to be careful. You can't just pick shit up. You have to wipe stuff down or get rid of the original packaging. As our ammo got low it got harder to clear towns. We had to change our tactics, drawing the dead out with distractions and then raiding. Not all of the zombies would get drawn away but at least we wasted fewer arrows.

Outside the town of Los Vegas New Mexico, not to be mistaken for the more famous Sin City, we came across Jeff Wilson. He was trapped on a rise by a band of dead. We cleared them out and I went up to talk to him. Keeping my distance I asked him if he was from the area. He told me he was and I asked if he could direct me to anyplace that had a clean water supply and was defensible. We talked and after a bit he suggested a place to the north. It was a broad high shelf of rock with a small spring. The ground was suitable for planting and there was ample space to build on top of it.

The next morning he was gone when I went to check on him. I was impressed. Our guards hadn't seen a thing and sneaking past them was hard. Without any other options we headed towards the rise he had described. I was surprised when we found it was exactly as he had described it. We spent about a year there, building homes with material scavenged from nearby and planting some basic crops. Then the damn dead came. We should have known they were back there. Somewhere. Never giving up, relentlessly pursuing us.

I guess part of us wanted to imagine they had gotten distracted or just stopped. They came slowly at first and then in a regular deluge. Soon we found ourselves in the same predicament that we had saved Wilson from. And like a fool I had set up a refuge for the first time without any sort of escape path. It was then that Wilson reappeared inside our camp. I was shocked to wake up one morning and see him sitting in my tent. He told me that he had been watching us for his superiors. He had told them all about our travels and they were impressed. They wanted to extend an invitation to join their refuge.

I was pissed. It felt like I was being railroaded into servitude. I had danced to that beat before and wasn't having any of it. He was surprised at my anger. The timing of the invitation was coincidental. While it was obvious that we were in trouble and needed help he would be more than happy to lead my people through an escape tunnel away from the dead. But, if we chose to join his people or not that offer was being extended in repayment for the favor we had done for him. In fact, the original idea to watch us had been his. After seeing how many of us had survived a trip across the country he wanted to know more about us.

It took a few hours but we worked out a meeting at a neutral location. The first time I met Phillip Kane I was surprised. He was barely older than I was and he was leading an entire refuge. After meeting Wilson I figured the leader would be some old fart. Instead there is a guy that looks like he could be part of my crew. We talked for days. We each shared our stories, our triumphs and setbacks. He really wanted us to join. I really wanted us to join. But the how and when was a problem. My people didn't want to give up what they had built. Even with the dead surrounding them. He didn't want them to stay because their presence attracted undead thereby compromising one of his refuges exits. There was also the real concern that we would find ourselves prisoner in our new home.

Philip listened to my concerns and suggested a compromise. My people had a unique set of skills. We were able to survive and travel the waste. He offered citizenship in Vigilance, and the only person we would report to was him. I countered saying that I would report to him but my people would report to me. It was a small concession but I could see him playing it over in his mind. He countered that we would train some of his people as well, including his son Jack. In turn he would have some of my people trained in other skills. That way if we decided to part ways eventually both sides would have benefited from the endeavor.

It made sense to me. I went back and told the group and they argued about it for two days. Some of them were tired of running and being afraid. They wanted to be settled. Others, like me, were not content sitting around. In the end I pointed out to them that while we could head out and find a third option out in the world we would be hard pressed to find something better than what Philip was offering. So the crew came to Vigilance.

At first there were issues. The existing populace didn't like the fact that we were above most of their laws. All transgressions got judged by me and no one else. This pissed more than a few of them off. The wave of discontent got so bad that one of them got into a fight with one of mine and got their ass kicked. That made it worse. Things were reaching a boiling point about the time we got done training Jack and a few of his friends. It took almost a year to train him. We had to unteach him a few things. When he graduated he suggested the name Hunters for our crew. He said it was a way to join the old crew and the new recruits together. The name stuck and the presence of some of the original populace in our ranks changed the perception from privileged newcomer to elite force.

It also probably helped that later that same month my people brought back the single biggest supply run the town had seen to date. They found a warehouse at the edge of Oklahoma City that hadn't been touched and lured away most of the dead. Then they used a few nearby trucks to haul everything back. We had boxes of medical supplies, dried food, seeds, books, materials, all manner of tools. Once they unloaded it the townfolk's attitude took on a permanent change. The naysayers were suddenly our biggest supporters. We found our next class of Hunter recruits so big that we had to hold trials to weed some out.

When Jack stepped up to lead the town many years later, after his old man died of pneumonia, he did a fine job. It only seemed natural, especially with me not having any sons of my own, that I named him my successor to the office of Lead Hunter. With that act the final schism between our two people was closed. We were no longer the crew and the townspeople. We were simply the people of Vigilance.

Ziu Xhau

THERE WERE MANY IN MY village who thought me a spoiled child. While they worked and toiled I was given time by my parents to carve things. From a very young age I showed what my grand-mother called an astonishing gift. People were amazed by my ability to call forth the essence of a material. Each item I made was pro-claimed a stunning work of art. The praise did not mean as much to me as being able to create beauty. My grandmother was the wealthi-est woman in our province. So she was able to indulge my gift. First with sandstone and wood and later with crystal, metal and gem-stones, she had me make her things. Never asking for anything spe-cific, she would give me material and let me create whatever moved me.

I never thought of my art as anything special. To me anyone could do what I did if they simply took the time. I later realized that I was unique. My creations were cherished by my grandmother and highly sought by many others. She never sold or gave away anything I made for her. Instead she would tell those that wanted something to provide the material they wanted their item crafted from. I would create something that spoke to me from the material and she would sell them the finished piece. By the time I was twelve my grand-mother had tripled her fortune.

I was never exploited. She simply encouraged me to do what I loved. The few times I did not feel like creating something she sent everything back and told the person to pick something else. Rarely did anyone end up disappointed from what I made for them. When it came time for me to go to university, I finally dared asked my grandmother for something in return. I wanted to see the world. She agreed that it was necessary for an artist's soul to touch many others and bought me a year tour around the world. When I was done traveling, instead of returning, I stayed in the United States in the City of New Orleans. Grandmother understood that the city called to me in a way that I could not explain. When my father demanded I return, she spoke to him and he relented.

This magical city was an amalgamation of art, culture, history and spirituality. Over the years it had been in French, Spanish and American hands and had a people as varied and interesting as its history. When I first came here it was to wander the streets trying to soak in as much as I could. It was almost as if I had finally found sustenance for my soul. The city itself was like a work of art. Sometimes upsetting, other times wonderful, always evoking an emotion. It was during this first visit that I met the friends that would bring me back to the city after I finished my year long journey.

I first met Billy Bob Mason, a giant redneck man with brown hair and eyes, at a bar called Bull Riders Paradise. The bar was built around a mechanical bull and Billy Bob was riding it when I walked in. Fascinated, I watched as he was thrown into a pile of foam rubber. A rude fellow nearby asked me if a zipper head like me had ever seen a mechanical bull. I told him I had not and he seemed put off by the way I spoke English. My mastery of the language was obviously far better than his. He told me that if I was a real man I would take a turn on the bull. Even though I knew he did not have my best interest at heart, I thought it would be a fun experience. However, I had not counted on him going to the controls and pushing it all the way up once I was aboard the bull. I was thrown over the foam and landed hard on the floor. When I came back to consciousness the owner and Billy Bob were crouched over me. Billy Bob made sure I was okay and then walked over to the man who had turned up the controls. There was a loud confrontation which ended with Billy Bob punching the man, knocking him cold.

After that, the two of us became friends, though we must have looked very odd to those around us. A giant redneck and a pencil thin Chinaman. Billy Bob told me to call him a redneck. I thought it was insulting, but he insists that a man knows who he is and embraces it. Billy Bob was also a skilled artist. He could make anything out of clay. I stopped by his house the next day and was amazed at the sculptures he had created. My favorite was of a half-naked cowgirl in a leather vest atop a bucking bronco.

Through Billy Bob I met some talented artists many of whom I became great friends with. First there was Jena Penny Fredon, a petite Caucasian girl that went by J.P. When she sang it was, as Billy Bob put it, as if she had swallowed a large black woman. Next there was Polly Garcia, a Latina street dancer whose performances have wowed tourists for years. The last of my friends was an actor by the name of Jack Bowers. Billy Bob said that Jack could charm the pants off just about anyone. He was what is known as a con artist. I have to say after watching him work that there was truly an art to see him run his cons.

It was this group of friends that I was eating with when we heard the news that overseas flights had been canceled. I tried calling home and managed to speak to my grandmother. She told me that the stories from my childhood, the ones about vengeful ancestors, had come true. The dead were walking and they were hungry. My family was retreating to the old stronghold on the mountain and she told me to find a safe place. The conversation got cut off just after she told me that crossbows were the best way to stop them. A bolt to the head.

I tried calling her back many times but the overseas lines were unavailable. The news seemed to be keeping things back based on what she had told me. They downplayed issues that were occurring down the east coast. When I talked to my friends about it they decided it might be a good time to get away from the city for a bit. Jack told us about a boat that he knew of that we could 'borrow'. When we got to the marina and cast off I could see we had made a good call. Many others were taking to the sea to escape the growing threat on the land.

We sailed out into the gulf and headed for the Caribbean. Polly told us of a wonderful chain of islands where we could live a quiet life of eating fruit from the trees, fish in the ocean and drinking from the natural springs. As we got into the clear waters of the Caribbean we realized three very important things. One, we were not the only ones who had thought of this plan. The place was swamped with ships. Two, the waters of this place were clear and beautiful. You could see all the way to the bottom. Three, there were tons of dead already walking around on the ocean floor. Chances were that any island we landed on would end up over run. We had a brief conference about our options and Jena told us that she had heard on the radio that the military had a few bases in the west set up as refuges.

It was decided that we would get off the water and take our chances on land. We headed back into the Gulf and landed the boat not far from Richmondville Texas. Jack hot wired a car and we started west. The landscape was surreal. Deserted except for the occasional abandoned car or wandering zombie. To see the dead walking was upsetting on a spiritual level. Grandmother had always told me the old stories. It was known that when the dead come back to avenge themselves on the living it is for a great wrong. What had we done to cause such a mass return by our ancestors?

Our vehicle ran out of gas in the middle of nowhere. There were no other cars so we were forced to walk. We continued traveling for almost a week stopping each night somewhere out of the dead's reach. Soon the walking truly began to take its toll. All of us had blisters on our feet, sunburn on our faces. We had run out of food a day before and water that morning. Our skill sets were very lacking. I cursed my ignorance for not learning more practical skills while in school. For all I know they had offered classes in desert survival, something that would have been far more helpful than music appreciation.

When we came to the general store in the middle of nowhere we were very happy. Billy Bob and Jack checked it out and it was locked and empty. It had a sliding sheet metal door that covered the front. Billy Bob smashed the lock off after he and Jack were done checking it we went inside. There was a back door that Jack went out and closed the front sliding door before coming back in. At the back of the shop we found stairs leading to a second floor.

It was an amazing discovery, this store in the middle of nowhere. The roof held solar panels and when we checked the building had power. There was water pressure and on demand hot water. We all had showers for the first time since leaving the boat, and washed our clothes and dried them. It felt good to be clean. The stores refrigerators and freezers had continued to run, off the solar panels. We ate pizza, hot wings and drank beer. For a week we rested up and tended to our feet.

Jena noticed them first. She was on the second floor and called us up. Zombies were roaming around down below. One that caught my attention was dressed in the clothing of a surveyor. Shambling to different spots he would stand for a moment holding a pole with a box at the top before moving on. He was the only one that I saw that was holding something, the rest simply shambled around with their claw like hands clenching and unclenching. Also, unlike the others he did not approach the store. Instead, he made his way across my line of vision traveling from south to north. The rest of the zombies clustered around the store.

At first there were just a few but within days there were hundreds. We were trapped in the store. It was not something that truly caused us panic. We had power, water, food and entertainment. The owner had a collection of videos and games to play. For quite some time we were content, happy even. However, it was only a month before I pointed out our food would not last forever. Another month and we had gone through most of the frozen food and were started on the canned goods.

I was sitting on the roof, contemplating my fate, when I first saw him. There among the furthest dead a figure moved among them. A madman swinging two machetes drew the dead from us to him. I called the others up to witness this. Everyone agreed that the man would be a zombie himself by morning.

The next day we returned to the roof and were astonished to see the man still at work. Behind him lay hundreds of zombies, their heads split open. Throughout the next few days we watched him work through the dead. As they drew away towards him Billy Bob spotted a truck that was parked behind the shop. It was parked facing us and Billy Bob used his binoculars to look at it. The truck looked empty from our vantage point. He and Jack waited until the dead were far enough away and went out the back door to look at it. They came back and said it was locked but empty. Jana told them she found the keys in the drawer of the cash register while they were outside. Billy Bob went out and opened the truck, making sure it was clear.

Over the next hour we loaded all the food and water we could carry into the truck. When the truck was ready we went back inside and locked the door. We all agreed it was worth the risk to get a good night sleep and make our escape in the morning. The next day I went to the roof. The man had made amazing progress. I took Billy Bob's binoculars with me. I wanted to try and see the face of our savior. We would not stay to thank him. The chance of infection was too great. But I wanted to make a statue of him as a way of thanking him, for that I need to see him closer.

I wish I had never raised the glasses to my eyes. I wish I could unsee what I have seen. My grandmother was right. The ancestors are angry. We should give thanks for any help they give us and be-ware our own curiosity. I pray that I have not angered him. I will pay him homage but the details I saw this day will not be included.

We are leaving soon. Billy Bob says that we have a straight shot from here to one of the refuges. I hope he is right. The world is not what it once was. Perhaps the ancestors have no use for us anymore. Where do artists fit in a world gone mad?

HUNTER PHILATIN – JOURNAL FOUND NEAR wreck of large pickup. Occupants appear to have missed a turn at high rate of speed and left road. Bullet holes in truck indicate they may have been chased by hostiles. Truck was stripped of all useful gear. Journal gives location of secured general store. Solar panels and on demand hot water system. Various supplies. Site checked and found undisturbed. Large contingent of dead zombies in area. Supplies earmarked for recovery.

Roger "Doz" Pental

IF I GET MY ASS killed I hope whoever finds this and reads it gets a fucking laugh out of it. This life has been shitty so far and I don't see it getting any better, only worse. For everything I've given in service of others I got jack shit back in return. My name is Roger Pental, but my friends call me Dozer, Doz for short. I'm a big guy and back in basic I knocked down part of the obstacle course instead of climbing over it. The drill sergeant yelled that he was supposed to be training a soldier, not a goddamn bulldozer. The guys started calling me Dozer and the name stuck.

Other than the grunts in my squad I didn't have many friends even back before the world slid into the toilet. I showed aptitude above and beyond and moved up after basic to extended training. By the time I mustered out I was a Naval Special Warfare Operator Master Chief Petty Officer, what civilians would call a SEAL. I spent twenty years in the military. I ate more dirt, pissed more blood and ended more lives than most battalions do during active wartime. I also lost more friends than I can count in little hell holes that don't appear on any map.

When I hit my twenty years some little pencil pusher showed up and gave me my walking papers. I was no longer operationally viable as an asset. Thanks for your years of service old man, now get the hell out so someone younger and smarter can take over. Little prick. I could have snapped his neck like a pencil. Instead, I saluted and left behind the only life I had ever known. Hooyah.

Adjusting to civilian life was a nightmare. I was surrounded by a bunch of soft, whiny, lazy little peckerwoods that seemed to have no control on their mouths. All around me was verbal bankruptcy. People writing checks their body can't cash. I soon realized that something an old friend of mine used to say was true. Soldiers should never retire. We should die. Those few of us that have given everything to the service end up with nothing to live for after we get out. Tom Handle. He bought it outside a little town in Lebanon. Funny bastard.

The only jobs I could get were mind numbing and pointless. I checked into freelance work. Mercenary work. But the pencil pushers had me flagged and I couldn't even get a passport for ninety days. Something about having to update my files. Bullshit. They wanted me to get soft sitting around. I ended up driving across the country aimlessly. One night I ended up in a bar in Mikery Texas, some little bunghole in the desert. Here I ran into an oil field wireline crew heading back from a job. One of their boys took issue with me and ended up unconscious on the floor. Instead of bum rushing me his friends laughed and bought me a drink. They were uncouth, viscous and crass. In other words, my kind of people.

Their crew consisted of one engineer and three hands. They went out on jobs where they worked outside no matter the weather, doing heavy labor for big pay. I liked the sound of that and headed over to their office. The guy running the place was a dog faced old coot that used to be Army. I tried not to hold that against him. We shot the shit for a while and he finally broke down and asked me the question. Why the hell did I want this job? I had a military pension and could live fine off that.

I told him that I would try this out and if I didn't like it I would move on. But a man needs to work and I had no interest in getting soft. Besides, I told him there were tongs in the fire, I just needed something to kill time and stay in shape. He hired me on the spot. I had to go through a bunch of bull shit medical tests and a piss screening for drugs. Then I took a test to get a CDL and get checked out on a crane. I did harder things than this on a daily basis when I was still in.

I was out on a crew within a few days and within a year I was the crew lead. They offered me an engineering spot a few times and I told them to go screw themselves. I wanted to work, not sit on my ass inside some air conditioned box playing with my joystick. I picked my own crew once I was lead. I had worked with all the guys over the course of that year but the team I chose were guys I could count on. Dan Larson was a solid older guy. Well, he was ten years younger than me but older than the rest and could run a crane in his sleep. The other guy, Mike Bain, was one of the youngest at the company. But at twenty he already was a better worker and more trustworthy guy than any of his coworkers. The three of us worked hard and played hard. The only rub that I had was that we were forced to work for this jerkoff engineer named Ricky.

This guy was a douche. Lazy, self-centered, opinionated, under-educated and never knew when to keep his mouth shut. He went to the owners a week before the end bitching that I threw him across the location. Stupid asshole got in my face and started screaming. If he had clue one what he was doing he never would have needed to do it. If he had any common sense he would have known better than to do it.

It was all bullshit anyway. He was showing off for the company man and it blew up in his face. We left in the pickup and he was stranded out at the site. So a week later, when he left us out on location and took off in the truck, I figured it was payback. He had to sit on site for a few hours waiting for someone to come get him so he figured we could do the same. Instead the zombie apocalypse was in full swing and no one answered the phone at the shop. I don't know for a fact what happened to him. But I hope he stopped somewhere to take a piss and a zombie bit his pecker off.

After an hour of trying to get a hold of the shop I started calling around but no one was answering their phones. When I started get-ting a fast busy signal instead of a dial tone I knew something was up. I have a satellite cell phone. They cost an arm and a leg but when you have been some of the places I have been you come to appreciate a clear communication device. I told the guys to grab all the water they could find. We hoofed it ten miles to the nearest town, Takers Point, Texas. The place had ten houses and a bar named Benny's. It was also deserted.

We had come through four days ago and there were at least fifteen people in the bar when we stopped. Now the place was locked up tight. After the walk through the desert my boys were pretty much done in and we were running low on water. I decided that I could buy the owner another door if necessary and kicked in the front. The jamb snapped out nice and clean, so I figured if he bitched I could give him a twenty for a new two by four.

Inside, the place was dark and deserted. I turned the lights on, grabbed the boys a few waters from the cooler behind the bar and told them to drink slow. It is always tempting to drink cold water fast, especially when you are hot. Most people only do it once. Massive stomach cramps have a way of educating you really fast on what your body can handle. To the guys' credit they didn't even roll their eyes at my mothering, they just nodded quietly. Truth is they were probably just glad to be out of the heat and into the A/C.

I flipped on the television over the bar and started flipping through the channels. The first thing I noticed was that some of them were missing. Major channels were not on the air. I flipped over to the 24 hour news network and saw why. Someone had uncorked hell while I was playing out in this sandbox. Footage showed heavy teams fighting what looked like rabid people. The talking head was spouting about zombies. Zombies. Well, that's a new one.

It didn't take long to get the big picture. It started overseas somewhere, guess it doesn't really matter where now. The outbreak was out of control, the east coast was falling and people were in full retreat across the country. The disease was spread by being bitten, scratched or getting 'zombie goo' on you. Nice term. Even at the end of the world we got asshats being cutesy.

Killing the bastards was easy enough, a bullet to the head. But the rub seemed to be that they were attracted to movement and noise. There isn't anything that makes noise quite like gunfire. I could see it on the footage. Regular army was taught to aim, shoot and repeat. They didn't seem to realize while they were doing it that every zombie in the area turned and came towards the sound of gunfire. That was sloppy. Someone in command was asleep at the switch to have missed that. Or maybe it was so bad they didn't have a choice.

They were losing, that much was obvious. There was no fire support, no air support to speak of or rear guard action. Not that air support would do much to things immune to pain and damage. Destroying the head looked to be necessary to destroying the threat. Most of the ordinance we had in the military was about destruction based on pain and injury. If you faced an opponent like this most of it became useless. The troops were running. They were running for their lives. I had seen enough and started looking for food. Most of what they had were chips and peanuts but food was food.

I tossed what I found on the bar and we ate in silence. When we were done I scrounged around the back and found some black trash bags. One I filled with the rest of the food, the other I loaded with water. I left the bags and told the guys I was going to look for some transportation. There was an old truck a few houses over. It was gassed up but there were no keys. I knocked on the door of the house but no one answered. I tried the door and it was unlocked. It looked like whoever had left had done so in a hurry. Rummaging around I found a few bottles of booze and hanging on a hook in the kitchen a set of keys.

After starting the truck, I backed it out and drove over to the bar. The guys came out, threw the trash bags in the back and jumped in the cab. It was a tight fit, older trucks aren't roomy, but it was better than walking. Our shop was about four hours away. I figured with the gas in the tank we should be able to make it with a bit to spare. As we drove, the guys filled me in on what I missed on the broadcast after I left. They were evacuating everyone to safe zones. The closest to us was a military base but they said everyone had to go through quarantine. I told them if they wanted to head that way when we got back it was up to them. But military bases meant gunfire, gunfire drew zombies, and I wasn't going anywhere near them if I could help it.

By the time we got back to the shop the guys were ready to head home. Each of us lived out of town up in hill country. There weren't a lot of people around, so we figured we would be alright at least for a while. Once we rested up, we would figure out what to do. At the shop we left the truck outside the gates and got our pickups. I locked the gate behind me when we left and we all talked by CB until we got home. The boys told me all was clear on their end and I signed off.

My property set up is a little irregular to say the least. I err a bit on the side of the paranoid. The life that I've led has given me plenty of enemies. My perimeter starts with a regular barb wire fence. Then about two hundred yards further in I have a bar barrier, steel bars set two feet up from the ground, enough to stop a heavy truck. Beyond that is a heavy section of razor wire. Next there is a flagstone wall, original to the property that I repaired and reinforced. It is my last forward line and will provide cover up to anything short of a 50 caliber gun. Each fence section had an electronic gate with a keypad that ran off solar power. I could also control them remotely from the house. If I locked them you would be hard pressed to drive a Mack truck through one of my gates. Overkill? Yeah, but I'm still alive. The terrorists groups have an open bounty for most members of the teams since back in the day. I figure this will give me a bit of security from the undead. I guess we will see.

WELL IT'S BEEN ABOUT TWO days and I just got a call from Don on the CB. Zombies are all over his place and he is bugging out to Mike's. He said it started with just a few and before long they were all over the place. I'm going to go check my perimeter and make sure it is solid.

MIKE AND DON ARE ON their way here. Less than a week after Don got to Mike's the dead started showing up. They're freaking out, so when they called to ask if they could come to my place, well I can't leave my guys swinging out in the wind now can I? Not with the dead showing up in numbers at Mike's as well. They shouldn't have even had to ask. But, I've never had the guys over to my place. I either went to their house or met them in town but I never had anyone over. I like my privacy. Still, there is nothing for it so I told them how to get here.

AN HOUR AFTER THE BOYS called they showed up at the back gate. I buzzed them through the gates, talking them through the many turns on the warren of roads that ran through my property. By the time they rolled up to the house they both looked a bit frazzled. The house on this property was a five bedroom ranch that I had bought more for the location than the size. So other than my bedroom there wasn't any place to sleep. I pulled a few cots out for them and they set up two of the bedrooms. We had slept in much worse conditions than this and I was encouraged that neither of them complained. That night as we sat down to eat we watched one of the last cable channels still on the air reporting the news. The east coast was gone, the Midwest was written off and zombies were marching steadily westward. I quizzed the guys on the number of shambling corpses they had seen. The count was surprisingly high. Leaving them to watch television I went down to the basement.

One of the oddities of this house, at least for being in Texas, was it having a basement. After I bought the place I cut a hole in the wall and extended down to add a command bunker, just in case. Here I had close circuit wireless cameras set up all over the property. I had infrared, night vision, and high level zoom capability on each of them. Checking the grounds I saw everything was quiet. I booted up my laptop and started a perimeter program that I had kept from back in my days on the teams. It would register any movement on the cameras bigger than an animal and send me an alert through the wireless network. Satisfied that I had set up a decent sentinel I headed off to bed.

The next day, about lunchtime, my alert system chirped in the living room. I jumped to my feet and ran down stairs. What I saw boggled the mind. There were hundreds of zombies on screen wearing everything from formal wear to a burger chain outfit. Some were already hung up in the barbed wire. As we watched over the course of the day a few made it past to the low wall and from there got hung up in the razor wire. I could see where this was headed. By sheer numbers alone they were going to overwhelm the defenses. Maybe it would take a week, hell it could take a month or more. But they were going to get through.

I sat Don and Mike down and we had a serious talk about our situation. Obviously, staying in one place wasn't going to work. We were going to have to bug out, but to where? Going to the military base had its appeal. Then again I could find myself being called back up and answering to some pencil neck. No. I was well and done with that bullshit. No more following other people's orders. That would just get me killed. I told them I figured the best bet would be to go out and find a more defensible place. Maybe the dead would follow us and we could double back. It felt a damn sight better than sitting here waiting to be overrun. If they wanted they could strike out on their own. Both of them laughed and said they were sure sticking with me was the way to go.

From the jump I made it clear, if they were coming with me they were going to do what I said when I said it. No way I was gonna get killed because they didn't feel like following orders. They both told me they were so used to me telling them what to do it should be second nature. I had to laugh at that. I took them over and showed them my armory. Just a few odds and ends I picked up over the years. Some experimental weaponry from the teams that never quite made it back onto the books. They were suitably impressed. I had enough C-rations to feed a platoon for years. We decided to load the three trucks equally with food, water and munitions. I was going to make sure we made enough noise leaving to draw the dead after us. This place should be clear the next time we needed to resupply.

I had enough camo gear, mostly desert, that the boys found something in their size as well as a week's worth of changes. Never know when you get a chance to do laundry I told them. It is always good to have extra gear with you. Most of what they had packed would be useless outside the local bar and grill. The next morning we went to the front gate and drove our three trucks through. I told the boys by CB to head up to the top of the hill and wait for me. Then I parked my truck and popped out the top through the open sunroof. My truck is a converted 2500 Ram. It has a lift kit on it that sets the cab three feet off the ground which kept my windows well out of the dead's reach.

Pulling out an M16 and a few clips I started dropping the dead starting from the interior and working my way out. The more I killed the more came towards the truck. I cleaned out the property and drew the rest of the zombies to my vehicle. When I had their attention I started the truck and drove over a few shamblers that were in my way leaving a zombie conga line stretched out behind me. Our engine noise attracted every zombie within earshot to follow us.

Over the next few weeks I taught Don and Mike everything I could from my training that was still useful. Like moving as quiet as a ghost and keeping out of sight behind cover. The same tactics we were taught to avoid being spotted by surveillance cameras worked just as well for zombies. If they didn't see you and you didn't make a noise there was nothing to draw them in. We also worked on testing the zombie's limits. I found out quickly that they were extremely limited. Their big strengths were being tireless, not needing to sleep and being very strong. That and their numbers. But they were really stupid. Using a sinkhole as a test I even tricked them into walking right into it. No hesitation, just lemmings off the side of the hole.

We started out spending a lot of time scouting and securing supplies. Since I had no idea how long this would go on, or if it would ever end, I figured hedging our bets was a good idea. There were caves all over the area. Mike was a bit of a geology nut so he actually knew where quite a few of them were, even a few caverns. The dry caverns became giant store houses, some were even big enough to put ramps up to and hide vehicles. We used the smaller caves to stash supplies and gear.

I honed the guys' shooting skills, which were pretty impressive to start with, as well as their survival skills. Our raids took us to grocery stores, pharmacies, big box and sporting goods stores. We lured zombies away before killing them to avoid spreading gunk all over the place. But we still used flashlights and gloves to make sure we avoided getting infected. I told them the rule was simple. You turn and you get shot. Me included.

We upgraded our transportation to include electric motorcycles we found in a dealership outside Houston. Don helped me rig up solar panels on the trucks so we could charge the bikes whenever we weren't riding them. Portable gas tanks got filled at service stations and hidden all over so we could refuel later if the gas stations ever got heavily over run. During our down time we worked on noisemakers to help distract the dead. A favorite of mine was a simple whistle, the round cheap plastic one that made a higher scale noise the harder you blew them, attached to a gas cylinder from an air gun. I made little spring activated devices to pierce the gas tube slowly causing the whistle to get louder and louder. They were great for pulling large groups of undead away from an area and simple to make.

Within a month of being on the road the guys had hardened into soldiers. They could run for miles, dig a hole, run back to the start and barely be tired. We ate pretty well, having cached the C-rations for emergencies, from what we got out of all the stores. There were hiding places for hundreds of miles where we had secreted every-thing from ammo to candy bars. It was about this time that we no-ticed a distinct change in the area.

There were still dead all around, but there was a noticeable hu-man presence. We would come into a town we had been to before and the place would be wrecked. The signs were obvious, tons of destruction, bodies and mayhem along a fairly erratic path. Mike found the remains of a teenage girl in one town that had him on his knees puking. Hell, it was pretty damn barbaric. The things someone did to that girl went beyond torture to pure evil. I started having the guys carry side arms and M16s after that. I didn't want to run into these guys and be caught with my pants down.

It was about a week after Mike found the girl's corpse, that we ran into one of the groups. A petty little band of wannabe bad boys and girls who seemed to think that the end of the world gave them an excuse to burn what was left down. I was scouting ahead of the truck on one of the bikes when I rounded a corner and saw the roadblock. I hit the brakes, spun in a circle and sped away. But not before three bullets whizzed by my head. I stopped the bike just after the turn and radioed the boys to come quick and ready. Then I grabbed my M16 and headed back to the corner. There were five of them jumping in a jacked up Toyota truck getting ready to chase after me. I let them get up to speed and as they came around the curve I shot out their front tire.

By the time their truck stopped rolling the three that had been in the back were pancakes, but that left two in the cab. I came up slow-ly and the driver tried to shoot me. I shot him in the arm and leg and accidentally blew the passengers head off in the process. Down to one prisoner I pulled the bastard out, ignoring his cries of pain. He looked like he was in his twenties, skinny and pale, with a scraggly attempt at a beard and really bad teeth. Before I could say anything the little prick started threatening me. Telling me his gang was going to make me pay, I was already a dead man, blah blah blah.

I stepped on his leg, on top of the bullet wound, and he was suddenly too busy screaming to make threats. I held the still hot muzzle of my rifle to his lips hearing a distinctive sizzle. He whipped his head down and away so fast he almost bashed his skull in on a rock. If it wasn't so pathetic it would have been funny. Now he was crying, begging, trying to figure out a way to save his pathetic life. I humored him. I told him I wanted the details, all the details, about his gang. Before the end I knew everything from the leader's birthday to what they had for dinner last night. When he was done he looked at me with that same arrogant look he had given me when I pulled him from the truck. I think he figured I couldn't kill him since he told me what I wanted to know. What an idiot. I popped a round through his head and turned in time to see my guys roll up.

I reloaded and put the bike in the back. I wanted a bit of protection if someone took a pot shot at me and being out on the bike felt too vulnerable. We slowly drove down the road with me in the back of the truck with my head on a swivel. When we found them they seemed surprised to see us. They probably figured they had the area locked down. What a bunch of clueless fucks. I've got anger issues with people that shoot at me. It puts me in a very unforgiving mood. So I suppose that would excuse the fact that I emptied a grenade launcher into the bar they were in and the vehicles nearby. Don and Mike seemed a bit surprised by the act. Maybe they thought we were coming to talk. So once I was sure the bad guys were dead I stopped to have a necessary conversation. I explained that we couldn't let anyone like that go. I had seen their kind the world over. They were insane. To them it was better to destroy everything. You couldn't reason with them. You couldn't talk to them. They were bat shit crazy. The only way to deal with them was to put them down like the rabid dogs they were.

I could tell later that night that Mike was not on board. Don seemed to be reserving judgment but Mike looked like he had something to say. So I told him to spit it out and he obliged. He was incensed that I had acted as judge, jury and executioner and never even bothered to tell them what I was doing. Don looked worried, like he was afraid I was gonna tear the boy's head off. But he shouldn't have been concerned. I have trained a lot of green candidates in my time. His beefs were normal. I let him finished and asked him what he would have done differently.

After I shot down all of his options he got frustrated, just like I wanted him to be. Then I told him about the three bullets that went by my head. They didn't know that the scum had tried to ambush me. Once the facts were out even Mike had to grudgingly admit they had it coming. I told him part of being a good soldier was to trust your commanding officer. If this was going to work he was going to have to trust me. I let him sleep on it and the next morning he apologized. I told him to forget it and we headed out.

We ran into another group of assholes a week later. They were in the process of attacking a town that we frequented. During our wanderings we had made contact with quite a few survivors still making a go of it on their own. One such place was Sugar Flats, Texas, population 85. When the evacuation order went out most of them ignored it. They were on high ground with a deep well and decent stores. They blocked off the approaches and hid from the dead. When we happened upon them they were in need of medical supplies.

As we had more than we would ever need I traded them for some fuel. The town had a few guys that made their own bio diesel and it worked in my truck pretty well. Within a few visits I met Samantha Green, a feisty thirty year old divorcee who ran the local bar. She had no kids and her ex-husband was in Boston when things went to hell. The two of us hit it off, not in a settle down and start a family kind of way, but our nights together were still pretty damn memorable.

So I was more than a little pissed to see these jackholes trying to kill her and her neighbors. After my run in with the other gang I had upped my ordinance to an M60 mounted on the truck's roll bar. I started off by saying hello and popping off all my grenades into their vehicles. Then I mowed the survivors down with my machine gun. We stopped long enough to make sure everyone in town was all right. Samantha blew me a kiss and waved. Then the boys and I headed off to deal with the consequences of our noise.

Sure enough the dead were drawn in like fat kids to a dinner bell. So I took one of the portable CD players, a Yanni CD (god I hate that shit) and a speaker and set them up on a rock that sat eight feet out from the edge of a canyon wall. We carried an aluminum extension ladder that worked great for setting up dead traps. This one was going to be hard to beat. The dead would come right for the caterwauling Yanni and fall into the canyon without disturbing the music. For good measure we put a small solar charger on it. The thing would play for long time letting a lot of our problem zombies in the area take a fast drop off the canyon wall. Circling back around we got to high ground and watched the show. It was like having our own nature channel. Here you see the zombie in its natural habitat. Tricked by the wily hunter it falls off the edge of the cliff to wiggle and moan below. It was some funny, if macabre, shit to see.

We kept watch around the town for a few days from outside. When no zombies came and no new gangers showed up we went into town to visit. They boys took the accolades from the townsfolk and did a little trading. Samantha and I retired to the room above her bar and stayed there for three days. When I came out I felt better rested than I had in years. She was still sleeping. The boys were restless now from being in one place for too long, and we were on the road ten minutes after I came downstairs.

I set us on an irregular patrol pattern of sorts. There were areas we hadn't raided yet for supplies and we could move between them by hooking up a portable fuel tank behind a pickup. Now it is true that we may have stopped by or at least been within sight of Sugar Flats more often than we ever had before. But the boys to their credit didn't say a single word about it, though I did catch them grinning at each other from time to time.

A few weeks later we came across the bicycles. More than twenty bikes abandoned on the side of the road. Near them were the bodies of eight teenage boys, all with gunshot wounds. In front of the boys was the body of a preacher, I could see the collar. His head had been blown clean off. I stood there and felt a cold rage come over me. I'd seen this before, many times. A priest standing before men with guns, it almost always ended the same. But that was in Africa, the Middle East, barbarous places. That was when I realized that everything was really over. We were now living in uncivilized lands with uncivilized people. Don was weeping and Mike just stood there gaping like a fish. I told them to load up while I looked around. They stumbled back to the truck and sat there waiting for me.

The signs were easy to read. The bikes were riding along and vehicles came up behind them. There had been panic but no gunshots initially, at least not at anyone. None of the bodies were dragged. They had forced the boys and the priest to walk over to the ditch and then shot them there. Based on the number of bikes they had taken some prisoners with them. Checking the priest's body I found a list inside his jacket. Damn. They had been choir kids. Fuck my life. Girls. The bastards had probably taken all the girls back with them. It would have been kinder to shoot them. When I walked back to the truck something in my face caused the guys to jump out.

I told them what I knew. It wasn't in me to walk away from this and let those animals have their way. I was going after them. Alone if necessary. The boys wouldn't hear of it. We would find the gang that took these kids and make them pay if nothing else. Mike wanted to take time to bury the bodies. I told him we would worry about the living. The dead were beyond our help. Tracking a band of assholes is harder than you think when they travel by highway. We headed back the way the vehicles had come from and almost missed the trail.

Luckily, the jackasses drove for shit. There were rubber burns at almost every turn they made. Thanks for leaving such a clear trail behind you. Otherwise we might not have found you. It was dark when we found their camp. They had set up on top of a hill in an old RV park. A few RVs sat up there and I shuddered to think what they did to anyone they found there. We broke out our night vision gear and I went out to scout. The camp had a roaring bonfire in the middle that was so bright I had to take off my headset. They were drinking, acting like fools and gang raping two girls in the center of camp. I went back to my guys and sent them to side positions to flank and give cover fire, then I went straight in. The first guy that saw me had a look of absolute surprise on his face right before I blew his head off. I had selected a short barreled assault shotgun with a barrel clip. One hundred shells took an immediate toll on the gang. A few shots came from either side taking down anyone trying to get a bead on me. It was over in less than a minute.

The two girls lay dying in the middle of that camp, abused beyond my ability to save. The best I could do for them was to dose them with morphine to ease their passing. We found the rest of the them, six girls and a boy named Nabian, locked in two of the RVs. None of them had escaped unscathed but at least they were alive. They lost it when they saw the girls near the fire, even more so when I told them there was nothing I could do to save them. Hell, even before the world went to shit it would have been touch and go. Now? There was no chance for them.

I let my guys deal with them while I figured out how to transport everyone. The gang had a pickup truck that ran on diesel so I fueled it up and went back to get everyone loaded. We stripped the camp and gang of anything valuable as a matter of course. The teens looked to be in shock so I had Don drive their truck with Mike riding in the back with the kids and took Nabian with me. He didn't say anything for the first few hours. Then he asked me my name and how I found them. I told him about finding the bikes, the others. He didn't cry or yell. Just nodded and looked out the window. It was about another hour, as we were getting close to Sugar Flats that he asked me if I could show him how to protect himself. I wanted to say no, the last thing I needed was more people to be responsible for, but one look at his face and I had to say yes.

When we got to Sugar Flats the townsfolk had a house ready, Mike had radioed ahead. The kids were fed, allowed to shower, change into clean clothes and then sleep. I asked Samantha if she would watch over them while I made sure any dead that followed us were lured away. Two days later, when I got back to town, the kids were waiting for me. Nabian had told them that I was going to train them all. I thought about telling them to forget it, but again I looked at their faces. There was a need there. They had been stripped of their humanity by the gang and all of their control. It was hard for them to face a world as dark as theirs had become. I had seen it before. Everyone needed to have a purpose, to be able to see a future worth living for. These kids had nothing now. Everything they knew had been shattered. So I said yes.

I know I was probably too brusque about it, at least from the way Samantha acted as she listened, but I wasn't going to sugar coat it. The training would be hard. They might not be able to complete it. There would be no whining, no talking back and absolutely no questioning orders. It was my way or the highway and I wasn't going to waste my time with a bunch of spoiled kids who wanted to play soldier. What I taught them would get them killed. The purpose of being a soldier was to die obtaining an objective. Those of us lucky, or unlucky, enough to survive had to live with all that we had done. Samantha looked like she wanted to stab me. I guess she thought I was being needlessly callous. I was just laying it out as plainly as I could.

Each of them agreed to do exactly what I said, although I think a few of the girls thought that I might try and take liberties with them. To put them at ease, and to make sure I didn't have to deal with any unnecessary drama, I told them sex was off limits for all of them until they completed their training. When I was done training them they were free to leave and make their own decisions. Until then their asses and everything attached were mine. And there would be no sex of any kind until they were soldiers. Most of them seemed relieved. I'm sure that was the last thing they wanted to think about right now.

I pushed them hard. I made Don and Mike the sergeants. We ran until they puked, then we ran some more. They were taught to move quietly enough to sneak by zombies and humans alike. From handgun to assault rifle they were taught to strip, clean and reassemble every weapon we had. I revisited hand to hand combat, even training Don and Mike, to use with any human resistance we met in the future. Classes on tactics, camouflage, how to decoy the dead and making noise makers followed.

Nabian had a knack for making clockwork devices that while simple made a hell of a racket. His best was something called a clacker, based off a percussion instrument. Two hard blocks of wood that were thinned out would rattle together while the spring ran down. A second spring would run up while the first ran down. The end result was a simple device that could make noise for almost ten minutes with no power. And they were fairly simple to produce. By the end of our six week course the kids had gone from church choir to bad ass killers. Their graduation was a raid on a gang of violent thugs two hours away. My squad showed a lot of poise and imagination. They all killed at least one of the bangers themselves. When the smoke cleared the gang was dead and they saved two women that had yet to be abused.

One of them asked to meet me and the kids had me come down from my observation point. She introduced herself as Betty Samuels. I recognized the name as I had traded with her brother Randy on multiple occasions. When the kids saved her she had pumped them for information and they had started running their mouths. I made a mental note to add a class on shutting the fuck up to my curriculum. Their skills seemed to have made an impression on her. When she heard I was the one that trained them she wanted to thank me personally. She was nice enough but god she was a nosy broad. Wanted to know if any of the people I trained had experience, how hard it was to train them, all sorts of pushy shit. I ended up losing patience with her and handing her over to Mike. He looked like he was in love with her anyway. Or at least her ass from the way he had been staring at it.

When Mike came back the next day he was grinning like an idiot from ear to ear so I guess she liked his ass too. The kids, having graduated, decided to stay on with me as their commander. Can't say that says much about their brain power but having trained them I was willing to accept responsibility for them. Besides, more hands make light work. And I'm no spring chicken anymore. I set them up going around doing the trading and out scouting for supplies. They were pretty good at it and enjoyed the work. I decided to go fishing.

I was gone a week and, wouldn't you know it, things went to hell while I was gone. A huge group of crazy asshole came through and destroyed two of our trading partners. A hippie commune and a bunch of uptight religious folks. My new recruits came back and told Don and he got on the CB and ruined my trip. About the time I got back the assholes hit Sugar Flats and destroyed the place. I got there just in time to see it going up in flames. I went in and found tons of bodies, quite a few of them gangers. And Nabian. The crazy little man had gone through about twenty clips and killed a hell of a lot of people before he went down. Do I know how to train them or what?

The bar was the only place not engulfed in flames. They had stripped it of everything and Samantha was gone. I radioed the guys and headed to base camp, a big cavern nearby. I walked right by everyone and pulled a tarp off the Humvee in the back. I had found this baby abandoned at a cross roads, out of gas and stripped of ordinance. I had plenty to restock it with. And I had loaded it for bear. I called everyone together and laid out my plan. They grabbed sniper rifles and ammo and we headed out.

When I found the camp it looked like the gangers weren't even done setting up. That was good because I didn't want to think about them putting their filthy hands on Samantha. The squad deployed out to high ground to set up covering fire. One sniper with one watcher, both for distance and to keep an eye out for zombies. I cranked the radio and told Don to drive straight into the camp. Popping up top I got the 50 caliber ready to rock. We blew into their camp with Highway to Hell blaring out external speakers on the Hummer. The look on the faces of those psychotic assholes was priceless. Like the devil himself had come to claim them. And maybe he had.

The combat was ugly. They fired at me, my snipers took them down or I cut them in half with the 50. We finished them off with small arms fire and knives at close range. One stupid ass threw his gun down and came at me with a butterfly knife. Seriously? I was laughing at him when I took it from him and broke the blade off inside his skull. Most of them weren't dead. They were injured and I had the squad relieve them of their weapons and then scavenge everything of value from the camp. I found Samantha along with twenty other townsfolk locked in the back of a panel van. She told me that it was damn good to see me.

I had the squad take the gangs vehicles out of camp, those that were roadworthy, and once we withdrew I lit them up with my grenade launcher. The noise was horrendous. Then we loaded up and drove away. My last image of the camp was a few of them getting to their feet and trying to stumble away from the zombies approaching. I knew it wouldn't be long before they realized they were coming from every direction. Noise attracts them after all. They are going to really wish they had at least one bullet soon. For themselves.

It was about a month later when the damn horde got out of hand. It's my fault. I should have just killed the damn gangers, but I was pissed. Beyond our normal contingent of dead more kept coming. It was like a damn convention. There were too many zombies to count. They must have been walking our way from multiple cities. We spotted them coming with plenty of time but with Sugar Flats in ruins there wasn't a good place to retreat to.

That was when Mike got the call from Betty on the CB. He told her our current situation and she said she might have a solution. A day later she had Mike get me on the radio to talk to her boss, Phillip Kane. He was the leader of a refuge not too far away and Betty had been regaling him with my wonderful training program. See? The zombie apocalypse and word of mouth advertising still sells. He had a proposition for me. Full citizenship for me and all my people and in return I train his people. No more life on the road, three squares a day, hot showers. I told him I would think about it.

Later that night when I told Samantha she smacked me in the arm. Didn't I want to stop running around? Well, I suppose. Didn't I want to have a place to feel safe? Sure, who doesn't? Don't I want my son to be able to play safely with other kids? Yep, that last one threw me for a loop too. Seems that all of our nocturnal activities had some unexpected, but entirely reasonable, results. I wanted to make sure that everyone was on board for the idea so I called a meeting. I told them what was on the table, what was expected of us and asked for everyone's feedback. I guess I shouldn't have been surprised at the unanimous vote to go to the refuge.

SO I CALLED PHILLIP BACK and we worked out the terms. He balked a little at the twenty townsfolk coming with me but I sweetened the deal with some of my caches. After that it was simple logistics. Two weeks after our last conversation on the radio I was sitting in my new home in Vigilance. I had taken my first hot shower in forever and was watching a movie on television. They had a huge library to pull from. I was watching an old action flick and laughing at some of the things I had forgotten about. The people he had me set to train were more skilled than the people I was used too. And they were even more eager to learn. Samantha is happy here. She told me she feels safe when I am around but this place makes her less concerned about us having a baby. But she has been hinting about us getting married. She has no idea what she is getting herself into.

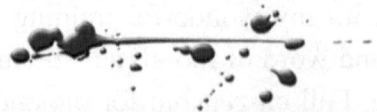

ARCHIVE JOURNAL OF DOZER PENTAL, first Sgt of Vigilance Training Corp.

Michael Patterson

ALRIGHT. LET ME GET ONE thing out of the way right out of the chute. I know I'm a god damn monster. I could sit here and blame the end of the world for becoming a world class prick but that would be a lie. I was already a full grown fiend when the zombie mob invaded. When they showed up things became a lot easier. No more cops looking for me, no more feds setting up electronic surveillance. Law and order was one of the first things to disintegrate when good old Shambling Sam came calling. What do you care if I steal your food if there is a zombie trying to eat you? It really puts things in perspective.

As for a name? What does it matter? I was born Michael Patterson but I've had more names than most people have hairs on their head. The system once had a file a mile long on me with each of my alias carefully notated under the heading A.K.A. Not that I have to worry about that stupid file anymore. The bullshit we called civilization fell in less time than it takes to build a house. No more assholes telling me what to do. No more worrying about carrying fake id's, using false names and hiding out in out of the way locations. No more hiding. I got to say I like being about to be out in the open. My current name is Cameron Braseon. I'm thirty years old, and I'm the bad man that most people warned their kids about.

By the time I turned ten, I was a master thief. When you grow up on the streets in a society that either wants to brainwash you or ignore you, learning quick is a necessity. I was eleven when I first killed. Jimmy Travers, a big asshole that loved to shake down the street kids. He was a piece of shit beat cop and loved taking what little we had. I stabbed him through the eye with a sharpened bit of rebar. It took him about five minutes to die. I held my hand over his mouth to keep him quiet until he shut up. Then I dumped his body down in the sewers. By the day of my thirteenth birthday I was running a mob of kids, had killed almost a hundred people and owned an entire block in Milwaukee.

In addition, I had a warren of old bootlegger tunnels that had been sealed up. I had stumbled upon them when I was young and used them from time to time to hide hot merchandise. When I could afford it, I fixed them up and had my own secret travel paths through the city. A few of the tunnels led into buildings that were now high end stores. Those places drove themselves crazy trying to figure out how stuff was going missing. Some of them even added more employees during the day, absolutely sure that people were shoplifting the stuff. Little did they know there were secret doors inside the storerooms. I shopped after hours to my heart's content, totally bypassing all their security and cameras.

By the time I could legally drink, I had my fingers in a lot of lucrative pies. Drugs, gambling, kidnapping, extortion, slavery, and I had killed more people than I would ever be able to count. I had tortured over a thousand people. I burned entire families, including the children, inside their homes. Cops, priests, judges, anyone that got in my way. A lot of people told me I had no conscience. I usually told them to fuck off, and then shot them in the face.

It was a few months shy of my twenty second birthday when the zombies showed up. By the time my birthday came around, most of the people I knew were dead. Or were shambling dead. As the world burned down, I used my people without mercy. Tricks, threats and outright lies got me everything I needed. I had most of the suckers around convinced that I had a sweet sanctuary lined up. This con was one of my best. I started a rumor using an honest citizen who didn't know me. I let him overhear me talking on my cell phone. He heard me say that there was a high end, really safe, refuge to the south. You had to buy your way in with supplies.

What an idiot. Not only did he bite, he ended up recruiting thirty of his friends. They then told the 'secret' to their closest friends who told others, and so on and so on. Pretty soon my secret was one of the hottest tickets in town. Even a local rapper tried to buy his way in. To me, it didn't matter who you were or what your sob story was. If you had supplies I happily took them, then you got a "map" to the refuge. I warned each sucker to keep the map hidden and destroy it rather than letting anyone take it. The more I lied my ass off the more they ate it up.

By the time the city was overrun I had my tunnels stuffed with supplies. I kept a light crew with me, all unattached and loyal people. I used every trick in the book against the other survivors in town. I traded a fake vaccine to three different groups and then sabotaged their defenses to let the dead in. A few survivors spread the word that I was not to be trusted but by then I had already claimed most of the city. What can I say? Lying is like breathing…and just as useful.

I managed to keep the wheels on the bus for almost five years. The entire time I kept a few of the smuggler tunnels secret. Here I kept my personal stash. It never hurts to hold some stuff back for a rainy day. And pretty soon it was pouring. One of my lieutenants, a smart fellow named James, got the idea to take over the gang. He gave this speech about how we were the last survivors of humanity, we needed to band together and nobody should be tricked or used. Etc, etc, etc. I shot out both his kneecaps. Sadly, I underestimated how much his bullshit had inspired the troops.

They tried to kill me. So I decided to kill them right back. I slipped into one of my secret tunnels and pushed the button. Not nearly as impressive as the nuke button they had in the old days. Still, it did the job. See this button was attached to some explosives that I placed near the main tunnel entrance. When I blew it every zombie for miles came shambling. They massacred my old crew. Serves them right. No one fucking crosses me.

I decided about a year later, when my remaining supplies were running low, that I should bug out. The radio had gone silent a long time ago so I had no idea if there were even any safe zones left. All I did know for certain was that the winters were getting way too cold, I was running out of heating oil and food was getting scarce. Also, as one of the only living people left in Milwaukee every time I went outside the zombies went crazy. After a bit of searching I found the perfect vehicle, an old hybrid SUV. It had the cargo space I needed for supplies and I was able to modify it so zombies wouldn't be a problem. But if you call me a soccer mom I will shoot your balls off.

When I was loaded up, I decided to set a little fire. All the remaining fuel oil got spread across a few buildings and I lit it up. One building was a cop shop. It went up like a tinderbox. They normally depended on sprinkler systems to keep fires down. Too bad there is no water pressure. When the building went the ammo inside went off and the noise drew all the dead away from my escape route. Still, getting out of the city was a serious fucking nightmare, even with my preparations.

I almost bit it at one of the bridges. Damn zombies are everywhere. After one of them almost grabbed me I decided I would waste the gas driving around until I found a good route. I slept in the truck and in the morning I had to nudge zombies with the bumper to keep moving. I ran over a few that were too slow to move out of the way. Who gives a crap? They are already dead. Am I going to kill them twice?

Traveling was annoying. Vehicles left blocking the road, zombies shambling all over the place. It made it hard as hell to scavenge along the way. I was starting to question my decision in leaving the north when the first winter storm hit. It was cold. Damn cold. I quit screwing around looking for useful things and headed due south until my balls were no longer in danger of falling off.

THE SOUTH SUCKS. I'VE NEVER liked it. Winter is still cold, just not freezing. The summers are hot and dry as hell. And the zombies are free range. Damn things were everywhere. Anytime I stop at a gas station to refuel I have to deal with their bullshit. I have been stealing gas since I could walk. So tricking some stupid shamblers away so I could siphon it from the powerless stations? Way easier than watching out for cops or cameras. Getting gas is annoying without power but far from impossible.

Living folks are scarce, but I do run into them from time to time. Trading caravans, rolling whorehouses, psychotic gangs, you know, the usual. The second week down in what used to be Oklahoma I ran into The Knights. These guys were a fucking trip. All dressed in white, they surrounded me and asked me my business. I eased my .38 out of its place on the seat next to me and told them I was just passing through. This big guy stepped out where I could see him and said he was Sir Galvain Zombieslayer. The rifle on his back led me to believe he was dangerous. The fact that he was acting like an insane D&D player reinforced that. So I shot him in the face and blew out of there.

Those assholes followed me for two days. Then I ran into what looked like rejects for an S&M movie. All leather and metal studs. I kept driving and listened to the gunshots as the Knights and new gang tore into each other. That racket attracted every zombie that could hear it while I headed due south. What shamblers I saw I avoided and kept moving. When I hit the ocean I had to stop for a minute to admire it. So I could see what everyone made such a fuss over. It was beautiful . . . until the first zombie came stumbling out of the surf. I started the truck and decided to head west.

I was in the middle of nowhere when something blew up. The SUV flipped and I blacked out. The next thing I knew I was hanging upside down and it was really dark. Somewhere below me I heard a moaning that I recognized. Zombies. I heard this asshole start talking a little while after I opened my eyes. What I caught of his speech was not encouraging. The entertainment for the night was about to start. Unfortunately, I was going to be part of it.

Do you know what the greatest thing is about never relaxing and going soft is? You never get soft. So while I was tied by the feet, and I was upside down, I was in no way helpless. Whipping my head up I pulled myself up in a gut wrenching sit up and grasped the rope. Before anyone could recover I went hand over hand until I felt the metal beam they had the rope over. Grabbing hold of the beam I flipped onto it and slipped the rope off my feet. I heard the asshole yelling at someone to cut the rope and a second later it suddenly slithered over the beam and fell into the dark.

As the rope hit below the dead went crazy and there was a light that flipped on below, aimed down into a pit swarming with zombies. The area the glow revealed looked like a rough arena. A bunch of leather clad men and women were cheering as they craned their necks to try and catch a glimpse of me in the pit below. Too bad for them I was on the high ground. By the time they figured out that I wasn't in the hole I was out of the room.

The morons were in an old barn with one exit. I blocked the door once I was outside. Then I used my lighter to set the dry grass on fire. The structure went up quick. It started so fast that I didn't get a chance to scrounge through their supplies. Instead I had to jump in the truck with the most gas and roar away. There was no way that the dead would ignore the bonfire I had lit.

With my adrenaline wearing off my injuries from the SUV crash were making themselves known. My ribs were killing me. I was bleeding out of my left ear and I was having trouble focusing on the road. I knew that I was hurt bad, I needed a place to rest up. If I hadn't burned the barn down it would have been perfect. I'm used to the dead moaning nearby. Less than an hour later I turned off the main road, running down a mailbox. It was the mailbox that had caught my weary eye. It was high end, almost a grand worth of iron and steel. Whoever had that mailbox would have a hell of a house.

Three miles later, I almost missed the turn, I would have if I had not been looking for it. The drive was hidden by rocks and I had to slide the truck sideways to make it. When I got up to the house I was impressed. Adobe style with high windows and three big doors set evenly around the house. It was almost three thousand square feet and was set up high on a hill.

I pulled up to the front and pounded on the door. When no one answered I tried the knob and found it locked. That could be good or bad. I looked around the front door and found the hide-a-key in no time. Fake rocks look a lot different from real ones. Once inside I made sure no one was home. One of the garage stalls was empty and the house itself was vacant. Going back out to the truck I hid it in some big rocks away from the house. The jeep in the garage had keys in the ignition so I figured it wouldn't hurt to have a backup vehicle stashed.

The kitchen had a bunch of canned and dry food and a hand pump for water. I used it to drink my fill and get cleaned up. Then I found a good room, barricaded myself in, and crashed. When I woke up I was parched. My head was killing me and I went looking for some pain killer. I was surprised to find a really well stocked medicine cabinet. After some more water and five painkillers I went back to bed.

I stayed in the house for three weeks. When I was healed up I started scouting the area. The remnants of the gang that had me were holed up in a farm house up on a hill near the barn I burned out. I decided that the rest of them needed to die. No one fucks with me. No one.

Sneaking back before dawn I saw they had three sentries. I ran one down with the truck. The two others came to check on him and got knifed. The house wasn't well guarded. There were seventeen people sleeping in there, with lights on. Not only could I see them sleeping there, anyone that goes past can see the glow of their windows. I suppose they thought they were the worst thing nearby. Surprise! I poured gas on each of the doors and windows making pools on the ground in front of them. Then I lit that bitch up.

Two people tried to jump out of the place from one of the ground floor windows. I shot both of them before they could get out and that seemed to make everyone else pause. But if you pause in a fire, you die. And they did. When I finally drove away there were zombies all over headed towards the new bonfire. Good hunting shamblers. I doubt you are going to get fed.

I headed back towards my new house, but wrecked just before the turn off of the road. Some asshole had left a car sideways in the middle of the street. I mean, who does that? Inconsiderate pricks! So here I am, in the fucking desert, hurting like hell, again. How many damn car accidents can one man have? Seriously? And the noise of the wreck attracts a bunch of shambling opportunists. I managed to keep ahead of them, but I swore the whole way that I would kill the bastard that parked in the road if I ever found him.

There was a beat up old Jetta sitting on the side of the road with the keys in the ignition. Once I was sure it was empty and looked clean I climbed in. The tank was half full. What in the hell? Well, thanks to whatever idiot left me a ride. Because of it I got back to the house. The pain started to get better, but that wasn't a good thing. I checked the mirror and I show all the signs of joining the shambalmba ding dongs. Fuck my life. Or my soon to be unlife. I could do the responsible thing and eat a bullet. Or carefully clean the house and walk out into the desert. Nope. That isn't me. I walked around the house spitting everywhere. I cut my hand and flung blood over everything. Then I went out to the garage and smeared blood all over the base of the car seat and filled the tank with the remaining gas from the cans.

If you are reading this and you have been driving the car? Fuck you. Serves you right for surviving me you useless fuck. If you somehow managed to avoid getting infected and are reading my book anyway? Fuck you blind. I hope you get sack or tit cancer and die slow. Or better yet die from one of your loved ones biting out your fucking throat.

I deserved to live and this is a crock of shit. If I could figure out a way to do it I would burn this fucking world down before I go out. Launch all the nukes, whatever. Instead I'm going to leave a bio booby trap for the next fucker to come along. I hope I infected you and you are reading this and cursing my name. My fucking head hurts. How about yours? The infection spread yet? Are you feeling sleepy? I am. Time to finish this up and hit the road. I am taking the truck and driving away as far as I can. If I can get far enough away my trap should work. As for my last words? Fuck you.

BOOK FOUND BY HUNTER TALIEN. Safesuit not compromised. Book decontaminated and taken to Archive. House burned. Hunter's rule #72 instigated for checking for bio hazard booby traps..

Johnnie Ringo

MY NAME IS JOHNNIE RINGO. Well, that isn't my real name. I was born Hector Richardson, but that name was lame. So I changed it to Johnnie Ringo, even did it legally when I was older. I was born to be a con man. My mom was a hooker and my dad was a pimp. It was totally out of character for pops to get all sentimental but when mom got preggers he put her up in a little apartment. Sure, once she had me he put her on the street again working. But he made sure I was taken care of. And when I got old enough he made sure I actually got to school. Who knows what would have happened if he hadn't gotten knifed by another pimp? I might even have had a somewhat legit life. After he bought it mom got out of the business and started working as a secretary. This from what I hear was just her trading many johns for one john that wanted her to type the rest of the time. Whatever.

Life sucks and if you got no one watching your back, you watch your own. When the daylight starts to fade, the only one that is going to fight off the monster under your bed is you. When I got scared, I started sleeping with a knife under my pillow. These days it is a solid 9MM I call Betty. Whatever gets you through the night. You know what I mean? By the time I hit high school I could have started pimping like my old man, but that wasn't my thing. I had more bitches riding my jock than I could handle most days. The good girls were the best. They all wanted to break a piece off the bad boy. It was way too easy to get them to give me money or clothes, hell one chick even bought me a car.

After graduation when all the brainiacs headed off to college I was already working at my full time job. Conning the old folks out of their money and stealing identities full time. Then some damn old coot went running to his son who also happened to be a cop and I ended up getting pinched. They couldn't pin much on me but I still got a year. That ended up being the best year of my life. I met Victor Michiko, an eastern European mafia boss. He was building an old school mafia. Fear and retribution were the cornerstones of his sales pitch. But he wanted a young guy with style to help soften the image a bit. For the next twelve months he had his guys show me how to fight. They also taught me their secret language, an obscure dialect of Russian that was hard for the cops to understand.

When I got out, I met up with some associates of his that took up the next chapter in my training. Guns. I had no idea how much there was to learn about guns. Not just shooting. But cleaning, loading, stripping them down and putting them back together. They even showed me how to cast my own bullets and reload my own brass. Victor believed it was better to reuse brass and reload it. Harder to trace them that way for ballistics. In return, I taught them how to schmooze like a mofo. The end result was a collection of charming guys that could go to any club or restaurant. I clothed the wolves in sheep's clothing. Then they took the whole damn herd. Within a few years they had a tight grip on organized crime in most major US cities.

Fast forward to just past my thirtieth birthday. Victor and I went to Vegas for a meeting with the heads of the different cities. There was a lot of fear going around with rumors of zombies out east and Victor wanted his intel first hand. Be careful what you wish for. We were only there for about ten minutes when one of the guys excused himself to go to the bathroom. Fifteen minutes later someone went to check on him and got his throat ripped out. By the time we put him down half the room was splattered with zombie goo. Victor and I bolted. He told me to head to the mountains and he headed to the airport to board his private plane. He was going back to Portland to get his wife and kids. From what we could figure someone on the plane was infected, maybe even Victor. It went down in the mountains after the pilot reported that one of the passengers had gone crazy.

I ended up in Victor's place in the mountains with thirty guys and their families. We were pretty well set and as the second in command I should have been in charge after Victor died. I might have been if the world hadn't come to an end. One of the guys decided to make a play and had a few of the others on his side. I ended up driving away with a full tank of gas and an empty 9MM. The three that tried to take me weren't going to do anything like that ever again, but I missed the ringleader. And I couldn't be sure who it was. No way was I going to sleep in that house with someone looking to ice me. The first chance I got, I stopped and bought more bullets. The store was pretty low on ammo so I bought what they had. Then I bought all the gunpowder and primers they had and all the stuff I needed to reload my own brass. Threw it all in the trunk and headed for my safe house. With the roads in the condition they were in, namely full of abandoned cars and undead, it would be a week of hell to get there.

Near Wheeler Peak in New Mexico I had bought this great place. Built into the side of a hill it had a spectacular view. It was self-contained with solar power, a deep well and two lifetimes worth of supplies. As I figured it would be, there was a bit of a hassle on the way there. I was forced to shoot about twelve people including two cops. In the end, I got where I was going, parked my car in the garage and went to bed. Imagine my surprise when I woke up with a shotgun being pointed at my head. The lady holding it seemed a bit nervous so I gave her my best scared act.

"Hey lady . . . just calm down okay? Whatever you want, it's yours."

She stared at me pale and shaking. "Look man, I don't want to hurt you. I've been on the road and I saw the light from your window. I jogged up the hills to get here. There are fricking zombies out in the desert. Not a lot, but enough."

I realized looking at her that she looked a lot like that prick Micky Vinto did before he went off to the bathroom. Pale with a red ring around her mouth and eyes. I smiled at her and nodded.

"Sure, hey I get that. We should be safe up here though right? I heard on T.V. that they can't climb, yeah? So they can't follow you up the hills, right?" She seemed to relax a bit. I stared over her left shoulder and let my eyes widen in fear. Just like the sucker I thought she was she turned to look. Leaping out of bed I threw myself back against the wall and raised the blanket to shield myself as I emptied the clip into her head. Her brains flew out and coated the wall to the bedroom. I slid out of the room and closed the door making sure to stay clear of any splatter. I quickly checked the house and then doused the light. It was stupid of me to leave it on but old habits die hard. In this new world old habits can get you killed pretty damn quickly. The next day I went outside and covered the windows with brush. Then I did the same thing to anything that might reflect light. I didn't want anyone coming this way day or night. I spray painted the windows black on the outside, leaving a few squares to see out of that I taped cardboard over.

It took two days to do it, but I hid the driveway and entrance down near the road. A couple of boulders rolled down the hill and some smaller stones scattered around and it looked just like the surrounding landscape. An hour after I finished a van came creeping down the highway. Whoever it was drove pretty slow and wove all over the road. I saw them turn off a half mile down and go up to my closest neighbor's house. I heard shots a short time after that. About an hour or so later I saw the van drive away. I waited a bit and then took a quick jaunt over there. The terrain around here is hilly enough that I wasn't worried about the zombies. I was much more concerned that someone might drive by and see me.

The scene in the house down the way was brutal. Shotgun blasts at close range to the husband. The wife and daughter had their throats cut and now I understood why the van hadn't left for an hour.

Sick bastards whoever they were. They had taken their time with the women before they finally killed them. What a waste. Other than the bloody front room and the kitchen being emptied of food the house looked mostly undisturbed. I hoofed it back to my place trying to make sure I wasn't leaving a trail. Over the next few weeks I placed traps around the property and loaded all the brass I had. This new life I was leading made me suspect I was going to need all the ammo I had soon.

Being near the road had been a selling point when I bought this place. Now it was a huge drawback. I found myself thinking about one of the other properties I had looked at around the same time. It was an old army bunker built at the edge of an abandoned military base. The base itself was dust and rust by this time, it had been abandoned in the 1950's. But the bunker had been built to last. Some guy bought it and converted it into a sweet pad. I remember thinking they would have to hold out for a kook who wanted to live in the boonies. Who knew, right?

Since I knew where it was I headed out that way. I went overland until I got to another road. Cutting over I found a for sale sign still stuck into the dirt near the entrance road. It was masked behind a tumbleweed. I pulled the sign and headed cautiously up to the old base. The shelter itself was inside an old fence, something built of iron rods welded together. The fence was rusted but when I kicked it the metal was solid. The gate had no chain so I went through, closing it behind me. Near the entrance to the bunker was a large area for parking vehicles. The ground dipped so that even a semi would have been hard to spot from outside the fence.

Parking my jeep I headed over to the cement stairs leading down to the entryway. The door was a massive metal relic from the cold war. When the realtor had opened it for me he had been sure to point out it was a foot thick. Now I found myself wracking my brain to see if I could remember how to get in. The door didn't have a lock on it. Instead there was a keypad that you had to enter a code on. At first I couldn't remember the code. I was drawing a flat blank. I knew I had watched the realtor put it in, more out of larcenous habit than really giving a crap at the time. It took me ten minutes to remember it. I clicked the numbers 9, 8, 7, 4, 5, 2 and the door clicked. Sliding open on heavily greased rails it slid into the wall. I whistled in appreciation once I was inside. The place was just as slick as I remembered.

Twelve bedrooms, four living rooms, thirteen bathrooms, a bar, a library, a few huge store rooms and tons of corridors. You could jog around this place it was so big. That had been another negative at the time. Big places are for lots of people and they are a pain to clean. Now though? This place was an awesome back up pad. There was a hardened conduit that ran up to a rock shelf full of solar panels. Power, water and security. What more could you ask for during the Zombie Invasion. And the best part was that it was free. Over the next few weeks I will split my supplies between the two places, making sure to mask my trail. Once I am finished setting up the second place, I will go out and explore.

FOR BEING IN A REMOTE desert area, there are zombies freaking everywhere. Slow, stumbling, dead folks. Everyone that you could imagine in life was there in death. A housewife, kids, business people, a fry cook. Hell, I even saw a guy in full clown gear. That certainly upped the creepy factor. For the last month I have been criss-crossing the area. When I got back to civilization I was amazed at how many of the shambling pricks there were. There hasn't been much on the radio. Two religious zealots talking out there ass and an automated recording with information on the emergency. Zombies 101.

Don't let them bite you. No shit Sherlock. Don't let them touch you. Again, no shit Sherlock. Their body fluid is infectious. Anyone infected would turn within ten hours. That was a good bit of advice. I had suspected as much but it was nice to have confirmation. There was a list of refuges and then the recording started over again. I plugged my phone into the outlet and started blasting Vivaldi. Screw the Apocalypse. I need some beauty to counter all this ugliness.

The good news is that not everyone became a zombie. Good fucking thing too because my ass would have been whacked a long time ago. My first week out I saw mounds of inert corpses, especially in the urban areas. Most looked like they got shot and stacked. I didn't stay around to find out by who. The bad news is there are still plenty of shambling dead walking around as well. More than I could understand until I found the jammed interstate twenty miles over. There are also a few small groups of people hunkered together for protection as well as a few large refuges nearby. Once I had the lay of the land, I decided it was time to start being proactive.

I had discovered a big box store, one of those trough stores where the lazy can get their jumbo bag of cookies and a big screen television, while I was wandering around. I figured grabbing up the electronics might be worth the risk. Plus there was food and water out the ass in there. Even though the parking lot was hopping with zombies, it didn't look like they had gotten inside. The metal gates were down in front of the windows. Weighing risk vs reward I decided it was worth checking out. Part of my arsenal in the house was a large supply of silencers. This made it a lot easier to quietly smoke the shamblers. Sure I attracted some nearby zombie looky loos. Silencers aren't exactly silent. But I took them out and proceeded to the store.

Around back, I found what I was looking for, the loading dock. The store and the trucks parked there were locked up tight. Back in the day this place would have been kept secure by cameras and alarms. That explains why they had a crappy lock that I bypassed in about two seconds. Inside, I took it slow. The sun was bright outside and this store had been built to take advantage of natural light. Still, I didn't want to get surprised. By a zombie or squatters who got here before me. So I made some noise and waited. Nothing. I went out of the loading dock area into the store proper and did the same thing. Not a thing. When I felt relatively safe, when most people would have called an all clear? I did a complete search of the place. I found a dead guy in one of the upstairs offices. Looks like he blew his brains out. I stayed outside that room, just in case.

The keys to the trucks were nowhere to be found. They were probably in the office with the dead guy. Fuck that. I am not taking the chance of getting infected for some keys. Still, it would have made moving stuff so much easier. I hitched up a huge trailer that I found in the stores back lot. By the time I was done I had boatloads of supplies. Food, toiletries, towels, blankets, video game players and discs, movie players and discs. I am in this for the long haul after all. I shuttled stuff back to the mostly empty bunker house, filling it from floor to ceiling. I set up one of the bedrooms and the kitchen but everything else was pure storage. Now I am going to take some time and hide my tracks. Just in case. This is shaping up to be a pretty good apocalypse.

OVER THE LAST FEW MONTHS I have been like a fat kid in a candy store. I'm the robber baron of the desert. I've cleared out the big box store, a strip mall, a few gun shops, survivalist stores, liquor stores, porn shops. You name it, I took it. Granted, it isn't like the old days with the cops trying to pinch me. But the zombies provided their own brand of danger. Even having to dodge the shamblers it didn't take me long to stuff both my house by the road and the bunker. I was out looking for a third stash house when it happened. I ran into Benson's Marauders. I know right? That's going to strike fear into your heart. Oh! Look out! Here comes Benson! They were just a two bit gang of idiots who thought writing a name on some jackets made them tough. Are you kidding me? Why not the Jackals? Or the Dragons? No, you decide to go with Benson's Marauders? What a fucking joke.

The little bastards tried to ambush me. They about got me too. I'd been getting a little soft, so it was good we ran into each other. I hadn't killed a living soul in a long time. During our little dust up I reaped about thirty of them. Once the survivors had high tailed it out of there, I collected my brass and then rolled the corpses for anything of value. Turned out they had a lot of guns and ammo for my collection. Almost as an afterthought, I decided to follow the survivors back to their base. What a bunch of amateurs. They were holed up on the second floor of an old building in a small town nearby.

I watched them for part of a day and saw there weren't many of them left. I headed back to my house by the road and spent the night sorting through their gear. It was lame. These guys were going to ruin their guns. They obviously had no idea how to clean them properly. The next morning I came to a decision. That building was of no value to me, but I was getting lonely. It would be nice to have a few women around to keep me company. And hey, I could really provide for a chick, you dig?

I went back to their shit hole the next day and made contact. Turns out I had killed all but two of the guys during the ambush. Those two had died of their injuries. So here were eight ladies looking for a guy to take care of them. That's when the lessons my old man taught me came flooding back. The smooth bastard had drummed the lessons in, even if he hadn't actually been trying to teach me. I was a bright kid that kept his eyes open and his mouth shut. And I had learned more than enough to do the old man proud.

There was profit in the women before me. There had to be other mercenary groups around, probably run better than this. They would have things of value to trade for services rendered. Granted, it wasn't like I was hurting right now. But it was always good to plan for the future, right?

I took it slow. The one thing pop always said was that you had to sweet talk them at first, get them dependent on you. So I was sympathetic. They were low on supplies so I brought them some great food. They ate better than they had in months. Next, I brought them some nice clothes. Not really functional but pretty. They loved that shit. Then I gave them a movie player and a few disks along with a solar charger to run it. They ate that shit up. Finally, I hooked up power so they could have hot showers, lights and warm meals. I schooled them on covering the windows to keep from attracting zombies and people at night.

When they were good and dependent on me, I announced that I was leaving. They practically begged me on their knees not to go. I was all like, hey this stuff doesn't come from a vacuum. I helped you out now you gotta get by on your own. I really played up the injured victim part. Made them feel like they had really been taking advantage of me. Then once I had the hook sunk deep, I offered them another option.

They were women, and pretty. There were people out there, men mostly, that would trade things we needed for services they could provide. It was a pretty simple transaction. They could stay there and fend for themselves. Or they could come under my wing and I would protect them and provide for them. In return I got all the shit they got for their services. To administer for the group at large, of course. In short, I became their pimp. They became my hoes. Naturally, we spent a few weeks with me sampling their wares and instructing them on how to improve. As a movie once said? It's good to be the king. I decided it was too dangerous to bring people back to the building. Instead we would have to make a circuit to get what we needed.

So began the Traveling Ho House. I retrofitted a few RV's that had been left in the area to run on electricity. Not hard to do when you have so many cars to pull from. The end results were ugly but functional. They had solar panels and batteries on top of them and three bedrooms each inside. There was a spot for a driver and three girls. I figured a girl could drive each of them and could use the cab area to entertain a john. Some guys even get off on that.

We hit the road and every time we stopped I made sure to find a suitable vehicle and prep it. Just in case I needed to ditch the girls and make my own retreat. Business is business but survival is golden. Things were a bit dicey in the beginning. Folks were skittish of newcomers. Most of the mercs would have been happy to kill me, rape the girls and then kill them. So I had to make contact on my own. The solution I came up with was simple but effective. I had hundreds of solar rechargeable walkie talkies I picked up at the big box store. They had few miles of range and were pretty durable. When I got to a camp I would throw one over the wall to where it would be found. Then I retreated to a safe spot and called them up.

My pitch was clear. I was a pimp, did they want to use my hoes? Fair trade, girls were clean, no infection. We would stop outside the town and sit for ten hours. They could prep a spot that would keep zombies from being able to approach. The RV's would back in and we would wait. The next day, we would start entertaining customers. This would go on for as long as we wanted to stay or as long as they had stuff to trade. Then we would move on. Damaging my girls would result in compensation or a penalty. Trying to keep us from leaving? A penalty. When asked what that would be I mentioned I had all the RV's wired to explode. And that the detonation didn't require my being alive. There was also a few rocket propelled grenades that they could count on being launched at their walls before I took off if they tried to dick me around.

Like I said, negotiations and first contact was dicey. I had a 9MM on my hip for the first few visits and every visit after that. My message was clear. You fuck with me and you die. Your whole family dies. I built our reputation during the second circuit. By that time people had started to believe that I was all talk. I blame my bitches acting like what I said wasn't a big deal. So some over puffed punk named Frank Bates decided he was going to take me down. He tried killing me in my sleep. Really? Like I have slept soundly since I was ten. I caught him and his guys before they even got in the RV. Dead.

All of them. Shot Frank in the crotch and let him bleed out. Then I had my women fire up the RV's and we took off. Once we were outside of town I stopped and got out. I told the girls to drive straight back to base. If they weren't there when I got back, they could fuck off and fend for themselves. Then I went back and took care of business.

Last time through, I had found a kick ass all-terrain vehicle. It was solar powered but was missing the keys. I did a little research in a remote dealership and found out they had a backup key in the owner's manual. When I checked, there it was. So I had set this up as a getaway car, just in case. Now it was going to help me get away, after I settled a score. Taking the ordinance I had with me I tossed it in the back seat and drove back to the outpost of the now deceased Frank Bates.

The place was in chaos, as I expected it would be. The gunshots, unsilenced and loud as hell, had drawn every zombie in the area. They were trying to silence the place up so the dead would wander away when I came back. Activating the sliding sunroof, I waited for it to retract and then popped up. In less than sixty seconds I shot six rocket propelled grenades into the outpost. I made holes on three different sides. The dead just poured in. So much for that place ever screwing with me again.

I turned around and caught up to the RV's pretty quickly. I radioed them to follow me and we got back to our base camp in no time. Then I disciplined them for running their mouths. For two days I made sure they knew who the fuck was in charge. Then we took a few weeks for them to heal up and show me how sorry they were. When we hit the road again they knew to keep their lips zipped unless their mouth was in use. The circuit had stood up and taken notice of what I had done. Survivors spread the word pretty damn fast. You screw with Johnnie Ringo? You gonna die.

Respect came flowing out like rain from the sky. I was a serious player and a dangerous man. Beyond the hoes I started procuring things for people. Hard to find things. Hell, most of them were sitting under dust in one of my stashes. But I never let on. It was always, hey that is some hard to find shit it is gonna cost you. They always paid five times more than they needed to. Not because I needed it, but you get respect in many ways.

The nice thing about traveling? There aren't a lot of people that do it. Those that did, the bandits and the like, gave me a pass. Either because they wanted my hoes to keep coming back or because they were worried about me being out for blood crazy. Either way, I got to places no one else could. So it was pretty easy for me to find out of the way buildings, houses and warehouses to use as stashes. I used my bitches as laborers. Had them ride locked in the back of the panel trucks I used to haul stuff so they never knew where the stashes were. Also, made them less likely to try and rat me out because they knew I would let the truck go over a cliff before I let anyone hijack it. I would get away and they would take a ride to the bottom.

Encouraging loyalty by not giving a choice has always been my favorite method. Within a few months of starting my traveling business we had more stashes than I could count. I had to actually keep a ledger, written in a certain obscure Russian dialect (thank you Victor). Between trading the girl's wares and scavenging along our travels I was constantly adding to my trove. I became known quickly as the go to guy for what you needed.

I expanded from prostitution and black market items to guns manufacturing when I located a machine shop out in the desert. It was set pretty far out, but it had a water well and I put in solar power. Then I put ten young guys out there with an old grizzled machinist. This guy was mean and ornery but he knew his shit. I showed him how to make silencers and he not only started making them, he improved the design. There weren't any vehicles out there and they were pretty far from anywhere, exactly why I picked the spot. Isolation kept them protected, elevation kept the dead away, and lack of transportation kept them trapped there.

The old coot taught the young guys how to make the silencers. I brought them raw materials, food and let them have time with the girls whenever I visited, if they made their quota. Missing quota meant no girls for you. Missing it by a lot happened once. You got a beat down that focused on your torso (can't hurt the hands) and told if it happened again you would be replaced. There was no retirement plan. There were a few replacements but for the most part they stuck with the program. After a time it was less from fear and more from wanting time with the girls. The ladies are very, very skilled at what they do.

From silencers, we went on to modifying guns to shoot better ammo, quieter ammo. When people saw my manufacturing capabilities I got requests for other shit. Valves, all manner of brackets, braces and locks. What I couldn't find by scavenging I was able to get the boys to make. By this time I had fifty RV's with a veteran ho in charge of each one. They had a quota to make and were fiercely loyal to me. This was because their children, and each had a few, were living in an undisclosed location with a few older women who were no longer attractive enough to be hoes. You screw with me and your kid gets fed to the zombies. Since I initiated the program I have had one hundred percent loyalty from my girls. Dad always said fear keeps a bitch in line.

Each girl gets trained in other things besides their main trade. How to repair the RV's is first. Salvaging parts and doing repairs leads to other salvaging. The second floor of the building I had found my first women in has become a way point for gear. I spend all my time shuttling things back and forth from there to my stashes. Either stuff waiting to be delivered by a group of girls or something they had acquired. Things were sweet. I had more wealth and power than anyone in the world as far as I figured. Then everything went to hell. All because of one fucking bitch.

That is how I came to be in my current predicament. Here I am, on the second floor of the building that I found my first girls in (I still don't know this stupid town's name) trapped like a rat. Alone and bleeding from a few well-placed bullet wounds. I think there is a good chance that I'm going to die here. I got a little cocky I guess.

Started thinking I was untouchable. This puts me in good company. Bonnie and Clyde. Hoffa, Al Capone. All of us got too big for our britches and got out ticket punched. Still, I haven't done too badly for being the son of a pimp and a whore.

The traveling show was celebrating its second decade in business when I came across the girl. Blond hair, long legs, deep green eyes and her body. Good lord. I haven't seen a body that hard in a long time. I decided I was going to have her. And I did for about a month. She put up a hell of a fight. Told me I would be sorry, but I didn't care. I just beat her until she seemed to give up. Then I took her in every way imaginable. Then I gave her to a few of my guys that had done a bang up job and they used her for a week. When she came back to me I had her cleaned up and gave her all the normal gifts, treated her really good. She seemed to come around, like they all did.

For the next week we had a great time, she was obedient, even enthusiastic in bed. At the end of the week I got bored with her and sent her to one of the RV's to replace a girl that was retiring to the kid farm. What an idiot I was. When I met her she had some impressive gear on. Told me she was a hunter, like that was supposed to mean something to me. She was wearing a bow and arrow as well as an impressive air gun. I didn't give her a chance to use either. I lulled her into a false sense of security and took her down.

When she woke up naked and locked in a cell she didn't react like I expected her too. Being naked didn't seem to bother her. She calmly tried to talk her way out. Even when she knew that she was screwed she didn't panic. Instead she fought back and damn near took my head off. This got her my special attention. It had been a long time since I had to break someone and I had fun doing it. Serves me right for having such a big fucking ego. In the end she played me.

Once she got to the RV, she waited long enough for them to get outside of town. Then she killed the two hoes with her and took off with the vehicle. The first I knew about it was when they failed to check in. I went out after them personally to track the RV. Hell it isn't that hard the thing isn't exactly a stealth plane. The trail led me to a couple of rock formations. The RV itself was empty and a search of the area turned up nothing. I figured that was the last I would see of her. Turns out I was wrong.

Three days later a group of people, outfitted just like she had originally been, came back with her at the front of them. They told my people they were there for me. Loyalty. Fifty people turned and pointed directly to me. Fuckers. The hunters pulled out those air guns of theirs and opened fire. My return fire caught a few but they filled the air with bullets. My people scattered and didn't look back. The bitch laughed at me from cover and said I was going to die here for what I had done to her. Turns out she is probably right. But I am not going quietly. They think they got me? Well there are three RVs parked behind them. Let's see how they like my little surprise…

JOURNAL FOUND NEXT TO BODY of the notorious Johnnie Ringo. Pimp, black marketeer and despot of Canyon Flats Arizona. At the time of his death he had over three thousand people in his employee, most indentured servants. When his ledgers were deciphered the Hunters were able to track enough supplies to refill the tunnels as well as ensure trade for the next century. Machinists were recovered and brought to Vigilance with their equipment. Given full citizenship. All but the oldest accepted. Oldest requested to be left behind. He was last known to be living at the location known as the Kid Farm with one of the retired prostitutes.

During final battle at Canyon Flats Ringo was able to detonate three RV's resulting in the deaths of twenty hunters and the injuring of many more. It is to date the single greatest loss of life in the Hunters guild.

Thomas Crandall

AS IS OUR CUSTOM I have begun a journal, starting with the day of my trial. My first and perhaps last day of being a Hunter. I have sworn the Oath of Truth to the Archivist and will record my actions faithfully no matter what light they might paint me in. My name is Thomas Crandall, I am 20 years old, and I am a Hunter Initiate.

The day started with the darkness being shattered by the harsh glare of the LED's turning on overhead. They burned through the thread worn blanket I had gripped around me, blasting sleep away. I came awake as I always do now, alert and ready. And grumpy. I am not a morning person. But my training has molded me to be watchful, careful and reactive. These days it is impossible to sleep soundly. The tiniest noise now wakes me like a gunshot next to my head. There are reasons for this-one day it could very well save my life-but I missed sleeping soundly. Deep sleep was something I barely remembered, but I do remember it. Fondly. I shifted my large frame, hearing the cot groan slightly beneath me. Carefully, I rolled to my side and swept the blanket off. At the small sound from the cot my mother appeared, opening the door with a look of apprehension. Seeing me sitting on the bedside she paused then glared at me. It was a mixture of exasperation and relief that quickly melted into something else. Her stern eyes silently chastised me as she pointed angrily to the worn message painted three feet high on the wall of the room.

QUIET, THE DEAD CAN HEAR YOU.

Nodding silently, I rose making no noise at all, no mean feat for one of my size, and followed her. We walked down the narrow hallway, carefully stepping over two pressure plates. Treading on them would cause dead weight panels to fall from above, blocking the hallway and destroying anything beneath them. Mother turned to the left and stepped sideways through a narrow opening, barely big enough to slip past. Over the years I had begun to hate that doorway. Stupid? Yes. Hating inanimate objects rarely helps. But as I grew older and larger I have found passing through the slip doors to be more problematic. My body has grown large enough to be a burden in getting through many of the safety measures against the dead. The only exception was stepping over the dead fall tiles. That is now much easier.

Through the slip door is our common area. Here my father and sister sat conversing in hand speak, the silent language of the Hunters. It is the only way to converse this close to the wall. For many who had been out in the world, like mother, speaking aloud is almost taboo. Even in the safety of the city most felt safer operating in relative silence. It is the way of the Hunter, the way of my entire family. Silent and unseen. The walking hands of death among the dead. As I entered I saw that my father and my sister Greta were arguing. Their hands flew so fast it was hard to follow. And they broke off as soon as they saw me so I suspect their argument was about me. Their behavior bespoke the actions of the guilty. As I sat they both began speaking to me using the hand language as if nothing had happened.

"Hello little brother. Did you sleep well?"

"Yes sister."

"Son, are you ready for your trial to start today?"

"Yes father, I shall work to do you proud."

That wasn't exactly what I wanted to say, but the hand speech lacks the nuances normally available in verbal communication. It was more effective for "Go there" or ""Kill now" or "Run" than it was for any sort of deep conversation. Father looked at me a little oddly, then spoke with his hands again.

"To be safe and sure in this is the most important thing. Pride is irrelevant." Father again gazed at me with that unreadable expression on his face before looking at mother. Something unspoken passed between them and when father's gaze returned to me, the odd look was gone. The food on the table looked wonderful, a true feast. Or a last meal. I felt my stomach trying to tie itself in knots. My sister nudged me under the table and caught my eye. She waited for our parents to be distracted, then her hands whirled in speech out of view of all but me.

"Nerves are normal little guy." She had always called me little guy. A name that was now ironic due to my massive and some said encumbering, size. It was well known that I had almost been denied the chance to train to be a Hunter. Many, perhaps rightly so, thought it would be impossible for me to pass the tests of moving silently or being unseen. She smiled at me and continued. "You will need all the fuel you can take in. Use the calm breathing exercises and clear you mind. The body throws up blocks to keep us from going into danger. A Hunter has to learn to push those back and do what needs to be done." Her lips quirked as she used a quote she obviously knew my instructors had beaten into my head over the last four years.

Closing my eyes, I focused on an invisible dot in the darkness. Taking silent, deep measured breaths I slowed my pounding heart. As my pulse lessened, the doubts and fears in my mind withdrew. The knots in my stomach disappeared and I found I was quite able to partake of the food before us. Once I had eaten my fill, I gave Greta a grateful smile as I rose from the table. Moving towards the door, I looked back at my family. Father, mother and Greta all looked back at me calmly and nodded their farewells. No tearful goodbyes, although I think I saw a sheen in their eyes. It may have been a fanciful trick of my mind. The way of the Hunter is stoic. I nodded my farewell in return and slipped quietly out the door.

My family lives in a module near the eastern wall of the city. While the city itself is elevated and in little danger of being attacked by zombies, guards are always present. The dead often posed less of a danger than the living. Though none of the guards were visible I knew that they were there. Each was a Hunter, silent and lethal. Any raiders that tried to breach the walls would soon find themselves joining the permanent dead. Every domicile here was one of the newly constructed modules. Each housed a Hunter and their families, the first line of defense against incursion. As such the houses were a bit more deadly than those found further into the city. Walkways here were filled with mazes of obstacles and barriers. They would confound the living and halt the dead from spreading further in to the city.

Glancing behind me, I was relieved to see I was leaving no trace of my passing. The things I had been taught were now becoming second nature. The ultimate test would begin today. A trek into the waste to find a black box. Inside the box was my Hunter's badge. The task was to find the box, retrieve my badge and return within the window of two months. I overheard among the other candidates that there is a pool running that has me at forty to one to return. Most of my class is small, agile and quick. Compared to them, I am a lumbering behemoth, sure to call down the dead with my earth shaking footsteps.

I am well aware of what the others called me behind my back. Giant. Godzilla. Paul Bunyan. Man Mountain. Thunderfeet. Many names that are far less savory. It hurts to know my fellows, the people that should be like brothers and sisters to me, hold me in such low regard. Even my own sister had doubted the wisdom of my path, but at least when she saw my commitment she took time from her own day to help me train. Thanks in no small part to her tutelage I am among the quietest in my class.

But nothing that she did could help me hide any better. My enormous size kept me from utilizing most cover techniques that the Hunters taught their recruits. What do you say when everyone else in your class can hide in a hollow in the ground but you stick out like an errant boulder. Still, I have persevered. Long past when everyone, including my instructors had given up on my cover training I kept at it, trying new things. This journey would prove if it was enough. I will prove myself, or I will not return. Either way it will be settled.

My days had normally been structured with morning physical tasks and classes in the afternoon. But now that I am done with my training all of that structure has fallen away. Each recruit is given a week to return home to visit with family and friends. It's an all too grim reality that not all of us would return from our journey. During the last trials the two most promising recruits had disappeared without a trace. Among the Hunters it was thought they fell afoul of dead sand, a nasty patch of quicksand that held zombies trapped within. Their families grieved for them and moved on. It is the way of the world.

Other recruits were standing at the Hunter Guild waiting for Headmaster Delmond to appear. It was still early, I was by no means the first here, and there were many others who arrived after me. After what seemed like an eternity Delmond appeared at the top of the stairs. Raising his hands he made sure that each of us was watching him before he began speaking in hand speak.

"Graduates, initiate Hunters, I cannot tell you how pride flows through me at the sight of you. My gift to you is the knowledge and skills that I have imparted. Your gift back will be to survive your journey and return to us stronger and ready to stand against the enemies of our city. I ask you all to say your goodbyes to each other silently and then pass within. Each of you will be met by your Mentor Hunter, the one that nominated you for training. They will outfit you with you gear and take you out to begin your journey. May you all return safe from your travels. Go silently, go swiftly and may your arrows never miss."

When I looked around me, I saw friends, acquaintances, even a few people I didn't like. They were all in the same situation, we were all equal here. With each of them, I made eye contact and nodded, imparting in that one motion my admiration, support and farewell. Each Hunter initiate knew the risk of death stood a mere heartbeat away. When my gaze had swept to the last member of the class

I stepped forward with the others and filed through the door.

Inside, a strong hand touched my shoulder to pull me aside. I turned to find my mentor standing behind me. Shock ran through me. I had expected father or maybe Greta to have been the one who secretly nominated me for the post of Hunter. Instead, I looked at the slightly amused face of the city leader, Robert Kane staring back at me. More than a few of my classmates gaped as they passed in abject amazement. It was a poorly guarded secret that most though the only reason I was here was because of my family's legacy as Hunters. Kane motioned for me to follow him and we slipped down the hallway to one of the small preparation rooms and closed the door.

"Well Thomas, you look like you have seen a ghost," Robert said. Still barely forty he was going gray at the temples and deep wrinkles lined his face. He spoke in the low tones normally used within the Hunter Guild, somewhere between a whisper and normal speech. I worked to swallow past the lump in my throat. I had never even spoken to the city leader before and here I was being mentored by a living legend. My voice broke a little as I tried to come up with something to say.

"Sir, I don't know what to say. I expected someone from my family…" Kane raised a hand to silence me.

"At the time of choosing, a lot of people had already decided that you were not suited for the Hunters. They were putting undue pressure on your sister and father to keep them silent. I took one look at you and, other than your large size, you had the skills necessary to do the job. Unlike the others I don't see your size as a hindrance. It could be a considerable asset out there in the waste." Kane looked at me seriously for a moment and seemed to sense my concern because he continued.

"Thomas, it's true your size makes it harder for you to hide. But going into a hole isn't the only way to take cover. There is a lot of cover out in the world that you will find can hide you just fine. As for the benefits of your size? I guarantee you that your added leverage and strength will make you capable of tasks beyond your classmates. Part of our charter is to find and bring back things the city needs. Books, technology, medical supplies. There are places out there that have not been explored simply because no one was able to get into them. I think this is going to be a situation you can rectify." The look I gave him must have expressed my doubt because he laughed good naturedly. I smiled in spite of the situation.

Kane clapped me on the shoulder, then turned to the task at hand. He opened a heavy locker bolted to the wall and pulled out a metal stand with a ring of metal at the top that he adjusted to be a bit wider than me. Testing this by running the ring up and down the metal bar, he nodded, then motioned for me to stand still. Reaching back into the locker he hefted a large metal box marked "Safesuit" and set it atop the ring high above my head.

"Alright son. I know that you have trained for putting on a Safesuit, but training and doing it for the first time are completely different animals. I want you to hyperventilate until you think you could hold your breath for a minute. Then give me a signal, close your mouth and slowly let the air out your nose. When I release the solution it will envelope you. Don't panic. There will be pressure as the nanites adjust the suit to your dimensions. All you have to do is breathe out and relax. But breathe slowly. All right?" I nodded back at him, focusing on breathing to keep myself calm. My heartbeat barely increased before settling back into a slow, steady rhythm. Once I had my center, I took several deep breaths taking the time I needed to prepare.

A minute or so later I gave Kane the signal, shut my eyes and started to slowly exhale. Liquid dropped down on me from above, but unlike water it clung and spread out over my body. Panic fought to break free, but I kept focus and allowed the gel like substance to envelope me. Less than thirty seconds later the gel had changed and I felt the pressure all over my body of the Safesuit hardening into its final form. From nearby Kane spoke.

"Okay Thomas. Open your eyes." Opening my eyes it looked like I had gauze over my face. We had trained in hoods made of the same material but this was very different. This fabric was snug against my skin, not quite uncomfortable, but tight. Carefully I moved through the exercises we had been taught to test the suits, to make sure they had formed correctly. The suit didn't hamper my movements at all, something I had secretly been worried about. A lot of the others had teased me that the material wouldn't be able to hold my massive frame comfortably. Quite the contrary was true. This was the most comfortable gear I had ever worn. The fabric covered my face entirely but allowed me to breathe normally through my nose and mouth. Breathing through the fabric was mildly disruptive but it barely inhibited my respiration.

Turning to Kane I saw the older man watching me. "It's something isn't it? I remember the first time I put one on. It is the damnedest sensation. Hard to describe to someone else. It is just the kind of thing you have to experience. Now let's test the tear off function. Take the thumb and forefinger of each hand and act like you are grabbing the collar of a shirt on the neck part of the suit." I reached up and did just that. The fabric stuck to my fingers and when I pulled the entire outer layer of the suit pulled off from foot to head. Balling it up, I dropped it in the trashcan near the door. Kane nodded at me then turned back to the locker.

From within he pulled a bow, two quivers, a tool kit, a rations bag and a canteen. Turning, he handed them to me one by one showing where they attached on the suit. "When you tear away sections of your suit they will split around these. When you come back from the field your gear gets sanitized and prepped for your next excursion. What is left of your Safesuit will get recycled by nanites to use again." Closing the locker he moved over and reopened the door. Switching over to hand speak he continued. "You ready to go?" I nodded and followed him out into the hall.

Pairs of Hunters and their initiates headed into different sections of the complex. There are nearly as many exits to Vigilance as there are citizens. Before long, Kane and I were walking alone. We emerged on a high bluff far north of the mesa the city sat atop. Kane stood inside the door and spoke to me in hand speak again.

"You may curse me for choosing you before the journey is through. I want you to know one last thing before you go out into the waste. Why I chose you. I don't think that what makes you different is bad. I think you being different makes you special. Be safe in your journey son. Return to us." With a final nod to Kane I turned and walked out into the world. Behind me the door shut with a soft thud.

The rise that I stood on had an almost invisible path that led to a small chimney of rock with hand holds cut into it. For the last fifteen feet, I had to brace my back hard on the stone and climb without the hand holds. When I was on the big rock below looking up the hand-holds were nearly invisible. Unless you knew what to look for this was just another outcropping of rock. Hiding behind one of the larger boulders I strained my ears to try and detect any noise. All was quiet. Taking a silent breath in through my nose I smelled nothing foul. Scanning around I saw no sign of anything moving, alive or dead. Swiftly and silently I left the exit being careful to leave no trace behind that I had ever been there.

Besides food my ration bag held a map and compass. The map detailed where I would find the black box that held my Hunter badge. Only after recovering the badge and returned to the city would I truly be a hunter. Pausing only to get a bearing for direction I concentrated on covering some ground. Though it had been early when I entered the Guild it was already nearing noon. Long past the cresting of the sun I paused to rest atop a collection of jagged boulders. Taking out the map I took a moment to study it in greater detail.

The map was a bit depressing. It showed that I had a lengthy journey in front of me. It was broken down into two sections. Long distance and then a detail map of the area the box had been placed. It was located in what had once been called Utah to the east of Abajo Peak. The box was in a town called Monticello. As far as I could tell there were three big problems with the location. One, it was on a major road. Or as the Hunters liked to call them, a "zombie artery," because anything flat would attract shamblers simply because it was easier for them to walk on. Second, roads normally meant travelers. Most would be people you would not want to meet. Third, it was remote. Getting there was going to take forever and I would have to travel through a lot of area with little to no cover. Well, no one said this was supposed to be easy.

Putting the map away I ate a bit, drank some water, and then continued on my way. Finding food and water was just a matter of course during the journey. Three days out I came upon a country store in a small town. The area was deserted, no bodies, no zombies, no vehicles. Something about that bothered me. Circling the area I discovered my hunch had been right. There were all sorts of nasty surprises peppered around the area. Snares, drop traps, some vicious spike traps. There was also a ton of old blood. There was so much of it that a rancid smell lingered in the area. On the far side of the quaint little country store I made another sickening discovery. A bone pit.

It was a feeding trap for a group of cannibals. Not an unheard of practice after the fall, but still disturbing to see up close. And to find it so close to home. Three days travel for me was likely a week for these people but I hope I make it back, if simply to report this. Skirting the far edge of the area I warily moved on. The reach of the cannibals was surprising. I was still seeing their traps for hours.

Because of this I bypassed the next few towns, giving them a wide berth. Anything close to the first town would likely be picked through anyway. Diverting around them took me up an old game trail which ended up being fortuitous. Two days travel through the wild brought me to an out of the way resort. There were no vehicles in residence and the road leading in was heavily overgrown, with fallen trees lying all along it. The building itself had been sealed up with heavy wooden covers, which looked to be part of the original design. They sealed the windows and doors. As it was still early I was hesitant to stop. After all, I am working on a mission with time constraints. In the end it was the natural curiosity that I think makes a good Hunter coupled with a sense of duty to see if there was anything valuable that made me pause.

For an hour I ghosted through the surrounding area looking for any signs of activity. I found no sign of anyone coming or going, no traps, or odors that concerned me. Climbing to the roof I found a door that wasn't locked. Opening it slowly, I slipped inside and carefully cleared the entire top floor. I found furniture, bedding, mattresses, a veritable treasure trove. Moving down the stairs I was almost disappointed to find the ground floor equally empty. More furnishings, tables, couches, desks and chairs were spread through the first floor. In addition, there was a huge pantry full of canned and dried goods. When night fell, I took the position from the stars using the small sextant feature on the compass. Before leaving the next morning, I again triangulated the location using landmarks as well.

With a full ration bag and canteen, I was able to make good time for the next few days. A bit over half way to my goal, I ran into my first horde of zombies. It started with a few here and there, most were easily avoidable. Then I topped a rise and saw zombies in the valley below spread from end to end. Slipping back into the trees I backtracked almost a day to find another path. This is where I ran into my second surprise. Hanging zombies.

Someone had taken the dead, tied cables around their waists, then hoisted them into trees. The result was a macabre collection of biting ornaments fit for hells Christmas tree. After the first one, I kept an eye out and climbed as high as I could. There were some dangerous moments climbing bare handed as I made my way over a few unpleasant crags. Once I was high enough, I found a good vantage point. I could see zombies spread out around some burned out structures. There didn't appear to be anyone living there. Noting the location for later report I continued on.

The town of Monticello was nothing like what I had imagined. A small main street, a big courthouse and a collection of destroyed buildings were all that remained of what I could see had once been a pretty little town. Burned vehicles lined the streets, blocking off most through traffic and in some cases penning zombies inside makeshift corrals. According to the map the black box was in the bell tower of the church. Based on the layout of the town the church was the most challenging building. Of course it was. Set alone, it stood on a large flat bit of land adjacent to a clear section of roadway. One of the few buildings that showed no damage, it had rings of debris that kept the dead at bay. Watching for an hour I was rewarded with movement in one of the windows.

I spent some time getting the lay of the land, looking for the best approach. On one pass, I saw an old metal ladder sitting at the base of the church. I had seen the type before. Durable, built to last and more than capable of holding my weight. That is, if it wasn't damaged of course. Most of the initiates would have had trouble lifting it, at least without help. I could move it easily and fairly quietly. Once I had the ladder up, I could slip up to the roof and get to the tower. The hardest part would be moving quietly once I was up there. Structures creaked when you walked on them, even carefully. After some careful consideration, I still couldn't think of a better way.

Slipping up to the building I shot an arrow over the roof towards the wrecks further out. Grasping the ladder, I flipped it upright and leaned it against the building just about the time the arrow clanged off metal on the far side of the church. I hoped it masked the small sound of the ladder touching the second roof.

Gliding up the rungs, I climbed onto the roof out of sight of the ground. Easing my way along slowly I moved to the tower. Once I was inside the bell tower, I saw the black box held in place on the railing of the tower by wire. Looking down, I saw the ladder inside the bell tower had been ripped away. Below, at the base of the missing ladder, a figure shuffled back and forth. Even if the walk wasn't a dead giveaway, the smell that wafted up left no question in my mind. The church was full of zombies. Had I tried going inside my task would have proved nearly impossible. Removing the box from the wire holding it down I silently backtracked, leaving the ladder up against the church.

Back in the relative safety of the ragged rocks above town I stopped to listen. After five full minutes there was nothing. Pulling out the black box I opened it and stared at the trinket within. After traveling so far, going through so much, it was a bit of a letdown. It seemed silly to have come all this way for an emblem that no Hunter ever displayed. It was pretty to look at but what was the point of risking so much for a little hunk of metal? Wrapping the box in cloth I slipped into an outside pocket of my ration bag. Heading to the west I took a different path back towards home.

As our training in evasion and tactics always reminded, the best evasion was to keep your travel pattern erratic. Being predictable got you dead. And scouting new ground was part of what a Hunter did. There wasn't much to the west. Most of the land had been national park, back when that meant something. Now it was just endless wilderness with very few roads, and some wandering zombies. Still, it was worth looking just to be sure.

Three days in I started to see troubling signs. Gore spattered trees. Snarls of razor wire pulled for hundreds of feet in a crude bloody line. Then I came upon ragged tents of every shape and size. Sleeping bags, many bloody, were strewn all around. A few of them were wiggling and issuing the low moans of trapped zombies. I moved as quickly and safely as I could to high ground. As I went I watched the trees for signs of hanging dead not wanting to get surprised again.

I had a bird's eye view of the valley floor below. It was obvious that a lot of refugees had taken shelter here. Most of the valley was a festering den of infection and death, but something on the far rock face caught my eye. Half way up the far slope was a flat area with an old metal building. It looked like an old miner shack. The risk was obvious. If there were so many zombies it was likely there were zombies at the structure. Maybe even inside it. So the place could be infected. I'll be honest. I almost walked on, went home and called it a day. I actually took one step away from that snarled mess of a valley.

Then I saw Kane's confident face, Greta's look of encourage-ment and my father's solemn eyes watching me. Danger was part of the job. If I didn't check this place out someone else might have to come back and do it. Carefully I made my way around the rim of the valley until I was above the shack. It took two days to circle the val-ley. Two long days of choking on the stench of death and decay while listening to the thumps and moans of the zombies below.

It was near the end of the second day that I came out onto a rocky shelf above the metal building. From up close I could see that it wasn't a miner shack at all. It was in fact a heavy metal building with US Army stenciled in cracked paint on the side. I got so excited that I made a horrible mistake. I slid down to the shack and started around towards the door. As I turned the corner, I came face to face with a sleeper. The zombie had been standing there quietly, waiting for something to set it off. Before I could retreat the festering corpse clamped a hand onto my arm and bit down on my shoulder.

Pain blossomed and I lashed out, kicking the creature, sending it crashing down the hillside ass over elbows. Goo coated my foot, arm and chest. Pinching the neck of the suit with both hands I tore five layers away, making sure to discard the old layers over the edge of the drop. Panic rose in my chest putting cold knots in my stomach. Forcing it away I checked to make sure that the area was clear. There was one more zombie near the door. I dropped it with an arrow, not-ing where the splatter went with detached calm. Somewhere inside my head a voice was screaming at me. Screaming about my stupidi-ty, about being infected, about becoming a zombie.

It took all the control of my Hunter training to push aside that panicky voice. If the zombie had somehow broken through my Safesuit's protection then I was already dead. All I could do now is finish my work and try and clear this area. If I was sick, there was time enough later to deal with that problem. Now it was vital that I make sure that my stupidity actually counted for something. My se-cond problem, after making sure the area was clear, was getting inside. The door was locked by two serious looking deadbolts. Steel constructed walls and ceilings appeared to be bolted together. In short, it was a very secure structure. Whatever was inside was likely untouched since the fall.

Time was an issue, namely the fact I didn't have much if I was infected. Hours before I got sick? Maybe. Rage filled me and I think I lost it a bit. What is wrong with me? The first rule. The very first thing I was taught. NEVER RUSH! Always check the area. Check twice before you risk exposure. And I get caught like an idiot by a sleeper. Sleepers were one of the common dangers we were taught about among the zombies. Without anything to agitate them a zombie could stand quietly for years. That was why it was so important to never rush in. Forgetting that, even for just a moment, might have cost me everything.

Ripping a giant metal post from the ground, I beat the hell out of that door. I made more noise in two minutes than I think I have made in my entire life. The anger boiled out of me and by the time I was done the zombies in the valley below were whipped into a frenzy at the racket. At the end the door gave way with a scream of metal. The hinges broke, leaving the door hanging loosely by the deadbolts. The gap left let me see into the interior. It was dark but there was no movement. I figured it was a pretty safe bet any zombie inside would be at the door after all the noise.

Wrestling the door out of the way was almost as hard as opening it in the first place. Heavy steel it weighed so much I was forced to lever it out of the way with the metal post. By the time I was done I was exhausted, every muscle in my body hurt. My hands felt like they had been stomped on repeatedly. Fear rose up in my chest as part of me wondered if it was a symptom of being infected.

Was I going to turn? The suit had seemed unbroken when I had stripped off the outer layers, but there was only one sure way to tell. Time. And if I was infected my time was running out. Inside the first door was a second normal door that opened in. Thumping the door I stopped and listened. The racket the dead were making down in the valley made it impossible to hear if there was anything inside making noise. Shrugging I turned the knob and peeked in.

Dust layered racks lined the interior of the building. A good start, but the visibility was obscured by the racks and what was on them. Even with all the dust there could be a sleeper or two inside. Reaching back I pulled my bow out and thumped the shelf near the door with it. Waiting a moment I thumped it again. Nothing. No movement, no noise.

Slipping inside I nocked an arrow. It took five minutes for me to clear the building, ten to check out the contents. Jackpot. This was a military supply depot. Weapons, ammo, rations, parts, manuals . . . every last bit was high value. I took the better part of an hour getting the door back in place. Covering the building with branches took another hour. Hopefully this will protect the cache until it can be collected. By the time I was done I was pretty well exhausted. Whether from the sickness or the activity I wasn't sure.

Deciding it was time to face facts I climbed up and found the tallest tree on the ridge. Breaking off the top I tied it in place, pointing it in the direction of the hut. This was the kind of thing that the average person would over look, but a Hunter would see as a sign. Taking out my map I made sure my discoveries were detailed on it. I am making sure to put as much detail as possible here in my journal as well. I will put it in my ration bag and hang it from a branch on a nearby tree. I plan to position myself in the first tree, tying my waist to the trunk. Then tie one arm to a branch so it points to my ration bag. I hope this will help the next Hunter that comes along. I am going to put a loop of wire around my neck. I will brace my legs on the branches beneath me then triple checked my preparations. If I turn into a zombie my feet will shuffle off the branches, I will fall and the wire will drive the arrow tied under my chin through my skull.

As deaths go it will suck, but at least I will die knowing I don't have to worry about hurting anyone. My body will be the best sign I can give to the next Hunter to find the cache.

THAT WAS A HARD NIGHT. For ten hours I stood in that tree, in a hell of my own making, waiting. I didn't want to sleep, afraid if I moved in my sleep, I would kill myself unnecessarily. Eventually, when there was no longer any chance that I could turn I dismantled the death snare.

I retrieved my ration bag, ripped down the broken part of the tree and found a place to sleep. When I finally awoke it was almost a full day later. The dead were moaning so loudly that I was amazed I had managed to sleep at all. Before I left the valley I set up a line of noisemakers to lead the zombies out of the valley. That should make it a bit easier to get the cache. Then I headed home.

Other than a roving band of psychos that I saw heading to the north east and a few zombies the return trip was uneventful. I used one of the most remote entrances, taking an entire day to make sure that I had not been followed. Hidden in a large rock cleft, I patiently watched until I was absolutely sure. Knocking on the door I waited while those inside verified my identity and that I was alone. When the door opened, they led me to the quarantine area where I stripped off my gear to be decontaminated. Three layers of the Safesuit went into a disposal before I entered the isolation room.

Ten hours later I walked to the edge of the room and removed three more layers of suit, threw them away and walked down the hall with my handler. Moving into the debriefing area I stepped into the suit removal booth. Liquid showered down on me from above and the suit melted down my form and disappeared down a drain in the floor. From there it would be decontaminated and then nanites would break it down to be recycled into a new suit. Nothing was wasted when it could be helped. Dressed in new clothes I walked down another hallway and sat down in one of a set of comfortable overstuffed chairs.

A few minutes later Robert Kane and Headmaster Delmond entered the room. I rose to offer the Headmaster my seat but the man waved me back. "I am sure," he said. "That you are far more in need of the seat than I." He stood behind and to the right of the other chair and Kane sat down in it. Looking at me he grinned widely. "Welcome back Thomas. Congratulations!"

It took hours, during which food and drink was brought for all of us, but I told them my story. As hard as it was to tell I left nothing out, spared no detail. Even my embarrassing and almost fatal encounter with the sleeper. When I was done the two men looked at each other and Kane nodded. "So," Kane said. "You had a very eventful trip. Your emblem has been cleaned and is ready for you to collect." I looked at Headmaster Delmond, waiting for the rebuke.

Delmond looked at me and actually laughed. "Don't look so downcast my boy. You not only passed your test, you also found a few good caches and gained some hard won insight. I myself was almost caught by a horde on my journey, and had a few close scrapes over the years. It's part of being a Hunter. Granted, in the old days you would have been lost to us. And you should never depend on the suit to save you, but we use it for a reason." Clapping me on the shoulder Delmond strode from the room leaving me alone with the city leader.

Kane turned and looked at me for a moment before he spoke. "So, how thick was that door," he finally asked. I looked up at him thoughtfully. "It was about three inches thick with reinforced deadbolts." I said finally. Smiling he slapped me on the arm. "Some might call a door like that impenetrable. You are a hell of a Hunter Thomas."

Hubert Barnes

THIS IS THE JOURNAL OF Hubert Barnes. I take pen in hand to record my experiences during this, what I feel may be humanities final days. While some have accused me of being melodramatic in the past I am self-aware enough of the events of the past few months to realize that I may be understating things. I am currently a resident of the town of Vigilance. Remote and well situated Vigilance is the brainchild of Jeremiah Kane, a wealthy businessman with vision. His unique insight made him a fortune in the first big oil boom in the late seventies and early eighties. It helped navigate him through the dot com and technology boom era as well as the second oil boom in the teens of the new century. It has also served all of humanity by providing a thriving refuge for what may be the few remaining humans left on Earth.

When he saw the news coming out of the first outbreak areas, he acted decisively as was his way. Liquidating all of his assets but a cargo company and the town of Ten Talk he used the cargo company to rush supplies to this remote village.

Ten Talk, a small community in New Mexico started its life as a native village. During the gold rush in the nineteen hundreds the small town became a thriving boomtown almost overnight. With a deep natural aquifer it sat atop a mesa with only one long sloped approach. Quite the defensible position from anyone that would do you harm. Even after gold was exhausted in the area many residents stayed. In the latter part of the twentieth century the town experienced another boom, this time with oil found nearby. A refinery was built down on the desert floor with pipelines from all the surrounding claims running to it. From there, large tanks of fuel, set in a salt flat far from the aquifer, were then pumped through a huge pipeline out west to the coast. The new industry helped swell the town's population even further to fill a good part of the mesa.

The city founders, having already experience the bust that normally followed such prosperity, tried to develop for the long haul. Their caution proved fortuitous as the market for oil did come smashing down and the debts owed by many in the town ended in bankruptcy. Jeremiah Kane then stepped forward and purchased the town's debts, along with many of the residents' personal debts. Overnight he became the area's largest landowner. It was a boon for those that lived there as he had plans for the small town.

Jeremiah had visited the area many times during the oil boom and had fallen in love with Ten Talk. The picturesque views of the desert, clean air, and good hard working people had made quite the impression on him. Some said that it was the first truly benevolent act of his business career to take the town under his protection. Many in the business world scoffed at him, saying he was getting senile before his time. Others jadedly waited for him to drop the other shoe, and show how he would exploit the town for money. It was this latter group that penned poison editorials when Kane got government money to have the highway to Ten Talk resurfaced and the bridges over the gorges replace. They attacked him for using taxpayer dollars-all perfectly legal mind you-to retrofit the electrical system. Further vilification was elicited when he used a little known program to remodel every home and building in town to be energy efficient.

Most of them I suspect were suffering from sour grapes. While Jeremiah Kane was indeed a gentle benefactor to the city of Ten Talk he was also a very shrewd businessman. His success was often at the failure of others. That simple fact made him a lot of enemies in the business world. Any program the state or federal government had that would benefit the town, he used. When the second oil boom came surveyors were sent out to look for oil. They did locate a copious deposit easily recovered with modern technology. It was processed, using locals only to work the fields. Besides the oil discover the surveyors came back with surprising news. They had found something else. An enormous deposit of a mineral that had never been found in such abundance in our country. Arideam, worth ten times what the oil was worth.

Jeremiah closely guarded the secret discovery. Constructing a company lab and manufacturing plant in the remote location was relatively easy to do without anyone finding out. The secrecy allowed his scientists the time to find the proprietary mix they needed to make a new ceramic pipe he called Arideam Multi. The pipe tested well beyond the specifications of anything available on the market. It was suitable for everything from water to gas and anything in between. Larger ceramic pipes could be used for purposes as varied as sewer lines to food manufacturing. And they were theorized to last for hundreds of years.

By the time he revealed the product to the rest of the world Jeremiah already had a working concept model to show it in action. He had retrofitted the entire town of Ten Talk with the pipe. From the smallest house to the largest building everything was changed over to the new pipes. Again, he suffered attacks for using government money to do the work. However, he showed that his product was not only superior but that the taxpayer money spent would be recouped in the first ten years in savings on maintenance. Some of the greatest labs in the world were invited to stress and safety test his pipe. Even the most pernicious of them had to grudgingly admit that it was an amazing product.

Ten Talk had money rolling into its coffers in such vast amounts that the city fathers were not sure what to do with it. The people had elected Jeremiah to the office of mayor many years before and they now turned to him for his wisdom. The first thing he did was eliminate property and income tax in the town. Then he poured money into improving anything that needed it. The schools became state of the art and had the best teachers. Salaries for workers were higher than anywhere in the country. Old structures were torn down and replaced. An indoor, state of the art aquatics center was constructed. The old movie theater was retrofitted with the latest technology. The entire town had an electric streetcar system that almost entirely eliminated vehicle traffic. After tackling these civic problems he then set about shoring up a forgotten danger that could have caused the ground to crumble beneath our feet. This last endeavor had far reaching benefits, beyond anything our founder himself could have imagined. It would end up being a vital resource for the town.

You see, back in the gold rush days, there had been tunnels carved through existing cave systems. Between that and the vast amounts of oil that had been removed from the ground there were areas of instability. An old mine tunnel with crumbling wooden supports was just a sinkhole waiting to happen. Jeremiah brought in engineers and specialists who quoted him astronomical amounts to fill the tunnels in. When he asked them how much it would cost to repair them they had been surprised. His ingenious solution to a difficult problem created a warren of reinforced concrete tunnels for a fraction of the cost of filling them in. When they were designing them Jeremiah had brainstormed that they might be used for civil defense, a computer server farm or simply temperature controlled storage. Each tunnel had doors installed every hundred feet to ensure if there was a collapse it would be contained as well as vents and sensors for harmful gasses to prevent accidental exposure.

It was during the completion of the vast labyrinth of tunnels that I came to live at Ten Talk. A graduate of Cambridge with a double major in English and Literature, I had been working on my debut novel. "New Yorker" magazine contacted me requesting a piece on Jeremiah Kane. They were impressed, and rightly so, with my past articles in such publications as "The New York Times", "The Wall Street Journal" and yes, "USA Today". I did my background research on him from my office however when the time came to write the story I contacted the man himself. I told him I was writing an impartial piece and wanted to get his side. He invited me out and put me up in a rental house in Ten Talk.

I could definitely see why this town had won him over. The location is awe inspiringly beautiful and the people, though a bit rough around the edges, are good hearted. They made an intellectual feel welcome, even if they didn't understand half the things I said. My accommodations were in a beautifully restored arts and craft style home. The restoration process had kept all the wood and natural beauty while updating the rest of the house with every modern convenience imaginable.

Jeremiah kept nothing from me, I had complete access. I walked the floor of the plant, talked to his scientists and workers. He took me to the tunnels and showed me how extensive they were. He had even begun additional excavations to connect all the tunnels together. The end result was a huge underground maze not unlike a human sized prairie dog warren. At the time, I honestly thought it was a wasteful folly. How wrong I was. I toured the city, spoke with the people and soaked in the culture. It was surprising how much history this one little remote town had. Early settlers had been here when Indians still killed white men in this area on sight.

During the Mexican-American war this site changed hands more times than could be counted. The gold rush saw no less than twenty attempts by bandits to rob the town, none succeeded. I found myself with enough material for a book on Kane and a book on the town. So I set about writing both. Besides, I was in no hurry to leave. As I said the place is beautiful and the people are very warm and welcoming. And there were other, more esoteric distractions.

In the spirit of full disclosure here, I must say I am not completely impartial in telling this story. During my time before the fall I had already met Janice Green. We had been dating for quite some time and she changed my view on a great many things. I do feel that I can still objectively tell Jeremiah's story as well as the story of the city. I just felt it is important to record for posterity my relationship status. Janice is singularly the greatest creation that has ever graced this mud ball of a planet. The owner and operator of Janice's Cafe just down the street from the rental house I was staying. Had it not been for her I fear I would have starved within the first week here. I am an absolute menace in the kitchen and had not realized that there were so few restaurants in town. Thankfully, Janice came to my rescue and I have been her culinary slave ever since. Her restaurant is a cornerstone of this great community.

It was to her establishment that Jeremiah invited me to dinner one night to hold a lengthy discussion about what was going on overseas. I had some friends who had emailed me their experiences and it read more like a horror movie script than reality. The few I had been able to get in touch with had told me that unfortunately the emails were not works of fiction. In point of fact things were much worse than they had originally reported. I admitted to Jeremiah that the events unfolding frightened me to the very core of my being. It was then that he told me he had a plan, albeit a very outlandish one, for protecting the town from the coming darkness.

We spoke for hours. I offered what counsel I could, gave insight where my expertise was valid, and by morning he was ready to act. He first called a halt to work in the oil fields and factories. Everyone was sent home to be with their families. Individually, he contacted managers and supervisors and within a few days set the defense plan in motion. Fleets of vehicles from his cargo company including all the company's planes began delivering supplies to the town. Flatbed trucks with crane lift arms were sent out with crews of men to every junkyard and metal supply business within five hundred miles. Indescribable amounts of wealth changed hands to secure the town for what Jeremiah saw coming.

Over the next week the man orchestrated moving mountains of supplies. He offered a place in our town to some of the best minds in the country. Most of the fools declined his generosity, some even laughing in his face on videophone. The town itself was fortified by crews that began building massive metal walls ten feet out from the base of the ramp leading up the mesa. Then they built five more walls spaced twenty feet back from the previous one. Gates were put in each to allow a semi sized vehicle to pass.

Supplies ranging from seeds to solar panels flooded into the city. Massive metal buildings were built on hastily constructed, yet carefully crafted, slabs of concrete. The buildings were to house anything that was not impacted by temperature. Everything else found a place underground in the many tunnels. The area surrounding the town was protected by derelict cars brought in and welded into place. From the top of the mesa you could see these great rings of cars, on their sides and overlapping, forming three great barriers around the mesa. From the ground they were hard to see until you were nearly on top of them.

The welders constructed great metal devices they called hedgehogs from large I-beams. These devices were able to stop tanks and had been used extensively in Europe during WWII. Jeremiah said that while we had to fear the dead the living might end up to be no less of a danger. He wanted to be sure a crazed desperate or daring bandit was not able to ram our gates down. By the beginning of April our supply train dried up and most everyone that was coming had already arrived.

The speed with which the infection spread took even Jeremiah by surprise. It had started simply enough in January with the first official reports from overseas of infection. Media blackouts and internet blocks had made it difficult to get a picture of how truly dire the situation was. It was not until March that we truly realized how the world had begun to spin down.

On March, 19 2033 flight 2044 from London to New York crashed into the Atlantic Ocean two hours after the last radio contact. That contact had reported a fatality, a passenger that had died of an unknown ailment. Speculation was rampant as every so called news anchor tried to titillate the masses with their vapid reporting of nothing. No facts or true information was gleaned by watching these pretty talking head speaking far beyond their intellectual ability. After a day of this dribble the only thing I was sure of was that I was losing IQ points the longer I watched.

A few days later, came stories of fishing boats, pleasure cruisers and cruise ships that had missed their check in times in the Atlantic. Normally after a stop at a port. The ports themselves had also become unreachable. Jeremiah told me that he had a very bad feeling that trouble was headed our way. That night he called a town meeting and set up the beginnings of our Domestic Defense Force or DDF. Each household had at least one member who would represent them on guard duty, either on the wall or in the street. They would coordinate through the Sheriff's office, what would now be known as Central Command for DDF.

March 23rd saw more stories of disappearances, this time all up and down the east coast. Homeless people, joggers, early morning commuters. All were disappearing without a trace. Flipping through the channels I managed to catch what was going on. People were becoming infected and attacking others. The military would mobilize and in each area a media blackout was enacted. If they were quick and you were watching then you could glean a bit of what was going on before they were muzzled. I am not sure who had the idea that bottlenecking information was a good idea. I firmly believe it was directly responsible for the speed of which the virus spread. How many times do you have to tell people that knowledge is power?

On April 1st, April Fool's Day, Dr. Johan Meiticoff head of the CDC went live on every television station to brief the American people on what was going on. How I wish it had all just been some elaborate joke on that day. Instead, I watched with others in horror as he showed us footage of the outbreak and its results. We saw zombies reanimating. Grabbing people, biting, clawing and in some cases eating their victims. That poor man faced the world and told us what was known about the spreading doom.

The virus had an incubation period of one hour to eight hours. Severity of the infection, for example a bite or scratch, would speed up the incubation process. The virus could also be spread by body fluid of any kind from an infected. This fluid remained virulent for some time after the infected was killed. It was suggested that any dead were burned to prevent spreading the disease. With a few rare exceptions the infected were violent. They attacked the nearest living thing they could when the body reanimated. Then he said the phrase that I knew was true already but had not wanted him to say out loud. There was no cure. None. All attempts to synthesize a cure had failed.

The acceptable quarantine suggested was eight hours. Once the broadcast ended there was a meeting and Jeremiah set a harder standard for our city. Anyone that left town, or new additions, must sit through isolation for ten hours before they would be allowed back in. There would be no exceptions. Anyone that failed to comply would be killed. A system was designed for holding cells that could become incinerators if someone turned. A few of our last minute arrivals were guinea pigs in the new quarantine area. None of them enjoyed it, but everyone felt safer for having it in place.

Nothing that was done seemed to slow the zombies' spread across the land. Martial law had been declared in my beloved New York. Zombies now infested the river, sewers, subways and streets of Manhattan. All attempts by the military to contain or destroy them had been unsuccessful. Footage showed bridges being blown up to prevent the dead from spreading. It was less than effective. Zombies simply walked off the bridge, hit the water and later came ashore in a level spot. New York had been abandoned. The entire east coast was heavily infected and news stations were disappearing from our television like soap bubbles popping in midair. The country was now under martial law. The Emergency Broadcast System had been activated and was transmitting details of the disease, locations to evacuate to and the current advancement of abandoned territory. This last was updated almost hourly and showed a slow foot march of death spreading towards us.

Jeremiah began to get calls on his satellite phone as well as urgent communications over the internet. He sent me out to help coordinate the different groups we had in town to provide him with a single stream of coherent communication. This was the very beginning of our hierarchy command structure. I became liaison to the Sheriff's office and city works. Truly there was not much to do. The town was secure and remote. However, it was good for morale for people to see their government in action. So I walked the streets, inspected the walls and checked the stores in the tunnels.

We had a few HAM radio operators in town that began receiving reports from the east. Most of the people they talked to were in refuges already when things got really bad. Information trading became an imperative part of our radio operators' daily lives. One interesting thing that they learned was that the virus sometimes had an odd effect in people. To crudely estimate I would say one in a million had unpredictable side effects. There were stories of people that were infected and turned but never became violent. A few of the crazier stories from the east spoke of a zombie walking back and forth with a dog leash and a zombie mailman walking the route it walked in life. It was hard to believe these stories. Many believe it is simply people telling entertaining stories.

The fall of humanity was quite difficult on Jeremiah, who was already an elderly man when this all occurred. Watching so many struggle and die seemed to drain him of his vitality. His wife, Talia Bugh of the New England Bugh's, told me many times she had tried to get him to stop taking all the calls. "Let someone else do it," she had told him. He had just smiled at her sadly and told her one of the downsides to being in charge is that you have to take the good with the bad. I think that the stress of the apocalypse caused his health to fail. Had the world kept spinning he might have lived to the age of one hundred or more. Instead we lost him a scant few years later. At least he had the comfort of knowing his children would carry on in his stead. They shared his love and reverence for the city and her people.

Before tax day dawned that year, the United States was starting its death spasms. Most major cities had been abandoned. Countless were already dead from the disruption of food and services. Hundreds of thousands were stranded, left behind with dwindling supplies to fend for themselves by those evacuating. Even military units tasked with providing a window of escape for everyone else were abandoned. Most of the satellite phone service went down and all the television stations went dark. The only people on the air were ham radio operators. We had quite a few enthusiasts in our town, due to the remote location. They set about forming the HAM NETWORK that we have today. Jeremiah credited them with saving thousands from the dead by keeping information flowing after the government collapsed.

On April 15th 2033 Jeremiah Kane called a city wide town meeting. It was held in Founders Park, the beautiful square of green in the center of town. There was a huge barbeque that Jeremiah himself worked over. Everyone brought side dishes. There were games and a dance. When everyone was settling down in the afternoon Jeremiah handed off his tongs and walked up onto the gazebo stage. I have recorded below what he said to the best of my ability.

Speech at the Green:

My friends.

It is a great day in our fair town, a gorgeous day to spend time with those that we love.

I do not wish to trouble you on such a wonderful day, but I must.

It is with a sad heart, close to breaking, that I must tell you that the United States of America is no more.

Our government is fallen. Our people are scattered. Millions are dead. Some have become the walking dead.

Never, in all my years, had I thought to witness such unspeakable horror.

Never, in my exploration of this world, had I ever thought such carnage could exist.

But it does. Our old world has ended. What we have known and taken for granted means nothing now.

It is up to us to adapt or die. Of all the animals that exist on this planet none is more adaptable than we are. So we move forward into this harsh new world faced with a grim reality. Change or die.

Our town is in a very unique position. I believe that we are singularly prepared for the current situation. Our improvements, made mostly for comfort, have nonetheless given us advantages that many others would kill for.

I can see from your faces that I have upset many of you. Well, I wish I could say that I was done.

As I said, we now live in a new world. A frightening world populated by the walking dead. Their touch not only kills us and the ones we love. It adds to their numbers that which we have lost.

Also in this world there are the lost. Other members of humanity that are out in the darkness looking for a place of sanctuary. Some of them will come in peace to join us, others will come in violence to try and take what we have. Then there are those, driven mad by the world they find themselves in, who may simply come to burn it all to the ground.

These are not possibilities. These are facts. Already I have word from the east coast of zombies overrunning refuges. Of people tearing down the very walls that could protect them fighting over resources. And tales of mad dogs, men and women who are consumed by the need to destroy.

Our town will not allow this fate to befall her citizens. If they come to us in peace we will quarantine them, question them and make sure they can be a part of our community. If the dead come we will lure them away or slay them. If the living come to try and take what we have or simply destroy it we will show them no mercy.

Make no mistake. Each and every one of you. Man, woman and child. Young or old. Strong or weak. Each and every one of you is vital to the survival of our town. Of our species. Together we will act to make tomorrow possible. Everyone works or everyone plays. There is no place for laziness or dissension in this new existence. We will work as one to ensure that we not only survive, we will thrive.

We will do this, not by losing our humanity, but by embracing it.

Our strong hands will lift up those that would be our brothers and sisters in the common cause. They will strike down those that would seek to harm us and eliminate anything that threatens our existence. There will be changes, things are quite different than they were, and it will be hard.

You will need to embrace ideas and actions that at one time would have seemed abhorrent to you. It will be necessary. These actions will be what ensures our survival. Balancing these necessary acts with retaining our humanity will not be easy. But nothing worth having is ever easy.

Our very existence will be imperiled on a daily basis. To flourish in this new and harsh world we shall be forced to metamorphosis like a caterpillar into a butterfly. From simple townsfolk we shall become strong warriors. Each of us standing as a flame against the coming darkness.

To that end, every citizen of the city will be trained in warfare. Not the old kind of warfare, the days of mortal combat have passed. Instead, you shall be trained to kill from a distance, safe behind our walls. Whether dead or living, any that threaten this town must be slain by our people without hesitation.

Everyone will be taught new skills, survival skills vital to our daily safety. It is now everyone's responsibility to keep our city safe. It is now everyone's duty to protect those that they love and cherish. From the oldest man to the youngest girl we are all here to stand against that which would destroy us.

Today, my friends, the city of Ten Talk itself has passed with the old world. Our beloved old town has lain down with its brethren and passed out of existence. Today we all, citizen and town alike, are reborn into the wasteland of our world. Stronger, more determined, wiser.

In the spirit of this change I have selected a new name for our town and in turn its citizens. One that better reflects the vast changes that we have embraced this day for our very survival. A name that will carry us forward into the future and remind us that our exist-ence is not a gift. It must be earned every hour of every day.

Today we all become citizens of the town of Vigilance.

Vigilance against infection.

Vigilance against incursion by the dead.

Vigilance against internal strife and division.

Vigilance against laziness and sloth.

Vigilance against invaders who would take what we have.

Vigilance in everything at all times.

This is the price we will pay in blood, sweat, tears and loss for our survival. It is the price I have already paid, the price I have lis-tened to so many brothers and sisters pay out in the darkness. And it is the price we will all have to pay daily if we want to keep mankind from being wiped from the face of this planet.

Tomorrow morning you will each receive instructions. You will each be assigned, regardless of age, to a post inside the new citizen structure. Compliance is mandatory. Military service is compulsory. This is no longer a democracy. I will have the final say in every-thing. This is not up for debate, it is a simple fact.

Looking out at you I can see many of you are already bristling at these words.

These words are so different than what you have lived under in the old world. They stir feelings of resentment or thoughts of rebel-lion in your heads. To those of you I say this. Without my vision where would you be? Where would your families be? Alone in the dark against the coming storm, that is where. I love each and every one of you. But I will stand for no insolence or insubordination driv-ing a wedge between us.

Still, I recognize that change this sweeping will require every-one to make a choice. So I offer this one chance for any of you that disagree with these terms. Leave. Now.

Go home and pack your things and leave the city forever. No one will attempt to stop you from leaving. Know this though. If you leave you will never be allowed to return. If you stay you will be ex-

pected to fully comply with all orders from this moment forward.

I give you all the rest of today and this evening to think it over. Anyone still in town by noon tomorrow will have accepted these terms and be full members of the citizenry of Vigilance.

Thank you all for your attention. Enjoy the rest of your evening.

The next few hours were filled with turmoil. Two distinct factions rose out of the speech. The pro-Vigilance faction made up of the oldest citizens and families. The anti-Kane faction that was made mostly of recent additions to town, including a few who had been asked by the founder himself to join us when the trouble started. This second faction quickly began trying to secure itself a foothold in the town. They were of the opinion that since they disagreed they could take over and run things themselves. Before it could get bloody, the leaders of the anti- Kane faction suddenly changed their stance. Both men were charismatic leaders Benjamin Frink and Paul Sorenson. Both men's wives were conspicuously absent from their concession speeches advising that they were leaving town immediately

Very few knew the truth of what had actually happened. The night before his speech Kane had called an impromptu meeting at the Sheriff's house. Besides the lawmen he invited his son and myself to attend. Here he laid out what needed to happen. The changes he proposed must be made for the town to continue to function. Democratic rule caused too much chaos. Many of the refuges out east were in disarray because nothing could get done because of the leadership structure. After a lot of discussion, it was surprisingly the Sheriff that came up with the solution. Kane had saved us all as far as he and many of the old families were concerned. He had led them wisely in the old world so he should have their trust and fealty in the new one.

The use of the word fealty coming from the man's mouth shocked me to my core. But it made perfect sense. We were, in effect, already living in a monarchy. It was a town that Jeremiah owned, and it had been rebuilt by him using his funds. The supplies had all been purchased by him. He employed everyone in town in one way or another. He was in truth our liege lord. Once the ball began rolling it was impossible to stop. Our small group pledged our service to him, each in his own words. It is far different from the oath that each citizen takes or the secret oath that each Hunter gives when they graduate.

As it was inevitable that there would be dissenters in our ranks Jeremiah came up with a plan. We would give everyone a choice. Faced with certain death out in the waste or swearing fealty he was sure everyone would make the right decision. I pointed out to him that there were two or three other things they could do. They could falsely swear and then betray him later. They could leave and bring others back to conquer the town. Or they could simply dig in and refuse to leave.

The debate on these issues lasted for hours. In the end the decision was made to identify those that were either known to be disloyal or voiced loud dissent. Once we knew who the troublemakers were, we could mark them to be sent away if they tried to swear. Those that would not swear would be sent away as well. Any that wished to leave on their own would be allowed. Once they were beyond the confines of the city, there was only one nearby town. The Sheriff was sure they would head that way.

One of the old gold mine shafts that had been upgraded to a solid concrete tunnel led in that direction. The Sheriff and his men would take that route and get ahead of those that left. Then they would kill them. The bodies were to be dumped in deep ravines nearby. This way the secret of Vigilance could be kept. I could tell the founder's soul hurt at this draconian decision. But he knew the only way to protect the town was to make sure it had the chance to change.

The next day, during the speech, the Sheriff's men mixed with the crowd in plainclothes. They identified the radicals, those that would never bow, even a few that thought to assassinate the founder.

When those men and women tried to enact their coup they were stopped. Hostages were taken to ensure good behavior. Once they were all safely out of the city, the hostages were released to them. I stood at the outside wall with the founder and listened to the men and women below.

The threats, insults and general bedlam continued until the Sheriff pointed out to them that noise attracts zombies. His exact words were "Quiet, the dead can hear you." This sentiment was later painted all around the interior of the perimeter wall. The traitors were indeed silenced by that thought and simply stared daggers at us and spoke in stage whispers. What about the children? The women? They were being sent to their death. The founder shed a tear when he was faced away but the face he turned to them might have been carved from stone. I will never forget what he said to them.

Founder's words to the wicked driven from Vigilance :

All of you were my brothers and sisters. I cared for you and your families as if you were part of mine. I saved you. When the darkness was coming I prepared the way for you and yours to be safe. All I demanded was your obedience. In a world that is tearing itself apart I asked you to give me your trust. To see that I know the way and follow me into the new world. Instead, you sought to kill me. To destroy what I have built and take it for yourself like thieves in the night.

That was your choice.

You ask me now what to do? Now you look to me for sympathy, guidance or relief?

It is too late. The time for choices has passed. The time for consequences is upon you.

Go now from this place. Do not return. You are no longer our brothers and sisters.

Now you are dust.

The founder wanted to travel with the men who went out to take care of that terrible task, but his health was beginning to fail. His son, a strong young man who had sat in on many of our recent councils, came with us instead. When we were ahead of the group, he looked at them through binoculars. Many in that group he had called friends. Some of the young women out there he had danced with . . . even kissed. Now he was part of a group that would end their lives. I found myself curious as to what kind of man he was, how he would handle this burden. I feared that he would not have the steel of his father and would falter when the time came. In truth this was from the tears he shed when he thought no one was looking.

When the group got close enough he told us to wait and the Sheriff and I exchanged glances. Was he losing his nerve? I soon realized that he was every bit the man his father was. When the group got past our position, he instructed our riflemen to start at the outside and work their way in. Half would fire on the front of the group, the rest on the back. This way they would not run back to town and they should stay grouped long enough for us to finish our work. There was an open gorge that was next to them. He had picked the perfect killing field. Running back towards town would make them an active target. Running away from town would do the same. Approaching us would do them no good as long before they got to our elevated position we would shoot them. Fleeing away from us would drop them down the ravine. It was an inspired, calculated choice and I silently applauded his sharp mind.

There were only fifty seven men women and children in the group that had left Vigilance. We started with the youngest and worked our way up. The idea was that taking the smallest quickly would lessen their terror. We shot sixty eight times. Eight of those were mercy shots to speed a target on their way. When the deed was done we sat in silence, crying. It took some time for our group to collect ourselves and venture out to the site. The bodies were grouped together, mothers shielding children, men shielding their families. It had done them no good. With as much aplomb as we could we rolled them into the gorge using rubber gloves to avoid direct contact with the bodies. Then we returned home.

After showers to decontaminate us we sat vigil in the quarantine cells. Ten long hours alone with our thoughts. By the time I emerged I had cried more tears than I had thought possible. I could tell by looking at the others that they had been similarly distraught. Regardless of how right the action had been the toll it took on all of us was extreme. When we returned to our homes, we did not speak of what was wrong, but many who knew us commented that we were changed men from that day on.

Our founder, Jeremiah Kane, died some months later on December 12, 2033. His passing was not unexpected. Thankfully, he had spent his final months getting the town ready for his son picking up the mantle of power. Still, there were those that saw this as an opportunity to rise above their station or escape. After Phillip Kane took power the population of our fair city dropped by thirty people. All were suspected to have fled the city. Only a few knew that while ten did flee, the other twenty attempted a rebellion. The rebels were swept up before they could seize the weapons they needed to cause mayhem. They were sent out the gate and told never to return.

Thirty bullet ridden bodies ended up in that same ravine. It has come to be the resting place of several groups since then. As have a few lesser known locations at the end of some of our tunnels. Since I began my service to the Kane's as adviser no less than twelve plots or rebellions have been quashed. Most of these have been caused or started by refugees that we have taken in out of the waste. They chafe at our way of life and seek to change it to something else. None thus far have come close to succeeding. I claim no small bit of the credit for that. My ideas for monitoring our population have provided advanced warning on all of the schemes.

I hope that this record of what has come before will serve our historians in the centuries to come. Let history not make gods of us for our lofty ideals, but realize that we were but men, exceptional men but still men, that when faced with tremendous adversity rose to the occasion. The truth is necessary so that those that lead can help us to find the way. As I am often fond of saying, knowledge is power.

JOURNAL DONATED AT DEATH OF Councilor Huber Barnes.

ACKNOWLEDGMENTS

TO MY WIFE. THANKS FOR being my critique partner, beta reader and sometime shrink. Without your daily support I would be a quivering ball of psycho in a dark basement somewhere.

To Robin. You brought an awesome cover to a project that wasn't even partially done. And you did it on the sly without even talking to me to help my wife bring me a great surprise Xmas present. Well played.

To my dad, thanks for reading the rough and being my alpha reader. You really helped me form this into a cohesive book.

To my betas, each of you helped in one way or another. Some big. Some small. But every bit was helpful in getting this from the brain to the page. I thank you all.

To Joyce, thanks for taking the time to go back through this and help me clean up the end product.

ABOUT THE AUTHOR

L.G.PACE III HAS SPENT several decades pouring creative energy into other things besides writing. He began his current journey by telling his two daughters bedtime stories about a magical realm and a hero named Terel. Though that story is still sitting unfinished in the electronic universe he has managed to bring two other stories out of the dark maelstrom of his mind for others to enjoy.

He dwells in the great state of Texas with his wife, novelist Michelle Pace and their children.

www.ingramcontent.com/pod-product-compliance
Lightning Source LLC
Chambersburg PA
CBHW020914200626
46814CB00001BA/334